BY RIGHT OF ARMS

Books by Robyn Carr

Chelynne
The Blue Falcon
The Bellerose Bargain
The Braeswood Tapestry
The Troubadour's Romance
By Right of Arms

BY RIGHT OF ARMS

ROBYN CARR

LITTLE, BROWN AND COMPANY
BOSTON   TORONTO

First Edition

Library of Congress Cataloging-in-Publication Data
Carr, Robyn.
By right of arms.
I. Title.
PS3553.A76334B9   1986   813'.54   85-24001
ISBN 0-316-12969-0

RRD-VA
Designed by Patricia Girvin Dunbar

Published simultaneously in Canada
by Little, Brown & Company (Canada) Limited

PRINTED IN THE UNITED STATES OF AMERICA

This book is dedicated to my California support group, my soul sisters, Kate Bandy, Beth Bowker, Linda Bradford, Elsie Feliz, Lou Foley, and Donna Mitchell. Thank you for finding me, changing me, and staying with me.

BY RIGHT OF ARMS

PROLOGUE

THE call from King Edward III for a private meeting held the element of intrigue for Sir Hyatt Laidley. News that there would be such an event was whispered to him at a banquet several days before by the king's son, Edward of Woodstock, the Black Prince. Hyatt had awaited the order since, bristling nervously, excitedly, at every sound that might be an approaching page with a message from the king.

Hyatt had just celebrated the anniversary of his birth, which marked thirty years. In his short life he had accrued a great reputation as a warrior, not the least of which was a valuable service to the young prince in the battle of Crécy nine years before. Since that time the Black Prince had been his devoted ally and undoubtedly had sung Hyatt's praises to the king.

Hyatt listened abstractedly to the sound of his chain mail jingling as he passed through the arching galleries of the palace on his way to the king's bedchamber. Behind him he could hear the loud thudding footsteps of Sir Girvin, the giant who accompanied Hyatt everywhere. Hyatt stopped before the king's door and nodded to the guard, stiffening his spine and holding his head proudly. He was instantly admitted.

Hyatt found the king, the Prince of Wales, the king's third son, John of Gaunt, and a few men he did not know seated about the room. He fell to one knee before his king. "My liege," he saluted.

3

"Rise, sir knight," the bold King Edward ordered. "You will find that this is an informal conference and you may abandon all airs."

Hyatt stood quickly and Prince Edward came forward, extending a hand in friendship. "Be at ease, Hyatt. I have told the king about your astute wisdom and enviable battle skills. These are ministers," he began, waving an arm toward three seated men, "and," he continued, "my brother John. And this is a baron of Flanders, Lord Lavergne. Now a cup, my friend, and a chair. We'll be brief and secret."

They were determined to be quick, as if the time set aside for this meeting had been minimal. The king launched immediately into his discussion. "My son tells me that you are a good knight, strong and rich . . . in fact, he is pompous, for he calls you the best there ever was." King Edward chuckled. "This was said, no doubt, to save embarrassment, since you saved his life in Crécy and he maintains it would take a warrior more fierce than he to save his life. True?"

"I don't know that I saved him, Sire. We fought together that day. Perhaps he saved me."

The king lifted a brow. "He did not say you were humble, but he did admit you were wise. Will you go with him to Bordeaux to form another attack against France?"

"I answer every royal call, my liege."

"Good enough. What is this business that you are rich, but without family or lands?"

"An argument with my father had me cast from his house, Sire, though I was wrongly accused and there was no proof brought against me. I have not carried his arms or banner in many years, but I made my fortune in Calais on your behalf. Nay, there are no lands, and little time for them since I have been occupied fighting."

"But you are rich enough to support property, should the crown bequeath it?"

"Yea, sire."

"Good, then. This man, Lord Lavergne, is of the Flemish allegiance that grants us homage. He comes to bargain with

4

me for a piece of land on the border of Aquitaine, strangely unconquered. His daughter, it seems, resides there."

"She is wed to the Sire de Pourvre," the old man broke in. The king glanced around at the noble, a soured expression on his face as if he disliked being interrupted.

"Edward," the king said to his son. "Explain to Sir Hyatt what you wish of him."

The prince walked from behind his father to seat himself on a stool near Hyatt. "The castle De la Noye of which Lord Lavergne speaks is a large and stout keep. The land is fertile and rich and there are many residents, but it has been mismanaged for many years. Our armies have not conquered so far east, but now I lead a new assault on France, and after the first battles from Bordeaux, I would have you secure De la Noye for England. Will you do it?"

"Yea, my lord."

"Do you have the means to enlarge your own forces? More men will be required."

"Yea, this can be done. There are those who desire to carry my colors."

Young Edward smiled. "I don't doubt it; you have both a good reputation and the ear of the prince. It is only the money I have worried about, for buying the weapons and horses, and paying knights and archers is costly. You made enough at Calais, eh, Hyatt?"

"Calais has seeded the wealth of many."

"Among them your enemy, Sir Hollis Marsden. That is why I have asked for a secret conference. Hollis must be carried to France along with many others, for I have need of the best soldiers. If he fights well, which I assume he will, he as well as you will secure a piece of land. You must not tell anyone where you are bound, nor your intention, nor our agreement, until you are nearly there. I have given my knights leave to take what they will when the plunder begins, but it is *you* I want in De la Noye."

"Sire," Lord Lavergne whispered with urgency. "My daughter."

Prince Edward looked over his shoulder with annoyance. "The old man despises his son-in-law, but pleads for the woman's life. You need not make any promises."

Hyatt chuckled. "Indeed, I cannot. 'Tis not a fair I journey toward. Rest easy, old man. If the castle is to belong to me, only necessary death shall occur. Will the lord who holds the land surrender to my arms?"

Lavergne snorted. "He cannot fight, that is sure. He is an odd, weak little beggar who has kept from war by means of money — all the money I sent for a dowry with my daughter twelve years ago. I have come all the way from Flanders to ask that a knight of some repute be sent to De la Noye, for it is apparent the castle must fall to the English soon. And in that conquest, my daughter must be spared."

"Why do you not give your daughter haven yourself?" Hyatt asked.

Lavergne looked down as if in embarrassment. "She will not leave the Sire de Pourvre. She refuses to betray him. She wrote to me that strong or weak, good or bad, stalwart or cowardly, the Sire is her husband by oath before God and she cannot return to her father while he lives. And . . . she cannot leave De la Noye, for all who reside there depend on her."

Hyatt listened with interest. "Do you claim her to be a worthy dame?"

"Yea, if foolish. She does not owe this loyalty to Giles de Pourvre; he has done nothing to keep her safe or well."

"If possible, I will let the beldame go," Hyatt said.

"Beldame?" Lavergne laughed. "She is but one and twenty. I sent her to De la Noye when she was nine years old."

Hyatt frowned, finding it impossible to believe that one so young had principles so strong. He shrugged off his curiosity, for the larger intrigue was the battle and the gift of lands, something he had waited and hoped for for many years. "When do we depart for France?"

"Can you gather plentiful forces in one month?" Prince Edward asked.

"Yea, and then?"

"When we have subdued the borderlands you have my leave to advance to De la Noye. If you accomplish this to my liking, you will be handsomely rewarded. And if you can keep Sir Hollis or any other scourge from taking it away from you."

"Sire, do any other of my enemies threaten? Does any member of my father's household take up arms?"

"Ah, do you mean Sir Ryland Laidley?" Edward chuckled. "I think that clever knight has avoided fighting long enough to assure us all that he will never raise a sword on my behalf or England's. But it is well known that he supports Sir Hollis against you. Beware of that strange brotherhood."

Hyatt rose and saluted the king. He shook hands with the prince again. "I am in your debt," he said quietly to the young prince.

"Nay, Hyatt. I am in yours. That is why I have offered you this chance for wealth and a homestead."

"But my daughter," Lord Lavergne said, rising to his feet.

"Direct me to yon castle, my lord, and if your daughter is as wise as you claim, she will escape death by the route of her good sense. I despise useless killing. No serf of mine could raise a hoe or scythe from the grave."

The king smiled shrewdly upon Hyatt's statement. He stood in the knight's presence, pleased by his son's choice.

"Remember, Sir Hyatt, to tell no one of our plans until it is too late to be tricked out of your booty. And watch your back."

"I have a worthy ax at my back, Sire." He bowed his way out of the room, his chest swelling proudly as he departed the chamber. Outside he met Girvin and they walked through the galleries to leave.

"Did a good offer come from the king?" the huge knight asked.

"Good, but costly. If we can fight our way through much of France, we have a place to roost. But silence on this, Girvin. No one is to know."

7

"While I waited for you, two crows came squawking by the antechamber. By my presence they assume you were closeted with the king."

"Crows by name — Ryland and Hollis?" Hyatt asked.

"Aye, Hyatt. The same."

Hyatt sighed. "Forsooth, if I can win the place from most of France, I have to hold it against my own countrymen. A good offer? It is too soon to say."

"Did you accept?"

Hyatt stopped walking and looked at his long time friend and ally. "When has anyone ever refused King Edward and the Black Prince? Yea, I accepted their offer. Now we go to war again. But this time, God willing, I do not carry my booty home on my horse."

ONE

APRIL 1356

HE banner of the English army was sighted from a high parapet at dawn and reported immediately to Lady Aurélie de Pourvre and the seneschal, Sir Guillaume. Giles, Aurélie's husband, had departed with his troop of men-at-arms to venture toward Bordeaux twenty-nine days prior, to meet and hold the landed English armies.

"Is there any word of my lord?" she asked. The page shook his head mournfully, but Aurélie had expected this answer. Had Giles sent a message, it would have been delivered to the lady instantly, even in the dark of night. "Do you know their colors?" she asked.

"Madame, the French lilies on blue are quartered by the gold lions on red. King Edward's forces . . . from England."

Aurélie had prayed through the long nights that the de Pourvre army would be victorious and her lord would be delivered safely home. This English troop had either conquered Giles's army or cleverly bypassed them. For many months she had heard the tales of the carnage spread by the forces of the English king's son, the Black Prince. Edward had laid waste from Bordeaux through the Limousin, and the stories promised that any of the Black Prince's forces would be fearful to meet.

Aurélie climbed the winding stairs to the top of the donjon, the central citadel of the castle De la Noye, to view the approaching army for herself. Guillaume was close behind her, as always. She was only one year over a score, but had been the lady of this estate for twelve years. Perhaps in the early years of her residence her authority was second to the counsel of the seneschal's wife, but since she was as young as four and ten her power here had been unquestioned. Aurélie had learned quickly and accepted responsibility readily. When Giles was away, she commanded even the soldiers, with the seneschal's assistance. And she did this very well.

She looked over the vast de Pourvre demesne, the lush green hills of spring. The wind at the high citadel tore at her hair and gown, and tears glistened in her eyes. Guillaume held her elbow, more out of affection than assistance. "How is the wall manned?" she asked softly.

"Archers, madame," he returned, his voice low and coarse. "We have no other means."

"They carry the English banner of Edward," she stated flatly. She turned and looked up at the seneschal's hard gray eyes. "They come to fight and they number one hundred or more. Guillaume, are we already fallen?"

"We are not so well fixed as they, but we have the bridge and wall and we have not endured days of battle, as I suspect they have."

Aurélie turned her gaze back to the sight of the army, already topping the farthest knoll and moving cautiously toward De la Noye. The banner was carried ahead of them and the troops were positioned in a large arrowhead shape, the shields of the horsed knights fixed toward the outside to protect the inside of the V, where their leader rode. Marching archers banked the riding knights and behind the troop they pulled mangonels on wheels, for hurling large stones or burning missiles. Foot soldiers pulled weapons and battering rams on carts at the rear. The slow convergence at midmorning did not speak of weariness, but of astute battle-consciousness. Had they been less than completely confident, they would have charged the wall in the dark of night or have used some other method of surprise.

"Send someone to meet them," she instructed.

"My lady?" Guillaume questioned.

"Let us learn their intention before they reach our door, Guillaume. If they kill my messenger, we will cover the walls and parapets and fight, though all of us will die before the day is out. But since their approach is so brazen, perhaps there is another way. Send a rider at once. I will wait here."

Her eyes did not move from the English forces and she held her hands clasped tightly before her. Guillaume hesitated but a moment before doing her bidding, and then he moved quickly from her side to find a messenger.

As Aurélie watched the advance her heart threatened to break with their every step. She had prayed hard for Giles when he rode to battle, for he was not as soldier-wise as his father had been. The old Sire de Pourvre had been powerful with his lance and sword; a fearsome and well-known knight. He had been dead now ten years. Giles, his only son, was more scholar than soldier, his religion being his consuming passion and his knightly skills lacking. He was weak in battle. Two things had saved them this long: the money that King Philip had accepted in lieu of arms when he was still alive, and the stout army that the old Sire had left behind. Giles would not have taken up arms even yet, but King John II had commanded the gathering of forces just after Christmas. Giles had to fight or allow his family estate to be confiscated. Sadly, Aurélie knew it had not been for France or De la Noye that Giles went to war, but because he had no choice. "I may die upon the field or be executed as a traitor," he had said to her upon leaving.

She tried to believe that Giles was safe and would arrive soon, but the dagger of fear penetrated her mind. To lose Giles and De la Noye in one thrust of a lance seemed more than any mortal woman could bear. Yet this dreadful possibility had loomed on their horizon for a long time. England wanted Guienne, their Aquitaine. Edward had launched total war upon the land, chevachie, the tactic of winning the king through the people by so depleting the countryside of booty, life, stock, and land, that there was no further source of revenue with which to raise armies. Calais had fallen nine years before and it was said that the English left nothing living or standing there. De la Noye was already weak from debts and deaths, for Giles had spent too much money buying freedom from war and benefices to assure his own eternal peace.

Giles should have been born to another family; he would have been happier as a monk or priest. His Church spending allowed no extra money to fortify their men-at-arms.

Aurélie had been delivered to this manse as a nine-year-old chaperoned bride with a heavy dower purse from her Flemish father. The marriage took place and the dowry was given to the Sire de Pourvre, the vows to be consummated when Aurélie and Giles reached maturity. Two years later the old Sire had died and Aurélie had grown up with her husband. It was all she knew and held dear. Giles suffered the ridicule of many, but he was the only man to whom she had ever been close.

She heard the sound of the bridge as it was lowered before she could see any change in the scenery. Within moments a single rider carrying the de Pourvre banner rode alone toward the advancing army and the English slowed to a stop. As she watched, she prayed, not for victory, for that was impossible. "Holy Mother of God, let us live."

Guillaume came up beside her and again took her elbow in his large, strong hand. She did not look at him, for if she saw fear on his face, she too would weaken. She licked her wind-dried lips and held her jaw tight, waiting.

The rider stopped ahead of the army and the knights separated to let their leader advance. Only a few words could have been exchanged when Aurélie saw the English leader draw out and raise his broadsword. The metal flashed in the sunlight. She gasped in sudden terror. She expected to see her messenger's head roll upon the turf, but instead she saw the English knight dismount and plunge his broadsword into the ground. The messenger turned and began riding back to the castle, while the English army held fast behind their leader.

Aurélie looked at Sir Guillaume. "The English bastard is confident," he growled.

"He can well afford his confidence, Guillaume," she replied somewhat sadly. "Let us see what he demands."

The distance from the tower to the courtyard was great and Aurélie arrived just as the gate was opening for her messenger. She was satisfied to see that Guillaume had sent one of their strongest archers and not a boy who might, in fear, have garbled the message. The man fell to one knee before Sir Guillaume and Aurélie. She braced herself for the news.

"The Sire de Pourvre has fallen, my lady," he reported. "Dead by the English blade. 'Tis Sir Hyatt Laidley, knight of Edward, who claims De la Noye by right of arms."

Aurélie felt her stomach jump up to swallow her heart and a dull gray began to envelop her. She swayed slightly against Guillaume, but would not let herself swoon. In her soul she screamed — *Giles! My Giles, my husband! My beloved friend.* But she straightened and lifted her chin, holding back the painful tears she wished to shed.

"Are there survivors?" she asked, her voice sounding distant to her own ears.

"Some, madame. They travel toward us under English guard. There are more of the English than those. This army is only his advance. This knight, Laidley, will hold his troops until you are given word of your husband's death. He says it is his intention to offer you decent retirement for yourself and . . ." He paused a moment and then, looking down, continued, "Yourself and your heirs, if you will surrender the hall and lands."

Aurélie's pain was like the point of a dagger; her eyes brightened with tears. "Did you tell the English bastard that the lady of this hall is barren and has no heir?" she asked bitterly.

The messenger did not bother to answer but simply looked to the dirt at his feet. Aurélie had asked the question knowing full well that none of her people would speak personally of her, most especially to a conquering force. "My lady, I pray you beware; he carries the bend sinister on his shield. He is a bastard true."

Aurélie gave a short, bitter laugh and turned her watering eyes to Sir Guillaume. "Mother of Christ, there are so many bastards born." Her knees threatened to give way and spill her to the ground. She felt Guillaume's hand move to her waist to hold her. He feared that she was becoming distraught. What matter her absence of children when her life and all the lives within her walls faced desperate peril?

"Fetch Perrine," Guillaume commanded over his shoulder, holding Aurélie upright, trying to give strength. The command from the seneschal was sobering. She knew Guillaume called for her woman to have her taken away and tended, and however grieving her heart, she meant to command her walls until they were hers no longer.

"Why does this bastard knight delay his attack?" she asked the messenger.

"He says his armies are well paid and he does not wish to break down his own walls to have his booty. He stabbed the ground with his sword and promised that if the gate does not open to him when the shadow cast by his sword is gone, he will take the castle. He bade me hurry the message that the choice of life or death is yours, my lady."

"Guillaume . . ."

"By God's bones, I would rather die on the English blade than abide his chains," the seneschal growled.

"How many would you sacrifice?" she asked him in a whisper.

"How do we know the vermin will allow us life if we lay down our arms and bid him welcome?" the knight retorted hotly.

Aurélie loved Guillaume well and had known and trusted him for over a decade. He was a wise and noble man who would not lightly abuse the men entrusted to him. But he was proud as well and could not easily give over this domain.

14

In truth, Guillaume was more the knight of the old Sire and had suffered in trying to serve the young, religious heir. He had never before faced a choice such as this.

"You saw for yourself, Sir Guillaume. They have a greater force than we. And ours are dead or captured."

"Do we believe him then, my lady?" he asked in a voice heavy with sarcasm.

"Do you see our men-at-arms?" she countered.

They looked at each other for a long moment. Aurélie could not find reason in the knight's eyes and he could not find the power for war in the soft blue of hers. Yet, of all the people housed in De la Noye, these two were by far the bravest. Guillaume had served here for over thirty years, ever since he was a young and hot-tempered warrior. Aurélie, having come to this place as a child bride, had learned to be the strong ruler her sensitive and cowardly husband was not. Although she had a gentle tongue and graceful step, she moved quickly through this massive keep to see her quietest command followed or her punishment meted out.

Aurélie turned to the messenger. "Go again to the English swine and ask him for the full measure of his shadow, so that the Sire de Pourvre's widow might hear a mass for her husband's soul. Tell him I request this above any civil retirement he offers. If he has not the honor to allow me this brief mercy, let him attack and win De la Noye at the cost of some of his men." And in a quieter voice, she added, "If Giles is dead, the wall is *mine*."

The man nodded and mounted his horse again. Aurélie raised her arm to the guard, giving her consent to open the doors again.

"My lady, I know your grief is deep, but a mass for Sir Giles could . . ."

"Sir Guillaume, my lord husband might wish a mass and my mourning in lieu of every other thing, but we cannot oblige him this time. Come and let us quickly ready the hall. Our time is short and I will not see that English snake slither about my halls in my husband's linen. We must burn his accounts and clothes and hide what little money there is. Give your men their orders to hold the gate against the Englishman until we are ready."

"And you will bid him enter, lady?"

"You will forgive me one day, dear Guillaume. I cannot waste more life in a futile battle that will only reduce our beloved De la Noye to ashes. The Black Prince has left naught but rubble and death in his path and he will not cease. Yea, I will invite the devil in, but I do not surrender yet. If but one of us is left alive, he will find his new conquest more a burden than a prize."

❧

The castlefolk somberly moved through the tasks that were assigned to them. There had been deprivation, sorrow, and fear within the halls of De la Noye, for the fighting had been close and Sir Giles had clung to his estate by the weakest rule since his father's death. The threat from England had worsened, for Edward had a foothold in Guienne and Gascony and sympathy from Flanders. Indeed, much of Flanders wore the English wool on their backs and the English drank good French wine. King Edward had made it clear he wanted complete sovereignty, a right he boasted through his mother. He was attempting to control the Channel and the Bay of Biscay and had many victories to his credit. The de Pourvre army was weak and weary. In a mood of resignation, the servants and soldiers saw the beginning of the great change of command that had been coming for a long time. Some hid their relief at not having to fight behind the sadness and mourning that came with the loss of De la Noye to an Englishman. Aurélie knew that not many would mourn Giles.

There was a cautious and watchful surprise throughout as the English knight held back his army for the full course of two hours.

Aurélie unlocked her husband's bedchamber. In the anteroom he kept his accounts and a box of money. The hearths in the hall and cookrooms burned bright as the Sire de Pourvre's records, letters, and clothing fed them. The portion of Giles's belongings that Aurélie most vehemently wished destroyed was the monk's habits that her husband often wore. She wouldn't share with this English foe Giles's peculiar obsession with his faith. The small amount of silver that was stored in Giles's coffer was distributed in seven different hiding places, none of which were close to the lord and lady's chambers.

Madame de Pourvre walked through her own chambers in a numbness that worried her woman, Lady Perrine. The young widow touched each piece of furniture she passed with an affection one would show a child or favored pet. She quietly asked her maids to fill her coffers with her clothing and sentimental items. She would beg the English conqueror to allow her retirement to her father's demesne in Flanders. She dressed herself in the black she had worn for the mourning of Giles's father and pulled her hair away from her face to be hidden under a black shawl. All jewelry but the ring bearing the de Pourvre crest was packed away.

Perrine watched her mistress with pain and doubt. Guillaume was Perrine's husband, and the two had been close at hand since the marriage of Giles and Aurélie, through the death of the old lord and during the ensuing hard times. They cared for the young couple as though they were their own children. At the news that Giles was slain, Perrine had cried her helpless tears, but Aurélie did not give in. Her stoic mien and slow, agonized movements, with an army camped on her stoop, confused Perrine. She had begun to fear her mistress was losing her sanity.

There was no conversation between the women. The chores Aurélie ordered were swiftly and silently done while outside the lady's chamber the fires destroyed Sir Giles's personal effects. Finally Perrine answered a light tapping at the chamber door and admitted her sadly beaten husband, Guillaume.

"I fear our time is come, my lady."

Aurélie looked at her seneschal with clear blue eyes. She was more than aware of Perrine's suspicious glances and chose to disregard them. Many, she supposed, considered her mad with grief. Her love for Giles was assumed by all who knew them, for she had served her husband well and faithfully, despite his shortcomings. Madness was not her malady, however. Her head was clear and her intention strong. "Sir Guillaume, you know my purpose is to let the Englishman enter this castle. You are my most valuable vassal. I give you leave to flee, if you will. If you stay, you must obey me until my rule here is over. Guillaume?"

"I would not leave your side, my lady."

"If he does not kill you, he will chain you," she said evenly.

"Do you know what he may do to you, lady?" Guillaume asked.

"I know. I have lived this last hour knowing."

The knight gave a nod toward the door and they moved together through the long corridors and down the stairs until the ground level was reached and the courtyard lay just outside the hall. Here Aurélie paused and questioned Guillaume. "Have you told our people we will surrender the hall?"

"Aye, my lady."

"Will they obey?"

"They have seen the number of English knights, lady. Many think you are wise to surrender."

"And you, Guillaume?"

"I gave my oath to fight for this hall to my death, lady. It is all I know. And by your order, my death would come easy."

She touched his arm in affection and then gestured toward the door. They passed beyond the inner bailey and through another wall into the courtyard of the outer bailey. There was room here for a thousand horsed knights . . . but there were none. She surveyed the wall and parapets and saw that her men were ready with bows should the foreigners attack. She drew in her breath and tried to still any fears that threatened to rise. Then her voice came softly. "Give them the order, Sir Guillaume, and meet the bastard at my side."

As she watched the opening of the doors and lowering of the bridge, she willed her eyes to dry and gather all the blue from the clear afternoon sky. She allowed no outward sign of weakness or grief. Her pale ivory skin was touched by the red of a rose and her lips were bright as if in fever. The black she wore did not enhance her beauty, but her fairness was too bold to be concealed. She let her eyes lightly close and tried to form pictures in her mind of the good days with Giles. They read and sang and rode together. They shared secrets and experiments. Inseparable as children, fond companions as young adults, theirs was an easy camaraderie all the years of their union. She knew nothing of passion in her marriage and the only romance she had known came from listening to traveling troubadours' songs. But there had been so much else she had loved because of Giles. She loved De la Noye and her people. She had learned to be content with this. She knew life would never be the same for her.

She held her chin high and posture proud, as Giles would have expected. He had always admired her strength and courage. She would show her scorn, but never let them know the infirmity of her fear.

As the English drew into her courtyard her strength was more difficult to maintain. Their size and number pitifully dwarfed her own soldiers. They were clearly ready for war; only destriers entered and no knight rode his palfrey. The war-horse was used only in battle and never ridden on any travel or errand.

The huge beasts bore their fully armored knights gracefully. Shields and swords were brightly brandished and their livery was red and black, making it difficult to see the stain of blood. The English entered in pairs and separated to line the walls, their eyes casting about furtively for the slightest sign that arms would be raised against them.

Along the ground and wall, as well as in the parapets, Aurélie judged her men to be still and acquiescent to the conquest. Some of her younger archers showed their awe of the invading army by their gaping mouths. She knew her decision, however cowardly, had been the only one. The brutish strength that circled her would have wiped out her people in little time. Even the thickness of De la Noye's outer wall would have crumbled under this force of arms. The survivors of such a battle would have suffered far worse than these unresisting few.

Fifty men soon lined her inner walls. They held their tense bodies still, watching; silently waiting. Aurélie sensed their number and immediately knew the clever battle tactics of this invader. Half of their army remained outside the outer wall, prepared for any trickery on the part of the inhabitants. Long, quiet moments passed and even the destriers were motionless. Then the sound of a single war-horse crossing the bridge could be heard.

Into the center of the courtyard, protected on all sides by the army, a lone knight rode. Aurélie assumed him to be the leader. He was massive in size; larger than any man Aurélie had ever seen. He would be called a giant in fairs and festivals and was easily four hands higher than she. His livery, too, was black and red and she strained to see the blazon on his shield, but he held it away. His face was covered by his helm and only a glitter from his eyes within gave proof that he was human. His voice rang out in clear, beautiful French. "Where is the lady of this hall?"

Aurélie paused a moment and then took one small step forward. She felt Guillaume, stiff and ready, join her. The conqueror bent his shielded gaze toward her for a moment before he dismounted. He looked around once more before pulling off his helm. The face that bore down on her was the face of the devil. His eyes were of slate, his skin was scarred and deeply bronzed, and his black hair fell errantly over his brow. He smiled an evil smile and his eyes glittered. Several teeth were missing and his lips were thick and swollen. Aurélie knew a mixture of fear and hate so intense that she could not find one emotion without colliding with the other.

He strode toward her, still smiling, then bowed. "Madame de Pourvre. Your mass was a long one." He looked skyward. "The incense you burned filled the sky."

She narrowed her eyes, for she knew the knight taunted her. When he saw her frown, he laughed loudly.

"Madame, is this man your servant?" he asked, indicating Guillaume.

"Sir Guillaume, the seneschal," she replied.

The knight inclined his head toward one of his warriors. The man dismounted and dropped his shield. A second knight followed the first and they approached Guillaume.

"Does this man command your army?" the conqueror asked.

Aurélie nodded her head.

"Command him," the knight demanded.

Aurélie looked toward Guillaume and spoke in her gentlest voice. "You are to be the example, beloved Guillaume. Let them take you." She saw the pain in his eyes. He was no match for the giant who stood before them, but he could surely cause a few bruises to these lesser knights. The will to fight was strong in him; yielding to bondage such as this destroyed the greatest part of him. She nearly wept in pity. "Forgive me," she quietly pleaded.

She imagined she could hear hearts breaking all around her as her people watched Guillaume, so brave and strong, allow these English to restrain him. Her hatred for the bastard blossomed and grew as Guillaume was pulled away from her side.

She turned on the huge knight with renewed fury. "Will you bind them all, Lucifer?" she asked, her voice heavy with ire.

He smiled tolerantly. "If they make it necessary, madame."

"And how will you bind me?"

"While you obey, your hands will be free."

"You killed my husband," she gritted out through her teeth.

His eyes took on a feral gleam. " 'Twas my sword and no other," he said, full of pomposity.

Aurélie spat at him. The spittle struck his face and the insult brought four men from their steeds, banners and shields falling abruptly to the ground. Only two were required to stay Guillaume, but in the instant it took to spit in the face of her conqueror, Aurélie found herself seized by four large, armor-clad men. Guillaume strained against his ropes and guards, but it was futile.

"You court death, *demoiselle*," he growled.

"Ha! Do you expect me to weep? My blood should blend on your foul blade with the blood of the Sire de Pourvre!"

"But I do not wish it so, *demoiselle*," he said, his voice low and mocking. "One so lovely as you should not die . . . so soon."

"I will await the moment; I will pray for it."

He looked at her for a long moment, a patient smile growing on his lips. "For each time you spit at me, one of your villeins will die. We will begin with him," he said, nodding his head over his shoulder toward Guillaume.

A broadsword slid out of its sheath the moment the words were spoken. Aurélie gasped in disbelief. She could not fathom their power. The men responded to their leader as if he sent them silent messages from his mind. "Mercy, sir knight," she pleaded. "It is my crime, not his."

"Need I spill his blood, *demoiselle,* for you to believe I will do it?" he asked.

"I beg of you; do these people no harm on my behalf."

"Will you fall to your knees before your lord?" he asked.

Instantly she let herself sink to the ground, though her arms were still held by knights on each side. "I beg of you, my lord."

The knights holding her arms jerked her to her feet, her black shawl falling away from her head and lying in the dust. She faced the victor again.

"I am not your lord," he said evenly. "I am his messenger. And if you fear me, do well to fear him the more, for his heart is not so tender as mine." Aurélie's eyes widened. This was not the fearsome bastard? The question formed on her lips, but she was not allowed to ask it. "Take her to her chambers. Tie her there, lest she foolishly anger Sir Hyatt by some wickedness. Guard her door."

As Aurélie was being led toward the hall, she was aware

of the commotion behind her. Several knights followed with swords unsheathed and ready if the battle lay within, and more destriers began passing through the gate and into the courtyard. The silence was replaced by the shouting of orders and the collection of arms. What she heard all around her was the sound of De la Noye falling to the conqueror.

TWO

HERE were screams among the women and the sound of running. Doors that had been fearfully bolted against the English knights were ruthlessly shattered. The clanking of armor and weapons, shouting, and wailing filled the corridors and galleries.

Aurélie heard men's laughter from her chamber and it stung her deeply, for the English army seized her home with victorious revelry. There were chortling and whooping as each family prize was discovered, or a woman servant ripe for assault was encountered. Before long the smell of roasting meat rose from the cookrooms, and she knew that her provender was being pillaged to feed the conquerors in grand style.

She had been bound with her hands behind her back. Her women were removed from her sight and she was left alone. She worried about Perrine, whom she did not think strong enough to endure much abuse from this army. And Baptiste, a young maid within her care, would likely fill the night for some ruthless warrior. There were the old and infirm among the castle people, and children too young to understand the expected behavior of the vanquished. She had been their mistress and caretaker all these years and now was locked away from them. It was only this worry that kept her from the fear that would paralyze her if she thought of what might happen to her.

The sounds dwindled as the day grew late. The violation

of everything on the upper level of the castle was complete and the English, she guessed, were gathered in the hall for feasting. She could sense the presence of the guard outside her door, but he made no sound. She was brought no food or drink and left no fire or candle to light her room against the gathering darkness. The skin at her wrists was chafed and sore; she tried in vain to loosen her bindings.

She heard a sound outside her chamber door and saw the latch move. The door slowly opened. She sat on the rushes before a cold hearth. Straightening and peering into the dimness, she could make out the form of a man in a short cape standing silhouetted against the torchlight of the corridor.

"Light this room," he instructed the guard.

The guard moved past him and into Aurélie's chamber. Aurélie almost laughed aloud as she saw the guard still uncomfortably clad in full armor. Against whom? This conquered mistress left alone and bound? The weight of the battle accouterments made his simple task of lighting candles a difficult one.

Aurélie kept her eyes fixed on the figure in the doorway while light began to gather around her. He was not huge like his messenger. He was generous of build, but did not wear his armor, or carry a weapon. He, she thought with contempt, was confident that his men could protect him now, and he had left behind his mail and helm and gauntlets. He stood poised in the frame of the door, garbed in a short, dark gown, a quilted gambeson, and chausses. His style of clothing was not ornate, but neither was it modest. Even at first glance she could judge his apparel to be of high quality.

He frowned at the sight of her. Then, turning, he spoke to his guard. "You may leave us now. I shall be here only a short time."

"I would stay, my lord, lest she has some weapon hidden in her clothing."

The man laughed lightly. "If I am felled by a woman of such slight strength, I deserve my wounds. Go. This business is between the two of us."

The guard shrugged and passed his lord, closing the door as he left. The man did not advance quickly, but leisurely contemplated Aurélie. His serious expression did not change and, if she could fairly judge, there seemed to be something of pity in his brown eyes.

"I am Hyatt," he finally said. "I have claimed this hall and all the possessions and goods herein. And the people."

"And my husband's life," she said.

"Aye, and other soldiers of your house." He made a half bow. "I am grieved to deliver the news. Many were killed. I bring to you the knowledge that Sir Giles died a warrior's death on the field of battle. You may bury him with pride."

His words came so easily, with such a beautiful command of the Gascon language of her homeland, that her chest swelled with pain anew. There was nothing to grasp but this confirmation that all was lost. He did not scorn her, laugh at her, abuse her, or even take much boasting in his accomplishment. She wished to see the ugly face of his messenger. It was easier to bear the cruel mocking of the victor than abide this young knight's compassion and courtly manners. In the wake of losing all she valued, he stood at ease in her bedchamber, looking down on her.

"Will I be allowed to bury my lord?" she asked quietly, a slight catch in her voice.

"Perhaps on the morrow."

He approached her, pulling a small knife from his belt as he came closer. He held it before her for a moment, judging her expression. She showed no frightened surprise; she feared neither him nor death.

He knelt and turned her so he might cut the straps that bound her wrists. She pulled her arms loose and rubbed the soreness with her fingers. He was still kneeling, his face close to hers, and she could see in his eyes a softness that she did not understand.

He took one of her hands in his and judged the redness for himself. "Had you not strained against the ropes, you would have suffered far less," he said, his voice as smooth as a polished stone.

"It is my nature to strain against so cruel a thing as this," she returned, lifting her chin.

He smiled in a quick, fleeting manner before his face grew serious again. In that brief smile, his eyes lit and his expression became momentarily bright. For an instant Aurélie forgot why he was there, leaning so close to her. Had the moment occurred at a dinner or joust, her heart would have leapt in some aroused excitement. His handsome face, tanned no doubt by many days of travel toward her home, was strong and flawless. There was nothing of weakness in his hard and implacable warrior's expression; his beard was thick brown, his brows heavy and brooding, and his mouth wide and firm. "This I understand, madame. I am likewise plagued by a natural fighting will."

She instantly found fault with his beautiful strength. She imagined that the women of his English court yearned for his attentions. She ardently wished him ugly and stupid, two qualities that would be easy to ridicule. But it was *her* bindings he cut. She could not decry his wisdom, strength, or even his appearance. He was older than Giles, perhaps thirty years of age.

"Will I be allowed retirement?" she asked.

"My ears deceive me. Did your messenger confuse your request? I was told you desired the time for a mass above all other concessions." He smiled. "This I have obliged."

She pulled her hand out of his. "Perhaps I will flee," she said.

"Where, madame? To a harsher master?" He chuckled. "Even an approved sojourn would be difficult. There is war on the land."

"Or join my husband in death, as I honorably should."

"Shall I leave you the blade, *chérie?*" he asked gently, turning it over in the palm of his hand. He shook his head. "Nay, I will not kill you. I dislike useless death and do not desire yours. I honor your right to die valiantly, if that is your choice." He shrugged. "But I think it would only cause greater suffering for those captured in this hall."

He laid the knife down on the rushes before her and turned his back to begin arranging the cold, brittle sticks and logs on her hearth. The sight of his back aggravated her more. He did not fear her, as if she lacked the courage to attack him. She picked up the knife and gingerly tested the blade, causing a bright swell of blood to appear on her finger. The instrument was worthy of the task, and in a swift motion she drew up on her knees, holding the knife high, ready to bring it down into his flesh. As quickly, with but a slight turn and deft movement, the knife was struck from her hand and sent flying across the room. It landed with a clatter and she was sprawled beneath him in the rushes.

His eyes, dark and smoldering, bored into hers. His jaw was tense and his mouth set in an angry line. He held her arms over her head in one hand, the other free to beat her senseless if he so chose.

"If some sharp dagger lay hidden in your mourning gown, *chérie,* use it quickly and well, for two score of your people will die with each missed mark."

"There is no weapon," she said slowly. "How many of mine will you slay for this?"

He shook his head. "This I yield to you," he said softly. " 'Tis your nature, is it not? But from now, madame, I will tie you in the courtyard and you will watch each of your villeins suffer as they pay the price for your foolish acts. Do well to hear me and know that I speak only the truth."

"You are clever, *seigneur.* My life means nothing to me now, but those abused by your men are tender souls who have never been helpless under a demon rule before your cruel arrival."

He raised one brow and a half smile touched his lips. "I could have sworn the guard stood fast outside your door, Aurélie. How is it the peasants already bring you complaints?"

She wiggled slightly beneath him, knowing he taunted her. "I heard women scream and the breaking of doors. Do you play me for a fool?"

He seemed almost amused by her anger. "To some, the defeat has come hard, but most already serve. Your tender souls have had no rule here; the fair Giles was too busy about his prayers to . . ."

She began to fight him in earnest when he maligned the memory of her husband. Her arms strained futilely against his hand and she tried to kick, writhe, push. He was large and as solid as a stone statue.

"Cease!" he commanded her. "Hear me, wench, for I will not spend much time teaching you. Your villeins do not suffer, but for the stupid few who test my wrath. I give you more consideration than you deserve. Indeed, I have allowed you much. You think I gave you leave for a mass for the dead?" he laughed. "Nay, my clever vixen, I gave you leave to rob your own stores and flee if you would. And I give you more; I will give you a short time to do your worst. Tear at your hair, scream, rend your black gowns, and wallow in ashes. I will leave you this chamber for your choice of torture. And, I will leave you the blade; if you do not value life, use it."

"You will wear my blood on your soul," she growled.

He smiled suddenly. "God will never know yours from all the others', *chérie*. If my soul is damned for killing, your blood will not damn me any further." His smile faded into a frown, almost pitying in its quality. "I suppose this is a poor time to remind you, for my losses were not so heavy as yours . . . but the de Pourvre army took a few lives with them." He shrugged. "Who of us, madame, loves war? Even though I make my own living from the booty, I would rather hold my land against armies than travel endlessly in search of victories. It is land that causes us to fight, and surely the victor finds it easier to bury his own dead than the vanquished. But this land is Edward's, from the Duchy of Aquitaine first brought to England by Queen Eleanor . . . a long time ago."

"England pays homage to the king," she argued, her words remembered from Giles's testimony. "John is king here."

"The battle is nearly over, *chérie.*"

"Nay!"

He looked down into her eyes, holding her firmly beneath him. His weight, full upon her, pressed her hard against the floor. His thighs lay heavy on hers, his belly was flat and as hard as his shield, and his broad chest crushed and hurt her breasts. To her horror, she felt his bold desire and knew that he could find many ways to punish her. He let his cheek brush hers, his beard tickling her neck and causing her a sudden shiver. The knuckles of his free hand brushed the skin of her jaw and neck and he ran one finger down over her chest to touch the valley between her breasts. She thought surely she had bought her rape with her waspish tongue and her eyes were wide with sudden fear. Yet, he went no further.

"But if you choose life, *ma petite,* must I bear the mark of your pleasure on my heart?"

"I hate you." Her mouth formed the barely audible words.

"I don't doubt it, Aurélie. But I think you are more clever than this. I think you will conceal your hatred for a time, if only to catch me unaware." And then in a very deep whisper, he asked, "Did Giles know the full measure of his good fortune?"

The question stirred a memory that held deep sorrow within her and she turned her face away. Although she knew her marriage to Giles was different from most, there had been some happiness for her here, with him. She could not mourn the loss of something she had never known, but she did not want Sir Hyatt to look into her eyes. She believed him a devil who might be capable of seeing her secrets.

He lifted himself from her quickly and she took in a deep, freeing breath. He walked toward the door and once there, paused to kick the knife toward her. He smiled, bowed, and quit the room.

Aurélie looked down at the blade, knowing it was a worthy notion to pierce her breast and end the torture of watching this cocky knight usurp her home. But she did not reach for it. She crumpled to the floor and wept until the tears would come no more.

❧

Though Hyatt had barely slept, he was summoned hours before cockcrow by the arrival of the carts bearing the dead. He had left his remaining forces, supplies, servants, and others to follow after De la Noye was taken. Their task was to bring those dead who wore the de Pourvre colors to the castle town for burial.

To return the slain lord to his demesne for burial was a great act of charity on the part of the conqueror, but this further concession of returning all the dead, some forty men, was a time-consuming and burdensome chore. Those whom Hyatt had left behind with the instructions were hard pressed to understand his action. This kindness would also confuse the survivors within De la Noye.

A lengthy entourage of people followed him to the castle, arriving in little groups throughout the night. Among the first to join him was his illegitimate son, Derek, and the boy's mother, Faon. Derek was almost two years old, and Faon mothered the boy closely, and for this reason Hyatt acquiesced to her continued presence. He was amazed by his attachment to his bastard son, but he still lamented that first attraction to the fiery-haired vixen who had borne him. Many assumed that Faon provided him with much pleasure, warm nights and spirited amusement. But he would have no more bastards from her.

Faon was from good merchant stock, clever, and some thought of her as beautiful. Any woman less so would have been settled with and left, but this woman he kept and supported so that he could supervise the rearing of the child. While many of his men believed Faon provided some carnal relief, it was the child who became a more significant part of his life with every passing day.

Although Faon's place with him was misunderstood by almost everyone, Hyatt was not inclined to explain his behavior. Sometimes he regretted his silence, for she was given to haughtiness as being the leader's woman. He chose to ignore this because he considered the benefits of her position few. When she arrived ahead of the others, a bevy of guards protecting her, he was certain she had used some privy authority to accomplish this grand entrance.

She rushed toward him, disregarding his frown of displeasure. He had hoped to see his other instructions followed before hers.

"Victorious again, my lord," she cried. Then, nuzzling his ear and neck, she added more softly, "I will make your night of victory very special."

"On this night, Faon, I am otherwise occupied. A room will be found for you and the boy."

She gave her head a toss, the reddish curls bouncing around her shoulders. Her eyes narrowed and she moistened her lips with her tongue. "Have you found some French whore to ease yourself upon?" she questioned flippantly.

Hyatt laughed loudly. Her saucy confidence had originally attracted him and, his memory being sound, he chafed at the knowledge that he'd not found a better bedmate since. He condoned her nearness only because of Derek, for he did not love her and seldom approved of her behavior. On occasion she made him angry enough to strike her, and one day might yield to the temptation.

"There is no French whore," he said. "Not yet, though I look long and hard. The victory is not complete. I am hard at work, and the little time I spend abed tonight will be used for sleep."

He felt the urge to fondle his son, who sleepily reached chubby arms out to him, but instead he turned away. He was careful to let no witness other than the boy's mother see how vulnerable he was to Derek. He made an impatient gesture with his hand, indicating that Faon and her servants and the child be installed somewhere to sleep.

Hyatt's distrust of women was understood, but left his

acceptance of this one unexplained. He heard confused whispers, for he had been seen in generous acts toward her and also as he scorned her. Some spoke of his lusty demands and some, he imagined, even envied him this fancy harlot, for she was pleasing to the eye and brazen in her appeal. But Hyatt was discriminating, and not weakened by these hoyden flirtations.

He was relieved when Faon did not rise early to press him for company, or some other demand . . . always on Derek's behalf. It was true that he had much on his mind, and a goodly share had to do with Aurélie. While he did not think she would end her own life, he had been told of her pride and her devotion to Giles. His knowledge of her was far greater than hers of him, for Lord Lavergne had met them in Bordeaux and given the location of the castle and a great deal of information about Giles and his troop. If Aurélie did not kill herself because of the siege, she might attempt to do so when she learned that Lord Lavergne supported Hyatt's attack.

Many Flemish lords were at odds with the French king and the Papacy. From Flanders to Gascony it was easy enough to find a friendly beachhead. Lord Lavergne was more merchant than nobleman and needed the English trade. All of his people were clothed in the English wool, and the English guzzled his wine. Giles, more an aristocrat than a warrior or merchant, did not see the advantage of making an ally of his enemy. He was all for France and the Church, whatever the cost. The cost had proven dear.

Lavergne had continued to plead for concessions on behalf of his daughter. Although Aurélie had abandoned her father's principles for her husband's, Lavergne was desperate to protect her against death or imprisonment. Hyatt had not given his word to that. He refused to weaken his position on any issue. But it was in his mind from the first that only necessary death and bondage should occur. He did not fear the mistress of De la Noye, this child-woman of whom Lavergne had spoken so affectionately. The fact that she was steadfast behind Giles to the end only made her more admirable in Hyatt's mind. Loyalty, especially from a woman, had come to mean a great deal to him.

When he saw her, ravaged though she was by the destruction that encompassed her and the effects of honest grief for her husband, her beauty was manifest. She was small and trim, though by no means frail. Her face, even in devastation, had a healthy glow, her eyes bright enough to glitter in the dark and as blue as the clearest sky. Her thick brown hair was streaked with honey-gold and fell below her waist, curling seductively around her face. And her tenacity spoke of passion. This was, as Lavergne had claimed, a worthy dame.

He had earlier found the woman, Perrine, and allowed her to fetch her mistress for the early morning burial. He instructed his men to let her pass. Although he wished it otherwise, he found himself compelled to watch her from the wall, assuring himself that there was sufficient strength in her stride. She endured her hardships well. He was disappointed that he lacked a better view, another chance to look closely at her face and alluring form. Hyatt was never trapped by a flirtatious smile, but there was something about Aurélie, something more than her obvious fairness, that occupied his thoughts. From the moment he had issued her the blade, he had hoped he was accurate in assuming she was made of surviving stock.

He returned to his own work while she was busy with the burial. He had serious matters to deal with, though most of De la Noye had fallen into place better than he expected. These simple castlefolk and even the men-at-arms had suffered a rule so weak, they were resigned to Hyatt's shocking power almost immediately. Little was needed in the way of educating them.

The greatest disappointment of his conquest lay in the continued poor behavior of one of his own, Sir Thormond. The knight was a cockerel who was consumed by self-importance. He had acted outside of Hyatt's authority on several occasions in the past, the complaints and crimes attributed to him many. Although he had been warned, Thormond was feeling a victor's zeal when they took De la Noye. He was reprimanded twice for actions he took against the residents, and Hyatt began watching him more closely. He discovered Thormond hiding some of the booty for his personal use. Now he must deal with the man. He knew the punishment must be harsh and swift for two solid reasons. Thormond had earned punishment befitting a thief, and the example to the other knights and residents here might save future retribution. If all were sufficiently shocked into awareness, only the foolish would dare steal from Hyatt in the future.

Yet Hyatt vehemently wished that he had never taken the knight on, or had turned him out long ago, on perhaps the first or second offense of usurping his master's authority. Against his better judgment, Hyatt had paid the man, purchased his battle gear and horse, and provided a squire. He needed men and had been in a hurry to appease Prince Edward. And Thormond had once ridden with Hyatt's estranged brother.

However, Hyatt would not give the fallen knight another opportunity to betray him. At just after daybreak, when the prisoners and injured were all returned to De la Noye and littered the inner bailey, Hyatt ordered Thormond delivered to the yard.

That the stench of death and the pitiful state of the conquered ones sickened him were weaknesses Hyatt did not share with any comrade; soldiers did not wince away from death and injury and despair. These were his thoughts as he entered the yard: that no one would know by his action or expression that his stomach churned against his duty. When he was noticed emerging from the hall, the prisoners were poked and ordered to stand taller, and Thormond was dragged forward.

He saw Aurélie. She stood far back, behind many captured soldiers. She watched the flurry of activity that took place the moment Hyatt inclined his head. He saw her face, pale and drawn, her head covered by the black hood of her cloak. For a moment he wished she were not there; he would spare her this. But it was a fleeting wish. *Let her see,* he thought. *She will know my strength and I will know hers. Until then, we know nothing of each other.*

Thormond wore the colors of red and black, but he was stripped of his sword and shield. As he was brought forward, he looked down at the ground. Only his chausses, shoes, and gambeson gave him away to be one of their number, yet he was being held as an offender. As he was pulled to the center of the yard to face Sir Hyatt, he slowly looked up, his expression full of hatred and defiance. Hyatt saw the stinging truth again, there in Thormond's eyes. He knew Thormond would kill him, if it met his needs.

"Thormond," Hyatt shouted in a voice that caused his prisoners to stand taller if the guard's prodding had not. "I would break the arm of any man who steals from me, but one of my own —" he shouted, looking all around him. He judged the reactions of those present. Then he spat in the dust at the feet of his soldier. "With one of my own, one whom I've trusted and tried to teach truth and honor, my judgment would be harsher."

He looked toward one of his knights and the man unsheathed his sword and tossed it to Hyatt. He caught the heavy weapon with ease, as if it weighed no more than a scythe or hoe. In a flash of action so swift many would wonder if they had even seen it, the prisoner's arm was held out and whisked off just below the elbow. A shriek of pain left the victim before he crumpled to the earth in agony.

Hyatt stabbed the bloodied weapon into the ground beside the severed limb and looked around again, his voice ringing loudly over the cries of the injured man. "To test my justice, test only the edge of my sword. They are equally sharp." Then in a voice only slightly subdued, he added, "Mend him and turn him upon the road. He betrays my shield. He betrays my word."

The cries stopped as Thormond was quickly hefted over

the shoulder of one guard and carried out of the way. Hyatt judged the observers again, looking for one in particular. She stood. He could not see her closely enough to know if she gaped, but her arms were still at her sides. Perrine hid her face and seemed to retch, but Aurélie faced the loathsome deed. He kept himself from showing a prideful smile and turned, striding back to the hall as confidently as he had come.

Hyatt had acted quickly; there should be little doubt he would not dally over tiresome testimony. He was grateful to find some of his men in the hall, finished with their early morning meal. He desperately needed any diversion they would provide. He wanted to scour away the memory of Thormond's betrayal and severed limb. Only a few of his most trusted men knew that he had doubted Thormond; they had helped him watch the errant knight. But the punishment was hard earned. The residents of De la Noye would consider him ruthless. That was his deliberate plan.

He called for cold ale and spoke with Sir Girvin, his closest vassal. "Thormond is finished," he said sourly.

"It should have been done long ago. It is a necessary example," Girvin grunted.

"A costly one," Hyatt said. "My hard-earned monies bought his sword and ax and horse. I could not teach him to follow, and now he shall never lead."

"You kept the destrier and weapons, did you not?"

"I would rather have a good soldier," Hyatt grumbled.

Girvin seemed to sense his friend's melancholy. "Does this promised castle prove too much trouble?" he asked, smiling.

"It does not bode of great plenty," Hyatt said, adding a curse under his breath.

Girvin began to laugh. He had been with Hyatt for many years, and the younger man often became surly when faced with a lord's responsibility. In truth, De la Noye was his greatest conquest thus far and Hyatt had no cause for any such coltish pouting. "Who will carry this poor lad's burdens?" he asked the men standing about.

Offers went up around the hall and within a moment there

was jesting and toasting, the very thing Hyatt had hoped for to ease his distaste. He was laughing over a good retort when he noticed the slim, darkly clad figure cautiously and quietly enter the hall. He thought she must pass this way to gain her chamber, but not knowing the keep well, he was not certain where he might cross her path next. Perrine stayed close behind her, the attendant's face still white with disbelief. He held a cup of cool ale in his hand and hoped he appeared untroubled by the fact that he had just maimed a man.

Aurélie met his eyes. He smiled and made his way to where she stood.

"My lady," he said, his voice even and smooth.

She lifted her chin but could find no words.

"I trust the departed are blessed and resting?" he asked. She nodded, looking up at him. "Good," he said. "We could not look to the morrow for fruitful harvest until yesterday's tragedy is past. I expect each soul yearns for only good to befall the fair De la Noye now."

He tried to speak as though those buried were but losers of a joust and that, as in all good sporting, he held no grudge. Women knew little of war — they sent their men away to fight and either welcomed home victors or buried the dead. Hyatt wished her to know that he held no contempt for those slain. Indeed, he had respect for those who fought valiantly. As long as kings argued, knights fought. His eyes remained softened toward her. War was work, a matter of necessary action, not meant to be enjoyed nor to destroy all that might be left.

She shook her head numbly, showing great confusion. "I . . . I could not help but see . . . in the courtyard . . ."

"I am sorry you must witness such, madame. A lord's chore is often ugly."

"I think, Sir Hyatt, that it must be a terrible demon who drives you," she said softly, searching his eyes.

It was as before, when he looked at her face. There was a catch in his breast and he felt a strange tugging. He was taken by more than her comeliness. From inside he could feel the urge to cradle her in his arms and drive away fear and pain she might have. But he reminded himself that her delicate appearance was not a true indication of her strength. She had stood through the cursed event as well as he, and did not weaken.

"Perhaps, madame, all that is different about me is that I am free from demons."

"Nay," she replied. "A fearful devil, surely . . . and one we shall all know quite well."

Hyatt let his eyes bore deeply into hers for a moment and then slowly he let his gaze drop, giving her body a long, leisurely appraisal. He wanted to touch her, but did not. In time, he promised himself, he might let her see beyond his ambition and calloused determination. And he would look beyond her pride and strength. He began to taste a tender moment, but forced himself to have patience. His eyes again focused on hers, and he did not smile. "You will know me quite well, Aurélie. Rest assured."

THREE

URÉLIE was aware of Hyatt's occupancy of the former lord's chamber. She could hear his movements and wondered at his strange hours, for it seemed the chamber was never without a variety of voices, heard from early morning until late at night. More confusing to her was the fact that he left her alone in her private solar. She expected this modest luxury to be revoked at any moment.

Isolated, by her own choice since the hall was not denied her, she gave herself to hating the victor and mourning her husband's death. She saw only a few servants, and that they seemed to endure their captivity well did not ease her mind as it should, but only increased her fury. No one, it seemed, mourned Giles or resisted Hyatt's rugged occupation.

"My lord insists that you rise from your grief and prepare for a visitor," Perrine told her when she delivered an early morning tray of food.

"My lord?" Aurélie said, aghast. "Perrine, have you made him your lord?"

"I have little choice, madame," she returned. "He makes it clear his rule here will not be questioned."

"Does the madman expect me to visit the kitchens for his guest? Am I to don a costume to serve the vermin? I will *not* do his bidding. I will not discard my widow's black."

The door to her chamber slowly opened and Hyatt stood there, looking in at her with an amused smile on his lips. "I was told of your stubbornness, Aurélie, but I was not warned about your impudence. I suggest that you set aside your belligerence and do as I have asked."

"Never," she cried, stamping her foot in emphasis. "I am your prisoner, not your servant." During her days of solitude her anger had built into a seething rage. She foolishly forgot the people she intended to protect from him and was insulted by his passive tolerance. While she might have cowered from his hostile treatment, she bristled under his smooth control.

He raised one brow and crossed his arms over his chest. "I am willing to force the issue," he said.

She stared at him with childish insolence. "Will you cut off my legs if I do not serve? Beat the villagers if I fail to oversee the hall? My arm," she said, thrusting it toward him. "Will it be sacrificed if I will not put aside my black? Or will it be my head?"

"None of these," he said easily, shrugging his shoulders. "I will simply dress you myself."

She was stunned into silence. She had learned, and heard from Perrine on her brief visits, that Hyatt meant to be taken seriously. And that his command was most frequently issued in a soft and patient voice that only covered a more brutal action he would not hesitate to employ.

"I would not bemoan the task. If it were unpleasant to me, I would simply send my guard to do it."

She whirled around and presented her back. She wished for a moment that he would simply beat her, rather than employ his boyish charm, this courtly solicitude of asking for her compliance. And then the memory of the man's stump and his arm lying in the dust came to mind, and she shuddered.

"I will not dally with you, Aurélie. I'm not a patient man. Your staunchest vassals have come around to my ways and means quicker. Dress yourself and come to the hall. And I know you can make yourself look pleasant, if you try."

She whirled to face him, her mouth moving well ahead of her head. "Perhaps my staunchest vassals were not widowed by your army and find your demands easier to meet."

He took two steps into the room, a frown on his face, and she took two steps back, wondering why she had foolishly tested his temper. Had she not seen his quick hand move to maim? "*Seigneur,* I will dress and come to the hall," she said quickly.

He stopped immediately. "Have a care with your appearance, my lady. My guest is your father . . . and he is concerned for your health."

"My father," she gasped. "Dear God, does he bring arms?"

"He is a welcome guest," Hyatt returned. "And a friend."

"But when he learns that you . . ."

"He knows Sir Giles is dead, madame. He wished it had not been necessary, as did I. But that is a hazard of war."

"He cannot approve your . . . your . . ."

For the first time since she had seen him, Hyatt seemed uncomfortable. He looked away and shifted his weight, but he regained his composure quickly. "He approves my occupation of this hall and lands. The Flemish are not much for your French king."

The depth of this betrayal left Aurélie standing mute and awestruck. Did no one understand her pain? Did all the world excuse thievery and murder by right of arms? Even her own father?

"I do not ask pardon," he said, the line of his jaw stern and his voice, as usual, calm and even. "You need not forgive me, respect me, or even set aside your grief for me. You will obey me as you value your life, for any survivor of this occupation treads on the lord's mercy."

She watched him as he spoke, noting that there was no struggle to form his words; no regret or vulnerability. He spoke as if giving simple instructions to a falconer or messenger.

"I have been told you have a grain of wisdom, or I would not trouble myself with such lengthy explanations. Were you a hostile knight or simple village craftsman, I would beat my intention into your foolish skull and mayhap you would die before learning. But lest you think yourself more clever than those able to usurp this keep and town, listen to me carefully.

"You may cleave to your hate and grief and pain for as many years as you deem it your right, but every action you take, madame, must show me that your desire for peace and prosperity for this land and the sorely molested people equals mine."

She looked at him closely. The words did not quite settle. He killed and maimed, yet longed for peace? He brutally ruined towns and families, but desired prosperity? Yet the entirety of his message was not lost. She was certain this was his final warning. He would stop using reason and begin using force if she did not acquiesce.

"Dress," he said slowly. "Our concern is no longer winning; the battle is won. Our destiny is in building. By the grace of God, you will never see conquerors cross your bridge again." He bowed most elaborately. "Adieu, for the moment, Lady Aurélie."

As the door to her chamber closed, Aurélie turned glistening eyes to Perrine. "I will never forgive him," she murmured. "I will not take a breath without praying for his comeuppance."

❧

She chose a gown of pale cream, trimmed in gold. It was a total departure from the black. She allowed her hair to be brushed until it shone, had it braided and wound around her head. A veil of the sheerest silk, fastened to her head with a modest cluster of pearls, trailed down her back. Her sleeves were wide and flowing, her bodice snug to accentuate her trim figure, and her train pulled around to be attached to her wrist for freedom of movement. That she wore no jewels to adorn herself did not detract from her beauty. The low neckline and her gently swelling bosom embellished her appearance more than any sparkling gem.

"Let him think I am resigned to healing this burg," she said to Perrine when her dressing was complete.

"I beg you, madame," Perrine whispered. "Take great care with your scheming. This Hyatt is not a man to deceive lightly."

"I will use cunning," she murmured.

"He sees more than . . ."

"Hush!" she commanded. "I am not so simpleminded as to be foolish with my methods."

She went to the hall, telling herself that she made this concession for the sake of future vengeance; in no way did she strive to please his eye. Rather than lose her temper and openly fight him, she would try to trick him into believing her behavior obedient. Even docile and tractable. When Hyatt rose to greet her, his eyes glowing appreciatively and a smile on his lips, she thought she had been very clever.

She curtsied before her father. He took her hand immediately, causing her to rise so that he could embrace her. "Thank God, Aurélie," he said hoarsely. "You must believe I suffered with worry."

Three years had passed since Aurélie had seen him. When his mighty arms encircled her, it nearly brought her to tears. Her ambivalent feelings tore at her. Her beloved father! Her betraying father! She could not find her true emotions as they bombarded each other with painful, crashing doubt.

"But you are strong," he went on, crushing her in his zeal. He held her away from him. "I beg forgiveness for Giles. I did not think he would take up arms; I thought he would yield the day."

"You must have known he would defend De la Noye," she said softly, trying to keep the bitterness from her voice.

"My daughter," he sighed, his tired, wrinkled eyes beseeching her understanding. His beard had bleached whiter, his skin was looser and sagging, and although he was generous of build, he crouched slightly now and she felt his aging bones as if they splintered in her hands. He was too old to live through many more summers. "What did I think?" he went on. She saw the tears gather in the fold under his eyes and for a moment she pitied him. "I thought Giles would send troops, that he would lose a fair number of archers and knights. I thought there would be sufficient damage to De la Noye.

44

I knew, my Aurélie, there would be war. . . . I have seen much of war in my life.

"But I thought Giles would surrender when he knew he was beaten."

Aurélie looked down at the floor, trying to still her threatening tears. She could not have expected more from her father. He appreciated Giles's scholarly wisdom but criticized his lack of knightly skills. He had expressed his worry for her safety for years, accusing Giles of being unable to protect her. Had it not been for the vast richness of De la Noye and the power of the de Pourvre family, she would not have been given to Giles in marriage. But all that had changed when King Edward proclaimed himself King of France and the countries were at war. Her situation worsened when the old Sire died and Giles was left to manage armies, a prospect for which he had no talent. Giles had, many times in the past, chosen any alternative to fighting. Although her losses were great, Aurélie had to accept that her father neither desired nor aided her widowhood.

In a surge of grief, her honesty broke through her barrier of cunning. She completely forgot Hyatt's close presence. "I begged him not to go," she admitted. "His men-at-arms would have done better without him."

Lord Lavergne clung to her again. "I did not think he would. God rest him, at least he died an honorable death."

Again the aging lord held her away. "All is not lost, daughter. There is still much to salvage." He looked at Hyatt. The younger knight nodded and moved to the stair. "We are allowed a private conference; a great concession from a man who cannot be sure he is among friends," he confided softly.

Aurélie's eyes were drawn to a movement across the room and looked past her father to see the large knight, Girvin, rise to his feet and begin to cross the room. His hand rested lightly on the hilt of the broadsword belted at his waist. His narrow, glittering eyes scanned the room and he came to stop just behind Aurélie and her father. His intention was clear; he would be closeted with them.

She let her eyes move from the fearsome vassal to Hyatt. "He does not jeopardize his safety, Father," she said, an edge to her voice. "We will make all the concessions. Rest assured."

Hyatt smiled at her remark and reached a hand out to her as if he would escort her.

She chose obedience and took the proffered hand, going with Hyatt to the lord's chamber, Lord Lavergne and Sir Girvin close at their heels. The door was tightly shut and Hyatt seated her before the hearth. Lord Lavergne slowly found a place near his daughter, and Girvin stood at the closed door, his arms crossed over his massive chest.

Aurélie's father sighed heavily as he adjusted himself in his seat. Hyatt stood a generous distance from them, leaning casually against the wall.

"Ahem," Lavergne coughed. "I am most grateful to see you are fit. You, above all, have some right to this keep. Your dowry saw the building of the church and much of the outer wall. It shall be preserved in your name. There is no heir save the widow."

Aurélie looked down into her lap, trying to keep her hands demurely folded and her heart still. "There are no heirs in war, Father," she whispered.

"That you are mistress of this hall need not be questioned again. You shall remain so."

She looked up at her father in astonishment. "That will be most awkward, Father," she said, trying not to ridicule him too openly for this absurd suggestion. "I doubt Sir Hyatt could bear my chafing presence."

"But he insists on your presence. You know the town, the people, and the lands better than any servant."

She quickly looked at Hyatt to find him listening to the conversation with quiet interest. She tried to read his eyes, but they concealed his thoughts.

"Then we must soon find another," she hastened, feeling her pulse quicken. "We must leave this man to rule his conquered lands."

"You are best suited to aid his leadership, daughter," Lavergne said. "And best suited to protect the interests of these people. You know them."

She neared panic at the thought. Hyatt's gaze, resting on her with enough heat to warm her, did not betray him. He seemed perfectly calm. "I am the enemy," she said slowly, trying to keep the anger from her voice. "With all best intention, with the help of God, I cannot be suited to aid Sir Hyatt. Father, I would not be a good choice. The people here would suffer as I would."

"Daughter," he softly pleaded, "pray do not further injure yourself by rejecting Sir Hyatt's compassion."

"Nay," she nearly cried, feeling herself becoming more agitated, more afraid. "It would bode ill for me to remain a prisoner here and . . ."

"You shall wed the man," Lavergne said evenly.

Her breath caught in her throat and her eyes widened. She looked quickly at Hyatt, the question on her lips. His mouth was firm, his eyes level, and she thought she noticed an almost imperceptible nod, but she could not be sure.

Her eyes were on her father again and she reached out to grasp his hands. "Oh Father, you must not. If I cannot leave here with you, let me take the veil. I shall never ask another thing of you." She looked pleadingly at Hyatt. "My lord," she nearly choked, "I yield all, but I beg of you, there is not wisdom enough in all Christendom, nor grace enough in all heaven for me to yield this. 'Twould be a bed of thorns."

He looked at her for a long moment, his expression unchanged. He appeared as unmoved by her plight as though he were watching the shoeing of one of his horses. "We shall manage, lady," he finally said.

Aurélie felt hysterical laughter coming to her lips. "But I am barren," she said victoriously. "Surely a knight so powerful must wish to sire many sons?"

"It is better thus, for I have a son. In himself, he is the equal of ten."

She looked back at her father, angered at finding no help

in his resigned expression. She whispered in strained agony, "Flanders or the convent, Father. I beg you!"

He simply looked down and shook his head.

"Father," she whispered urgently, "you would have me wed this English bastard and . . ."

"Bah! He is no more bastard than you or I. 'Tis but a family disagreement. Perhaps it will be eased." He looked uncomfortably toward Hyatt, then back to his daughter. "His family denies kinship, but he is not baseborn. Take heed."

"You must not agree to this, Father. On my mother's grave, I appeal to your kindness . . ."

Lord Lavergne closed his eyes as if contemplating his next words. "It is difficult for you, Aurélie, but in time you will see the wisdom in this. Marriage is but a means of ensuring your safety, protection for your dower purse . . ."

Her ears began to ring and his words blended one into the next. Lavergne droned on of marriages used to form alliances, to bridge rent families, to end wars. Brides could purchase peace, ease conflicts . . . all a matter of sound negotiation as estates changed hands or were won and lost in the event of war. She shook her head violently, her hands going to her face as if she would press back the tears. "I cannot. I cannot. I will *not!*"

"Enough!" The command came as loudly and unexpectedly as any bolt of lightning. The stammering Lord Lavergne and weeping Aurélie both jumped in surprise, became silent, and looked at Hyatt. He no longer leaned against the wall in a relaxed manner, but stood to a full menacing height and held clenched fists at his sides. There was an angry scowl on his face and he appeared to struggle for control.

"Your reluctance comes as no surprise, madame, but do not carry the game to dangerous lengths. You do not have to love me or approve me. I need your close presence to lessen the rub on these villeins. I did not plan your husband's death, nor did I intend your misery. In taking De la Noye in the name of my king, I allowed a sum to retire the deposed lord in some humble dignity. For the last time I tell you, I regret it was impossible. But 'tis over. English and French must parley if there is to be profit. There is no discussion."

Aurélie swallowed hard and looked at her father. He shook his head. However angry she might be at his involvement in the matter, it was clear he was no match for this man. All the arguing Lord Lavergne could do in a lifetime would not alter the decision or strength of rule.

She fearfully drew a new breath. "Would you have me, so recent a widow, prepare the hall and see the priest for a wedding, or will I be allowed some time for . . ."

"There is no need for further preparation," Hyatt said flatly. "It is apparent you will judge me only as the conquering foe and refuse to see me as a man, flesh and blood, like any other. Neither will you show gratefulness that you are to be *wed* to protect your father's hard-earned dowry and thus kept safe as is your right through marriage, when I could as easily turn you out for wandering armies to feast upon. If you will cleave only to your hatred and ignore your advantage in this proposal, then we shall not celebrate the event, and we shall have it done. We shall go now to the priest."

"But . . ."

There was a sound behind her and she turned abruptly to see Sir Girvin change his posture, indicating his intention to enforce his lord's decision by any means necessary.

Hyatt walked toward her and reached out to her. She eyed him cautiously and moved her slight and trembling hand into his. Her flesh was cold and clammy all over and she stood on shaky legs.

"I am not an ignorant woman. Only one who has suffered grave losses," she said with as much dignity as she could muster. "You are not a patient man."

His eyes warmed as he looked down at her, but his mouth remained stern. "You are wrong, Aurélie. I am more patient than most. But it is clear to me that you dislike my patience, for you test its limits. Had you but opened your mind to discussion, we might . . . But never mind. If you choose to see me only as harsh and wicked, certainly you shall." He tucked her hand in the crook of his arm and led her to the door.

For a moment she felt as mindless as a puppet, for her actions were not at all her own. He led, her feet moving by his order, her passage by his command. She knew her options to be death or agreement. He would own her by law, rule her by power, and violate her by a husband's right. Even God would not come to her aid.

An odd shiver passed through her as she walked beside him. Never in her life had she been controlled by such power. She had been the only strength, but for her there had been no strong arm to lean upon. She judged her feelings to be born of the most wretched despair. But she could not place the genesis of the strange tightening of her stomach, the lightness of her head. When he momentarily released her arm, she felt peculiarly alone.

Her mind soared out of control. *When it is just we two,* she wondered, *and he has left his sword and shield, when his man does not stand ready at the door to beat me into submission, when he is as naked as God made him . . . will he prove to be a man . . . or a beast?*

⚜

The hearth burned low in the lord's chamber. The few remaining candles flickered as they died. A bright spring moon filtered through the window and cast a beam across the bed.

Aurélie stood before the hearth, distractedly watching Hyatt as he removed his tunic and laid it carefully away. The day had exhausted her will to resist him in any way. Father Algernon, though stunned and appalled, had blessed the reluctant union, with only her father and Sir Girvin present. The meal in the hall, served without any special flair or celebration, had taken long to pass. Aurélie was not sure whether anyone knew there had been a wedding. She had whispered the news to Perrine, who blanched white and covered her gasp with a shaking hand. It seemed as though Hyatt's men were considerate with their jesting and drinking, but having

58

spent little time in their company, she couldn't be sure if they were more than usual.

As the moon began to rise, Hyatt bid Lord Lavergne a good night and led his bride to his bedchamber. She stood awaiting his command or demand, whichever might come. *Perhaps he will never know,* she thought.

With his tunic and chausses discarded, he presented an exquisite figure of a man. Even in fear and grief a woman would notice his magnificent, hard-muscled body. He was lithe and graceful when not clumping about in armor; his shoulders were broad and his arms thick and strong. She had never seen a man in any state of undress and found herself curiously staring at the thick mat of hair that covered Hyatt's chest.

As he approached her, she steeled herself and closed her eyes. Her fate was sealed and she would be used. Silently she prayed that he would not hurt her too badly. She felt his hands on her hips and the softness of his beard on her neck.

"You make this difficult, Aurélie," he breathed in her ear.

She stiffened in his arms. "Call your man," she offered, the edge to her tone as sharp as a knife.

His seductive laughter filled the room. "Though he would be willing and all my men serve me quite well, there are some things a lord must do for himself."

He tilted her chin and lowered his lips onto hers, catching her off guard with his gentleness. He moved over her mouth slowly, using tenderness to disarm her. Although thus far only his words had been brutal, she had not expected him to be kind; she had expected to be conquered. Yet he caressed and fondled, as lovers of her dreams had done.

She felt the veil drop from her hair even as his hand began to unloose the braid that adorned her head. His other hand pressed against the small of her back, forcing her against him. Her cheeks flamed; a fiery trembling possessed her. This was not the ruthless warrior of her nightmares. As if he felt her change, his lips demanded more. She would not let her slackened arms rise to him, but it took great effort.

He released her mouth and methodically began to undo the fastenings of her gown. She felt dizzy and knew that her body betrayed her. She gritted her teeth in shame and frustration, trying to remind herself that this man was the enemy, the murderer of innocents. Her mind taunted her — does he truly regret Giles? Dislike killing? Detest the ugliness of war? She tried to suppress such speculation. His feelings did not matter. He *had* killed . . . and captured her home. But the desire she had learned to suppress began to rise in her, causing her flesh to tingle from his touch.

She looked up at his bearded face above her. His eyes, black in the dimness of the room, glowed in passion. "You must not . . . ," she heard herself whisper, though she knew it would be foolish to resist. He laughed softly, and the sound was cruel to her ears. He was forcing her spirit in lieu of her flesh and her agony worsened with every moment.

"Please," she whispered. "Have your way quickly and be done with me."

His eyes burned brighter and his smile was illuminated in the moonlight. "Nay," he breathed. "I married you to protect your fortune and keep you safe from future ills. I would have better than thorns, Aurélie."

"You wed me to work in this hall," she countered.

His lips touched her brow. "Your labors will be handsomely rewarded, if you would but cease to wound me with your spiteful tongue."

His hands deftly pulled the gown over her shoulders and it was instantly gathered around her feet. Her chemise quickly followed and before she could gasp at her sudden nakedness, he lifted her in his arms and carried her to the bed. Feeling his naked strength gently pressing her down, she opened her eyes wide, as if in wait for the worst. But he kissed her, caressed her, and murmured words he could not have meant, words spoken only between lovers.

His hands, gentle on her body, stirred her. His mouth, warm and moist and insistent, lured away her fears, and the demon desire ruthlessly possessed her. With a moan of despair, she allowed her arms to embrace him and she returned his kisses. Her breasts firmed eagerly under his hand and her body rose to his with a will of its own.

"Hyatt," she breathed in a sob, "do not do this to me. Do your worst and be gone."

"Our life need not be all pain, *chérie* . . ."

"I beg you," she cried. "Do not shame me so. Have done."

His laughter was soft and mocking. "A husband's right," he murmured.

"Right of arms," she answered him.

"Do I hurt you, *petite?* I would have better than your hatred . . . if only here . . . if only in my bed . . ."

She sobbed, but her mouth met his and her body strained toward him. She felt his hand gently part her legs and she despised his smooth experience. Better he should brutally force her than to throw her own weakness at her in this way. Her response gave lie to her earlier rejections.

Drifting, helpless in the wild sensations his touch brought, she contemplated the many women he must have loved. Thousands, she thought distractedly. He knew how to arouse, he knew the art of sweet torment. She knew nothing of this intimacy and could do naught but float in the rapture of his carnal skill. She longed for the end of this torture and felt it near as his gentle tempting was replaced with eagerness. His hands began to demand roughly, his body was hot with urgency as he entered her. She gasped as the pain, as sharp and searing as any dagger, flooded her womb and spread through her. Her eyes clouded with tears and she could barely see Hyatt's face as he rose above her. He loomed over her, motionless and astonished. As her vision slowly cleared, she could see the shock in his eyes. She turned her face from him and quietly wept.

His fingers gently brushed her hair from her face. He carefully lowered himself, moving with great temperance, but the pain was no more and neither was the hunger. Aurélie's struggle with shameful desire was gone, for his startled discovery left her listless. She neither aided nor discouraged him, but passively let him have his way.

It was a long while before he eased his weight from her, and she rolled onto her side. He did not completely release her, but curved his body around her back, raising himself on one elbow to look down at her profile. His hand casually toyed with her hair.

"You might have saved yourself much misery, had you told me."

"What difference?" she flung. "Would it have delayed you?"

"Nay," he said softly. "But there are certain remedies . . ."

She turned abruptly and looked at him. "You would not have believed me."

He laughed a bit ruefully, shaking his head. "Even now I do not believe it."

She rolled away from him again, this time trying to put some greater distance between their naked bodies. His hand was quick to find her hip and draw her back. "Aurélie," he said, again the master of the smooth but commanding tone. "Whatever tragedy marks your past, you may bury it now along with your Giles. I share your secret, *chérie*. I don't know what Giles was to you, but I know he was not a husband. You have one now, and I shall remain. You must not expect me to show great patience with your anger and hate."

"I expect nothing," she wept.

He gently nuzzled her neck. "In that event, my lovely Aurélie, you will be very surprised."

FOUR

URÉLIE heard the reigning cock of the yard crow and warily opened her eyes. The curtains were yet drawn in the room and there was a suspicious absence of morning chill, but she lay alone in the bed. She rose slightly and turned. Hyatt had pulled a chair near to the bed and sat there, one foot casually hoisted up onto the straw mattress as he silently observed her. He wore his chausses, leather boots, and a linen shirt, holding of cup of some steaming brew in his hand. It looked as though he had been awake for a long while, for the fire was stoked and his eyes were clear.

"Good morning, my lady," he said softly.

She settled back against the pillows again and pulled the covers up to her neck.

"I was going to wake you in a moment, for the castle will be astir shortly. I have noticed that your people rise with the rooster at dawn."

"Have you been awake a long time?" she questioned.

He laughed ruefully. "You have inspired great thought, Aurélie. You, and your keep, are full of surprises."

She felt the color come to her cheeks, but kept her eyes fixed on his just the same. "Do you say that you had no idea what you conquered, sir knight?" she asked with no small amount of sarcasm.

He leaned forward toward her, a frown of puzzlement wrinkling his handsome brow. He firmly planted both feet on the floor and leaned his elbows on his knees, holding his

55

steaming cup in both hands. "If you wish to address me formally, lady wife, you may assume my lordship. When the villeins are settled and word of this occupation is delivered to Edward, I will carry full title in his name. Yea, I will be your lord." He took a sip from his cup. As he swallowed, his eyes burned into hers. "What was Giles to you?" he asked flatly.

"My husband; my beloved," she replied without hesitation.

"Nay," he said quietly. "Whatever love you had for him did not bind you in wedlock. Why did you play me false? Was the truth so painful?"

She felt the sting of tears threaten, but forced herself to face him with strength. "I do not expect anyone to understand what I felt for my husband," she said defensively, hearing the tremor in her own voice. "That I loved him deeply is absolute. The consummation of our marriage was delayed . . ."

"Delayed? It is reasonable to shelter and protect a child bride, and I was told you were very young when delivered here. But, for twelve years? Aurélie, do you deceive yourself even as you attempt to deceive me?" He shook his head as if he pitied her. "Had you told me the truth, I might have dealt with you differently than I did."

She could bear no more and turned away from him. She did not understand how or why she had failed with Giles; she could not explain it to Hyatt, of all people. She felt his weight press down the bed and a hand on her shoulder turned her back to look at him again.

"I pity your grief, but, madame, I do not know what you grieve." His brows were drawn together in sheer bafflement. His voice was smooth and quiet. "Was it a brother you had in Giles? A friend? What things did he do for you that made you love him so? From all accounts he was a weak and incompetent leader, and there are many insinuations that he was strange. Was he kind? Gentle? I know he did not keep you safe, make you wealthy, or give you pleasure in bed. What, lady?"

"Surely, Hyatt, I cannot expect you to understand, if you think that wealth and carnal pleasure are the only things a pure woman desires," she said, her tears running down her temples and into her hair.

Hyatt shook his head and leaned away from her slightly. "Had I known your circumstances, I might have proceeded with you in other wise. But it is done. Perhaps one day I will understand what you felt for your Giles and can offer proper sympathy for your loss. For now, I would have you know that I was not temperate in my plans, for I thought you were a woman of experience, a widow true."

"Do you seek my forgiveness, Sir Hyatt?" she asked sarcastically.

He did not respond to the insult, but seemed to take it in stride. "The marriage is necessary to combine our houses and perhaps unite opposing forces . . . unless you think it better, more honorable, to execute those who cannot abide a change in rule. But never mind that decision, Aurélie. You will find me willing enough to offer apologies when I am wrong. This once, at least, you were wrong to withhold the truth. I am afraid you will have to bear the burden of it.

"Now, let us forget Giles and think of the troubles we should sort out. First, soldiers of the Sire de Pourvre are still held, some of them bound. You may be of some help in deciding which of those might, in time, swear fealty to me and which must be banished. If you seek to house traitors, there will be more bloodshed, and that is useless to us all. I have brought a mighty army, and they do not relax. There is no chance you or any of your remaining forces can overthrow me. I expect you to look to those who are held prisoner and make a judgment of their worth.

"Second, I have a son and he is here in your hall with his mother. That will be difficult for you, I imagine, but he must remain, and the woman tends him to my satisfaction."

"Your whore resides in your wife's house?" she asked, appalled.

He sighed heavily and returned to his chair. "It is unusual,

I admit. But the child is valuable to me. He is my only one. He *is* my firstborn son regardless of what your womb may yield us. But I assure you, I shall be fair with our children. If it is easier for you, you might imagine that I am likewise widowed and the child is the product of an earlier union."

"Do you share your whore's bed in my house? Will there be many bastards running about?"

Hyatt smiled leisurely. He propped his foot on the bed again. "Do you ask me not to, Aurélie, my beloved?" he questioned with humor. She turned her face sharply away, her cheeks burning again at the sound of his amused laughter. " 'Tis good that you want me, but I realize I have not earned such devotion yet. You shall have your pleasures in time, *chérie*. I shall prove a decent mate."

"My God," she moaned, keeping her face turned away.

She felt his hand on her hair, gently squeezing the full softness of it. His voice was soft and seductive. "I did not expect to marry a virgin. I did not intend it. But I will admit to only you that I find great pride in this. You served my pleasure well and I rest easier knowing that if a child is forthcoming, I need not question the sire."

She turned her head sharply, the action causing him to tug her hair inadvertently. Her eyes blazed beneath the tears. "My God, Hyatt, does Satan himself feed you the tender words you speak? I am to live with your whore and you are pleased that I, a married woman, served your pleasure with my virginity. Will you shout it from the highest citadel, that Giles failed with me? Surely even your cruelty has an end."

Hyatt sat back in his chair and looked at her, a frown wrinkling his brow. "You are a very difficult woman to please, lady. Most women like to be told that they are much appreciated for their chastity."

"Not I. Why would such please me? I do not wish to be your wife, nor do I find much solace in being a pleasing bedmate."

Hyatt put down his cup and raised a foot again to the bed, casually unlacing the straps around his boot. He drew it off and repeated the action with the other foot, speaking without looking at her. "You lie to yourself, Aurélie. 'Tis a pity. You delay any good settlement of our lot with your foolishness."

"You are not a man," she said angrily. "A beast from the forest, rutting aimlessly, keeping whore and wife and finding base pleasures where they lie."

"Aurélie," he sighed. "You are such a challenge." He stood and pulled his linen shirt over his head, tossing it aside. His chausses soon followed and he stood before her in only his loincloth.

"Hyatt, no," she murmured. "I beseech your kindness, do not hurt me."

He laughed and his knee was on the bed. "You hurl your insults, then beg me not to bring you pain." His hand touched her cheek tenderly. "I have not hurt you yet. Nay, your deflowering would have been painful with any man, for it is the way of such things. But with you I have been gentle and kind, giving far more than I have asked in return." He lazily pulled the fur covers down to expose her nakedness. His hand made a soft sweep over her bosom, resting on her flat belly. She trembled in spite of herself. "Ah, Aurélie, you may cry out your hate for me, but when I touch you as your lover, your body rises to meet mine. It is a good place to begin."

"You shame me," she whispered. "You torment; you hope to find this fleshly weakness in me."

"Nay," he said huskily, softly caressing her waist, her breast. He pulled her hand and placed it atop his, forcing her to follow his movements as his fingers became more bold. "When I do this, lady, I am loving you. You will learn to know the touch, the pleasure, and you will find that it eases the hurt. You may despise me in the courtyard, the common room, the corridors of our castle, but in my bed your venom will cease. Here, if you cannot answer my kindness with equal weight, you will at least be silent when I touch you." A half smile played on his lips. "Just let your body speak to mine. That will be enough for now."

"You . . ."

"*Hush*," he demanded. His fingers touched the soft mound of hair between her legs and she snatched her hand from his, the color burning on her cheeks. Her eyes closed as she gritted her teeth both in embarrassment and rousing pleasure. "There is ever accusation in your tone. In every word from your lips I hear pain, doubt, fear, hate. Yet in no action since my arrival can you claim I have been cruel to you."

His hands again brought to life the yearning. She moaned in misery, for the longing from deep within her womb had cried out for fulfillment. How did this devil know so much? She had craved to be in a lover's arms, to be touched, caressed. She had desired to take the seed of a strong man, to bring to life a child. For as many as seven years she had been ready for love, life, joy.

He played casually with her body and she opened her eyes to look at the hardened features of his face. He quickly stripped away his loincloth and his eyes smoldered with passion's fire. She could feel his probing manhood against the inside of her closed thighs. Her heart beat wildly, her breathing came in labored gasps, for his fingers brought the response from her body. Tears clouded her vision as she studied his handsome features. Why could he not be a knight of John's France, come to console her in her loss? Why could he not have been brought by her father when she was a girl, before she had committed so many years of loyalty to France and Giles? Hyatt was her lover now, and her body had taken him if her mind had not. Yet she was the vanquished, the prisoner, the captive. Why? Why?

"Let me in, Aurélie."

She opened her mouth to speak, but he would not have her oaths, denials, or insults. He covered her parted lips with his in a searing, hungry kiss that devoured her. He pulled her hips to meet his and with a deep, humiliating moan of resignation, she parted her legs to take him in. Within moments she clung to him, answering his thrusts with her own. Like a rising river, she felt the tide of rapture building and a glimmer of what lay ahead was relayed in this man's arms. A glow flushed her skin; a deep quivering forced her to answer his kisses and meet his thrusting hips.

He clasped her tightly to him and that which had escaped her on the night before filled her with astonishment now. The molten heat of his pleasure filled her. He moaned weakly, his muscles taut and trembling.

His lips touched her cheek, his glowing eyes looking deeply into hers. "It will come in time, Aurélie. In a little while you will share my joy. When you let yourself."

He left her to dress himself and she turned over and sobbed into the pillow. Her tears were wrenching and painful and she was thankful that he did not mock her. Finally, his hand was on her shoulder. "Rise, Aurélie. Enough of that."

She turned to look at him. He was fully dressed and just strapping a knife to his belt. Tears ran unheeded down her cheeks and her hair was a tangled mass that fell in a torrent over her shoulders and around her face.

"I'm afraid that I cannot allow you to indulge your self-pity any longer. This hall has been too long without the consolation of the lady. Your people, your soldiers yet in their bonds, need you now. You will have to endure better than this, if not for yourself, then for them, my lady." He held out a hand to help her from the bed.

She shook her head. Her whisper was soft and strained. "How am I to rise and go about my duties? As simply as that?"

"They have had losses as well, madame. We all have."

"You?" she questioned, giving a short laugh.

The anger glittered in his dark eyes. "Yea!" he snapped like the crack of a whip. "I do not bemoan my losses, nor weep as you are wont to do. I lost good men in the battle. I am set to the task of informing my son's mother that I am wed and bound by my own honor to act the husband to you. She has undoubtedly hoped that my conscience, if nothing else, would move me to marry her and give the boy a legitimate name. And, above all that, you seem to expect me to coddle you, when you should rise to ease the plight of the vanquished here."

"If I attempt to mend their bodies and hearts on your behalf, they will call me traitor."

"You are strong enough to take a blade to my back," he protested loudly. "You are brave enough to insult your captor, to bury your dead, to stand witness to the harsh blade of my justice. Where is your courage now? Can you not counsel these castlefolk on wisdom to save their hides because of what they may *call* you? They are conquered. If they do not bend, they will die."

He walked toward the door, turning back to her. "I have no more time for your selfish whims. Lavergne promised you were worthy of the task; he said you were both strong and wise. I tire of pleading my case to you."

"Oh Hyatt, why?" she questioned with a sob. "Why could we not be of at least the same army?"

He stood silent for a long moment, staring at her. "All in good time, my lady," he said quietly.

Aurélie sniffed back her tears and sat upright in the bed, clutching the pelts over her bosom. "Milord, will you send Perrine and my maid, Baptiste, to me? I should like to present a better appearance to my people."

"Baptiste? Is she the young, golden-haired one?"

"Aye. She is but three and ten. But she serves . . ." Aurélie stopped as she saw a flicker of emotion cross Hyatt's features.

"Your woman did not tell you? She is ill; I gave her leave to stay apart from chores."

"Ill? But . . ."

"She was raped, madame," Hyatt said impatiently, as if the words soured in his mouth.

Aurélie groaned, her mouth tightening. Her eyes took on a violent gleam. "One of yours, milord?" she questioned brittlely.

"Aye. They were told to respect the womenfolk who did

not fight them, and I saw for myself that the child was frightened into submission and did not deserve what she got."

"They obey you ill. Will he pay? Who did this to the child?"

" 'Tis odd that you ask for justice from me, the enemy, on behalf of your people, yet you have spent this week lolling about in self-pity. Is that what you ask of me, Aurélie? A lord's justice, quickly levied?"

"Tell me which of your heathens hurt the girl and I will avenge her," she returned hotly.

His eyes held hers for a long spell across the room.

"You saw," he said in a low voice. "It was Thormond, in the courtyard."

Her eyes rounded along with her mouth. "For Baptiste?" she asked weakly.

"That was not his only crime, but had it been, he would have paid. You are slow to learn, Aurélie. De la Noye is *mine;* her walls, her farms, her stock, her people. My word is the law here. Yea, Thormond paid for abusing what is mine. I could have forced him to wed the lass, but it did not seem prudent to give Thormond someone to abuse. He showed much violence toward the girl and would not have made a decent mate. I know that I am harsh, but I am not a fool."

Aurélie dropped her chin and looked down into her lap. She was suddenly ashamed of her self-indulgent grief, and sorry for even her criticism of his ruling. Her insides trembled in a quivering spasm. She had missed Baptiste, but had not asked after her. And there were others she had ignored. Guillaume. Sir Verel. Father Algernon.

"I am sorry, Hyatt. Should anyone ask, say I am resigned to my duty. I will come."

She heard the sound of the door as he left her.

❧

Aurélie found the best of her working clothes. She was cautious with her appearance, for she had learned that her dress signaled her people of her mood or motive. She would not wear her best clothing, but neither could she look threadbare and deprived. Her tunic was of a rough, durable cloth of dark purple wool over which she wore a heavy gray apron of sturdy linen. She chose a wimple to cover her hair and donned her leather girdle to carry her beads, pouch, paring knife, and keys.

Her mood was serious as she bathed and dressed. Once finished, she turned to Perrine. "Should this suffice? I do not wish to speak of either drudgery or elegance."

"Lady, they will be much relieved to have you about your duties again."

"Perrine, I am sorry. I should not have ignored the needs of this hall. This has been so hard for me to accept."

"Many fear you will fight the knight, lady."

"Fight him?" she echoed weakly. "I was afraid they would hate me for submitting to him. Now, I am afraid they will hate me for ignoring them."

"Lady Aurélie, they are too frightened for hate. They do not know what to do and most still move blindly through the hall, flinching every time one of these English knights orders them. They need your guidance badly. This Hyatt demands much of our people."

Aurélie had not seen Hyatt with her own people. Under Giles, Aurélie had been the only discipline. The Sire de Pourvre, too distracted by scholarly discussions and prayers, had left all management chores to her. The change for her people as they accustomed themselves to the harsh commands of a new lord must have terrorized them. "Is Hyatt cruel to them, Perrine?"

The old woman shivered slightly. "I do not know," Perrine whispered.

"You have watched him; you have warned me. Does he strike? Threaten? Rage?"

Perrine's eyes were filled with a frightened glitter, her voice soft. "Nay, madame. None of those." And again she trembled.

Aurélie sighed impatiently. The swaggering knight had struck terror into them all with his steamy glance, his clenched jaw.

He was crafty. He had meted out his punishment once, and in that single action all were filled with awe. She had thought him barbaric and ruthless; now she realized his intelligence. He had saved himself the work of fifty lashings with one swift slice of his sword.

"Come. I will see to Baptiste first."

The girl was more frightened than anything. In the week that Aurélie had neglected her people, the large bruise on Baptiste's face had dulled to a greenish hue and only the redness of tears marked her eyes. "He must have beaten you badly," she confirmed.

"I don't know why he hurt me, lady. I did not fight him."

"He had no cause. Can you come about your service to me now?"

"I am afraid of them, lady. I do not want to see the English knights . . . especially that one."

"He cannot hurt you further, lass," Aurélie assured her. "And no other will dare touch you, for Sir Hyatt has ordered them to be decent with the women. If you are able, you should find some solace in duty, for these English will remain. You cannot hide away here for long without going mad." She shrugged and smiled, for though she had only seen to one of her own, she already felt better for having some purpose. "It is easier to work, Baptiste, than to silently grieve. I did not find my part as a conquered woman an easy one to assume."

"Have the English hurt you, madame? Were you beaten?"

"Nay, Sir Hyatt has been cautious in his treatment of me, for Lord Lavergne is in residence."

"But he *wed* you. Did he —"

Aurélie's cheeks took on a darker shade of rose. She found herself almost wishing she herself had a bruise that would show. "Nay, he was civil. Now come, you need not worry about me. And this misery of yours will pass."

"Their master, Sir Hyatt, has told me to bring my troubles to his ear alone and they would be set aright. Does he plan some trickery?"

A half-smile tugged at the corners of Aurélie's lips. He was a difficult man to understand. Sworn, fighting knights were seldom soft and the gentle were unable to fight. Yet Hyatt could maim and kill without conscience and in the next breath, give tender counsel to a wronged girl of Baptiste's delicacy.

"I don't know, lass," she said honestly. "I have seen both his fury and his fairness. Keep safe; come to me with your worries and I shall help you."

"Do you accept this knight, lady?"

"It is only my wish to prevent any further death, and I cannot change their victory. Now, you must find your former strength, for you are needed." As Aurélie walked to the chamber door to leave, she stopped short, realizing she had echoed Hyatt's command to her.

Hyatt was not in the common room below, but Sir Girvin stood as she came down the stairs. There were only a few knights present, and none were lounging. Squires hammered the dents from their masters' armor before the hearth and fully fettered knights sharpened and polished their battle gear.

She approached Girvin. "The wall is held on your behalf; do these men never cease in their labors?"

"Not when the occupation is new, madame," he returned. "A soldier's greatest error comes when he thinks the battle swiftly done. These men of Hyatt's are always wary of comfort. They are a ready lot."

She smiled slyly. "You worry that King John will send troops?"

"He is well occupied by the Black Prince, lady." Girvin returned her smile. "And I do not think De la Noye will be among his first attempts. We are deep in Guienne and he would have to pass through too much of Edward's land. We encountered little resistance in coming here. Aquitaine is secure."

She felt her heart plummet. King John would not rescue them. It was hard to decipher relief from disappointment.

She would dance at a festival celebrating Hyatt's comeuppance, yet more fighting only meant more death, and she knew Hyatt would fight to the death of them all. Over and over, the message that it was finished assaulted her. The instinct to resist them would not die away. She bristled at the mere sight of the tall knight Sir Girvin; she despised his self-confidence, his control. It would help to see him frightened, if only for a moment. "You do not wear your mail or armor. Perhaps you will be caught unaware by some French troop."

"My duties lie within the castle, madame. But rest assured, I can quickly find my armor."

Aurélie looked around impatiently. "I have need of Sir Hyatt. Or my father."

"Lord Lavergne left the hall early and took a mount with some of his own men. I do not expect his return soon."

"Where has he gone?"

"His purpose was unclear, but I think he wishes to know the extent of the English occupation in Aquitaine. He will be a long time in finding any French settlement still intact. And Sir Hyatt is occupied elsewhere."

"He told me to see to my knights. How am I to do that when . . ."

"I will accompany you, lady. Our captives are held in the bailey."

"They have no shelter? Do you bother to feed them?"

Girvin frowned, but said nothing. He walked ahead of her, leaving her to follow him into the courtyard, around the large wall to the side of the hall. There, between the outer bailey and the keep, she found a camp. Canvas cloths and tents had been raised to give shelter, and a fire in the center of a large circle of men warmed a side of pork and boiled a large kettle of brewis. Their keeping was decent, but most were tied.

"They are untied in small groups that can be watched," Girvin said. "We know not which of these can be trusted. Do you come to help?"

She straightened proudly, holding her hands clasped before her. This was the hardest thing she had yet to face. Those knights who had gone with Giles were battle worn. Some wore bandages, but none here seemed badly injured. They had obviously not been released long enough to get any change of clothing and their unshorn locks and stubbled chins told there had been no grooming.

She located Sir Guillaume and met his eyes. "Bring him to me," she told Girvin, without naming the knight or pointing to him. With only a swift gesture from Girvin, two of Hyatt's men went to Guillaume, untied his hands, and pointed toward Aurélie.

She looked up at her vassal's face. She took note that the anger was still simmering, close to the surface in Guillaume's eyes. Girvin's close presence beside her must have chafed at her knight as well, for Guillaume would pay no regard to the English knight. She braced herself, for if Guillaume failed her now, she knew not what she would do.

"Are you well?"

"As well as can be expected, my lady."

"Not hungry, injured, or sick?"

"Nay."

"Do you serve me still, Sir Guillaume?"

"Yea, madame."

She took a stabilizing breath. "Do these English bring you word of what occurs in the hall?"

"They do not bait us much, madame. There is little word, but I was told you were unharmed and my lady wife was allowed to bring me food."

"Sir Guillaume, Lord Lavergne has come and now that it is done, he stands in support of the English siege. He mourns Giles, but he pledges to Sir Hyatt's rule on my behalf. My options were few, and the conqueror has wedded me with my father's permission."

Guillaume's eyes narrowed. "You are a widow one week."

"Aye. I know the length of time."

"Have you cast your lot with —"

She held up a hand to stop him, and slowly pinched her

eyes closed. Then slowly she opened them again. She had learned the way to control softly and she hoped Guillaume, who had taught her, had not forgotten. "Take heed, Sir Guillaume. I have been instructed to find those men who will follow my orders and serve the new lord. This I must do on behalf of Sir Hyatt for the safety of these survivors. I could not come here and ask for your release on my own behalf."

"And what will happen to us, madame? Are we expected to wield arms for the Englishman?"

"Nay, sir knight. You will be freed, but will carry no arms. This I do for you, for the temptation to strike will be strong in all those who have been loyal to Giles. For now, until your honor to your oath is tested, you may serve in other ways. 'Tis too much to ask you to defend Hyatt's lordship now, but yet you will remain bound if you cannot at least accept his rule."

"Must these men who are released swear to him?"

Aurélie turned her head and looked up into Girvin's eyes. The knight did not meet her gaze, but stared straight ahead, leaving the matter to her. With a sigh of resignation, she looked back to Guillaume. "Not yet," she said softly. "For now it will be enough if you do not fight him. But soon, Guillaume. I know you are too proud for this, my loyal man, but save bloodshed, I pray. Convince these men to take freedom. Do this for me. I cannot bear to see you so restrained. I need you at my side again."

Sir Guillaume looked deeply into her eyes for a long, difficult moment. His eyes slowly shifted to Girvin, and the two acknowledged each other for the first time. "It would have been better for me, lady, had Sir Giles taken me with him on the campaign." This was said to Aurélie, but Girvin and Guillaume looked hard at each other.

"It would have been a worthy contest," Girvin said in his impeccable Gascon tongue.

Aurélie knew what had happened between them. Intense hatred trumpeted, but the echo around the words demonstrated a certain mutual respect. She could not help but understand that Girvin had given in this exchange, for it was not necessary for the victor to bestow the merest word to attest to the abilities of the loser.

"You were left with me because in both wisdom and strength you were the best man. I am sorry for us all that Giles lost the battle, but I can do nothing to change that."

Her voice drew his eyes back to her. Then he slowly turned to speak to the closest bound knight behind him. His voice was too soft for Aurélie to hear, but the man turned startled eyes to stare at her. Her plight was being cautiously explained. The man's hands were tied in front of him and he looked several times between Lady Aurélie and Sir Guillaume, stunned by disbelief. Finally he swallowed and gave a slow nod.

Sir Girvin stepped toward Guillaume and withdrew the short blade from his belt. He extended it, handle first, to Guillaume. Aurélie watched with some relief as the man was cautiously released. Around the captives' camp, Hyatt's men stood back, weapons sheathed, for the release.

Aurélie looked at the faces of sitting, leaning, reclining prisoners. Some were too young to have gone to battle, some too old. There were linen bandages, the blood dried and blackened, that alerted her there would be injuries to tend in the hall following this release. Eyes that held grief, confusion, fear, and shame studied her and the tall knight who escorted her.

She sighted Sir Verel and her throat constricted. The knight had been with Giles for only five years and he was their best. At five and twenty, he was handsome, strong, and proud. After Giles's father's death and the subsequent deterioration of their army under Giles's inadequate leadership, some knights fled De la Noye in search of a stronger troop to serve. But Sir Verel remained and tried to groom a better army. He had worked hard to train and lead able soldiers, though much was against his success. There had been little enthusiasm from Giles, and no money to bolster them. In Verel's blue eyes there glittered a fierce hatred. A linen cloth stained with blood was wrapped around his upper arm and another at his right thigh. His mouth turned down in a sneer as he stared at her, and she shuddered. Surely Verel would choose his ropes, for here was a stubborn and driven warrior. She tore her eyes away from his and looked again at Girvin.

"Will that do, sir knight?"

Girvin smiled down at her and took her elbow, leading her away. "You deal with the beaten with experience, madame. It appears you have done this before."

"The terms I offered them meet with your approval?" she asked, carefully suppressing her distaste for what she had done.

"As I said, it is as if you have done it all before."

"Certainly Sir Giles brought captives here."

Girvin threw back his head and laughed heartily. "I find that hard to believe. Sir Giles did not appear much of a leader of soldiers, although I did see some worthy in his troop."

"Do not delude yourself," she snapped back. "Giles, for himself, was more scholar than soldier, but his men were not lacking. They were a strong, loyal force."

"Ah, Sir Hyatt has tamed you well. You warn me."

"Nay, you will not be warned," she huffed, stomping back to the main hall.

" 'Tis a pity. To warn me might save a life."

Aurélie stopped short. Over and over again she found her anger gained her nothing but more trouble. She stood for a moment in thought. Verel.

She sensed that Girvin had halted behind her, in wait. She slowly turned to face him again, and if her pain had been great in dealing with Guillaume, it was even greater in explaining Verel. Tears sparkled in her eyes. "There is one among them," she began, trying not to sob.

"Who?"

Aurélie faltered and her voice broke. She wiped at her eyes nervously, for it bit her deeply to beg mercy from this man. She wished to lift her chin proudly, but it was impossible for her.

"His name is Sir Verel. He served my husband for only five years, but as a good and strong knight. He often worked the other knights in contests and challenges and has never before lost a battle. He is young, sir knight, and his temper is short, his loyalty deep. Perhaps he is foolish; I do not know. But he does not deserve to die because of this. Give him his freedom. Banish him."

"And let him take the secrets of the keep to another army? Nay, it cannot be done. Will he attack Hyatt's men?"

"I cannot say," she answered softly. She looked into his stormy, unyielding eyes. "But if he learns the way of this conqueror, perhaps he would be a good soldier. I think his ways are much like Sir Hyatt's. I fear it will not be easy for him to bend."

Girvin gave a slow nod. " 'Tis good. There are those among the Sire de Pourvre's men-at-arms who are worthy of Sir Hyatt's troop and those are the same ones who cannot easily yield. Sir Hyatt looks for loyalty that is difficult to break."

"Will you be merciful?"

He shrugged. "It depends on what this Sir Verel will dare."

"But if you watch him . . ."

"You plead for so many lives."

"There *are* many. Holy Mother of God, say you will try to preserve rather than punish those things you admire. He is loyal. He is strong."

"I shall use caution."

Aurélie whirled away, dissatisfied with the response. She feared for Verel, who had often criticized Giles's lack of discipline with the men. Verel was a good leader. Giles often had said he would make a good lord.

"My lady."

She turned back as Girvin beckoned.

"If it is possible to bring him to the side of the victor, it will be done. The weight is on Sir Verel's shoulders, not yours, to find the side he serves. To give fair warning of the best and most loyal may save bloodshed and provide a better guard in your future." He smiled broadly. "Sir Hyatt will be pleased."

Her cheeks burned scarlet. She fled from him and gained the common room quickly, her feet putting the distance swiftly behind her. She entered and eyed the familiar scene of knights and squires working.

"Sir Hyatt's captives are being released and this hall will soon hold injured in need of ministrations. You will make room for them."

A few startled eyes rose to look at her. Clearly these men were not accustomed to taking instruction from a woman. The door behind her softly closed and she was aware of Girvin's presence, but it was to the landing at the base of the staircase where the men-at-arms looked.

She turned to see Hyatt, just descending. There was a faint smile on his lips as he regarded her.

"You have spoken to the Sire de Pourvre's knights?"

" 'Tis what you ordered me to do," she said impatiently.

"Did you offer to free those who can submit?"

"They are beaten. What more do you wish?"

"Your word that they will safely reside here."

"It will take far more than my word to make them heed your rule here, my lord. I offered them release without their arms to reside at your mercy. I can do nothing more. Perhaps one of them will slit your throat as you sleep."

His brows rose in amusement and he crossed his arms over his chest. "Then keep them tied, lady, lest my blood stain your naked breast, for that is where my bare throat is likely to be found."

There were a few chuckles about the room. She heard the shuffling of men gathering up their gear to make room for her injured. "Hyatt," she said in a breath, shamed to the core.

"They will make room for your men, Aurélie. Warn those you tend that I have no desire for more killing. But I will reward violence with violence. It is my way."

He came down from the last step and pulled his gauntlets

from his belt, passing Girvin to go outside. The hulking knight followed and Aurélie was left to look at the few men still getting their things moved. She struggled to control the rage she felt, clenching her fists at her sides. She did not know how to fight him. He left her no way to spar. She could not show her fallen knights any bruises, she could not swell with the bastard offspring of an errant knight, and she could not abandon them for her own solitary mourning. It would be easier to tend the wounds of those who had fought beside Giles if Hyatt had at least abused her.

But her anger fell abruptly away as the first of many knights of De la Noye entered the hall. She looked at Sir Delmar and pain dimmed her furious eyes. Sir Delmar was too old for fighting and the bandage about his head had started to yellow. He shuffled weakly, carrying his shield but no weapons. One arm was tied to his chest and there was suffering in his eyes. Vengeance would wait.

"Sit by the hearth, Sir Delmar, while I find women to help me here."

Again her emotions were steadied by work, for at least a dozen who entered the hall needed her attention. The women from the cookrooms came willingly and some village women were brought to the hall to receive their men. She learned that the more serious of the wounded were tended by squires and pages of Hyatt's and only those who could wait for tending were held as captives. But still she found infections among them, and unset limbs that would heal badly and remain deformed.

Many questions were asked of her and she tried, with painful difficulty, to explain that Hyatt's occupation was complete and she could think of no alternative save total surrender.

"He cannot turn us into English forces."

"Nay, but until you see some French army, let him think he can. I have seen his broadsword work. He is swift and will not ask you twice."

Almost two hours had passed and Aurélie was already

exhausted when Sir Verel came into the hall. He cast wary glances about the room. A few of Hyatt's men casually watched the mending of the wounded. Aurélie knew they were far from trusting even though none braced himself for any uprising.

She guided Sir Verel to a bench and bent to the task of cutting away the bandage at his thigh. She silently worked, not meeting his eyes. She found no problem with his injury and tied a new linen strip around his thigh. She rose to repeat the task on his upper arm, again avoiding his eyes.

"I will avenge your husband's death," he whispered.

"My husband is Sir Hyatt. Were you not told?"

"You coddle the bastard?"

"I obey, since I cannot fight."

"Do you invite him to stay? Here?"

"Nay, but he requires no invitation from me. He will not be beaten by any army, much less a single knight. Do not be foolish."

"He has taken your husband's place. He deserves to die."

"He will kill you, Verel. I cannot protect you."

He grasped her arm in his good hand, forcing her to meet his eyes. "Long ago Giles said that if he fell, I would take De la Noye and rule, since there is no heir. Guillaume was to be my seneschal."

Aurélie saw the vicious gleam in his eyes, and though she was unaware of any such arrangement, she reasoned it was possible that Giles had made such a promise. In any event, Verel was the most likely, even if he was among the newest to join Giles's men-at-arms. "And me, Sir Verel? Did Giles bequeath me?"

The young knight's eyes softened. "I have always been your protector. Have I ever lacked honor in my treatment of you? I would not have wedded and bedded you before your husband was cold in his grave."

"That has all changed," she said softly.

"I cannot bear to think that he . . ."

He was stopped in mid-sentence by the startled gleam in

75

Aurélie's eyes. "You speak like a lover, Sir Verel. Our conversations have been few; nothing ever bound us but Giles."

"I have *worshipped* you! I could not come closer, for my honor was at stake."

"Oh, Verel, stop! Say no more! I cannot endure these words. You must believe me when I say that Hyatt will surely harm you if he thinks you harbor jealousy for his place in my bed. God help us, I did not know of this greater bond, this desire. Swear you will never speak of it again."

"But my lady, the English swine does not please you. I know you wish to be free of him, even at the cost of life."

"Swear!"

"How can I? I . . ."

"I shall ask them to tie you, Sir Verel. I shall tell Hyatt of your desires."

"You couldn't do that. You wouldn't."

"To save you, Sir Verel, I would tie you myself. You are the best that remains of De la Noye's knights. I want you to *live*."

She was certain that she had not reached his better sense, for his eyes were aglow with both hunger and agony.

"I will do nothing. For now."

"Oh, Verel, I am afraid for you."

"Do not worry about me, Aurélie," he said, using her name for the first time in her recollection. She was shocked by the passion in his voice, the unconscious flexing of the muscles in his arms. She had not known this knight desired her. And she had not been aware that Giles valued him beyond his warring skills and that he had made promises regarding De la Noye. The shock of this revelation was almost as intense as the heartbreak of being overthrown.

She tore her eyes away from his and swallowed hard. She picked up a linen bandage with trembling fingers and tied it around his arm. "Your injuries are minor. You need not remain in the hall."

"Protect yourself, Aurélie," he whispered.

"I will not try to advise you past today, Sir Verel. I have warned you; that is all I can do."

"I expect nothing more."

She rose to leave his side and found she could not face any of the men. Without raising her eyes, she ventured to the stair. She nearly collided with Hyatt's broad chest. With a startled gasp she looked up into his suspicious eyes. She had no idea how long he had been standing there and she watched as his gaze drifted slowly from her face to Sir Verel's, then back to hers again.

"Your wounded are tended, my lady?" he asked.

"Yea, they are being cared for."

"Good. Are there any problems among them of which I should be aware?"

She shook her head, half frightened and half sad. "Please, milord, may I be excused? I can bear no more of them."

He touched her cheek with the knuckle of his finger. "Go ahead, madame."

She fled up the stairs toward her chamber, pausing at the top to look down at Hyatt. She imagined that his eyes were burning into Sir Verel, for he stared into the common room. Then he slowly turned to follow her up the stairs, leaving everyone who saw them to wonder if they bedded together in the light of day.

Aurélie knew he would follow her. She sat on a small stool in front of a cold hearth, struggling to collect herself. He came into the room, but stood just inside the door.

"What is it you should tell me?"

"There is nothing, Sir Hyatt."

"You are unsettled."

"Indeed," she flung back at him. "Would you be at ease in such a circumstance? I have had to explain to my dead husband's forces that I am wed to the conqueror and seek their docile acceptance of our lot. Lord above, Hyatt, I am ever amazed at what you expect of me."

"No more than I believe you are capable of."

"Please . . . give me a few moments alone, I beg of you."

She turned away from him, hearing the door softly close as he left. A shudder possessed her.

Her mind went over the years of companionship with Giles. She shook her head in disbelief. She had tried to bear her burdens graciously, while the villeins whispered piteously about her sadly barren state. And she had hungered for affection, craved physical love. Had she known that Verel, the most handsome among them, had lusted for her . . .

Her shoulders shook with her sobs. She had felt such longing that when the conqueror came, her body betrayed her even to the enemy. Surely she could not have resisted Sir Verel, had he but spoken his desire. And now, Giles, who had never touched her, was dead, and an honorable knight of France wanted her. But between them stood an English warrior who would not hesitate to kill. Hyatt held fiercely what he had claimed.

She wept piteously. The only time in her life that a man had spoken words of love and passion with the will to consummate such oaths, he was a prisoner and she was wed to the victor. The Englishman had arrived and acted quickly, branding her in vows and body as a wife, but there was nothing of love. All she had ever prayed for was the love of a good man, and the joys of intimacy and children such a love could bring. It had always seemed like such a modest prayer.

"Oh Verel," she cried, "had your passion been spoken sooner, I might have yielded all. Hyatt might still hold the power of life and death over me, but he would not know my secrets. Now, such spoken words will only be stained with my tears, and your blood."

She had longed to hear words of love. Now through pain and fear, she wished she never had.

URÉLIE looked from the window in her bed-chamber into the inner bailey below. Orderliness slowly fell over the castle. The cloths and tents that had housed the wounded and captive were being dismantled and villagers wandered in and out of the bailey doors. Everyone who had fought for Giles had accepted their freedom.

She heard the chamber door open and close and knew that Hyatt had returned. She had used an hour of time to compose herself, but it seemed not enough. Months, she reasoned, might not ease the plight in her heart. She did not turn to look at him.

"Sir Girvin tells me to be wary of Verel, and I know Guillaume would risk his life for you. Are there others?"

She shook her head. She knew of no others who were so driven. It amazed her that there were things she did not know of her own people. She had not expected Verel's spoken desire. What else had missed her close perusal?

"I know it is difficult for you. You did well."

Aurélie turned toward him. "It is difficult for them, milord. I would ask one thing more."

He gave a slow nod that she should voice her request.

"Please do not touch me so before my people. They look hard at my face and hands, hoping to see some marks that shows I fought you until I had no strength to stay you."

"I don't know why, Aurélie. Surely as they view us they

should see it would be very foolish for you to fight me. Women are not expected to die for nothing."

"There are those who think De la Noye is *something*."

He put up his hands, palms facing her. "If it serves some purpose for you, I shall keep my caresses to the privacy of our chamber."

"It saves me some dignity. Am I not allowed that?"

"There is seldom dignity in being captured, my little Aurélie. You are very slow to understand. And caution your hot young knight; I will not condone his appraisal of you as if he already tastes your sweet flesh."

"How dare you . . ."

"Did I mistake his eyes, madame? If his gaze had been fingers, I would have had to slay him for trespassing."

"What do you know of it? He was Giles's staunchest vassal. He mourns his lord."

" 'Twas not mourning, *chérie*. It was lust. Do take special care, for Verel can be replaced . . . and you cannot."

He strode out of the chamber, leaving her alone with his warning. Nothing was ever missed by this man. She sat heavily on her bed, staring at the wall. She, and each of her vassals, stood naked before him. He accurately interpreted every glance, gesture, whisper. She had seen confusion only once in his eyes, and that was his perplexity over how Giles had won and maintained her support.

She meant to learn Hyatt's weakness. However, she did not expect to gain any knowledge by sulking in her room. She would relearn this keep, as she had learned it twelve years ago. She would watch the organization of two opposing forces, judge the strength of her people, and observe the habits of this new troop of men. She meant to become as good at judging her foe as he was at judging her.

Aurélie made only cursory trips through the common room, entrusting the tending of the wounded to other women. She examined the cookrooms, spoke with the villeins for the first time since the coming of the English. She paid her calls to widows and children. She saw weaponless soldiers installed with their families or casting about in search of a place to bed down. Hyatt's men and additional servants had left little extra space in the hall, outbuildings, and stables. A knight who had once resided in the hall took his refuge with a recent widow. A page who had lost his knight was placed with another, but this time his role was to carry bales of hay. Where there had been four to a room, there were now ten. Wagons, tents, and mean shelters littered the outer bailey, for many residents had been rousted from their inner bailey or village hovels. Aurélie worried whether there was enough food to feed them all, victor and vanquished alike.

The sun was lowering when she moved through the corridor toward her chamber. She was halted in mid-stride by a shriek, a ringing slap, and the abrupt opening of a chamber door. Baptiste came stumbling from the room backward, tripping on the frame and falling against the opposite wall, a hand clasped to her reddened cheek. Aurélie was but five paces away. She saw the girl's tear-filled eyes and the shocked wonder on her face.

"I'll have you whipped, you belligerent slut!"

Aurélie looked toward the chamber to see a wildly enraged woman brace herself against the frame with both hands. Coppery tresses fell errantly over her bare shoulders, her eyes sparkling with fury. She looked ready to hurl herself at Baptiste, and Aurélie flew to place herself between the two.

"Nay, madame, do not harm her," she ordered, crouching to see if Baptiste was hurt.

"I would not have burned the child, madame," Baptiste choked.

Aurélie turned pleading eyes to the stranger. "Madame, the girl serves well, but it is her first day of chores after a battering from these knights. Patience! Please!"

"Bah, the ignorant whore deserves a battering. She is a fool. She meant to bathe my son with scalding water."

"Madame, she is a *child,* and she has never tended the

young for her duty. She usually attends to *my* needs." Aurélie turned to Baptiste. "Why have you not kept yourself to my rooms?"

"I ordered her to serve me. I am of Hyatt's house. 'Tis my right."

Aurélie's temper was slowly building. "You may enjoy a victor's right without destroying the spoils, madame. If you have needs, seek me and I will place the best servant in your hands. Baptiste is a tender lass and need not suffer your abuse."

"And who are *you?*" the woman demanded.

"I am Aurélie, and I *was* the lady of this hall."

The woman showed some surprise and then quickly collected herself, crossing her arms over her ample chest and leaning in the frame of the door. She leisurely surveyed Aurélie from her toes to her nose, a superior smile playing on her lips.

"So we meet. The wife and the mistress."

Shock etched itself on Aurélie's features, though she quickly chided herself that she should have expected as much. The woman was beautiful, almost exotic, with her fiery hair cascading freely over her bare shoulders. Her lively green eyes were animated, her lips moistened to the shade of a peach. Her gown was not only revealing, but elegant. She was not working to settle Hyatt's possession, but beating the servants.

Aurélie felt no superiority when facing Hyatt's vixen. Something inside her shrank convulsively. He had need of wifely talents as the keeper of the provender, but surely this woman could entertain him in his leisure time.

"Shall I send you a servant who knows how to tend the young?" Aurélie asked.

The woman threw back her head and laughed. "Please, madame, send a servant who can help mine. I have three to serve me, but I need another. Hyatt has one son now, but there will be many."

"There are needs in the hall. It may take some time to find

the right woman," Aurélie said, turning to help Baptiste to her feet.

"Then leave this wench. I will teach her myself . . . or beat her for her mistakes."

"Nay, madame, she comes with me. By Hyatt's order, she is to be left alone. She serves under my care, or not at all."

"*Hyatt's* order? He will let me have her."

"If he wills it, she will return. Otherwise, Baptiste stays with me. And I shall find a servant for you when I can."

"When you *can?* You must think yourself mighty here, *lady.*"

Aurélie turned to walk away. How could she be so cruel? But then Aurélie did not expect pity for her grievous losses. Especially from Hyatt's mistress.

"I hear you are barren," the woman chided. "Should you like to see my son? Hyatt's firstborn?"

Aurélie continued toward the stair without responding to the woman's wicked jeering. She pulled Baptiste along with her to safety. She heard the woman's door slam by the time she had led Baptiste to the top of the stairs.

"Did you hurt the woman's child?" she asked gently.

"Nay, my lady. I was about to add cool water to the boiling kettle when she became enraged and slapped me. I do not know how she could think I would hurt the child."

"Stay with Perrine, or keep yourself near me. You cannot please her — do not try."

"My lady, she is so evil. How did you keep from slapping her?"

Aurélie smiled ruefully. Her own justice in this hall had been swift and sure. She had not often had to resort to physical punishment, but poor Baptiste remembered well that Lady Aurélie did not condone such disrespect. "My poor lamb, you cling to useless memories. I only appear to be the mistress here, but I am a servant like you. My role is to serve Sir Hyatt's whim and I have already seen what he does to people who abuse what he owns."

"I do not believe he values her. She is a shrew."

Aurélie touched the girl's sore cheek with a loving, grateful caress. "She is here, sweet Baptiste. Sir Hyatt would not keep her close if it were not his desire. Believe me, he values her. Tread carefully."

❧

Aurélie's second meal in the hall since Hyatt's coming was a strange experience for her. Lord Lavergne occupied the seat on one side of the conquering knight and Aurélie was placed in the other. The woman, who she had learned was named Faon, occupied a lesser place at the end of the lord's table. But oddly, the woman seemed in lively, entertaining spirits. She had dressed herself elegantly and laughed and joked with Hyatt's men. Aurélie was confused by the woman's acceptance of this role, but she kept her questions to herself.

Lord Lavergne was not so gracious. "Hyatt, I perceive a grave mistake in keeping this woman, your mistress, in residence at De la Noye."

"Oh? Do you?"

"Aye. It should prove a poor example for other men, leaving them to think that they might freely take any number of women that suits them. Many, I suppose, will join mistress and wife in the same family."

Hyatt chuckled ruefully. He looked between Faon and Aurélie. "If they think they can, who am I to forbid them?"

"This strange situation disgraces my daughter," Lavergne pushed.

Hyatt raised a questioning brow. "I could have sent her fleeing the English armies in rags. Now there, my lord, is a disgrace."

"But Hyatt . . ."

"Enough of your judgments. It is my problem. I shall handle it."

"At least you admit it is a problem. Have you asked your wife for her preference?" Hyatt refused an answer. Instead, he banged his empty tankard on the table and a page rushed forward to bring him ale. "Daughter?" Lavergne pressed.

Aurélie sighed. "Father, you must leave these things to Sir Hyatt. He will not condone your interference," she said quietly.

"Do *you* accept this arrangement, Aurélie?" her father asked her.

"Father, I have accepted a great deal worse."

"The woman should be sent away from this hall. Back to her people. This will breed trouble. Your wife could tend your son . . ."

Aurélie's surprised eyes focused a long moment on her father. She couldn't believe what Lavergne dared. "Father, please . . ."

"Well, you would do it, would you not? Tell him. He is your husband now. You are entitled to some authority in such matters."

She looked warily at Hyatt, surprised to find that there was a tolerant amusement in his eyes as Lavergne pleaded his case.

"Well, Aurélie . . . tell him your preference."

"Father, I have no children, but if I did, I would not wish for them to be taken from me. Leave this to Sir Hyatt, and place none of this problem on my shoulders. Now be still, lest she hear you."

"Why would I care who hears me? I . . ."

"You," Hyatt interrupted, "must carefully recall that there is a difference between an ally and a vassal. A very large difference. And I am not your vassal." He quieted his voice. "Take your daughter's advice, my lord. Leave the matter to me."

The discussion at an end, Hyatt resumed his meal, eating heartily and hurriedly. Lavergne was finally quiet. When Hyatt had finished, he rose and went to speak with Girvin. While her husband and his knight were in conversation at the other end of the room, Aurélie turned to her father.

"My lord, you must heed Hyatt's words. Believe me, you do little to help me when you come to my colors in such a way."

"I have a right to . . ."

"My God, you are more difficult to teach than I have been. We have no rights here, Father. Hyatt has made it clear that he will not tolerate any question as to his rule. If he chooses ten whores to place at the foot of my bed, I have nothing to say. Do not try to match him again."

"How can you abide such indecency? I have raised you above the likes of these base habits."

"I have buried my husband and seen my men-at-arms turned into stable hands. Believe me when I say that none of what you raised me for has been mine this past fortnight."

Lavergne's eyes dulled sympathetically. "Does he treat you badly?"

She looked down. "There is very little joy in this marriage."

"And this business with his whore, Aurélie? This surely hurts you deeply."

She raised her eyes and looked at her father. "Father, I do not love Hyatt. Why would I care?"

"He is your *husband!*"

"He is the lord of the hall. If I am dissatisfied with his habits, where do I plead my case? To King John? To the Black Prince?"

"To *me.* I am your father; I am his ally now."

She shook her head. "One more word from you, Lord Lavergne, and you will be sent from De la Noye on the back of a mule. Hyatt has no need of your alliance."

She rose slowly to fetch a pitcher and fill her father's cup. She carefully poured the ale. "While you enjoy the food from this table, Father, I bid you remember, you do not eat from Giles's storehouse. Nor from mine. Everything you touch belongs to the Englishman now . . . until some French army comes to wrest it away from him. Should that happen, I fear there would not be much for either of us to enjoy. Hyatt would likely fire the keep before he would turn it over to anyone."

She returned the pitcher and sat beside him again.

"Do you hate me for this, Aurélie? Did I do you wrong, giving you to him?"

"I know you meant to help, Father. Nay, I do not hold any grudge against you or anyone else. You thought to restore my position and my home to me. Yet I do not forget for one moment that I polish Hyatt's cups, roast his pork, keep his house. And you must accept this, or we shall have more trouble."

She stole a wary glance toward Hyatt and found that as Girvin spoke to him, Hyatt's eyes were upon her. She ended the conversation with her father after one glance at Hyatt's suspicious frown. He did not trust her. Of course he should not, for she would undermine him if she could. But did he not realize how totally he had intimidated her? If she could think of the slightest way to plot against him, she would. But alas, he gave no sign of any weakness. She had spoken the truth when she said that he held his conquest firmly.

Hyatt left Girvin's side to speak to others in the room. He braced an arm with one comrade, partook of a toast with another, and paused to inspect the repairs that a page had made on a bridle. It was a long while before he returned to the table, but he did not sit. He stood behind Aurélie and placed a hand on her shoulder. "Have you eaten your fill?"

"Aye, Hyatt."

"You leave so much on your plate. You will become too thin."

She turned to look into his eyes. She couldn't help but think of Faon, whose soft, round curves must be more to his liking. "My appetite will return, given time and fewer wars."

"Good enough. Bid your father good night."

Aurélie merely nodded toward Lord Lavergne once and then went with Hyatt toward the stairs. She was grateful that there were very few of her own people in the common room, and those few present were frantic in their service to the demanding knights. It was better that only Hyatt's people could judge his impatience to take her to bed, since she did not care what they thought of her. In her resignation, she had forgotten Faon.

"My lord," the woman's voice interrupted, causing them to stop on the third step.

Hyatt turned toward her.

"My lord, I have need of another servant, and your lady wife will not give me one."

"Oh?" Hyatt questioned.

"I had ordered a maid to help me in the care of your son, but your lady wife took her away and will not allow her to serve me. I have explained my need, but she refuses." Faon placed her hands on her hips and looked up at the twosome. "She makes her decisions in your name, Hyatt."

Hyatt crossed his arms over his chest, leaned against the staircase wall and looked suspiciously between Aurélie and Faon. Aurélie met his gaze without a tremor. "I have offered to look for a woman to help, but there are so many needs in the hall, it has been difficult to find the right one."

"Return the girl to me," Faon said, smiling victoriously at Aurélie.

"Sir Hyatt, 'tis Baptiste she wishes, and the girl knows nothing about tending to children. I'm certain her work would not please Mistress Faon."

"I will attend to that," Faon said. "I do not like it when I am chastised by your lady wife, Hyatt. It places me in a poor light among your people. You said you would not have me ridiculed."

"I did not . . ." Aurélie stopped herself. She chewed her lip in indecision, realizing she would be treading on shaky ground by either defending herself from Hyatt's lover's accusations, or by criticizing Faon's actions. "Perrine," she finally said, her eyes brightening as the thought came to her. Perrine would not allow herself to be abused, as Baptiste had. She could smoothly duck an angry slap and would not be easily frightened. She unconsciously placed her hand on Hyatt's arm, excited and pleased by the clever way she could keep Baptiste safe. "Let me give her Perrine, milord. She knows much about caring for children. She would serve better than Baptiste."

Hyatt frowned. "You have only one attendant, and you would give her to Faon?"

"I will have Baptiste," she said victoriously.

"She is only a child. She will be of little help to you."

"She will learn. Please, milord? I do not need so much."

Hyatt's frown darkened. "The girl will not be very useful in our bedchamber, Aurélie. She quivers and shakes each time she passes me in the hall. She sets me on edge."

Aurélie laughed suddenly, an amused ripple that brightened her face. Her smile, which had been rare indeed in the past week, was captivating enough to melt even the armored heart of the warrior. "Oh Hyatt, she is frightened of men. When she discovers you mean her no harm, she will be at ease as my servant. You'll see. Please?" She tilted her head and lifted a brow. " 'Tis better than what you will endure with Perrine's motherly fussing. At least Baptiste is shy."

Hyatt sighed. "I dislike problems between women." He looked pointedly at Faon. "You now have four servants. Treat them well or you shall have none. And bring as few complaints to my ears as possible."

He took Aurélie's arm and began to climb the steps again. Aurélie looked over her shoulder at Faon and met with the woman's venomous glower. Aurélie felt as if she had won. Hyatt had not actually taken her side over his mistress's, but she was learning that there were some things she could wheedle out of even this stubborn knight. She allowed herself a winning smile and took great pleasure in the way Faon huffed away from the stair.

The sight that greeted her in the bedchamber caused her smile to fade as amazement took over. Two pages whom she had seen in the hall were hurriedly stacking Hyatt's things in her room. They had even brought in the writing desk from the lord's chamber. Hyatt viewed the chaotic scene and threw his arms wide. "Can you do no better than this in two hours' time?"

"Pardon, my lord, but we should have it set aright shortly."

"Come tomorrow after I have gone. I am not going to sit about and watch you . . ."

"Hyatt? What is it they are doing?"

"I told them to bring my belongings and some of the furniture into this room, since it is where I shall remain. But they cannot accomplish even the simplest . . ."

"But Hyatt, do you not desire your own chamber?" she asked.

"It is a luxury I cannot afford. Have you noticed the numbers we house?"

We? She almost started at the sound. He meant to stay with her, night after night? She was surprised speechless.

"The . . . the lord's chamber is larger."

"I have an aversion to Giles's bed. And the room will hold ten men-at-arms. This will do nicely, when it is in order."

"It will take only a few moments, with their help."

Hyatt looked around the room, frowning his irritation. "How long?" he asked.

"Less than an hour, surely. But alone it will take me half a day."

Hyatt whirled away from her and went to the door. "Have it done, then. You may instruct these morons before they do any real damage to my things."

Aurélie smiled at him. He dealt very poorly with domestic problems. "I shall see to it, Hyatt. May I ask Perrine to help me before I send her to Mistress Faon?"

"Madame, I don't care if you require Perrine for the next month. Faon does not need another servant and I know what game she plays. In fact, if it will get me sooner to bed, you may go to Faon's chamber to get the help you need."

"Thank you, milord, but I think we shall be able to manage."

He looked into her eyes with intensity and she knew it was not for want of sleep that he was impatient. Strangely, Aurélie felt a swell of pride in his act of moving permanently into her room. And she felt certain victory in his denial of his mistress. She admitted to herself, however, that this was beyond her own understanding.

"It is a minor chore, Sir Hyatt."

"Good," he said softly. "See it done in minor time."

ॐ

Spring faded into summer and a meager planting was begun. There had been so much hardship and resettling to be done that those farmers who would have tilled the land were fewer than on the previous year. Yet the available labor and skills were so well organized that to Aurélie's amazement, a larger portion of land was utilized. The weather warmed and would soon give way to a scorching heat, but De la Noye was becoming more settled, more resigned. Lady Aurélie suspected that there were a few peasants and serfs, if not her own men-at-arms, who would rather abide this Englishman with his strange ways than endure any more conflict . . . or return to the unsubstantial methods of Giles's rule.

Hyatt worked them hard, overzealous in his demands and control, but improving results were already within sight.

An early evening fire was allowed to die as darkness fell and residents slept, for the winter chill had left for good. Aurélie had begun opening the heavy shutters at nightfall to let the June breezes freshen the bedchamber while she slept. She had lain beside her conquering knight for over one month. It did not seem possible.

Hyatt had forgotten to extinguish the single candle beside the bed and she took advantage of the light. It was not frugal to let the candle burn low, but she raised herself on an elbow and studied the features of the sleeping knight. In his state of rest his face had a boyish innocence, yet she of all people knew his implacable strength.

The coverlet rested at his waist and she marveled at the finely developed muscles of his upper arms and chest. His brown hair was overlong now and streaked by the sun, as was her own. Their labors were driven outdoors for the planting and breeding of the stock. This knight, she mused, had a definite love of physical labors. She had watched him, albeit from a safe distance, at work in practicing arms, overseeing the pasturing of animals, directing the assarting of the wooded land, and inspecting the maintenance of the castle. In every task he displayed a singleminded attention, a fervor and commitment.

And remarkably, he had energy left when he came to the bedchamber. She nearly chuckled in recollection. The first time she had eyed him sleeping he had bolted awake as if her eyes were needles that pricked him. The second time he had roused to find her watching him. But now he slept. His sleep appeared peaceful.

She sighed heavily. Had his army not slain her husband and others of her house, making this home a booty of war, there might be no rift between them. He had not spent one night in his mistress's bed. If he visited Faon by day, he was discreet and it did not deplete his desire for his wife. She doubted the mistress was kept to her liking. And he showed fairness to the villeins, although he was stern. And he treated her well. He had rescued her, with his sword, from a lifetime of loneliness and longing. But she could not thank the English army, nor could she let herself be trapped by any deep emotion for him.

Ah, but he was a magnificent man. If he were French, he would be perfect.

Aurélie cautiously extracted herself from the bed and took light steps around to the commode. She blew out the candle.

"Aurélie? Why are you about?"

"The candle, Hyatt," she whispered. "It would have been a waste to let it burn." She gently crept back into the bed.

He opened his arm to her. "Come," he said sleepily. "Closer."

She hesitated for a moment and then snuggled closer to him, resting her head on his shoulder. There was little point in fighting him in the dark of night. Here, where they were only two people and not two countries opposed, it would be acceptable to share his warmth. No one would see that she indulged in the new feeling of a protective arm, though this arm belonged to the enemy. No one would know that she sometimes pretended, late at night, that this was a union of love, and not bondage.

"Ah, wench, you are the softest thing. Do you think that I am unaware when you watch me sleep?"

"Oh Hyatt, does nothing escape you?"

"Nothing. What rouses your curiosity so?"

"You are a curious man, Hyatt. You conquer, then coddle your prisoners. You make high demands, but demand as much of yourself. I do not know when you will be cruel or kind, harsh or soft."

He chuckled and hugged her close. "Be careful, Aurélie. If you find some tenderness for me they will call you traitor."

"I shall be careful," she promised.

"Perhaps you cannot help yourself. Women have this affliction; they fall in love with the nearest available man, exercising very little wisdom. Trouble is stirred by these feeble notions. It will be better for you if you realize that I cannot be controlled; not by brute strength nor love."

"Oh, Hyatt, you need not warn me. It is not too late for me yet."

"Beware, *petite*. Women are foolish bondslaves to this malady; they crave this love and delude themselves that it cures some ill. Then they become vicious when it only brings pain. I warn you freely — I am not a likely victim."

"And men, Hyatt?"

"Men work. Women pluck the strings of hearts. 'Tis the way." A sound escaped her, but there was no word. "What say you, woman?"

"Naught, Hyatt. Go to sleep."

❧

Hyatt stood in the open window and watched the sun rise over the farthest knoll. The countryside did not appear war-torn or ravaged, yet not far behind them there were battles between the forces of Edward and John. Other keeps were falling . . . or English knights and soldiers stained the fields in blood of failure. He feared for Aquitaine; Edward's forces were fewer than John's. Aquitaine was Prince Edward's possession now, but the rest of France resisted.

Yet De la Noye had passed from the French to the English. Hyatt had planned it well; through Lord Lavergne he had learned that the Sire de Pourvre had been a weak, strange, incompetent lord. And he also knew that De la Noye, if managed properly, could be rich. He looked at the makings of such richness from the window — the grove of fruit trees, the good roads, the stout wall, the fertile acreage. Had Giles put energy into work rather than prayer, money into seed and stock rather than the buying of benefices, Hyatt would not have been able to take the castle.

What he saw from the window was not unlike his homeland. The fine sight that spread before him turned his memory to a time early in his youth. It was faint, now, but buried in a private place whence he could still retrieve it, if he dared. The remembrance of lush fields, blossoming trees, strong horses, happy villeins, and family love came to mind. He chose to ignore the memory because all that had been lost to him and was painful to recall.

He had had joy as a small child, as a second but favored son. He was stronger and quicker than his older brother, Ryland. He vaguely remembered the warmth of his mother's arms, and a vision of her sweet face would not be subdued, no matter his desire to forget. He was only ten when she died and Lachland Castle and towns fell into mourning, into a long-lasting despair. His father seemed to have lost his will to live and ruled poorly. Ryland was too young, at thirteen, to take responsibility. And Hyatt remembered being jolted more by what his mother's death had done to destroy the happiness of everyone, than by the pain of her loss.

Both Laidley sons were sent away to earn their knighthood as squires to neighboring barons and, upon returning to Lachland, found the place deteriorated.

And then a new woman came to the castle. Faustina, a strong young woman from a rich Welsh chieftain's family, married Lord Laidley and changed the face of the castle and towns. Hyatt was pleased, at first, that his father's spirits were lifted, but his comfort was temporary, for Faustina was treacherous, selfish, and cruel. She had a harsh, punishing hand that Lord Laidley would not attempt to stay. She was possessed of a brutal greed and squeezed every family in their domain for more wealth. And while Lord Laidley had been satisfied to answer the king's call, Faustina urged him closer to the king and counseled him in politics. Her schemes and plots were many; she once had a Welsh heiress whom she had hated since childhood kidnapped and ransomed at a high sum.

Hyatt was appalled by her, but his father and Ryland allowed her and even took her advice. And of course, Lachland was returned to its former wealth and status. But there was no happiness. Hyatt quietly disapproved until his scorn for her vile habits burst from him in a temper, winning only his father's anger. Not long after, Faustina claimed herself with child and named Hyatt as the sire. Lord Laidley punished his wife severely and banished his son. Hyatt was then sixteen years old.

Life since then had been only struggle and work. Girvin followed Hyatt out of Lachland and they worked as mercenaries, slowly building their reputations. On a campaign in Wales, Hyatt fought so fiercely it was said he would have been satisfied to win singlehandedly, for he imagined Faustina's face behind every Welsh wall. He had joined Edward's forces in taking Crécy, protecting the young Prince Edward and being credited with saving his life. He had made a good fortune in Calais, allowing him to hire a larger troop. His reputation was strong in England; he was regarded as one of the best.

Hyatt slowly collected men, modest victories, but he had never held any lands until now. And as to women, he had never made any commitments of any kind. He turned from the window and looked at Aurélie; even in that commitment he had been driven by a harsh purpose — he had meant to get everything that De la Noye could offer. It offered wealth, prosperity, higher influence, and a place to roost, to leave to sons.

Aurélie did not know, he mused, that until this marriage, he had never spent an entire night in the same bed with a woman. He'd entertained himself with Faon, but he knew her to be ambitious, conniving, and capable of being quite dangerous.

When he had found Faon, he had succumbed quite easily to her seduction. Yet she had attempted to trap him into marriage. She took the tale of her lost virtue to her father, Montrose, and Hyatt had been called out for the deed. Montrose lost the contest. Hyatt, being the winner, was offered the woman. But Hyatt refused to take her, and Faon's father promised he would kill his own daughter, rather than be disgraced by a bastard. Hyatt took her out of her father's home and carried her along with his traveling troop of soldiers.

Faon was well guarded, since Hyatt was very suspicious of her, and when she came with child he knew he was the sire. He saw her cared for and she stayed in his camp. Derek was born in a tent at the edge of a battlefield. He bargained with Faon. He would keep her, pay her way, accord her a few benefits, or he could as easily settle her in a home with enough money to keep her and the child. He gave her a free choice and suggested that she could as easily play the widow and live a free and shameless existence, but he would not marry her. Never.

Faon argued for her son, Hyatt's firstborn child. This Hyatt found agreeable. "I will bequeath firstborn rights to this child, if you give him to me. If you choose a life apart with him, his future is dependent on the estate you acquire through marriage. The choice is yours, but it is final after today. Should you change your preference in two years or ten, you leave my protection without my son. After this time, you may not take him with you."

"I must stay with him," she had insisted. "I must stay with you."

Had Faon proven, even for a little while, to be a good woman, he might have taken her to wife. But he knew she was bad. And he loved the boy. Several times he had considered sending her away, but she had pleaded with him on behalf of Derek. He damned his soft heart where women were concerned. It was foolish to become snared by them. Since Derek's birth, he desired no more bastard children and had never gone to her again.

"Why does she not see that I am generous with her, and respond with goodness?" he had asked himself many times. "Why does she seek to use my power to her advantage? How does she foolishly believe that I do not see her plots and schemes? How does she pretend there is anything of love? How does she live with this, that I only meet my obligation? Does she still perceive that she can bind me . . . though over and over she fails?"

He knew he had nearly gone the way of his father with Faustina, and this dragged his spirit low until he could overcome the fear with sheer willpower.

He found himself standing at the edge of his bed, staring at his wife. *Wife.* What had he done? Yet this one caused him deep thought, for her plotting was subtle. He did not find evidence that she used evil tactics to destroy him. Her schemes were of the softest sort, for he had felt a tugging at his heart on the first day he saw her.

They were opposite. Faon had triumphed in her plot against Hyatt and had been ceded much more than she deserved. And still, Faon was wicked and played dangerous games. Aurélie had been the strength in her husband's home, had been conquered, made a captive, and although her anger sometimes seeped through, she served in the castle better than any, although he knew she hated her role. Her position as his wife was more degrading than Faon's position as the mother of his illegitimate son. And she did not even openly battle Faon's treachery, but sought to soften the witch's blows with reason.

Aurélie stirred and turned over, mumbling something in her slumber. He lost the sight of her face and was left staring at partially exposed, round buttocks. *Women,* he silently cursed, ever seeking to tether and weaken a man, whether by means of wickedness or feigned sweetness. How could he doubt that they were all after the same thing, though their methods were varied?

He gave her rump a hearty *thwack,* bringing a startled yelp out of her and causing her to bolt upright in bed. She stared at him through sleepy, incredulous eyes.

"You may desire to lie abed all day, madame, but there is much to do. Lord Lavergne departs today and I would be ashamed to tell him that you cannot bid him farewell because you are lazy."

Her eyes narrowed and she rubbed her posterior, more insulted than hurt. "If my sleep offends you, milord, you have my permission to rouse me."

"I just did," he said, walking impatiently to the door. "Get up, woman. The sun has risen. I would prefer to see a little more spirit."

She threw her legs over the bed, glaring at him. "And I would prefer to see *less.*"

"You have complained that no mark of my beatings leaves you any dignity when facing your people. Perhaps you can throw up your skirts and show them that you are sufficiently abused. That will serve you well."

Aurélie sat in stunned disbelief for a moment. She had no idea what had caused this strange mood. She could think of no offense she had committed. But he stood there by the door, very pleased with himself, watching her.

She lifted a finely arched brow and an odd smile graced her lips. "You are ever a mystery, messire. 'Tis not that I expected to remain free of beatings, but I heartily doubted you would damage your own favorite sporting ground."

Hyatt threw back his head in sudden, unrestrained laughter. "Ah, woman, you are coming to know me too well." He whirled around and left the room, his mood changed yet again. She could hear his laughter as he went down the stairs.

"Aye, messire," she said to herself, "though it is a long, agonizing task. And to what end, I have no idea."

LTHOUGH Lord Lavergne had traveled to De la Noye with a troop of twenty men, Hyatt provided an additional escort for the old lord to the coast from which Lavergne would sail to Flanders. The journey from De la Noye to Bordeaux would take four to seven days, and in that time the redoubled troop could encounter hostile French or English. Lavergne could be attacked by one of Edward's armies if they did not believe he was an ally, or by a French army because he was. In addition, there were hundreds of locals, frightened by the threat of conquerors, who would fight anyone who came too near their villages.

Aurélie was content to see her father go. She sighed in audible relief when the group departed and the outer bailey gate was closed. Without his interference she might have been granted retirement, travel to Lavergne's demesne, or perhaps she could have taken leave to a convent home. Though she finally knew the secrets of the marriage bed, she had lost the peace, comfort, and gratification of ruling her own home. Her life was now a contradiction. Her father, in his good intentions, had only made things worse. She shared name and bed with her conqueror, and her people watched her warily, trying to judge her position as either for or against the English occupation. There was little dignity allowed her in this odd alliance; to fully yield her heart and loyalty to the knight would cause her people to think her fickle and disloyal, and to hold herself back seemed already futile and absurd. Although he was English and bound to Edward rather than King John, Hyatt was more of a leader in one month than Giles had been in a dozen years. She bid Lord Lavergne farewell gratefully, before he could confuse her situation any further.

"It appears that you will not miss your father," Hyatt remarked with some amusement.

"I think he has done enough for me," she replied flippantly.

Hyatt laughed, fully understanding her meaning. "Do not blame the old lord, Aurélie. Had he not argued for decency, I would have made you my mistress and let the bastards fall where they would."

"At least there would have been sufficient shame in that position to please the conquered, milord," she said with a curl of her lip, turning away from him. "Then my people would not wonder about me. A forced marriage to me does not give Guienne to England." She began to walk away from him and was jolted to a stop by a harsh thwack on her posterior. She whirled around to glare at him, her eyes glittering with blood-lust.

He smiled at her fury, crossing his arms over his chest. "You like pain, *chérie*. I only wish to please you."

"It would please me if you would not act like a knave."

"I am patient. You cannot go on pretending to be a mistreated slave forever, when you know you are treated as well as any treasured wife. Soon, you will have to choose: will it be I and the wrath of your pitiful vanquished people or will you choose their pity while you struggle against your husband?"

"Do you propose to choose, *seigneur?* Between making me a cherished wife and playing the conquering warrior?"

"They are one and the same, *petite.*"

"Nay," she flung back at him. "My people know that I was wed by force and all that I do is done to preserve De la Noye. I will *never* choose against my home. De la Noye is the babe at my breast."

She turned to walk away again and his words gently pounded her back.

"De la Noye is not safe until you make your choice, my lady wife. Not until you show these people by your actions and devotion that the castle and you belong to me. *Pretz, sabers, cortezia, umiltatz.*"

Her pace was slowed, but she did not turn back to face him with her astonishment. Hyatt's accomplishments continually astounded her. Most knights were warriors only; poor, unlettered mercenaries. Hyatt must have come from a very good house. He first struck her with the truth about De la Noye, which she loved deeply. She lived in a castle divided and she alone could join the opposing factions together. She had cautioned her people to submit, but she did not encourage them to accept Hyatt as their leader. Until Hyatt's army and her people stood side by side, they could easily fall to any attack. If the forces of France approached and Hyatt was overtaken, they could suffer under the next ruler. Would he be weak like Giles, or more ruthless than Hyatt? She knew there only true safety lay in a united people.

To further astound her, he recited the female virtues in the troubadour fashion; virtues she did not possess with him now, but had been reared to believe valuable and necessary. *Excellence, wisdom, courtesy, humility.* She had worked hard to display these womanly strengths while married to Giles.

That she could not be what she had always believed a perfect woman must strive to be, that she could not rise to her own desire to be virtuous as well as courageous, gnawed cruelly at her heart. She trudged slowly on, thinking how far from her intentions her life had wandered. In her honorable marriage to Giles there had been much missing; she had not been safe, ruled, protected, or bedded as a wife. And with Hyatt, the marriage forced at the point of the sword, she found that she was provided that which had been lacking before. Yet there was no genuine love, dignity, or honor, and the purpose for Hyatt was to secure material wealth on behalf of an English king.

Why could Giles not be *strong* . . .

. . . Or Hyatt weak?

❧

Aurélie entered the common room of the hall after nones,
the afternoon prayers. She had prayed overlong, for her
confession could not yet be fully drawn from her. She wished
to seek the help and absolution from Father Algernon for
her sin of cursing her dead husband for his weaknesses and
hating her living husband for his strengths. But lacking the
courage to bare her soul to a mortal man, she begged divine
inspiration, and still left the chapel feeling empty.

The common room was quiet, for all castlefolk were using
the best of daylight in their outdoor works. She was surprised
by the few who lingered there and stunned to see Baptiste
sitting on a rug of skins before the hearth, playing with Hyatt's
son. Aurélie looked around the room and did not see any of
Faon's servants, not even Perrine. She had only seen the child
a few times, and never at close hand. He seemed to be kept
mostly out of sight. She approached Baptiste and the child,
crouching down near them.

"Baptiste, how have you come by this chore? 'Tis not what
I asked you to do."

"I could not help it, lady. The woman threw the child into
my arms and told me to watch him here until she returns.
There was nothing to be done but obey her."

"She must surely intend to find some fault with your care.
Did you not think to seek out one of her other servants?"

"I could find none, madame. I would not dare leave him
unattended."

Aurélie ran a gentle finger along the child's chubby arm
and he turned trusting brown eyes toward her, smiling and
gurgling happily. There was little doubt that he was Hyatt's.
Though his face was roundly padded with baby fat, the set
of his eyes, his wide, strong cheekbones, and square chin
pronounced his paternity. His hair, thick and wavy brown
like his father's, fell in the same errant fashion.

"Baptiste, what is his name?"

"Derek."

"Ah, Derek," Aurélie said, smiling and putting both hands out. "Such a handsome lad."

The little one grasped her fingers quickly and pulled himself up on chubby legs. He began a rhythmic babbling of bah, bah, bah, swinging Aurélie's hands as if in a dance. Aurélie knelt, letting the little boy play his game, laughing with him and making equally incoherent sounds, adding a few "weeeee's" and "boo's" for his entertainment. Not two minutes passed before she was pulled into the child's games and oblivious to all else. Worry was dismissed as Baptiste played too.

They formed a triangle among them to roll a ball, Derek's effort bringing more giggles from Aurélie and Baptiste. There were hand clapping, tickling, and face making. For a moment Aurélie had forgotten that the child was Hyatt's bastard son and that she was a prisoner-wife. It was so natural to play with the child, to cuddle the softness of his baby skin, to listen and laugh at his crude attempts at words, and try to help him refine his speech.

A shadow fell across their play. Behind Aurélie stood Faon, erect and frowning. Her rich velvet gown lay in wide gathers around her feet and gold bracelets decorated both arms. Faon never covered her magnificent hair, but wore it fully curled about her face and falling in ringlets to her shoulders. She tossed her loose coiffure as if it were a lion's mane.

"I should have known I could not trust you," she said unpleasantly. "You've let the witch near my son, when this woman means him harm. Now you'll be punished."

Aurélie rose quickly, facing the fiery vixen bravely, though she was smaller and slimmer. "Nay, madame, she will not be punished. You forced her into your service against my word and that of Hyatt's, and she'll come away with me now. You may tend to your son yourself." Aurélie reached out a hand to help Baptiste to her feet, leading her quickly away and toward the stair.

"You think you fool me with your little games?" Faon

railed behind her. "Hah! The boy's presence frightens you as much as mine. Derek will inherit all that is Hyatt's and he will never deny my rights as the child's mother. You are a prisoner, nothing more. You are kept against your will, while I am invited to stay as an honored guest. Do not think yourself so superior, *lady,* for your time is short . . . especially now that your father is gone."

Aurélie turned before mounting the stairs. She judged the woman's brazen beauty and noted that her flashing green eyes were filled with fear. She wondered if Faon would display such a tantrum if the room were filled with Hyatt's men, but the common room held only two young pages seated in a distant corner with armaments to mend and polish. The well-trained English youths turned a deaf ear to the scene and kept their eyes downcast as good lackeys should.

Faon was losing ground. The child was the fulcrum on which she balanced the precarious weight of Hyatt's tolerance. In a sudden flash of truth Aurélie realized that it did not matter how Hyatt regarded his marriage, whether it was a union of deep feeling or a bond tied for material safety. Hyatt was selfish, stubborn, and strong. If he desired Faon he would have spent many nights with her.

"You are right, Faon," she said softly. "You are here as an honored guest, because you are Derek's mother."

Aurélie pushed Baptiste up the stairs ahead of her and followed, listening to Faon's outraged shouting behind her, soon turning Derek's pleasant gurgles of fun into cries of discomfort and fear. "How *dare* you speak to me so! You high-flown bitch! You have no children of his loins, but mayhap if they ever come from your barren womb, Hyatt will strike them down to preserve his son's demesne, and you will surely know what he *loves!*"

Aurélie closed her bedchamber doors on the cries of the mother and child. She felt pity and sadness for the boy, having to grow up in such a terrible, jealous home. Perhaps Lavergne was right. Hyatt's decision to keep faithful to his promises would breed trouble. Faon's presence might be more than even the stalwart knight could endure, and it was certainly a trial for Aurélie.

"Do not leave my room unless it is on some errand of my bidding," she warned Baptiste. "I do not know her purpose, but clearly you are the one person upon whom she can easily vent her anger."

"What am I to *do?*"

"Stay away, when possible. Perhaps it will pass."

"But lady, we did the child no harm. We . . ."

"Understand, lass, the woman sees the child as harmed by his mere knowledge of me. She fears that Hyatt's marriage will cost her too much. Only I know that Hyatt wed me at my father's request, to help him secure these castle walls on his behalf." Aurélie cocked her head and listened to the quiet. The ranting and crying had stopped. "Come with me to the weaving rooms, lass, and help me to look over the yarns and cloth."

❧

Faon burst from the double doors of the hall and ran into the courtyard, crying and hugging Derek close to her bosom. She passed a dozen serfs and fettered men-at-arms in her flight to the stable. Tears coursed her cheeks and she panted in sobs, not ceasing until she came to an abrupt halt at Girvin's solid chest. "Hyatt," she whimpered piteously. "I need Hyatt. Where is he?"

"He is judging a mare for breeding. What is it you wish?"

"*Get* him!" she demanded. She looked up into Girvin's fierce expression. "Get him, you overgrown lout!"

Girvin stiffened, his dislike for this woman eating like worms through his gut. "I'll decide if he is to be called out of the stable, Mistress Faon. Tell me your problem."

Faon pushed her whimpering son toward the huge knight. Derek squealed once at being moved so harshly. His nose was wet and his eyes were dripping with tears. She showed Girvin a chubby bare leg on which the delicate skin was scorched raw in a perfect line that ran from his little thigh to his calf and swelled with a blister of blood.

"The bitch found my child alone with one of her servants and tried to maim him. 'Tis the mark of a hot poker that burned him, and had I not come into the hall, she might have killed him."

"Lady Aurélie?" he asked, the sound more of an angry growl than a question.

"Aye, the *lady!* Do you doubt it, fool? Why would she allow a poor bastard child of mine to live, to take away all that she thinks is *hers?* Get Hyatt for me at once."

"You bring the injured lad here? Why do you not take the boy to be tended?"

"He must see," she wept. "Hyatt," she yelled in the direction of the stable. "Hyatt!"

"Get the boy tended," Girvin ordered. "I will find his father and send him."

"Hyatt! I want Hyatt!"

"Mistress, you — "

The stable doors opened with a bang and Hyatt took long strides toward the bickering twosome. His quilted gambeson was rolled up over his elbows and his hands were filthy with stable dirt. He looked in confusion at Faon, her tear-stained face, and at his crying son burying his face into his mother's bosom. "What the devil is . . ."

"Your lady wife, milord," she cried, her voice no longer shouting but wheedling. "I could not find anyone to tend the boy and left him with that useless child who serves your lady. The lady hates the child, milord. She . . . she . . . *burned* him!" She pushed Derek toward Hyatt and upon seeing his father, Derek burst into cries anew and reached for him.

As Hyatt's eyes fell to the injured leg, fury sparkled in his eyes. He took Derek from Faon, carefully holding the burned leg away. "You *saw* her do this?"

Faon gasped with sobs. "She *fled* as I entered the hall. Of course it was she. None of your own nor any of these pitiful swine you have conquered would dare, but she is so jealous of the flesh of your loins, milord. 'Tis because she is barren and cannot have children for you. What did you expect from her? You gave her this power through marriage. Oh, Hyatt, you hurt Derek so badly when you refused your name."

Hyatt's muscles quivered with the will it took not to sputter in rage. "He *has* my name! He may be called bastard by others, but I have given my oath and promise to my son and 'tis *you* without proper titles and names. Where is she?"

"I don't know, Hyatt. When Derek was crying from his hurt, she fled. Hyatt, you must end this with her . . . before she kills your son."

"Where is Perrine?"

"To chapel to atone for her sins. She is insolent and not to be trusted. I cannot depend on her to keep my son safe from the bitch who claims to be lady of this castle."

Hyatt looked over his shoulder to the stable doors where Guillaume stood, his appearance much like Hyatt's. The men had been hard at work currying destriers and making decisions about which mares to breed and which to keep fallow. At the slur against Perrine, Guillaume's features hardened, but he said nothing.

Hyatt stormed past Faon, the child clinging to him with little arms tight around his neck.

"Hyatt, where do you go? Hyatt, you must help us; you must protect us."

He heard Faon's cries and the sound of her feet, running to keep up with him, padding along behind him.

"Hyatt, say you will give me justice! Hyatt, promise me justice!"

He kicked open the door to the common room, nearly taking the heavy oak off its leather hinges. A page came running from the cookrooms in response to the noise.

"Lady Aurélie," he barked, his eyes bright with anger. "Where is she?"

"I do not know, my lord. I have not seen her."

Hyatt took the stairs two at a time, Faon close behind him. He could hear the sound of her heavy skirts, which she lifted in an attempt to equal his speed. He used his foot to open his bedchamber door, but there was no one in the room. He shouted once for her, his voice booming down the dark gallery. A frightened maid peeked into the hall. "The looms, milord," she said weakly.

Hyatt climbed a third flight and by this time Faon was losing her stamina. But Hyatt moved swiftly in the direction of his wife, cradling his son close to his chest.

Faon labored up the third flight, her eyes dry and her head clear. *She does not know what havoc his anger is,* Faon thought. *He values his son above all else and while I could be trod upon by the feet of any swine, Derek cannot be abused or Hyatt will surely kill. Perhaps on this very day the bitch will lose her head. . . .*

The door to the weaving rooms burst open and startled gasps rose.

"*Aurélie!*"

She rushed toward him with fearful concern brightening her eyes. She looked first at Hyatt's face and then at the child. Hyatt turned the boy and exposed the burn. "Dear God," Aurélie breathed. She did not consider but one reason for his coming. "Oh Hyatt, give him to me. Your hands are dirty," she said, taking the child gently from his father's arms. Derek was willingly transferred and put his head on her shoulder, his cries now subdued to tired whimpers. "My grease and salves from my chamber, Hyatt. You know the pouch. Hurry! Oh sweetheart, poor thing," she cooed.

Hyatt stood immobile, watching as Aurélie took Derek into her tender arms. She carried him toward the window ledge, where she sat on a long bench and held the boy on her lap.

"Baptiste, clean water and rags. Quickly now." She held Derek's cheek against her bosom while she held out the injured leg for a better look. Impatient for her maid to bring a basin of water, she lifted her hem and used the soft fabric of her shift to wipe the dirt of Hyatt's hands away from the sore, murmuring to the child as she did so. "Oh, my lamb, you are so brave, so good. Sweet little dove, it will heal quickly." She looked up impatiently at the boy's father. "Hyatt! My pouch!"

From behind Hyatt came a startled gasp. "Hyatt, get my son away from that witch. Hyatt!"

Hyatt walked into the room and took the basin away from Baptiste. "Go for the pouch that the lady needs," he said. He took the basin to Aurélie, noting that Derek sat on her lap without resisting, without crying. Aurélie did not even regard Hyatt, nor did she notice Faon. All of her attention was focused on the child.

Hyatt turned his back on Aurélie's ministrations. He stared across the room at Faon. The tears on the woman's face had dried and her eyes reflected this betrayal with cold accuracy. He took slow, pained steps toward her and as she watched him approach, she checked her temper.

"I will put the boy in your care only one more time," he said evenly. "Tread carefully, Faon, and understand that I do this as a debt I owe to you because you labored with his birth. But it is the last time."

"You do not even question her. You do not even suspect her."

He raised a questioning brow. "You said you did not see who did this thing to my son. Do you lie?"

"Nay. I found him thus, but it was she who hurried away from the accident."

"You should *never* find my son thus. I grant you servants to help you because it is my wish to be generous with you. But I keep you with me only because you are his mother."

She shook her head in denial. "You have cast me aside for that haughty witch, but before . . ."

"Nay," he snapped. "Before it was the same as now. I gave you your choice long ago, when you came with child because of my errant affection. I offered you sustenance and a strong arm to lean upon in deference to what you would give me — a son. But you had my word that I would never marry you. It is not too late for you to leave, but . . ." He turned and looked across the room at his wife and child. "But you will leave without him."

"How do you live with yourself, doing this to me?"

"You did not mind that we were unwed before. You even preferred it. You have used much authority among my men with your haughty behavior. And you have failed in the one thing I have asked of you; it is your duty and no other's to see him properly tended. If a lazy or stupid servant injures him, whether intentionally or innocently, 'tis you who must take blame for putting him in jeopardy."

"You know not how unjust your designs, Sir Hyatt." She gave her head an angry toss in the direction of Aurélie. "You will regret this, for you have put your son's welfare in the hands of the same one who will do him harm."

Hyatt chuckled at the woman's absurdity, his voice low and mocking. "Are you that much of an imbecile? I knew you to be conniving, but I never thought you were stupid. If Aurélie wished vengeance, she could make me a eunuch in the dark of night, for I lie bereft of armor at her side and, I admit, I sleep soundly. She would not have to stoop so low as to hurt a defenseless babe." He crossed his arms over his chest. "But what of you, woman? How low would you sink for vengeance? Would you harm your own son?"

"How . . . ?" She looked at him aghast, words failing her and her question stopped incomplete. Her eyes welled with genuine tears and she turned from him, fleeing down the stairs. He heard her sobs dwindle with the distance and in another moment Girvin was trudging heavily up the stairs. The knight's face was stony and dark.

"Hyatt, a page says that Faon was alone in the common room before the shrieks of the child were heard."

"Did the page see the accident?"

"He is one of ours, Hyatt. He sees nothing that he is not bidden to see. But I warn you that Faon . . ."

Hyatt held up his hand to halt Girvin, more than aware that Girvin had a severe dislike for the audacious mistress. "I have heard enough of blame and accusations. If no one saw it happen, we do not know how it happened. What matters now is that he is tended."

Girvin looked past him into the weaving room and far to

the rear, past the still and silent looms, a group of women were gathered around Aurélie and Derek.

" 'Tis not what the wench expected you to do," Girvin snorted. "You fuel the hate. Be wary, Hyatt. You, of all people, should know how treacherous a woman can be, if allowed. And yet you keep two, when both have cause to hate you. That I have failed to teach you is excusable. That you have failed to learn from your own life is unfortunate." Without waiting for any reply, Girvin turned and left his master alone in the corridor.

❧

Aurélie felt depleted of emotion by the time her duties were called to the cookrooms and common hall. She moved through her task of overseeing the dinner with an unusually soft voice. When a page failed to carry a tray filled with meats to a table full of English men-at-arms, she carried it herself rather than chastising the youth.

She served, or ordered Hyatt's table to be served first, then the English knights, then the knights of De la Noye who were now workers, and finally the castlefolk who took their meals in the hall. Her step was slower, but her vision more acute than ever.

When she had returned Derek to his mother's rooms, Perrine was there to take him. Faon was not in evidence in the chamber. The boy's leg had been bandaged, and Perrine surprised Aurélie with the news that within Faon's modest household there was a woman who was skilled in healing. She was old and doddering, but carried many herbs, balms, odd samplings of roots, weeds, and animal parts for her use in creating new cures. Why, Aurélie wondered, had Hyatt brought the boy to her? Aurélie's own skills with tending the injured or sick were very modest. She had learned a few things from Perrine, and while not afraid to try her best on any malady, she did not experience a great deal of success. It was for that reason that whenever there was a visitor, a troubadour, juggler, aristocrat, monk — anyone from another town — she questioned them about remedies they used.

112

Why did Faon's woman fail to share her healing skills with the rest of the castle? Those who knew the arts of tending the sick or hurt were usually a generous lot who held themselves above taking sides, but applied their talents to anyone in need. That was the way of her people . . . but perhaps not the English.

She waited until she was satisfied that the room was served before taking her place beside Hyatt. She met with Faon's hostile glare briefly, then turned her eyes to her plate. The food was tasteless to her, the conversations going on all about her sounded distant and garbled. In her mind, as in her heart, there was a faint thudding like a faraway drum, and all else was dark.

A month, she thought vaguely. A month gone, many to come, and I am too confused to make sense of all this.

"Pass the lady wine," Hyatt commanded.

She did not look up and he impatiently filled her goblet. She took a modest slice of meat, tore off a fistful of soft bread, and lazily swirled the gravy around her bowl.

"What ails you?" Hyatt asked harshly.

"I am tired, milord," she said, sighing.

"Only tired? What bites at you now?"

She sighed and looked at him. "There is nothing, Hyatt," she whispered.

Hyatt covered his displeasure by lifting his cup. He ate his fill, drank liberally, but his eyes were drawn to Aurélie more often than he liked. He was deeply troubled by her peculiar slowness, quietness, professed tiredness. Before even questioning her, he had noticed the way her head bent lower than usual, and not in a posture of obedience, but almost sadness. Her eyes seemed focused on a distant point, and she stared unseeing.

Hyatt had seen her beaten, raised up, chastised, praised. He had seen fury rage in her blue eyes, just as he had witnessed their sparkle when she had cleverly foiled Faon. And he had seen her moist, parted lips in the aftermath of passion. What he saw on this night was entirely new. It was a draining of the spirit. He had not counted on anything, her tenacity, her wisdom, her subjugation, her joy; but he had believed there would always be *spirit*. He had learned to recognize it in the men he trained and had seen it in very few women. It was like a candle glowing behind a drape; a light that shone from within that nothing could extinguish.

When the platters and bowls were emptied, Aurélie supervised the cleaning of the tables and floors. She loosed the hounds to pick up the scraps and sent the boys for dry wood, though a blazing hearth was unnecessary. Dying torches were replaced with new ones and pitchers were filled for one last cup of ale. The sun went out like a doused flame and darkness subdued the activity in the room. She took a place beside Guillaume on a bench and asked him if he was well, if he had any needs. Her voice was painfully soft.

Before Guillaume could answer, Hyatt stood before them. Many of the knights, squires, and pages had begun to leave the hall to seek out either late night chores or bed.

"Guillaume, your seneschal, has worked with me for many days," Hyatt said to his wife. "His talents far surpass simple warring skills."

Aurélie looked up at him. "A seneschal has more to do than hold the wall, my lord. During times of battle, Sir Guillaume fights well, but when there is no siege, he has managed the castle and selected the archers and guards. Every chore in De la Noye must be understood by a castellan."

Hyatt pulled a stool from nearby to sit with them. "You work well, even now," Hyatt said to the older knight. "Though I think I know the reason. Like your mistress, you work for De la Noye and not for me. How long has it been since you have resided in the seneschal's house?"

"Since your coming, my lord," Guillaume replied.

"Where do you sleep?"

"In the rooms behind the stable."

"And your wife?"

"She is ordered to Mistress Faon."

"Where does she sleep?"

Guillaume shrugged, confused by the questioning. "On a pallet on the floor in her anteroom, to be close when called."

"Perhaps you would like your home again," Hyatt offered.

Guillaume stiffened slightly and even Aurélie tensed. She worried that it was too much to ask Guillaume to defend De la Noye on Hyatt's behalf. "My lord, I should like a room with my woman, but I cannot pledge fealty to Edward of England."

"Did I ask it of you? You should hear me out, Guillaume, before you decide I am a fool. Can you pledge fealty to Lady Aurélie?"

"I did that many years past, and hold the oath as sacred."

"So be it. On the morrow I must take a troop northwest toward Limoges to judge the progress and mayhap lend aid to Edward's armies. I shall leave Sir Girvin to protect the hall, but I do not wish to overtax him with Aurélie's protection. Yet this you have attempted for a dozen years and, most times, done well. If I give you personal arms, will you guard her?"

"Hyatt, I am safe in my own . . ."

"Will you?" Hyatt asked Guillaume, cutting her off.

"Yea, Sir Hyatt. That is my wish even if you do not ask it of me."

"Good. Know these things; should you decide to escape, go far and fast, for I have good horses and can find you. Aurélie might be brought home, but it would be over for you and Perrine. If you allow another near her, if another man touches her in my absence, 'tis treason and wives are killed for the crime. And finally, if you plot against my rule of the castle while I am away, I will take De la Noye again, and I will take her with much more violence than before. Do you understand?"

" 'Tis only Lady Aurélie I would serve and protect, Sir Hyatt. I do not have the means to fight you . . . or pledge to you. But I can pledge to the lady herself."

Hyatt chuckled lightly, checking eyes with Aurélie. She held confusion in hers. "Guillaume, I swear it is the first time

I have been relieved to hear someone assure me they will not pledge to me. Forsooth, I could not trust your oath to me, but I think you will do right by her. And 'tis best for her that things proceed as they are." He stood from his stool. "The planting does not require me, the horses to be pastured for mating are selected, and apart from hunting parties that Sir Girvin will command, I am freed to go about my duties for Edward. Be it a week or a month, serve the lady's needs and upon my return, you shall have your house and Perrine." He held out a hand to Aurélie. "Come. I am not at ease when you whisper with your old castellan."

She went with him to the stair, allowing herself the luxury of looking over her shoulder to give a quick smile to Guillaume.

Until learning that he would leave De la Noye, it had not occurred to her to question him. Once in their chamber, she studied him as he removed his clothing and carefully placed it away.

"Why do you reward Guillaume?"

"Reward him? You misunderstood. I gave him a weighty chore."

"But you will give him the seneschal's home, and Perrine."

" 'Tis his home," Hyatt shrugged. "I have displaced as few as possible."

"The seneschal's is the richest single home in the keep. What of Girvin?"

"He is happier with the horses. Girvin prefers to ride and would not stay behind now, but that I insist. And Guillaume knows each nook of this place."

"Perhaps you should have wed him, Hyatt."

Hyatt threw back his head and laughed heartily. "A worthy notion, woman, but I think he would not bring me as much pleasure in the dark of night." He looked at her squarely, but she did not even smile. "You, however, have proven lively sport . . . when you forget yourself."

His hand ventured near and she turned away from him, taking a few steps to put distance between them and then, facing him again. "Sir Hyatt, did you bring your son to me for tending, or was it another trick you play?"

"Trick? The boy was badly hurt . . . and, I think, maliciously."

"You thought I did it?"

"I did not accuse you."

"But you brought him directly to me, when there is a woman in Mistress Faon's service who is more skilled than I. Was it to see if I would show my guilt upon spying the injury? Did you expect me to fall before you in shame? Hyatt . . . do you think I could do such a thing . . . to a baby?"

Hyatt did not answer, but kept his gaze level with hers.

"Hyatt, do you love Mistress Faon?" she asked brazenly.

"Nay," he replied easily, void of emotion.

"Do you love me?"

"Nay."

"Why do you keep her here?"

He raised a brow. "Do you know the answer, *chérie?*"

"Aye." She lifted her chin. "You set us apart, placing yourself in the middle, and you wait to see who will win." She shook her head. "You will be disappointed. I shall not enter the fight, Sir Hyatt."

He took two steps toward her. He touched her cheek with a finger. "You misjudge me again. If Faon thinks to fight for me, it is a useless battle. And I do not wish for you to pierce your own heart with love for me. I shall not pity you, but watch it bleed. In time you will understand my ways. I am capable of truth and honor, and my word is as good as hard silver, but I do not love women. It is beyond me." He cocked his head. "But I have found, *chérie,* that oath and honor are more valuable than love. Be grateful that I grant you these."

"You do not even pretend to trust me."

" 'Twould do you a grave disservice to offer you trust and thus place my life in your hands. It would make me weak, and I am not certain you know how to handle that kind of power. Nay, I do not trust you. Neither am I so suspicious that I must keep you chained to be sure of you."

"A man who lives without love and trust is weak, Hyatt. Not the other way around."

"My ways serve me well enough."

"Truly? And what about your son?"

His face darkened as if a cloud passed between him and the sun, but it was night and only two candles lit their room.

"A son is worthy of all these things: love, trust, honor, oath, and silver. A son does not pass a fickle moment when love is lost, as with a woman. A son takes his father's name, heart, arm, and hews of these things a life. Yea, Aurélie, I love my son. And I suppose I will love more sons. Even yours."

Aurélie winced slightly at the slur, but the words confused her. "Hyatt," she said softly, "if there is love between a father and son, why is it not possible for a man to love a woman? Especially the woman who would bear children to your name? Why, then, do you call yourself bastard, when Lord Lavergne tells of your true family?"

His eyes were as dark as a starless night. "I have found many loyalties possible between men, until women twist their hearts with jealous fingers. There is great loyalty possible between father and son unless stabbed and torn by a woman's treachery. I shall not fall prey to such, for I shall not place my promises to my son in any woman's hands — not yours or Faon's. In my experience, it is the woman who cannot remain true, and in her wrath, separates even fathers and sons."

He turned his back on her and went to sit before the fire, occupying a stool and staring into the flames. He did not acknowledge her as she put a gentle hand on his shoulder. "You have either known too many women, sir knight, or too few."

SEVEN

YATT rode with forty men and left sixty behind. They traveled with purposeful slowness along the best roads to judge the lie of the land and to keep approaching armies in sight. The worst of the fighting was north of Limoges and in Aquitaine the English now had a strong foothold. Still, Hyatt's army passed through little sects of houses that were dusted with the aftermath of a ruthless army's passage.

He halted his troop before a group of six partially standing houses and a burned barn. A dozen ragged peasants hid fearfully behind the rubble. Hyatt could see no evidence of farming tools, stock, weapons, or even cookery pots. "Come out and name yourselves. We mean you no harm; there is nothing here and I have no desire to kill defenseless serfs."

A long moment passed before an elderly man appeared. He approached Hyatt warily, the others staying well away from the monstrous, horsed knights. The man was dressed in ragged chausses and a dirty and torn tunic, and used a staff for walking. But he wore a sculptured silver beard that spoke of some previous prosperity. That and a glitter in his intelligent eyes were the only signs Hyatt had to read.

"Is this your village?" Hyatt asked.

The man's lips curled in a bitter smile. "Where do you see a village, sir knight?"

"Are you bound to Edward or John?"

"I was bound to my family and Guienne, and there is much brutal discussion about whose land this is. Yesterday this belonged to France, today to England, tomorrow . . . perhaps Rome."

"To England, now and forever, old man."

"Yea, that is what I am told." He looked at the rubble behind him. "I was told by the man who left us this, that England claims it." He spat in the dust. "You will rend a hearty tithe from this."

Hyatt leaned down and stared closely into the old man's eyes. "You should have surrendered and pledged, old fool, and perhaps something would be left for you."

The man threw back his head and let go with a wicked laugh. "Hah! Do you see a wall or bridge? A castle or donjon? Do you think this meager lot was ready to raise scythes to fight the English strangers? We are *farmers*. We are decent folk with no time for the arguments of kings, popes, and knights. I met the force at the cross in the road and pleaded for mercy. They burned everything that stood, slew everything with two legs, and led away everything with four legs. Your English brother has a fine pot of chicken brewing in some war camp, and yonder we have buried a score of babies."

Hyatt straightened in his saddle. "How many resided here?"

"Over fifty."

"And how did you survive?"

"We fled, O great knight. We hid ourselves deep in the wood and came back when there was no more smoke. No one was left to live and there is nothing with which to rebuild. How does England hope to profit from this conquered land? Do you sell the bones of the dead and drink their blood?"

Hyatt bristled slightly at the sarcasm, but did not let it show. Yet he despised the carnage that he saw for the very reason the man had named. It had been a foolish tactic to level the land and people to this degree, when a clever knight could use them well. Even this little village, though a minor quest, could wrest pâtis payment of a few livres in exchange for the protection of the nearest men-at-arms. Buried in crude mounds behind the ash there were probably boys who would have made decent pages and squires and girls who would have worked and bred more.

Here lay a common mistake of men bred for fighting. Chevachie, total war, was useful in its place. A king could be ruined as his lands were destroyed and nothing was left from which he could wring a tax or tithe. It was a method painfully learned by the English knights at war with the Scots, and the battle tactic had depleted the French king's stores, making France more vulnerable to Edward's onslaught.

But there was also a code of honor among the knights — that death would not occur upon surrender. Pillage would be the reward of conquerors till the end of time and all valuables were fair game, but with life the people could rebuild. The man who destroyed this village could have had all the booty he could carry without killing almost the entire town. It was, with some, like a parasite in the blood, a heat to slay the enemy, whether in a fair contest or otherwise. The sad fact was that women and children were frequently sacrificed when the men of the town raised up arms in a fight already lost, but Hyatt was more than wary of a man who would kill a child for the sheer love of murder. Yet it was a defect quite often overlooked if armies were engaged in a serious war.

He knew it was useless to chafe at the misdeed, for this was a common malady within the knighthood of men. He had known many who bragged at the flow of blood they could leave on the dirt, then bemoaned their lack of coin when the wreckage they claimed did not produce. Only a few had the true principles of lords; the hard-learned ethics necessary for good leaders in high places. Few men could feel a victor's zeal unless they had slain many.

Hyatt meant to draw his winnings from a full purse, not a pile of ash.

"Do you remember the arms of the English knight?"

"Yea, he carried two snakes on a lily. And unlike you, only one in his troop had the Gascon tongue. He commanded his men in Anglo-Norman."

"He took no prisoners?"

The man hung his head, sad rather than angry for the first time. "Everyone is accounted for," he murmured with a catch in his voice.

Hyatt knew, as did those men who rode with him, that the knight to destroy the village was the same one they rode toward. Sir Hollis Marsden had been bound toward Limoges, where a keep of great strength and wealth was rumored to be unconquered. Hollis meant to add that parcel to his conquests and gain much of the king's favor, for he almost always won in battle and seemed to be rich enough to supply good armaments to his men and their squires. But Hollis's wealth would be depleted soon if this was how he used his weapons and soldiers.

Here was the pact with Prince Edward that Hyatt had made. The prince had need of good fighting skills and found it necessary to look the other way if a knight of England had low morals, but was a good soldier. Hollis was a good one to take into battle, but one must not be too certain of his loyalty. And because Sir Hollis shifted his alliances to improve his wealth, here was a man who could threaten even a king if given too much power. That was why Prince Edward and the king had conspired with Hyatt for De la Noye. Hyatt was meant to hold a strong castle in Aquitaine to serve England, and to keep Hollis at bay, arrest his growth before he gained too much territory in Aquitaine. By the same token, Prince Edward would not openly protest Hollis's fighting, for Hollis still fought for England.

Hyatt's stomach felt sour and his brow was damp. He was confident in his ability to fight Hollis, if necessary, but he admitted a stronger adversary could not be found. He pulled off his helm and rolled up his coif, looking at the old man now with a full face.

"You have a dozen or more here and no reason to stay. Do you know the castle De la Noye?"

"I have heard, sir knight, but have never been there."

"It will take you five days walking. I will loose two palfreys for your sick or injured, and a knight named Sir Girvin holds the wall there on my behalf. If you can make the journey, you will be admitted."

"Does it matter to you that we hate the English?" the old man tested.

Hyatt smiled suddenly. "You will find plenty of company, old man. Hate whom you like, it is of no matter to me. But if it appeals to you to be dry and fed, you will lift a hoe and work for your enemy. Or —" He shrugged. "— You may stay here and build out of your ashes."

"You do not wish to kill us, as your brother knight desired? I was ready to die."

"Cease such lies. You did not approach me as a man ready for death, but as one with the wisdom to hold life as a great value. Even the lowest life can plant a seed, mend a pot, or produce a prayer. Any man who cannot do some small thing of value will die from his own lack of existence. My sword and lance are for the winning of battles, not to collect deaths as the queen collects jewels. Nothing worth having is wrought of killing for sport. Now, I hear a scholar's learning in your speech, though you claim to be farmers all. Is there some reason to send you to De la Noye, or are you as useless to me as you pretend?"

The old man smiled, showing a perfect row of white teeth against his aging face. He bowed his head slightly. "I am a teacher and planter. My son works with leather and my wife bakes bread. There are few of us, and made poor by this carnage you see, but our skills could not be burned. I am Percival."

Hyatt looked over his shoulder. "Give the man two palfreys and a bag of grain to see them through." He looked back to the old man. "I could give you my banner to carry, but it will do you ill against any French force, and I cannot promise that it will offer protection against the English knights."

Percival's eyes sparkled with emotion. "John's forces are

few in this part of the country. North is where the true fighting exists. I will carry your banner, sir knight, for I suspect it is feared by your friend and foe."

Hyatt nodded over his shoulder for a squire to fetch a spare tunic on which was sewn the blazon of his arms, a ferret and a star fashioned against a red background. It would do well enough to convince Girvin. He handed the tunic to Percival. "Beware, old man; the blazon will protect you best if you travel in brush and tall grass. Soldiers who feast on the blood of the helpless pay little regard to any threat. But it will open the doors of De la Noye."

Hyatt led his troop away from the demolished little burg, not looking behind to see what the few remaining villagers did with the horses and grain. He took the chance that they would flee to some camp deep within the forest and replay this scene for every passing troop. The investment was minute for a dozen good hands, and, in addition, had Hollis taken even a moment to talk to the old man, he'd have discovered at least one good head. In Hyatt's opinion, one intelligent man was worth twenty brawny morons.

As the troop traveled silently and watchfully on, Hyatt considered the ravages of war. Being quite proud of his own skills, he had slain many lesser warriors in battle. He had even laid a town or two to waste, when there was enough fighting to warrant it. It was not because of a soft heart that he left his enemies their lives, but because nothing could be gained from a dead man.

Hyatt had even intended to let Giles de Pourvre live, and had had nothing to do with his death. Did none of Giles's men-at-arms speak of their leader's death? Aurélie had accepted his warrior's departure in good faith, as if she did not know the truth about her husband's cowardice. Hyatt had ordered his own men to keep silent about the details of the battle, but they all knew that Giles could have spared many men's lives had he stayed behind the De la Noye walls or issued a surrender on the field. The questions came again and again: How did she love him? What had he ever done to justify her respect and loyalty? How had she kept herself virtuous? How had she managed the clever lie that she was barren? And why?

They made camp in a thick, protected copse at dusk. They were still days away from Limoges, and the rubble they had viewed this day had happened as long as a fortnight before. Hollis had surely passed through on his way to the richer conquest. How like the foolish knight to steam up his desire for battle by laying a path of carnage behind him. Hyatt assumed, already, that Hollis was victorious; if he had failed to conquer the keep he sought, English stragglers would be seen along the road back.

"Why venture on, Sir Hyatt? It is certain he has won."

"I do not go for Sir Hollis; that should have been clear from the start. He will resent my appearance, though he will be careful about his behavior for now. I venture onward for Edward. Hollis will lie about the booty and give less than the fair portion to the king."

"But he will not let you examine his stores," a young knight said. "And his troop is two or three times larger than yours."

"Aye, larger in numbers. But I should like to see for myself how Hollis holds them. I have been told that as many as a quarter of his men are dangerous criminals, freed by a pardon bought by Hollis to form a large troop. Most are indentured to him for some years to come. When he cast about looking for a sizable army to join Prince Edward, there were not many eager to ride with Hollis. Although he is frequently victorious, he does not pay his men well and he allows them a meager share of the winnings. But criminals soon to die will take life at any price, however low. It is important that I see for myself how many are there now, many months after the battle has begun, and how they regard Hollis as their leader."

They sat around a low fire, making their pallets on the ground, and passing around dry bread, pork strips, and water. Most of Hyatt's men were indentured to him for the cost of their arms, their ransom in tournaments, or debts Hyatt had cleared for them. But he did not have one man of whom he was unsure. This, compared to Hollis's two and a half hundred, was better.

"It is rumored, Sir Hyatt, that Hollis hates you and would strike your back," the young knight remarked.

" 'Tis not rumor. It is truth, and he has."

"Then why do you ally yourself with him?"

"It is with Edward that I am allied, and do not sheath your swords when any of Hollis's men are behind you."

"He would not do you harm when he fights now for Edward, as do you . . ."

"He would take what I have claimed in a moment, lad. And he would tell the king he took it from Guienne. But mark me, he could not succeed in such a lie if but one of my men lives. That is why we are safe in approaching him now; more than half my men remain at De la Noye under Sir Girvin."

"Yet we ride toward him? Sir Hyatt, if he is in trouble, we will have to fight for him, will we not?"

"Do not discount a good plan because it is not as swift as a single thrust of the lance. We go to see what damage Hollis has done, for I am certain he has won the keep. And what you see upon our arrival is a pure example of what he would do to you, for Hollis's enemies are not solely those few whom King Edward will name for him, but anyone whom Hollis thinks he can beat. When we arrive, look at the conquered demesne as you looked at the village. Know it. Taste it. Smell it. The only way to best a man in any contest is to know full well his manner of fighting, and Hollis is as much my enemy as the French forces of John. Only with Hollis it is much more dangerous, for we do not acknowledge it openly. Rivals, they call us at the tournaments. 'Tis far more serious than that. And remember, each knight has a style, and Hollis's is sly and brutal."

"Are we not on the same side after all?"

Hyatt sighed heavily. There was more than simple practice of arms to teaching a knight sound skills. "For the time being, while commands are issued from the king, we are of the same side. Hollis is not fair or prudent, but he is not stupid and he knows where to use his influence. Hollis will lay bare this land, taking ten conquests to Edward's court . . . but nothing he wins will produce for him. The king will own naught but a charred field where crops once grew. My victory belongs to England for generations. There is a difference. Edward desires a quick theft, but he also needs the property peopled with loyal vassals. What we have in De la Noye is an English encampment that will provide support in any uprising that threatens Prince Edward's hold on the land. That takes more than a good fight. It requires time and wisdom, not just skill in battle."

"But, Sir Hyatt, you were generous at De la Noye, and now there are two hundred or more who silently despise you. They are subdued, but how do you know they will change their fealty? Would it not have been better to lay them down, once and for all, and remove the threat, finally?"

"And hang up my bridle and lance, to spend each hour working the soil so that I might eat? Nay, the very serfs who hate and fear me will feed me. This is not a tournament, but a war. That which is won in a single stab of my lance is useless to me. Fealty pledged in a weak and fearful moment will cut my throat when I sleep. I have more respect for a man who comes to his loyalties through long and careful consideration than one who surrenders in sheer fright and is spared, later to reconsider and decide he was hasty in his first decision."

"Is that why you did not insist that the Sire de Pourvre's men-at-arms swear fealty to you?"

"Their lord was not yet cold in his grave. Any oath to me would have been wrought of sheer survival. I spared them the punishment I would levy for betrayal. Yet . . . I did not give them their arms. When fealty comes from any of them, it will be a true oath. And from some it will come."

"And those who will not swear to you?"

"Some will flee. Some will plot or attack and be caught. But in time, all will be accounted for."

The younger knight shook his head, trying to assimilate so many crafty designs. "You must be certain of your plan, Sir Hyatt, for you take your rest at the side of the former lord's woman."

Hyatt nodded, but silently his thoughts were protesting such a statement. Someday, he thought, she will admit that she was never Giles's woman.

❧

Father Algernon had never confronted Lady Aurélie on any issue since her first arrival at De la Noye. There had never been reason, for Giles so strongly supported the Church and this priest that no other ally was necessary to him.

Aurélie had expected some words from the ecclesiastic, and was frankly surprised that he had waited so long. But then, he had been silent only until Hyatt and his large number had departed.

"I have not heard your confession and you have not taken communion, my lady," he said to her as she was leaving the chapel after matins.

"I cannot partake of the Blood and Body without first atoning for my sins, and I cannot atone."

"I will give you absolution when you name them."

She felt a rueful smile touch her lips. "I have done nothing of which you or God is unaware. What is your penance?"

"My lady." He bristled. His voice was a subdued whisper, but she could not miss the anger in his eyes. "You could begin by confessing your hatred for your priest, and atone for that."

"It is not within my power to hate you, Father. I am pleased that you are unharmed, and that these English accept the mass and communion from you, though they know you were for Giles."

"They do not pay me," he complained.

"You have taken an oath of poverty," she countered.

"My own poverty . . . not the poverty of the Church."

"Ah," she said, remembering the argument quite clearly. That had been the cause for such depletion of funds, as she recalled only too well. Since the great site of ecclesiastic pomp resided in the Avignon papacy, there had been a priority on the buying and selling of favors. Philip of Valois had raised substantial funds for his armies by keeping certain offices vacant and selling positions. This blasphemy had helped Giles, for he had not wanted to fight and could buy his absence quite easily from King Philip. Only the highest bishops might wear cloaks of greed in their actual threads, and Father Algernon might indeed be dressed as if impoverished, but Aurélie had always known that their true wealth was in the power of the promises they traded. Giles, like Father Algernon, had been filtering money into the fleshpot of the Church for many years, attaining the purity of spirit and rising within the political ranks of the Church to guarantee a high level of eternity in heaven. Or so he might have thought. Aurélie's prayers were that her late husband had actually, finally, gotten some spiritual reward, for those left among the living had definitely paid the price.

Father Algernon did not fool her, and never had. But he was their only priest.

"Lady, do you mean to cut this castle free of the bonds of God and life eternal?"

"Nay, Father. We must continue to live as righteously as possible and pray for our salvation."

"What of benefices? The dispensation of Holy Rights? The salvation of the dead?"

"One of those dead is the Sire de Pourvre. I do not doubt his salvation. Could you?"

Algernon's face grew hard and dark. His shock of thick white hair stood like snow on a shady mountain. He did not like to argue with a woman. "He died unshriven. He died without a final prayer. Cannot you bring this Englishman to do the honorable thing and buy a final prayer for the dead?"

"Nay, Father, I think you are lucky he did not burn the chapel and turn you out. You will not find in Sir Hyatt what you had in Giles. He will give the Church only what he deems honest and fair, and he is little concerned about damnation.

He has already made many harsh criticisms of Giles's devotions."

"And I imagine you agreed," he said snidely.

"Nay," she shot back. "Nor did I defend him, but I bid you remember that while some bishop in Avignon wears scarlet robes, we are now the captured serfs of an English warlord."

"God will never forgive you," the priest solemnly confided. "You have always resisted the tithe and many times you hid money from your husband so that it would not fall the way of the Church. I think you urge the English bastard to abstain. I shall pray for you, for it is my obligation to be generous with sinners. It is not too late for you to amend this blasphemy."

"When I see the hand of God reach from the sky into the pocket of the Church, I shall change my mind. Now all I see is waste; had you urged Giles to spend his money on arms and food we would not be so helpless now. And you could have done it, Father. But instead you bought favors in the Church. If Sir Hyatt becomes angry and turns you out, will they take you in Avignon and make you a bishop?" When he did not answer, she smiled confidently. *"Homo mercator vix aut numquam potest Deo placere."*

The priest's eyes grew round with wonder as he listened to her announce, in perfect Latin, the statement that had won so much power and money for the Church. *A man who is a merchant can seldom if ever please God.*

"I think it does not matter what you are trading in God's eyes, Father. Whether it is forgiveness, mercy, power, or divinity, God must surely frown on the sale of it."

The priest was astonished at this ingratitude and it showed fiercely in his eyes. Aurélie almost laughed at the sight. "Could I have lived with him so many years and not know his rhetoric?"

"Giles was pure, but you are a whore to give yourself to the conqueror. Better you should take your own life and . . ."

"Even whoredom shines in the face of taking one's own life, as the Book teaches. Yea, Giles schooled me well in scripture, for 'twas he who was so tormented by love of divinity that he wished to die, finally, to end his waiting and reach that sparkling realm you promised to sell him."

"You take a very grave chance, woman, that you and every person in your demesne will be excommunicated."

"I have lost everything else, Father. Why not that? But you would do well to keep your own losses small. There are still those here who will give you what you demand . . . some of them, I imagine, are among the conquerors. Tread carefully."

She turned to go and heard his words at her back. "Your hatred finally shows. I wondered when it would. You were always jealous of the love and spiritual strength I shared with your husband." The words caused her to stiffen as if slapped. Jealousy had never been the emotion she felt. Even though she had struggled with what it was she had felt, not knowing its name, she knew the feeling to be much deeper and more violent than that. "There is nothing more dangerous than to share learning with a woman. I warned him of that."

She turned slowly. "Dangerous to whom, Father? A man in power . . . or just any man?"

"Why do you not urge Sir Hyatt to cast me out, if your heathenish sins can match his? Surely you would not miss me."

"There are those here who do not know that they pay you for what would be theirs freely, if they but sought it. And though you accuse me of cardinal sins, I still need the power of divinity in the walls of this chapel to shed light on my own prayers for myself and my people. The place was built and blessed in good faith, and your greed has not yet darkened the spirit in which it was raised." She smiled lazily. "My dower purse built it, which is why Giles urged his father to deal with mine for marriage. I was a child then and thought it was good to bring this, a holy place, as a marriage gift to my husband. I did not know what it would cost him."

She moved from the chapel slowly, her hands clasped and her head down. She walked across the courtyard and was not questioned or halted as she moved through the gate to the outer bailey. At the farthest wall she was stopped by a youthful guard whose cheeks actually pinkened as he detained her.

"I should like to visit the graves," she said quietly, keeping her eyes downcast to hide the rage that burned in them. "You should have no trouble watching me from the wall."

He thought for a moment and then reluctantly had the door opened for her, keeping the bars back as she left. "Don't be too long, my lady," he urged, but she walked steadily away from him without reply.

The graves were too many and she shuddered, wishing that they had forced her to consent to a burning pyre rather than this remaining proof by the stone markers of the numbers lost. She found the central one, bearing no name as yet, and looked down at the dirt, trying to understand the emotion that rose to choke her throat.

Giles, she silently screamed. Why has this happened? Were you gentle and good, little knowing how Algernon used you? Did you mean to achieve something of righteous purity, of everlasting light, but instead descended into darkness to be ruined? I kept it all as your secret, your knowledge and prayers, but I was alone in knowing how tormented and troubled you were. The others saw you dressed in your monk's habit, beating yourself in penance for sins you never committed and for which you should never have been forced to atone. If they do not scorn your memory now, they will soon, and they will speak of it more freely than in the past. And do you not see, now, from your place high on the wall of heaven, what it has cost? There is no de Pourvre son, no loyalty, or love. He came here *knowing*, Giles, that he could beat you because your only strength was that you longed to be weak.

"Oh Giles," she sobbed aloud, falling to her knees at the end of his grave. "I have tried." Her fists hit the dirt, which was already sprouting new grass. "I cannot pretend any longer. There was no value in what you did, yet I worked to hold together what you left untended, and even protected you from the slander that would surround your peculiar obsession. And now I work to hold your memory with a shred of respect, a small piece of decency. Dear God, let your soul be in peace. Let your years of pain and suffering have acquired you at least that much. Oh Giles, such lies. Such pain."

She held her face in her hands, crouched there on her knees, and wept. She had not known the darkness she lived in until there was light. She had not known how to name the quiet, dull pain of Giles's indifference, disguised as it was by impotent courtesy, a mien of kindness. She had always thought her husband selfless and pious, until Hyatt came and took their home as easily as one would bat a fly, and then finally, tragically, she could see Giles's humility and submissiveness for what it was: an ugly, vile, sinful indulgence to serve only his own needs, sacrificing the lives and wills of all those people who depended upon him for strength. He had handed his life to a priest who promised him the very hand of God, but when the warriors came, God did not appear to save Giles's people. But Giles was dead, and she missed him less every day.

It was not enough to see Giles's weakness and reckon Hyatt's strength. The battle cries may have dulled to whispers, but the war raged on. It was a hideous, secret war, a treacherous mistress who worked fervently to recapture her mate; deposed men-at-arms who carried hoes now, but in the fists of knights ready to fight and to set her home again on the battlefield; a conqueror in her bed who used her body with a troubadour's smooth experience in his touch, and his devout promise never to love a woman. And there seemed nothing she could do. She could not slay the mistress, remove the hate from her soldiers' eyes, bring Hyatt to love her . . . and even her prayers were made dirty by the silver that bribed the priest to buy them.

As she wept, she swore to do without even the costly prayers. If God could not hear her pleas without the tinkle of livres, then she would bear in darkest silence the agony of a deaf Savior. Yet, as if some inner spark of hope lay deep in her soul, she continued to pray as if God would hear. Save us from further tragedy. Let the end of pain come, dear God, let us live in peace and harmony. . . .

She was unaware of any presence, divine or mortal. Girvin stood at the edge of the trees a short distance away. A stag that would feed a hearty number was curled lightly around his shoulders as if it weighed no more than a woolen shawl. He watched Lady Aurélie in silence, but the urge to go to her was strong. He had never before pitied a woman. And he doubted that anyone could give her the comfort and peace she needed, least of all Hyatt.

He turned and went back into the woods. It was better that she mourn in private. And he could not bring himself to let her see that his own eyes mirrored her pain.

❦

"Come here, *slut,* and baste this meat."

Aurélie stopped where she stood. The cruel, mocking sound of Faon's demand sent prickles up her spine. She slowly turned from the bottom of the stair to assure herself that the command was issued to her, knowing full well that it was. Behind Faon, Aurélie saw the pained eyes of Perrine as she jostled Derek on her hip.

Aurélie had felt the need to tarry on her way back from Giles's grave, letting the cool late afternoon breezes dry her moist cheeks and steady her pulse. By the time she arrived in the hall, the dinner was nearly ready to be served, and she realized she was not ready to supervise. She meant to fetch a clean smock quickly from her room when she noticed that Hyatt's men had begun to filter into the room to take their meals.

Faon stood in the center of the room near the hearth, hands on her hips as if she were ready to dance in glee. Her fiery tresses bounced on her bare shoulders, her jewelry glittered on her arms and neck. She smiled much in the way a hunter smiles when he has landed a powerful beast with a single arrow.

A sound alerted Aurélie, and she turned to see Guillaume enter the room. She turned away to mount the stairs.

"Did you not *hear* me, wench? You have duties here; see them done."

Aurélie lifted her chin. "If you wish that the meat be basted, Mistress Faon, I will not be offended if you do so yourself."

"I cannot be ordered here," Faon chuckled happily. "My only duty is to take care of my lord's son."

"Good. Then do so."

Aurélie turned to leave again.

"Don't you dare turn away from me."

Again Aurélie stopped. She checked eyes with Guillaume and found that he watched Faon dangerously. She quickly surveyed the room and took note of the way Hyatt's men looked on in stunned wonder, little knowing how to react. Would they stay the mistress, or would Guillaume lose control and be punished for any act in defense of the wife? She could not fathom the answer, nor could she trust her instincts. She took a few quick steps across the room and picked up the ladle from the drippings collected in a large kettle under the meat on a spit. She carefully poured the drippings over the side of meat and, once done, began to leave.

"Wait."

She turned back to Faon and nearly winced at the devilish gleam in the woman's eyes.

"Turn the meat for me, and I will baste it properly."

Aurélie's fingers trembled as she took a knife to the well-cooked meat and began slowly to force it to turn over the kettle. Faon held the full ladle and slowly dribbled the contents onto the meat, moving her hand deftly and evenly to let the hot, greasy drippings pour onto Aurélie's hand.

Aurélie gasped as the scalding brew scorched her, snatching her hand away too late to save herself from a burn. The knife she had held dropped into the kettle and the grease splashed on Faon's gown. With a movement as quick as light, the ladle dropped to the floor and Faon grasped the folds of her dress. "Stupid bitch! You've ruined my gown!"

Aurélie heard Guillaume's fast-approaching footfalls before she saw him. She whirled to face Guillaume, raising her uninjured hand to stop him. She knew her seneschal well enough to believe he could kill Faon without conscience . . . and what Hyatt would then do to him, she dared not guess. She was so intent on protecting Guillaume that she missed the action of several knights, bolting to their feet in outrage. One even held the hilt of his broadsword. But no man of Hyatt's army knew which woman he valued the most, if he valued either one.

"Guillaume, nay! You must not . . ."

Guillaume stopped, but if his eyes had been red glaring pokers, Faon would be holed through her hide. Then, very slowly, his eyes turned to look at Aurélie's scorched flesh. Again the violence grew, for the top of her hand had already blistered under the crimson burn.

"Do you find the meat basted to your liking, Mistress Faon?"

Even Aurélie's head turned at the deep, gravelly voice of Girvin. He stood in the frame of the door that came from the back of the hall, the opposite direction from which Aurélie had come. Over his shoulders a dead stag slumped. The animal he carried was huge, but he gracefully strode across the room as if he carried nothing at all. Everyone moved as he passed, as if backing out of the way of Goliath. Knights who had risen in sudden but helpless fury reclaimed their seats. Girvin lifted the stag over his head and dropped it on the rushes, staring down at Faon. She was the only one in the room who did not react to him.

"I asked, is the meat now basted to your liking?"

She gave her curls a flippant toss, her hands going to her hips. "I suppose it will do."

Girvin's lips slowly parted as a grin developed on his mouth. " 'Tis well, since any more basting you require, you would do with *my* help."

"Hah! I would do it better alone than with anyone's help. The insolent witch purposely ruined my gown."

Girvin's voice came in a slow, dangerous rumbling. "You should be whipped, mistress, for what you dare."

She lifted her chin defiantly. "Who will whip me, Girvin? You?"

"Nay," he said, sharply. "Not for this, since I have not been bidden to protect Hyatt's wife." The last word was stressed and Faon actually blinked at the sound of the word that haunted her.

Girvin turned to Guillaume. "What did your master bid you do in his absence?"

"Guard my lady."

"From whom?"

"From anyone who would dare touch her."

"And have you done that?"

"I have tried."

"Try harder." Girvin threw an arm to indicate the room at large. "There are plenty of witnesses from Hyatt's own camp in this room. Your punishment would be worse should you ignore the duty Hyatt gave you, than should you slay ten of his best men in pursuit of your duty. Hyatt does not give command lightly, and never for his amusement. Take this to heart, Sir Guillaume, and hesitate only at your own risk. You must not fail again." His eyes narrowed as they swerved in Faon's direction, though he continued to speak to Guillaume. "You would be pardoned for anything done by Hyatt's order, on behalf of his wife."

"This French slave has a protector?" Faon demanded. "And whom, pray, did Hyatt name as *my* protector?"

Girvin's smile came again, and it was the evil smile of a beast who had just tasted fresh blood.

"Me."

EIGHT

OW do you fail me in this, Nima?" Faon asked, a near whimper in her voice. "You had potions and spells that served me so well."

The old woman slowly shook her head. "You have fooled yourself for so long, though I never lied to you. I have not misled you, Faon. Hyatt has never been moved by my balms or brews. You believed what you wished to believe — if he was more docile than usual, you decided some brew had worked at last. But it is all in your mind, Faon. The only time Hyatt was at your mercy was once, and you know when that was."

Faon frowned at the memory. When Faon had been desperate to have Hyatt with her for once, Nima gave her strong herbs to put in his wine. They had made him so seriously ill that he could not rise and required her care for a fortnight. She knew the chance she had taken, for if he ever learned that she purposely caused his sickness, he might have killed her. But she had thought he would be so grateful, so endeared to her. Instead, when he could rise from his pallet, he took his leave. Since he never discovered this deception, and to keep such aids at her future disposal, Faon held Nima's talent for mixing rare concoctions as a careful secret.

"I have told you, nay, *warned* you, that I know brews and mixes that sometimes fill a man with lust, or render him helpless to love, but there is a condition: the man must be weak of will. Hyatt is too strong. He denies his body's urges. He is capable of ignoring pain."

"Why would I want a weak man?" Faon asked.

The old woman smiled with knowledge. "Of course." In teaching this simple wisdom to Faon, Nima had failed. A strong man who was capable of great control could not be changed by potions or spells, yet a weak man would swoon powerless. However, the weak man would come around as easily with a wink, a swinging skirt, a seductive lie. Nima repeatedly pointed this out to Faon; every time Faon failed to see.

"You said you would try. Do you have *anything?*"

Nima's old eyes seemed to moisten as she sprinkled a few herbs into her palm and studied them. A crooked finger separated the different-colored leaves and twigs. She sat on a stool before the window in Faon's chamber and glanced hesitantly at the agitated young woman pacing the floor.

Once Nima had a reputation as a skilled midwife and healer. She knew balms to cleanse the bowel, cure the flux, both induce and stop miscarriage. She studied and experimented and invented new potions suitable for helping with common afflictions. People came to her from villages far away, for she could banish the pain of an unbearable headache, set a limb, dissolve a thick and dangerous cough into a harmless runny nose. Not every attempted cure was successful, but many were. And then an important man from a neighboring town had been thrown into seizures from one of her brews. He died a horrible death before witnesses.

Faon was Nima's daughter's daughter. The bond they shared preceded Faon's birth. And there was yet a tighter allegiance, since Nima was accused of dallying with spirits and potions by Faon's father, Montrose, and it was better that she followed her granddaughter, as Faon followed the knight. Where was an old woman of no means to go? No one of this household, not Hyatt nor Faon's other servants, knew that Nima was the girl's grandmother.

"He is married now, Faon, as he promised you he would be one day. There is nothing more to be done, but accept his offer of retirement and find us a proper house somewhere.

He has a wife; it will not matter even if he desires you again."

"It will," she insisted, whirling to face the old woman. "It will. She is barren. He amuses himself for a while and he has a proper mate, but I will bear his children, I will command his body, and I will spend all my days as his love."

"Hyatt does not love anyone."

"Hah, what do you know? He loves Derek. And as long as he loves Derek, my place with him is safe."

Nima looked again into her palm, shook her head and dropped the mixture into her pouch. It would not help to remind Faon that Hyatt was independent of her, as he had always been, even though he allowed her to follow him. At first, as the old woman remembered, Hyatt was attempting to be civil to an abused girl of six and ten. He had lain with her and her father threatened her very life. But once the boy was born, Hyatt's attention shifted quickly to Derek, and Faon's only link was through Hyatt's son. The knight was now chafing more with each of Faon's demands, but the foolish girl did not seem to see how shaky the ground was on which she trod.

He had never loved Faon; he would never love a woman. This Nima understood, for she watched the knight closely and learned his ways. He was hard put to trust a decent woman, but a treacherous one was poorly placed within his reach. If Hyatt had known half of what Faon dared, she would have been turned out long ago. Nima protected her granddaughter as she kept safe her own sustenance. There was nowhere to go should Hyatt lose patience and withdraw his offer of support.

"While he is willing . . . ," Nima began again.

"Nay. I shall never slink away, beaten, to find some hovel in which to spend my days alone."

"Faon, you must hear me. I do not think he loves this woman, this Aurélie whom he married, but I see that something in his manner has changed. You must use your eyes and ears and be cautious. He is less tolerant than he was; he has a woman who can tend Derek for him and he will not condone your trickery. For your life, dear Faon, be *careful*." Faon straightened in a show of confidence. "This will not last. The bony, screeching whore will cease to pleasure him soon. Despite all that Hyatt claims, he is a man, and men want sons. They take pride in their bastards; they only pretend that children burden them. You'll see, Nima. He will be mine again soon. Let her have the name and proper marriage." Her lips curved in a superior smile. "Even queens have learned that a king's whore can be more important than his wife."

"Once I thought, Faon, that it was better that you accept what Hyatt is willing to give you, rather than feeling misery and anger about it. Now I am worried. You are tempted to push him too hard. You forget that you have never outwitted him."

"But I have," she said slyly. "I gave birth to his son."

"Then," said Nima very slowly, in a warning, "take very special care of that prize, for if anything should happen to Derek, you will be gone like a dry leaf in a gust of wind."

The women fell silent as Perrine entered, carrying the boy. Perrine did not glance their way, but went straight to the fur-covered pallet to lay the sleepy baby down. His arms were tight about Perrine's neck and he resisted the separation with a tired whimper. But Perrine's gentle cooing and slow stroking of the child's back won over any protests and Derek laid down his head, obediently closing his eyes. Faon frowned, noting that the boy responded very well to Perrine.

Perrine did not so much as turn her head once to regard Faon and Nima. Instead she knelt on the floor beside her young ward's pallet and hummed softly as he slept.

Faon came slowly to stand behind Perrine, a smile curving her lips. Her eyes glittered as she looked down at the older woman. "I can see that my son benefits from your care," Faon said softly. Perrine looked up at the young mistress, confusion in her eyes. "It was Thea's chore before you, but she is not as talented in keeping him happy as you are. Poor Thea, I think she is jealous of you and has little to occupy her. Perhaps I shall let Lady Aurélie have her."

Perrine frowned, but said nothing. In one month of caring for Derek she had learned a few things, though she had never asked a single question. She found that the only person in Faon's company to cherish the boy was the old woman, but Nima was too withered and aged to care for a youngster of Derek's energy. The other maidservants, Thea and Aisla, played more the part of ladies-in-waiting to Faon rather than actual servants. And Thea was not even slightly jealous that Derek had taken immediately to Perrine. To the contrary, she seemed relieved and had more time to dally. It was hard to know whether Faon had found two wenches of the same selfish temperament as herself, or whether these girls had once been hardworking, good lasses who had followed their mistress's example of behaving in a haughty, superior, and lazy manner. Whichever was the case, more and more of Faon's household chores fell to Perrine.

Another thing that became clear to Perrine was that Faon was uninterested in motherhood and had not been softened by the velvety skin, large trusting eyes, sweet disposition, and dependent arms of her child. Perrine learned that Faon had not even nursed the child herself and seemed bored and petulant whenever she was with Derek. She was an impatient, intolerant mother; one would think she did not love her son. Yet Faon was aware of her precarious position, and rarely approached Hyatt without the boy in her arms.

Perrine had seen the knight's dark eyes grow wistful with longing when his son was near. It had not been her duty to take the boy to his father, for Faon was very protective of that right. But Perrine went in tow, for if the boy had some need, certainly Faon did not wish to be bothered. Too, Perrine suspected that Hyatt struggled to keep this devotion to himself. He forgot himself sometimes and hugged the little boy close, his eyes closing and his implacable expression softening with emotion, making him appear, for only a moment, like a protective young father with a gentle heart. Hyatt's appearance could be, in those brief seconds, like the face of an angel. The faint glow of giving, caring, and needing appeared like an aura about his strong features. It was the look, seldom seen, rarely shared, that a young bride might catch in a flash of early dawn on her husband's face; the coupling of fierce, powerful strength, and naked, urgent need. It was what happens to a warrior's face when he is beset by deep love.

Perrine recognized these particulars about Hyatt and Faon because she had loved and married a man who could equal her devotion with his own, and they had raised four sons together. Most interesting to her was how Faon would use her son's presence to wiggle closer to Hyatt, only to be effortlessly rebuffed. Hyatt was not even slightly intrigued by her any longer.

"The boy is sleepy, Hyatt," she would say.

Reluctantly, Hyatt would prepare to end the visit, yielding Derek to his mother.

"Perrine can take him to bed," she would attempt. "I can . . ."

It never went farther than that. Hyatt's expression would turn completely indifferent again. "Go ahead, Faon. See about the child." Hyatt did not unbend even slightly in the presence of his past mistress. It was a fact that his desire for her was long since past. It was also a fact that Faon was not nearly ready to give him up.

Perrine slowly turned her head away from Faon without responding in any way to the suggestion that Thea serve Aurélie. She resumed her humming and stroking of the child. Behind her, Faon paced about the room, mumbling. "That is what I shall do. Hyatt will think that very kind of me; I will ask Thea to go to Aurélie." She chuckled conspiratorially. "How good for her. Just as she deserves."

❧

The call came from the donjon and was echoed across the wall. A few men fled from the hall and mounted hurriedly saddled war horses. Aurélie sensed a rising panic, but could not name it, for the men seemed to prepare for war. Yet all that was called out was "*A troop approaches.*"

She rushed down three steep stretches of stairs and out to the inner bailey, following running knights toward the gate and bridge of the outer wall. She passed Verel, who stood in the doorway of the stable with a shovel in his hand, but she took no notice of his frown. By the time she reached the gate there were already twenty horsed men there, and an equal number lined the wall.

"What is it?" she asked. "Who comes?"

The young knight whom she questioned showed confusion of his own. "It appears to be peasants, my lady. Injured peasants."

"Do you require arms to let a few peasants enter?"

"It could be a trap." He shrugged. "There could be knights hiding amidst the . . ."

The man stopped suddenly as a shudder seemed to run through the crowd of men and horses. The knight with whom Aurélie had been speaking grabbed her shoulder suddenly to pull her back as Girvin's horse pounded through the bailey. As she looked up she was struck by a tremor of harsh memory; Girvin was fully armored as he had been on that day that De la Noye was taken.

He looked down at her for a moment, his gray eyes glittering through the narrow slit in his helm. A knight held her arms back, though only for safety, but in Girvin's eyes there was a sparkle of recognition. He winced slightly before his rumbling voice was heard. "Stay within the wall, milady, until I have looked over this approaching troop. For your safety, madame."

A few men who seemed to know without benefit of any command that they were the selected ones followed Girvin across the bridge. Aurélie's view was blocked until ten horses had cleared the gate and bridge and were stopped before the peasants. It was then that she saw approximately ten tattered people, one being pulled on a rude litter. She could not see their faces clearly because of the distance, but the white-haired, bearded man who stood before them had a rag tied to his staff. He met Girvin.

Villagers who were not busy in the fields had begun to drift from their chores toward the outer bailey to witness the source of such commotion. The gate was being pulled closed behind the knights when the old man pulled out the banner he had tied to his staff to be displayed for Girvin. It was Hyatt's banner.

She gasped and covered her mouth, a cold dread consuming her. "Wait," she cried, rushing to the huge gate and trying to get out. Two men instantly ceased their labor in closing the doors to restrain her. "Hyatt," she cried, straining against them. "The man carries Hyatt's banner."

She did not even think of the hysteria that gripped her until Girvin turned to look back at her. The panicked tremor in her voice had been loud enough for him to hear, though he was on the other side of the moat. She stopped her struggle instantly, wondering if he knew that she feared it was Hyatt these peasants dragged on a litter.

Girvin dismounted and removed his helm. "Let the lady come," he barked.

The men released her and she ran to the group, rushing past the old man to look at the face of one who lay on the litter. It was not Hyatt, but Aurélie was not completely relieved. She went back to the old man and faced him, an almost furious expression on her face. "Where is Hyatt? How do you come to carry his colors?"

"Our village was destroyed, my lady, and he sent us here. He gave us the blazon to help convince the gatekeeper we were invited. We were better fixed when he left us." The old man had a gash over his eye that had swollen and festered and he leaned heavily on his staff. "We were attacked by looters, and the two horses and food that Sir Hyatt gave us were stolen."

"Who attacked you?" she asked. "When?"

"Thieves. They were not knights, nor ever were, since they had no shields nor mail, and only shared four horses among twenty men. They were French." He turned and looked toward the litter. "My son, Stéphane, tried to fight them. I am Percival."

"Sir Hyatt? He sent you? He was not injured?"

"Sir Hyatt found us, questioned us, and gave up the horses and food and told us the way to De la Noye. He said we would be admitted if we could work for our keeping. He was gone, following Edward's army north, when we were attacked by the thieves." Percival tried to smile. "You are his lady?"

She looked around a bit uncomfortably, knowing full well how much she had betrayed. "Aye," she said softly.

"He was fit . . . then."

She gave a sigh of relief and turned to Girvin. "Do you let them come in?"

"Aye, it was what Hyatt desired. It appears that they need food and tending."

Girvin began to turn away, choosing to lead his destrier across the bridge rather than remount. Aurélie followed, also ahead of the tattered group, when a stifled gasp and a motion just barely behind her caused her to turn. Percival swayed slightly and clung to his staff, but he went down in a swoon. An old woman behind him rushed forward and knelt to the ground. She cradled Percival's head in her arms and looked up at Aurélie with tear-filled eyes.

"He has not eaten in days, my lady," she tearfully admitted. "There was so little, and the way through the forest was so long."

She had not seen Girvin pass his reins to a page or squire, but she saw the shadow he cast on the group as he strode toward them again. Girvin tossed his helm carelessly to the ground, and a lad scurried from the keep to retrieve it. The monstrous knight stooped and lifted Percival into his arms as if he weighed nothing at all, taking long strides to carry him across the bridge into the bailey. The old man was beginning to stir slightly. "I . . . I . . . ."

"Save your breath, old man. Hyatt sent you here to work. This is a place of plentiful food and work."

Aurélie struggled to keep up with Girvin, whose long foot-steps kept anyone who tried to follow galloping in his path. "Now that my family has found De la Noye, I can die happily," Percival muttered.

"No one here admires happy death," Girvin said brusquely. He stopped at the first hovel inside the gate, not far from the stable. He kicked open the door with one foot, sending a woman and two small children scurrying to a corner in fright. "We have wounded who need shelter," Girvin said to the woman. "Either make them welcome or find another abode."

Girvin placed Percival on a pallet in the middle of the room. "My lady," he called over his shoulder. "Who can best see to these poor wretches? Someone must care for this man if I am to get the others inside."

Aurélie stood in the doorframe and cast a concerned look in the direction of Milliva, the young farmer's wife, who quacked in fright at the intrusion of the huge warrior. She tried to smile in reassurance. "Be at ease, Milliva. Sir Girvin would do you no harm." Looking back to Girvin, she sought to reassure him. "You have perchance chosen the best place for them, Girvin. Milliva will help me tend to their wounds. She is a very talented woman, but will need food brought from the hall, though, for I am sure her means are slim."

"It will be done," he replied, stepping through the door. "Can you see to them now?" She nodded and he was stopped for a moment by her eyes. He looked down at her and kept his voice low. "He must keep you to your liking, if you worry for him so."

She lifted her chin proudly. "Perhaps it is more my fear of my next master."

Girvin smiled, showing that wide gap where a tooth was once rooted. "Wise as well as tenderhearted. You may fool the knight, but not I. I think he is as smitten with you."

"Why would you think so?" she asked impetuously, blurt-ing out the question before she even considered it.

To her amazement, Girvin's features darkened as if he

blushed. "I have never known Hyatt to make any oath to a woman, much less a marriage oath."

"But Faon . . . he has made promises to her."

"I think you misunderstand, madame. It seems that Mistress Faon clings to the fringes of some promises made to Hyatt's son." He leaned closer and whispered a secret. "Do not be afraid for Hyatt. He is well."

She nodded, a grateful smile tempting at the corners of her mouth. Girvin looked quickly away and hurried out of the hut.

Within a short time and with a little urging from Aurélie, five peasant huts were opened to the newcomers and the women and children were busily making room. Servants from the hall were quickly sent into the village with baskets of food to provide for those whom Hyatt had sent. Aurélie knelt beside Percival, whose wound was already cleaned and bandaged by Milliva.

"It will take some time, Percival, but there are enough hands here to build a home for you and your family. Until then, we'll have to make do with this."

He chuckled lightly. "My lady, a fortnight past, we did not dare hope for so much. Your husband is generous. And . . . your Gascon tongue is more perfect than his. One would think you had lived here all your life."

She lowered her eyes and looked down at her hands. "I have lived here for a dozen years, sir. I was the wife of the Sire de Pourvre, whom the English army slew."

Percival was quiet for a long moment, studying her closely. "And he wed you?" he asked in a near whisper.

"He means to secure this land."

"Above the whims of kings," the old man said.

She looked at him and saw his sympathetic smile. She tilted her head slightly in question, peering at him. He reached a withered hand into her lap and squeezed her hand.

"So," Percival began, his voice weak, "do you think yourself hit hard by the English, milady? Do you wonder where your true loyalty should lie?" He shook his head almost sadly.

"Your wall still stands, but beyond it there are whole towns reduced to ash. Be wise. Take this offered peace and live well."

Aurélie stiffened slightly, indignant at this uncalled-for advice from a stranger. "You do not even know how many we lost."

"Nay," Percival said, "but it is easy to see how many lived."

⚓

The commotion in the outer bailey and town brought even Faon from her high tower. She looked out of place in the streets crowded by soldiers, peasants, and servants. She wore a rich mauve gown embroidered in silver and a sheer veil that was held on her head by a sparkling collection of gems.

She lifted her gown to her ankles as she picked her way toward the outer bailey. She was almost there when a wayward flock of noisy chickens cackled in a rapid flight right in front of her, bringing her up short with a gasp. An ear-splitting squeal followed and a piglet, recently escaped from his pen, rumbled into the narrow street in confusion. The chickens scrambled in many directions to avoid the piglet, and one hit Faon squarely in the shins. Her foot was quick as she kicked the bird, sending it flying and dazed across the street. "Clumsy oaf," she muttered.

The sound of laughter caused her to look around. A handsome young man leaned in the doorway of the stable a bit down the road. He had a shovel in his hand and although he wore peasant rags, she could see that his hard-muscled chest and arms strained at the thin linen of his shirt. His face was tanned from working and his golden hair shone in the sunlight.

"If you do any real damage, surely my plate will go empty and not yours, my lady. Pray be gentle with the fowl."

She lowered her eyelids slightly as she smiled. "If you're worried about the chickens, you could collect them."

"Nay, I am bidden to the stables." He lifted his shovel slightly. "It is horse dung that I will be collecting this day."

She walked a bit closer to him. "Are you one of the de Pourvre knights?"

"No more, madame. De Pourvre is dead. I am the keeper of the dung heap. A slight but noble chore."

She could not help but laugh, and it was easy, as she found him to be quite handsome.

"I heard a commotion; some said there was a troop approaching."

"It was hardly a troop. A group of beggars were sent here by Hyatt. As if he does not have enough beggars to feed."

"You do not like the new lord, sir?" she asked, her eyes twinkling.

"Who am I to like or to . . ." His voice trailed off as a uniformed knight, bold in his red gambeson, black hose, and flowing black mantle, stopped short as he passed to stare at the twosome. "Pardon, my lady," the stableboy said quietly, giving her a slight bow and turning to go.

"Wait a moment," she said. She reached out, pinching a piece of his shirtsleeve to draw him back.

He looked warily at the guard and turned pleading eyes to Faon. "Please, my lady, I would not chance a beating —"

"You will not be beaten. He will leave you alone if you're talking to me." She threw a glance over her shoulder at the guard and after a long and scrutinizing look, the soldier walked on.

"You must be of some special influence here," he observed.

"Oh, perhaps. I am of Hyatt's house and I can detain any serf of my liking. What is your name?"

"Verel. Once a knight of De la Noye."

"Ah. And a good one?"

"I was the captain of a half-troop."

"Hah! You are too young to have been a captain."

He smiled and raised a brow. "Age has little to do with it. I am old enough. I was knighted on a field of battle six years ago."

"I suppose you wish to fight again? Do you seek a position from Hyatt?"

His jaw tensed and his blue eyes glittered. The hand that was wrapped around the shovel tightened, causing his muscles to stand taut. "I have a position, my lady."

Faon leaned against the stable wall, oblivious to the contradicting pose she created in the street. She was the only woman dressed in finery, the only one not carrying something or rushing to do some chore. But she was enjoying this young man, whom she judged to be in his mid-twenties. "Surely this does not suit you. You were telling me how you view this new lord."

Verel's eyes narrowed slightly as he looked at her more boldly. "Until this morning, my lady, I regarded him as the devil, landed with his black angels. But I had not seen you."

She threw back her head with a lusty laugh, her green eyes twinkling in delight. "You are a brazen lout, speaking to me in such a manner. How do you know I won't have you flogged for insolence?"

"I trust you would not detain me for so long, if you meant only harm. Tell me, my lady, how do you see the new lord? You must have traveled here with his people."

"I did. He is a good leader of men, but if he has overlooked your talents, he is not a good judge of strength. 'Tis obvious you are strong and able."

Verel looked at her closely, his eyes dipping to her swelling bosom and narrow waist. "I am able," he said softly.

"Are you chained at night?" she whispered.

"Nay, but I share a stable tackroom with seven other serfs; all were knights once."

"Are you guarded?"

He smiled. "Nay. The gate and wall are kept tight and we have no weapons."

She gave her head a toss. "Mayhap I will wander to the stable when the moon is set. . . ."

He lightly grasped her elbow. "If you tell me when you

will come, I will wait for you beneath the loft. These men who were de Pourvre's know how to look the other way."

"Do you seduce me?"

Verel chuckled. "I thought 'twas much the other way around. But if it pleases you, yea, I beg your favors."

"Then . . ." Her voice trailed off as she noticed that Verel's gaze was drawn away from her. She turned to see where he looked, for his blue eyes had clouded with anger and pain. Aurélie was backing out of a peasant's hut, a basket hanging from her arm. She seemed to be consoling the woman there, or giving instruction. She did not look about the streets, but was much engrossed in some mission.

Faon felt a moment of indecision and confusion. Aurélie's gown was less fine than her own. In fact, the lady's habit was conservative, roughly sewn of brownish wool. Her wimple covered her hair and the hem of her apron was frayed. It was typical that Aurélie did not adorn herself much, except on those rare occasions when she attempted to beautify herself for the evening meal or for mass on the Sabbath. Yet frequently the knights looked longingly in her direction. Faon thought her looks plain and ordinary, although when Aurélie wore finery and let her hair fall freely down her back, she was comely, but in a quiet way. What was her allure? Faon wondered.

She looked back at Verel. The handsome young man's eyes were misty with passion. But the object of his desire did not expose her bosom, swing her hips, or let her hair trail seductively down her back. She seemed to have captured men by some other means, unknown to Faon.

Aurélie departed from the hut and began a hurried step toward the hall. She paused when she saw Faon and Verel in discussion. "Why, Mistress Faon, have you come to help tend our injured?" Faon wrinkled her nose in distaste and looked away. "I thought not. Forsooth, your beautiful gown would be damaged."

Aurélie laughed lightly and continued on, Verel's eyes

following her with pained attention. Not a dozen steps were taken by the lady of the hall when a fully costumed knight of Hyatt's colors approached her, bowed and begged the chance to carry her basket as he escorted her to the hall. Aurélie willingly turned over her burden, gave a brief smile and nod, and walked with the young, besotted knight toward the inner bailey. She was out of sight before Verel could pull his eyes away from her departing form.

"You betray your lust for her," Faon said angrily.

"Lust?" he laughed. " 'Twould be an ill-fitted shoe, should I lust after the Englishman's woman. I do not seek death so eagerly as that."

"What makes you think he values her?"

"Only a fool would not, madame. And in addition, I see that she places high value on her husband, even if she tries to spare us all the agony of her final betrayal."

"What say you? She fears him, from all I can see."

Verel chuckled ruefully. "So I thought, but as the peasants approached with the injured bearing Hyatt's blazon, the lady fair tore asunder two guards to see who came. It was clear that she feared 'twas Hyatt who was hurt. Do you want to see how a woman cares for a man? Tell her that he is injured and you will know."

"Bitch . . . ," Faon muttered, looking down at the dirt.

"What ho! Do you perchance trouble yourself to be jealous of Lady Aurélie? Perhaps you had your sights set on the Englishman. I will tell you something, madame, to save you much misery. It is said that Hyatt does not do anything against his desires; he wed the lady. I know her well, and if he does not see the prize that he holds, he is a fool. I hate him truly, but I suspect he is wise, or we would not have fallen so easily."

"You have been watching her?"

"When I can." He shrugged.

"Do you think she comes to love him?"

"If she does not, she may in time. Women often look the

way of the man with the most power, and there is little question of Hyatt's dominion here. And I know something of the woman. She is steadfast, whether the man is deserving or not. It was her way with our Sire de Pourvre, even though he certainly did not deserve her. There is naught I can do now. I should have taken her when I could."

"When you could?"

"Aye. While the Sire de Pourvre paid me as the captain of his half-troop, there was talk that the woman suffered as his wife. He did not put much stock in women; he was more keen to young boys and priests. A sweet word in her ear might have turned her away from her spouse. The Sire de Pourvre promised the castle and towns to me, since there was no heir."

Faon smiled, but it was an evil gleam in her eye. "Would you get away from here if you could?"

"Do you lay some trap for me?"

"Oh nay, I would not harm you. But mayhap help you."

"Then I tell you true, if I could find some French force to reclaim this place, I would do to Hyatt what he did to the Sire de Pourvre. I would take the castle, make her a widow, and reclaim it all."

"But if you already had her?"

"Then, madame, this place would mean little to me."

Faon lowered her lids seductively. She ran a hand along Verel's arm, taking no notice of how passersby would look. The beaten people of De la Noye were very cautious with the way they stared at her.

"I think perhaps we will be friends, Verel. We will talk again."

"You take a grave chance in talking to me, lady. I am the one they watch most closely."

"I do not worry, Verel. I don't plan to talk to you in the light of day again. But the loft; now there is a place for whispering."

He looked into her eyes and his own came alive with

154

mischief. He made a sweeping bow, like a well-trained courtier. "I am at your service, my lady."

❧

The smoke from the Château Innesse could be seen darkening the sky from twenty leagues away. The keep was so named because the moat that surrounded the front of the enclosure was wider than the widest river. A full bridge rather than short drawbridge was built for entrance, and the rear of the wall and keep was built into the side of the hill. An approaching army could be seen on all sides from the highest citadel. At first sight Hyatt was struck by its magnificence, for it was easily twice the size of De la Noye. And his heart was somewhat saddened, for he believed the conquest had been successful days before, yet still she burned.

The stench worsened as Hyatt's troop neared. It was the flesh of the beaten that burned and filled the air. The outer wall was not battered, but within the outer bailey were the charred remains of wooden houses, wagons, sheds, and people.

Hyatt's bearer carried the banner of Edward, and they were admitted. A pitiful number of captives were chained or tied throughout the streets and pathways to the keep. Doors were torn apart and the stain of blood was everywhere. Armored knights clamored through the keep and stood watch on the wall. A woman lay in the ashes before what was once a house and wept. Her clothing was torn to shreds, and dried blood stained her forehead and hands. Only stone buildings still stood, but the roofs were burned.

The troop dismounted before the central hall and tethered their horses. All the men looked around, frowning, grimacing. Hyatt went directly through the doors into the hall to meet the captor.

"What ho! A knight of English blood."

Sir Hollis Marsden sat on a jeweled throne on a dais that must have once belonged to the lord of this estate. On the floor beside him was a woman, her dress torn completely open, her ankle shackled to the leg of the chair.

Hollis tipped a horn to his mouth while the other hand lazily held a whip. His jowls were sagging with plenty, his gut round and full, and one leg was outstretched before him in lazy indifference.

"You seem to have quelled the place, Sir Hollis," Hyatt said, looking around at the rubble in disgust. "You have little need of my assistance."

Hollis threw back his head and laughed. "As if that's why you've come. Give the man drink," he shouted. "Aye, give my enemy drink, for we will never drink together again, God knows!"

Hyatt smiled lazily and stepped into the room. A few of his men began filtering into the hall behind him, while others stayed without to keep watch. A young boy rushed toward Hyatt with a filled mug and, as he accepted the drink, he looked at the youth. The lad wore Hollis's colors and was likely a servant or page, yet his face was swollen from a beating. Hollis did not even place much value on his own people. Hollis did not rise, but cracked his whip lazily into the rushes on the floor.

"Did you let anyone live?" Hyatt asked.

"The useful ones," Hollis replied. He glanced at the tattered woman on the floor.

"Who is she?"

"She was daughter by marriage to the old lord's son. But he is dead. She is a widow now." Hollis began to laugh wickedly. "She had some high-flown ways . . . but no more."

Hyatt tried not to look at the woman. Her dirty blond hair was matted and covered much of her face. A bruise marked her cheek and her clothing was in unsubstantial shreds that might once have been a gown of quality. Dark, swollen marks dotted her exposed calves. Her feet were bare.

Inside, Hyatt began to seethe. He did not understand why anyone would take something of beauty and destroy it. The castle, the woman, the land, all ruined by Hollis's greedy hand. But he did understand that Hollis would do the same to him in a moment.

And the woman chained at the knight's feet could be Aurélie.

"Do you require anything of me?" Hyatt asked. "Some French adversary that may threaten from nearby?"

"Nay, we circled the area before I took Innesse. There is no one to attack us."

"How did you get in?"

"There was no trouble getting inside, once the entire keep was surrounded. I have two hundred and fifty now. One hundred are archers. The sky was black with arrows."

"I have long wondered how you could afford such a large troop."

"It is easily done."

"It must have been a harrowing fight." Hyatt smirked, looking around. There was little doubt that the place had surrendered and been destroyed.

"Three days and nights. But I lost only a few men. Ours are better, that is all. The word is that you have taken a castle south of here on behalf of the prince. True?"

Hyatt nodded. "But to your credit, Hollis, you did a great deal more fighting than I. We were engaged in only a skirmish. The castle surrendered." Hyatt shrugged. "Of course, not a door latch was broken and the people already work the fields."

Hollis began to glower, his cheeks pinkening. Little could be raised out of his plunder to make Innesse a decent place to live. It was as if he had only just realized his mistake in razing the place with Hyatt's mention of it. "What is the word from Edward?"

"There is no word as yet. He ordered me to secure De la Noye and look to your needs. Since you need nothing, we will depart."

"Not a meal? Won't you stay and share the spoils?"

"Spoils. Indeed."

Hollis frowned blackly. "Do you insult me? You are captive within my walls, Hyatt. Do you think it wise to be impolite?"

"I left a good army at De la Noye. They have my letters ready for the prince in Bordeaux. I will not dally with you, Hollis. If you kill me now, it will be murder, and Prince Edward will be told of it. He has two thousand. I will not waste my good men on you, even after death." He raised a brow. "I swear the king told me you gave your word to fight only England's battles until this demesne is settled for the prince."

Hollis glowered at Hyatt. "It is nearly settled." He cracked his whip once. "We will meet again. Soon."

Hyatt bowed. "I never doubted it." He turned and walked out of the hall. His men separated to let him pass and in the courtyard they mounted their steeds.

When they had cleared the bridge and were well on the road away, a young knight urged his horse beside Hyatt's. "I heard, Sir Hyatt, that Hollis means to attack you."

"Aye. Give the word to the men in the rear. Hollis will send out a troop immediately. We will go south until out of sight of the Innesse wall and then circle northeast. And there will be no fire for several nights. Until we are within sight of De la Noye, we will be the friends of the wolves in the forest."

"Is there no way to form a pact with Hollis? A peace pact?"

Hyatt laughed. "Did you not hear? There was a pact, issued by the king. We are ordered not to attempt to settle our dispute until these lands are secured for England."

"Sir Hyatt, why does he hate you?"

"Surely you've heard. I know my men are careful not to gossip within my hearing, but they talk."

"A contest of arms, I was told. Hollis lost."

"There was a tournament after the fall of Calais. It was witnessed by the king and his family in Ghent. Hollis was losing in the joust and when I turned to accept the token from the king, he attacked my back. Hollis not only lost all his gear and was ransomed for a goodly sum, but was disgraced. King Edward revoked his earlier promise to award the knight with admittance to the Order of the Garter. Hollis has sworn to kill me ever since."

The knight whistled. "Since that . . . how has he managed to secure the arms he has?"

"He has managed to get money from rich nobles, and I imagine he steals, kidnaps, and ransoms hostages. When a man is as determined as Hollis, there is nothing to stop him." He turned his head and smiled at the young knight. "Except, perhaps, me."

There was confusion in the young man's eyes. "But why don't you meet his troop, then? Even if they triple us in number, not one would live out the day."

"Because, lad, Hollis would have the advantage. His men are roiled up to kill and they would attack us by surprise. 'Tis Hollis's way and perhaps the way he has taught his men. Why allow any advantage to the wily fox?"

"You are certain he would come from the rear?"

"Aye. Under cover of dark, I suppose. Or from a forest or overgrowth. What did you notice about Innesse?

"It was destroyed. Completely destroyed. Hollis must have kept battering the place and the people long after the battle was won."

"Yea, and the charred wreckage was *within* the outer wall. There was not so much as the bruise of a battering ram on the gate."

There was a long silence as the wide-eyed youth absorbed this. Then, breathlessly, "They let him in."

"Or . . . he crept in somehow. Got their surrender, or crept past a night guard, or tricked them." Hyatt smiled. "You see, there is something else you must know about Hollis. Whatever values the leader boasts will often become the principle of the whole troop. Hollis is fierce, strong, ruthless, has no conscience, and is well oiled with the money to buy men and arms. But the most dangerous of his traits is this — he is a coward. And cowards use sneaky ways to fight, then lie about their methods." Hyatt paused and looked closely at the young man beside him. They had only ridden together since Hyatt selected his troop in England, less than a year ago, but the young man was good. And he was learning. The serious look in his eyes made Hyatt feel a little more secure. "Go alert the men at the rear of our party what to look for. Some of these men know Hollis, some do not. It is up to you to pass the word."

"Aye, Sir Hyatt," the youth said, whirling about on his steed to fall back in the ranks.

NINE

HERE was no sounding from the donjon when a lone messenger arrived in late June, a fortnight behind Percival's group. Aurélie happened to be in the town and heard the large, squeaking levers of the wheels turning to lower the bridge and open the gates. She stood back to see who came, since it was not time for the farmers to return, or their spouses to take them food in the fields. A lone rider, a sunburned lad in a well-worn livery, came across the bridge and into the bailey, giving a wave to those acquaintances among Hyatt's forces whom he knew. His teeth gleamed white against his rosy skin and he had already removed his helm as he entered. She recognized him at once to be one of those who had accompanied Hyatt on his campaign.

He dismounted when he saw her and left his destrier to a fleet-footed page, who took the beast into the stable. He approached her and bowed. "My lady, I was sent ahead to bring word of your lord husband's return. In two days, perhaps three, he will arrive with the others."

"Does he send some special instructions for me, in preparation for his return?"

"Nay, only that you be informed. And he did say that he hopes to find you well."

A half-smile appeared on her lips. "The courtesy was unexpected," she said, trying to explain away the sudden flush that came to her cheeks. "I shall see that extra game is set to roast for a hungry troop."

"He would be appreciative, my lady. The work has been hard on this ride."

"Oh? Were there many French to quell?" she asked hesitantly.

"None at all. The countryside is quiet. But did you not know he rode to see what Sir Hollis had done?"

"Who is Sir Hollis? I heard nothing of Hyatt's plans."

"Hollis Marsden is his enemy, my lady. They were both called to arms for Edward in this campaign, but when left to their own ends, the challenges between them are many. Sir Hollis is a friend to Sir Hyatt's brother, Sir Ryland."

Her eyes rounded with question. "Brother? Ryland?"

The sunburned face brightened more as he blushed. The young man shuffled his feet slightly. "I would be in your debt if you made no mention that I . . ." He straightened. " 'Tis only gossip among the men, my lady. And I have only lately learned of this rivalry between Sir Hollis and Sir Hyatt. Sir Hyatt does not speak of family, but insists he has none."

"I see. Do you know the reason for this?"

"It would be considered a breach of conduct for me to speak of rumors I heard, lady. Please forgive me."

"But was he in grave danger?"

The lad sighed. "We did not rest easy in Hollis's keep, and we spent many days evading Hollis's troop. But I understand now that Sir Hyatt was correct; we are safer to see what Hollis does than to sit idle here and suffer some bad surprise. Hollis would not be above attacking one of his own and reporting to the king that it was a French battle in which so many English were killed."

Aurélie shivered slightly, hearing something that had never occurred to her. "And Hollis's keep? Surely it is one that was French . . ."

"The Château Innesse south of Limoges. Do you know the place?"

"I have visited the castle twice in my lifetime; a more beautiful place does not exist." She noticed a sudden sadness in the young man's eyes. "Was the quest of your English knight hard on the people?" she asked with almost fearful reluctance.

"Sir Hollis is not a tender heart, my lady." He swallowed. "Leave it to say that it is better we know how he fights, and you may thank whatever divinity you worship that 'twas Hyatt, and not the other, who took De la Noye."

"It has been said that Hyatt was intent on De la Noye before leaving England."

"Aye, this place and others like it were once firmly held by the Duchy of Aquitaine; the plans were made well in advance. In kind, Hollis was aware of Château Innesse."

"Then why did Hyatt not push his forces to Innesse?"

The knight smiled. "Hollis's troop triples ours in size, and Hyatt kept secret his intentions toward De la Noye. In fact —" he grinned "— Hyatt did not tell any of us where we were bound until we were nearly here. If you'll forgive me, my lady, it has been said that your suffering was a good deal more than planned. Sir Giles was to be released and pensioned after a short imprisonment."

Her head snapped suddenly in attention. It was not the first time that there had been mention that pardons were the order of the battle rather than death, but she and Giles had always been mentioned together, as a pair. This young man specifically referred to only Giles. "And . . . I?"

"I . . . ah . . . that is . . ."

"What had you heard was to be done with me?" she asked.

" 'Tis only gossip, my lady, and . . ." Aurélie gave a sharp, insistent nod of her head to show that she was not willing to excuse this bit of gossip. "An old Flemish lord saw Sir Hyatt in Bordeaux after our troop landed. It is said that the marriage was arranged and De la Noye spoken for before we began our advance. But I think a divorce or annulment was planned."

"How did anyone imagine that Giles, held prisoner or freed, would agree to such a thing?"

His eyes held a glimmer that Aurélie thought resembled pity. "By way of retirement and pension to a monastery, my lady. A rich monastery."

She looked away from the young man, her eyes misting slightly. Giles need not have died. He would have gladly traded her and his home for a life of misery and want among monks.

"Had he known . . . and yet, he was killed. Poor Giles."

"Killed? My lady, he —" The man stopped himself and stiffened his lips. "I say too much, my lady, if you tell Sir Hyatt that I . . ."

The young man was so discomfited by his loose tongue that Aurélie deemed it wise to reassure him. "I will say nothing to Sir Hyatt. You must be hungry after your long ride. The evening meal is nearly ready if you wish to eat in the hall."

"Thank you, my lady." He started away and then turned back. "Oh, and Sir Hyatt did say he was eager to be home."

She smiled, though her lips trembled, and turned away to finish her errand. She collected a basketful of eggs for the next day from a peasant woman who owned six laying hens and was en route to the hall when she heard her name being called. She looked this way and that, failing to see who called to her, until she finally noticed Verel lurking behind a grain barrel at the side of the stable. "Aurélie! Here!"

She approached him warily, suspicious because of his sneaky manner. When she got near enough, he pulled her inside the dark stable and along to a stall in which bridles and saddles were stored for the knights.

"What is it, Verel? What's the matter?"

"My lady," he breathed. "Nothing is wrong; all is right. I have found a means of getting away from here. I can take you with me."

"You are mad."

"Nay! You, of all people, know that I cannot stay and abide this demesne held by an English warlord. Nor can I abide his possession of you. You deserve better than this. . . ."

In spite of herself, Aurélie burst into laughter. Here stood a ragged young man who smelled of horse dung, driven by nothing more than some farfetched vision of glory, enticing her to flee.

"Oh, Verel, forgive me . . . but the numbers of people who know how much I deserve seem to increase, yet my lot worsens with each good intention. Now, do you think I deserve to flee with you, to battle my way through the forests and marshes and . . ."

"I have a horse," he said defensively, straightening proudly. "And a shield, sword, and crossbow. I may leave without armor, but I can take you safely to Avignon, or farther. And we can secure a troop to bring De la Noye to her knees."

Her laughter fled instantly, noting that he was deadly serious. "How have you come by a horse and arms?"

"Oh, nay, my lady, I cannot tell you who helps me. But I can save you from the brute before he returns."

"He will hunt you down, Verel. Do not do this."

He grasped her suddenly by the upper arms and forcefully claimed her lips with his. The basket swung on her arm, spilling the eggs. His breath was desperately labored; his arms released hers only to go around her waist and pull her more violently against him. Verel's peasant hose and light linen shirt were little protection against desires that Aurélie could feel raging forth. Her innocence was fast disappearing; she knew he would take her away not for the sake of France and De la Noye, but because of his own lust.

"Let go of me," she demanded.

"I love you. Aurélie, I swear I do." His lips were hot and moist on her neck and she pushed him.

"My God, even *he* wed me before he tried to bed me."

He released her abruptly. "Aurélie, Aurélie, I have wanted you since I first saw you, so many years ago. I would have spirited you away long ago, had I believed you would go . . . but it was easier to serve Giles and be near to you, knowing that Giles valued me and that he would not last long."

"What do you mean?"

"Giles was destined to die in the first battle he fought. He knew nothing of fighting; he could not even protect himself. I stayed here all the while for you. I did not wish to serve de Pourvre as much as I wished to be here when he was gone, to rule this place as it should be ruled."

"I thought you were his most loyal. Verel?"

"I *was!* God above, I worked harder for him than anyone. But it was for you that I was fighting. I have always loved you. And I have always loved De la Noye. Can't you see that? I have wanted strength and order for this place . . . as it was in the old days, with the old Sire, so it is said."

"As it is now," she said softly.

"Nay," he said, shaking his head as if hurt. "You cannot cast your lot with the English bastard."

"He is my husband. He is the lord of this place now."

"Aurélie? Have you given up?"

"Given up?" She laughed again, but it was a bitter sound. "I have never seen the place better than it is now, only two short months after he has come. Even under the old Sire there was not such order. For once the priest does not run the town and is properly placed at prayers rather than counting his money. There is more broken ground for crops than ever before and while my villeins wear sour faces, they are plump with his food. Given up? Are you truly such a fool?"

"But you cannot abide his presence in your bed? In Giles's place?"

"Giles never used that place," she said hastily and angrily, wishing immediately that she could withdraw the statement after it was issued. Instead, she rambled on, hoping he would forget. "If you do not see what has happened, there is nothing I can do to change your mind about it. So you carry a hoe or shovel rather than a lance, but it comes to me that Hyatt is not the fool to ignore good fighting skills, and if you would but show your talents and that you could be trusted, he would use you better than Giles did. If you try to flee or plot against him, he is within his rights to slay you. It would be a pitiful waste, Verel. You are too good to die."

"You return none of my affection, do you?"

She bit her lip in indecision. It was in her mind to tell him that had he pleaded his case of passion before, when she hungered for love, for a touch, she was not certain that she would have had the strength of conviction to deny him. But now his admission did not tempt her.

"Would you have some useless prattle of love and longing and make me witness to the rivers of blood that would spurt from your neck? I would be forced to pass daily the place where your head would ride a pike on the wall. Nay, I return none of your affection and I bid you remember 'tis for your own good."

"You no longer mourn your husband?"

"Mourn him? He rides toward De la Noye now and will arrive anon! My husband, Verel, is Sir Hyatt. It is written in the vows of the Church, of property, and of my body as well. There is no one in all Christendom who will argue that he has wed me, albeit by right of arms. Do you know the penalty of an adulterous wife? The peasant's woman may be tied in the courtyard or stoned. The lord's wife is guilty of high treason. If I loved death so well, I'd have taken my life by my own hand. To speak of love is to speak of death. Nay, I return none of your affection."

"You love him."

"I speak naught of love. I speak of reason and life. Your choices are as simple as mine, if you will but see them. No French force will travel here; Hyatt has sent the marriage papers to both kings — De la Noye is a married estate, no matter the victor in war. If you flee, you will either be hunted down and killed, or spared only to starve along the road as you search for a sympathetic army. Do not be a fool. Hyatt has use for good men; you could prove yourself to —"

She was cut short as Verel spat in the dust. "I will never seek to win favor from the bastard. I would rather die first."

She backed away from him, conscious for the first time of the few eggs that had spilled from her basket and lay crushed on the stable floor beneath her feet. "And so you shall, Verel. I'm sorry I cannot help you."

"Will you betray me?"

"Nay. 'Twould only serve to quicken your death. I think perhaps it is better if you go. You will not return."

She turned to leave the stable, noticing that the sun was sinking as she reached the door.

"My lady," he called, "if I do return, for whom will you fight?"

"As I always have, Sir Verel. For De la Noye and the man who owns her."

⁓

The noise in the common room was louder than usual. There seemed a great deal of laughter and jesting and at first Aurélie thought that it was because word had been delivered of Hyatt's return. She passed what remained of the collected eggs to a servant, listening closely to the men. She soon realized that it was another matter that caused such riotous glee from the knights.

"Had she but ridden a bit farther into the copse, she might have worn the horse into exhaustion and been forced to ride him all the way to Brittany."

"Or better still, straight into Hyatt's camp . . . in which case her privy arse would've been injured by other than a fall."

"I only lament that she didn't break her bloody neck. 'Twould make for less bickering among the women."

Aurélie listened to the laughter, slowly approaching Girvin. He occupied a stool near the spitted fowl on the hearth and pounded dents out of his shield.

"What amusement so pleases these men?" she asked him.

"Faon," he grumbled. "She took a good stallion to mount, like the hellion she is, without permission or escort." He shrugged. "The beast threw her and left her to limp home alone."

"You do not share their jesting."

Girvin looked up at her, his eyes narrowed to slits. "It was a good horse," he said slowly, with much irritation in his voice.

"You truly hate her, don't you, Sir Girvin?" she asked.

168

Girvin looked directly into her eyes, a thing he rarely did. "There are women, madame, who are stupid enough to think that to disable their man will give them power. Faon is one of them. No act is too low. She is the fool to cut off Hyatt's arms to have his dependence on her, and then bemoan the fact that he can no longer embrace her."

"You are partly wrong about Faon. She wants Hyatt. She loves him."

Girvin grunted. "If so, she portrays her love in ignorance. I know nothing of women's love, nor do I wish to know more. But I have seen the likes of Faon before, under many a swinging skirt."

"Aye," Aurélie said. "You need not fear for Hyatt. He is more than aware of women's shortcomings."

Girvin looked at her long and hard. "I hope so, madame."

"Sir Girvin, I . . ." Aurélie stopped herself. "Never mind. You guard him well, from men and women alike, and he is the better for it. I will not try to convince you that I am any better than Mistress Faon."

She rose to leave him and heard his voice come softly from behind. "You need not." She wondered only briefly what was meant, before dismissing his words from her mind.

Aurélie listened to the banter, Faon absent because of her injuries, and realized very quickly what had happened. She suspected she was alone in knowing the truth, but wondered how many had seen Faon talking with Verel on that afternoon a fortnight past.

When the meal was done and Aurélie went upstairs, she paused before her door and then, upon further consideration, walked down the long, dark gallery toward the rooms allotted to Faon. She did not knock, but the portal was not latched. She pushed the door open very slowly and Faon, whose posterior was not too bruised to sit on a hard stool, turned in surprise.

"When does he go?" Aurélie asked simply.

"Who?" Faon asked with a toss of her curls.

"You know who I mean. I do not go with him, mistress.

But if it is not too late, perhaps you should. I don't think Hyatt would search for you."

Faon shot to her feet, staring at Aurélie with icy daggers in her eyes.

"I know what you have done."

"I don't know what you're talking about," Faon insisted, lifting her chin.

"I could go to Girvin now. He would relish a chance to throw up your skirts and see for himself how worn are your poor hips."

Faon stiffened and her mouth curled in a sneer. "Then go, bitch. I shall show that black devil my rosy butt and let him kill your young knight. We both know what will happen; Girvin may wish me dead, but he wouldn't dare harm me."

Aurélie slowly smiled. "I think I shall let it be. Verel can get to safety better without you, and I wish him no harm. Given enough time, you will slay yourself. You are too foolish to last long."

"Do you think to betray me to Hyatt? Hah! Do not try it or you will find that Hyatt does not —"

Aurélie slowly shook her head. "Does not trust women? I pitied him for that once, but I see now the reason and think him wise to distrust women. Nay, I will not betray you. You will betray yourself soon enough."

She turned away and closed the door, standing there for a moment. A chill in the corridor caused the hairs at the back of her neck to prickle in uneasiness. Faon did not follow to challenge her and she shrugged off the strange feeling. She walked back down the gallery toward her chamber. The hall turned and as she came around the corner she gasped in sudden fright as she came up against Girvin's solid chest. "Oh, Girvin, you frightened me half to death."

"Is aught amiss, madame?" he asked evenly.

"All is well, Girvin. I only wanted to assure myself that Mistress Faon did not need anything for her injuries."

"And how does she?"

"She is remarkably well, for someone who suffered a nasty fall."

"Do you suggest that I look in on her myself? Hyatt did ask me to watch her."

Aurélie laid a hand on his forearm. "Perhaps you should, Girvin," she said, smiling slyly. "If you leave her to her own ends, she may get herself in a good deal more trouble. She may even flee."

Girvin smiled down at Aurélie and then whirled about, presenting his back to walk down the stairs, making it quite clear that he could look the other way should Faon decide to leave De la Noye. Aurélie had no doubt that Girvin would watch, as he always did, to be assured that Hyatt's son was not taken away. She could not resist the urge to chuckle, though she kept her voice quiet. "Good eventide, Sir Girvin," she said softly. But the hulking knight did not turn or answer.

❧

There was no second messenger for Hyatt, and Aurélie had set out more food each night than was needed, yet she went to bed each night alone, for he did not come in the two or three days promised. Seven days passed before she warily approached Girvin.

"My lord is delayed somehow, Sir Girvin," she said softly.

Girvin looked at her for a long moment. His voice was nearly a whisper. "Do not be afraid for him, my lady. Bad news travels very swiftly and we would have heard something if he were in trouble."

"Sir Girvin . . . ?" She stopped herself. He looked at her with a puzzled frown and she touched him, laying a gentle hand on his arm. " 'Tis nothing," she said. "Thank you."

She turned to go and he called her back. "My lady, each night for four nights there has been more roasted meat than necessary and . . ."

" 'Tis my fault, Sir Girvin. I do not disregard your hard efforts in hunting, and I appreciate your talents better than anyone. I have only thought there would be a hearty and hungry troop, and perhaps I should wait until Hyatt is here in fact before ordering the roasting done."

Girvin smiled at her. "I do not criticize you, my lady. It is to your credit that you do right by the messenger's warning. I need an extra bowman on the hunt and I would ask for Sir Guillaume, if you think he can manage a spear and bow well, and if you can spare him from trailing at your skirts."

She was surprised and delighted by the request. It was also the second time that Girvin had used Guillaume's title with his name, as if the time of Guillaume's restoration came closer each day. "He is among the best huntsmen, Girvin, and is ill disposed to play nursemaid to me. Take him with my blessing."

"Do you carry a dagger, madame?"

She laughed goodnaturedly, a soft ripple of amusement that caused Girvin's stony features to relax into a complacent pose. "Only Faon would dare threaten me, and if she does I shall simply offer her one of our best horses for her amusement, and my vengeance would be served."

"Be careful," he warned before their conversation ended.

In the days since Hyatt had left, Girvin had stirred her curiosity a great deal. Of course, he was closest at hand to protect what Hyatt had claimed, for there seemed to be a bond between the two men that ran deeper than blood relation. And in Girvin's eyes Aurélie had begun to see that softness of love and devotion, much like what passed between brothers or fathers and sons.

She had almost asked him about Giles's death, for although Girvin was a terrifying, ruthless knight, there was something about him that was like a snag in her understanding of him. He seemed anxious to kill, yet he also regarded useless death as a waste, as did Hyatt. He struck terror in hearts when he loomed in his threatening position, yet she had never seen him act unfairly or cruelly. Upon her first sight of him, with his admission that his sword had dealt the final blow to Giles, she had decided never to forgive him. But she doubted, now, that Girvin had killed without cause. And, even more, she doubted Giles could possibly have possessed the courage to attack one such as Girvin.

Aurélie was cautious in her pursuit of information about Verel and was limited to glancing about the area of the stables and corrals whenever she was within the village or outer bailey. She did not see him, but neither did she hear anyone in the hall remark on his absence. These knights of Hyatt's were extremely attentive to details, and she doubted he had slipped away unnoticed. But she dared not betray her own knowledge of his plan and if she saw Faon, she skittered away like a frightened rabbit, not willing to exchange words or glances with the woman.

It was more than a week since the messenger had come when she stood at her bedchamber window and stared pensively at the stars in the clear black sky. *Hyatt, do you live?*

She doffed her chemise and crawled under the down quilt. She wondered briefly what would become of her if Hyatt were killed in some skirmish between Limoges and De la Noye. Would she be passed to a new owner, be executed, or be left as a dowager? Perhaps she would be dependent upon Girvin, who, she assumed, would act as a protector to Derek until the boy grew up.

But these questions quickly passed, since the real cause for distress lay in how she would grieve for the loss of this man's body's warmth beside her. And his strength would be gone . . . a strength she felt certain no one could match. She now truly belonged to a man, and she knew she could never belong to another. Yet he did not love her, so where was her purpose?

He has conquered me, she thought. *I am his, and it is as if I had no life before him. But he is not mine; I know nothing of this well-reared, well-lettered man who chooses to be known as a bastard. 'Tis plain he was highly born and has somehow learned the wisdom and justice of the highest nobles, yet he attacks and fights under the shield of a base-born knight and will not confide one moment of his past to me. I lie in this bed that was ours,*

missing him, wanting him, and for what? He goes to great lengths
to make love to me tenderly, and still greater lengths to remind me
that all I mean to his existence is what I can bring in service to
his cause. Oh love, if you are my love, will I ever be cherished by
you? Will you ever let me cherish you, or would my spoken word
only make you fearful that I am cut of the same cloth as Faon?

He filled her thoughts, which turned to dreams, as on many
nights before this. She dozed fitfully, torn with concern for
his safety, coupled with worry for her own sanity. She had
nearly come to cry out with longing for the man who forced
his whim on her lands, her home, and her heart. Every time
she settled herself again into the quilt, she saw his face in
her sleep.

In the blackest hour of the night she was startled awake
by the crashing of metal, and she bolted upright. Her chamber
was black; there was no candle and only a sliver of the moon
shone through the shutters. The summer heat made a fire
unnecessary and so she could see nothing at all. She reached
under her pillow and felt the handle of her dagger and drew
it, holding it against the unknown intruder.

The sound of scratching flint and then a spark and light
across the room caused her to let her breath out slowly. But
she was still poised upright, dagger raised, a torrent of hair
falling over her shoulders and curling to cover her breasts,
and the quilt at her waist.

"Hold, Aurélie," Hyatt whispered.

As he walked toward her, she slowly let the dagger drop,
resting on her thighs. "Hyatt? It is the middle of the night."

"Closer to dawn," he said, smiling down at her. "I dropped
my gear. This chamber is crowded in the dark."

"You didn't make camp for the night?"

He leaned over the bed and gently pulled the dagger from
her hand, putting it aside. He sat down beside her and in the
dim light she could see the harsh effects of many days on the
road. He had not been lolling about as some guest or wooing
any farmer's daughter. His beard was thick, his face burned
by the sun, and the dust and dirt on his clothes caused the

smell of the horses and leather to cling to him. But his hand deftly pushed her thick hair over her shoulder to expose her naked breast and she did not cringe from his touch. Rather, she welcomed it.

"I could not wait another night for you," he whispered.

She let her eyes gently close. "Do you treasure me after all, milord?"

He chuckled, a deep and seductive sound. "You doubted it? I do not know what games women play, but with men, I can assure you, their passion is only aroused when their minds are. 'Tis not a thing simply willed. Aye, wench, I treasure you. You pleasure me greatly."

Though it was not all that she wished to hear from him, she quickly decided that she would not press him further on this night, since the gentle touch of his calloused hand already sent ripples of pleasure spiraling through her. Her cheeks grew flushed in anticipation and she tilted her head back as his lips lightly touched hers.

"Is there a chance you have missed me as well, *chérie?*"

"I have been worried that some terrible battle delayed you —" was all she was willing to admit.

" 'Twas nonsense that delayed me, but we need not speak of it now. I could have made camp and waited another day." He kissed her again, a deeper kiss. "Nay. I could not have."

Her hand rose to rest on his chest. "You must be hungry."

"Aye," he whispered, covering her mouth in a searing kiss. He pulled her hard against him, crushing her breasts against the rough cloth of his gambeson. His lips dropped to her bare shoulder, his hands under her, urging her closer. "I am famished."

"I could fetch food," she breathlessly offered.

He chuckled softly and, without putting much space between them, removed his gambeson and tossed it aside. He shed his boots, chausses, and loincloth in one swift motion and was pressing her down into the bed. "What fruit would satisfy me when I only wish to taste your flesh? What wine can you bring me to substitute for the thirst I have, that only your body can quench? I have not slept a night that your rosy hips, teasing breasts, and witch's locks did not torment me. I am hungry for you, and I shall take my fill."

"Oh, Hyatt," she breathed, clinging to him. From deep within her she could sense the urgency of her own desire and she could choose no word of love more eloquently than his own poetic verse.

He nibbled at her ear, her neck, and her breast. Her sighs mingled with his seductive words, muttered against each curve of her body. What had once been acquiescence on her part was now a wanton craving, and she opened herself to him willingly, urgently. But he held himself at bay and teased her.

"Tell me you want me, *chérie*. Or deny it if you can."

Her hips rose with a will beyond her ken, desperate for him. "I want you, Hyatt," she obliged in a whisper. "Be my love."

His fingers handled her body with the finesse of a true craftsman; his lips tempted hers until she was wild with pleasure. "I will be your lover . . . until you can stand no more."

When her sighs of pleasure turned to gasps of desperate longing, he moved within her slowly, rhythmically, torturing her with some ecstasy she thought she could not bear. Her words began to flow as easily as his, as she lost herself in his lovemaking and murmured her own endearments against his ears. She clung to him in a fever, with the force she would have used to keep herself afloat against a raging river.

And the river swept her away in a wild, pulsing joy of brilliance that consumed her. She was frozen by the mystical shower of passion fulfilled, grasping him tightly in awe, in wonder.

He felt her achievement and she heard the confirmation from his lips in a breath. "Ah, my love, at last . . ."

Aurélie had never given or taken so much. She lay panting within his arms, their bodies covered with a mist of rapture past. It was a long while before her rapid breathing subsided, and longer still before she could speak. And when the words did come, they trembled with emotion. "Oh, Hyatt . . ."

"You did not know, Aurélie? What did you think passed between men and women? Where was the reason for sport, if not the reward?"

"I did not know," she said simply. "I suppose I should have guessed."

He rose on an elbow and looked down into her eyes. "There is the power which men are willing to kill for . . . and ofttimes women use to snare unwilling victims into their traps."

"It feels a little like death," she softly mused. She reached a hand to gently touch his cheek. "But it occurs to me, Hyatt, that it is not just a power that pushes men to kill and women to show their treachery, but mayhap a power so glorious that soothes what pain has been endured and gives men and women alike the courage to *love*."

He stared down at her for a long moment, considering this. When he opened his mouth to speak, she placed the palms of her hands on his cheeks and pulled his face down to hers, kissing his lips. "Nay, Hyatt, do not speak. I do not wish to hear you argue this point and spoil the moment. It is too precious to me."

A slight smile touched his lips before he returned her kiss, and let many more precious moments follow the first.

❧

Although Hyatt had suffered a lack of rest, both on the road and in his chamber, he was dressed and gone with sunrise. Aurélie stirred, finding herself alone, and almost laughed at his determined nature. He would not be weakened by love or love's play. His duties would never go undone.

She washed from a basin of fresh water brought by Baptiste and donned a clean gown. Her cheeks were pink, if not from a night of untold pleasures, at least from the chafing of Hyatt's beard. She made a silent, and somewhat cheerful, resolution to play lackey and see him properly shaved.

Hyatt was still at his morning meal when she descended into the hall. Several of his men stood around while he sat, talking and eating. He noticed her arrival and looked in her direction. "Perhaps Aurélie can tell you how he managed. Have you asked her?"

She stopped short and looked at Hyatt and some of the faces surrounding him. One young man flushed slightly before speaking. "Nay, Hyatt, we feared it would sound too much like an accusation."

He pulled the chair beside him out from the table for her to seat herself, his eyes studying her broodingly as she approached. "Sir Verel of Giles's troop is gone, Aurélie. Did you know he planned to escape?"

She looked down. "I strongly suspected from the first, milord."

"And you chose not to warn me? Or Girvin?"

She took a bolstering breath and met his eyes. "I am sorry for your loss, messire, for Verel was good and strong, and if he could have been shown the way to save his pride yet change his allegiance, you would have had a good man in your own troop. But he was an enemy and could not change. I think it is better he is gone, than in De la Noye, reduced to plotting against a force he could never best. If I said nothing it was because he is not a threat to you, but your justice would have forced his death. I have wanted to spare anyone from the old troop of De la Noye."

"Do you know who gave him a horse and weapons?"

"How are you certain he had these things?"

" 'Twas a small group of thieves or soldiers who delayed us. We found them leaving a village with their booty and though we chased them far, for two days, they had good mounts and evaded us. Left behind in one of their flights was a cloak with an initial on the collar. It belonged to one of my men. It was stolen."

"Did you see Verel?"

"Nay, but I have reason to believe he was among them. And we have found the hole he burrowed under the wall, behind the stable. The shovel given to him was to scrape the stable floor free of dung, but he put it to better use."

"Is it possible that the thieves came upon Verel, killed him, and relieved him of his gear?"

Hyatt slowly shook his head, his eyes boring through her. "Do you know who outfitted him, my lady? Do you know his purpose now?"

"Messire, I know that none of those knights whom you have reduced to beaten vassels gave him aid, but I cannot say from whence his help came. And he spoke of finding a French force north of Avignon to attack De la Noye, but he is dreaming. He will find no one to come this far, especially on his behalf. His anger bites him deeply, and he will not fare this escape well. I warned him."

Hyatt took his eyes off her for the first time and looked to his men. "Carry on and forget the knave. He is among thieves and scavengers now, and if that satisfies him more than an army, so be it. But fill the spot and keep your eyes sharper now."

When the men had drifted away he looked again at his wife. "Do you lie to me, my lady?"

"Nay, Hyatt. 'Twould be of no use."

"Did you ask Verel to stay and take up arms on my behalf?"

"I only said that it was possible, in time, for his skills to be proven and you had no use for talented stableboys. I have seen you command, *seigneur*. I know you to make good use of each man."

Hyatt slowly nodded. "Is there more?"

Girvin had wandered into the hall, glanced briefly at Hyatt and Aurélie with a slight nod, and gone to the barrel to dip a cup of cold water for himself.

"Nay, Hyatt. There is nothing more."

"You spoke of changed loyalties. Have you now changed yours?"

"Have you, my lord?"

"What? I cannot —"

"You swore your oath as husband for the sake of usefulness and alliance. Is that your allegiance still?"

"Aye."

"And so is mine the same; for the sake of this castle and its people, I am beaten."

As he looked at her, his hand slipped over hers in her lap. He gave it a slight squeeze. "You play the beaten one so well that I sometimes wonder if you mean to use it as a weapon, rather than a sufferance. Do you think that if you remind me over and over that I have won, I will forget there has been a war and you were a parcel of the booty?"

"I assure you, messire, I am not clever enough to use your victory as any plot against you."

"I wonder, Aurélie. You are an unusual woman. I will ask you again, do you know who aided Verel?"

"If she has suspicions," Girvin's voice interrupted, "do not insist that she make wishes into verdicts, Hyatt. You will not find the truth by demanding her thoughts. I have suspicions as well. Suspicions are hot for as long as a fire poker in the snow, and as useful. I will not name them."

"What do you say?"

"I have said enough. If I knew who spirited the boy away and could prove it, I would tell you. 'Twas not Lady Aurélie."

"You have earned the trust I have in your word," Hyatt said. "How am I to be assured that this woman, my wife by conquest, would tell me what she knows? She has not yet earned my trust."

Girvin laughed deeply, the rumbling noise causing Hyatt to stiffen and Aurélie to listen attentively. "I have seen how the whining accusations of women deepen your trust in them. Leave the lady be. Verel is better gone. He would have gotten himself killed had he stayed here. Lady Aurélie does you a service with her silence, more so than she could with wily and hopeful tales."

His task and speech finished, Girvin quit the hall, back to whatever labor he had been engaged in. Aurélie followed his departure, a smile tugging at the corners of her lips. When she regarded her husband, he was studying her closely and his eyes burned with many questions.

"Somehow, in my absence, you have brought my messenger simpering to his knees. I would know what dribbling honey your lips proffered that has won his loyalty. Girvin is less fond of women than I."

Aurélie let her hand rise to the table top and slowly close over his. "I would, Hyatt, that you spare me some dignity in your questioning. To trick Sir Girvin into some service on my behalf was never in my mind, since he has claimed responsibility for Giles's death. I am not weak, but neither am I strong enough to coddle, for my own ends, my husband's murderer. If Girvin has come to my colors in some small way, 'tis not of my doing, but his own." She shrugged. "Let me prove my worth any other way, but do not hurt me so deeply as to imply that I am such a simpering whore. Of all my weaknesses, that is not one."

As he listened, his eyes darkened. She spoke as eloquently as any high judge, as faithfully as a sacred tribunal. And she echoed for him what he believed, rather than escaping the question. "I think, madame, that you take my sharpest wisdom and twist it like a blade into my breast."

"Or do I take your greatest strength and wrap it like a warm embrace about your heart? It is for you to decide."

TEN

URÉLIE still walked the wall and viewed De la Noye from the parapets and high donjon as she had done daily when Giles was alive. Now, there was little question in her mind as to whom all this belonged. With Giles, she had known this possession to belong more to her than the lord, but her life as his wife was a secret, and a lie. Now she was a wife well used, but had no possessions.

She had lost more than a husband in the siege. She had lost control of the castle.

Hyatt did not need her at all. He ordered her compliance and asserted his husbandly rights. She had nothing to say of how the wall was manned for protection, of how the guards would spend their days and nights, nor did she have any dominion over the villeins, except to supervise their good service to Hyatt. But now she knew the secrets of the marriage bed. And in the dark of night when Hyatt's arm gently encircled her, she pretended that she was also loved.

If she were to consider Hyatt's treatment of her when they were in seclusion, she would believe herself cherished. But in the cool light of morning he faithfully resumed an aloof and commanding manner. He neither trusted nor coddled her. But then, he had never promised any more than he had given.

It was just past dawn as she walked her vigil to see the hall, houses, town, and farming plots. She viewed the perfect patches of fields. He had overthrown them, yet De la Noye had not been so well settled since her arrival twelve years ago. The heavy iron gate at the portcullis that separated the inner bailey from the outer bailey had not been in use for many years, for it had rusted and could not be lowered. Hyatt's troops repaired it, doubling the security of the main hall.

Even nature accommodated Hyatt, for the weather provided a perfect balance of sunlight and showers for the crops. Houses were rethatched and the stock and people were well fed. The summer was at its hottest now, and if the growing season continued this well, the harvest would be good and next spring's shearing would be the best ever.

The gates were being opened below her to let the farmers leave to do their daily chores. Armed knights accompanied them to the fields and pastures. From the high tower her people looked the same as ever. On closer inspection she could see anger in some of their eyes, but they no longer shuddered in terror as they had in those first days. Most, she was forced to admit, were better off than they had ever been. Father Algernon was the only person in all of De la Noye to make do on less than he had before.

When the gates closed behind the guards and farmers, Aurélie descended into the town. She stopped at a few houses to see how the occupants fared. Percival was mending nicely and his family already plied their labors to Hyatt's cause. Aurélie visited this household often, but not so much because she was needed. Rather, it was because of Percival's regard for Hyatt. Once he and his people had come inside the stout walls of De la Noye and were cared for, Percival had been ready to pledge allegiance to the Englishman. "My village was wasted and many lives were lost. Some may damn me, my lady, but I would pledge to the devil himself if that same one offered me shelter, a chance to work, and food for my family."

"There are some here who think that you would be pledging to the devil," she had said.

"Then they have not seen what I have seen. Your lord is not soft, but he is more generous than any I have known."

"Because he spared your lives? Do you see that as *generous?* To live is your right."

"Nay, madame. Anyone can spare a life; the choice is simple to kill or not to kill an innocent man. But there are few who are wise enough to help a man put his life to use."

Aurélie visited other houses and there was no doubt that what Percival said of Hyatt's wisdom was true. Delmar was retired from his duties as a guard and was denied the possession of any weapons, but he laughingly showed her his tools. The knights of Hyatt had helped him construct a work area behind his house and trees were felled to bring him fresh wood, from which he made furniture and utensils. "No sword, shield, nor knife, but hammers, chisels, saws, and axes. This may fool some of the serfs, but it does not fool me. If Hyatt feared I would raise a weapon against him, would he give me an ax?"

"You are happy, Delmar," she stated softly.

"Hush, my lady," he said with a smile. "To be happy under this new, barbaric rule would name me a traitor to France." But there was no question that Delmar was pleased and productive. He had always relished his time away from knightly duties so that he could carve, build, polish, and fashion eating utensils and furniture that made his wife the envy of the other women. "When De la Noye is settled and the needs we now have are satisfied, I will sell my wares. Even now I train my son as an apprentice."

"I think you prosper, Delmar. I am pleased for you."

"Who does not, lady? Ah," he said, holding up a hand. "I know the names of those whose positions were lost. The younger men-at-arms, the captains, watchmen, bowmen, and pikemen . . . not all are happy to have seen their swords replaced with scythes. But they are only a few. Not many from De la Noye would ever meet the king or travel to Paris. Most of the villagers never see the man who draws the gabelle tax from their salt to build his army. These people wish only to work, eat, and have the protection of the decent lord.

"I only say, give the man time and let us judge his worth

when we are done with war. That is when a man discovers the value of his overlord, when he shows his merit during peace."

By the time she had stopped at a dozen small houses and was en route to the hall, the gates were being opened again to allow escorted women to bring food to the men in the fields. She realized the whole morning had been spent in the village and began to rush back to the hall. What she had been looking for, she knew, were not problems and miseries that required her attention, but her daily surveillance was to determine Hyatt's growing acceptance by the people and the progress on the castle and town. Unless some work in the main hall delayed her, she went around the wall and into the town every morning. She had done so since the second week in May.

July had aged, drawing the harvest nearer, and she could not ignore the evidence. Hyatt's arrival had been a salvation for the deteriorating De la Noye. Very few still mourned the passage of the demesne from French de Pourvre to an English knight named Hyatt Laidley. Only a few families of knights killed in battle and certain deposed warriors held any hope that France would reclaim Guienne. She even witnessed the unexpected sight of a young woman of her village talking and flirting with a soldier in red and black livery. The resistance to Hyatt was slipping away. But the mistress of De la Noye held back. Not for France, but for the sake of pride.

Hyatt was seated in the main hall, eating more leisurely than was common for him. He had been home for over a fortnight and she had become accustomed to his habits very easily, for his rote was simple and predictable. By day he commanded her and everyone else, but by night when he chose to make love to her, he was not satisfied until she, too, experienced great pleasure. There were times when he studied her face in brooding silence as if some memory pricked his tender conscience. These troubled spells were short, and he did not speak of his burden. She wondered if she was coming to mean something more to him.

"Do you not ride out with your men today, my lord?" she asked.

"Not today," he mumbled. He turned to Girvin. "The hunting needs to be done in the south wood, Girvin. I think the forest north of the keep holds more French scavengers and meandering English troops who have lost their leaders. Those brigands and our hunters seem to have depleted the good game."

"Tomorrow at dawn, then," Girvin said.

"I will accompany you. It is not good for me to have too much leisure."

"My lord," Aurélie attempted quietly, "is it necessary to send guards with the farmers? I can think of none who will abandon their homes in De la Noye. And the women are escorted to the fields, as well. Surely you do not think they . . ."

"What is it you seek? Fewer guards?"

"It might serve to show them that you come to trust their honest labors and —"

"And open the gate for free passage? You forget, my lady, these people are not free."

Aurélie stiffened. "I believe they know that, Sir Hyatt."

"Of course," he said sharply, his tone implying that he was not in agreement. "Do you ask me to lighten my guard for a special reason, Aurélie? Does Verel plan to return with an army soon?"

"Oh, Hyatt, nay, that is not what I . . . Is that what you think? That I plot against you?"

"You give or withhold important truths at your will, and how can I be secure? You knew Verel's plans, yet told no one. You covered his path as he fled. You —"

"Nay!" Her voice was a sharp, angry denial. Hyatt was abruptly cut off. Aurélie did not argue further, but turned and fled to the stair, running up quickly to her bedchamber. It had taken great willpower not to cover her ears against his accusations, and she felt the heat of tears on her cheeks. He chastised her when it was Faon's treachery at work. He criticized his wife while his mistress wore gold bracelets and beautiful gowns. She ran into her chamber and across the room to the window.

The door opened soon after, as she knew it would. She flinched as Hyatt slammed the portal. "Do not *ever* walk away from me as I speak," he thundered.

She whirled to face him. "Even as you accuse me? Even as you call my word a lie? Even as you allow your soldiers and serfs to stand witness to your ridicule?"

"You did not deny that you knew Verel's plans. You admitted that he might have left as he threatened he would, rather than succumb and name me as his lord. Yet you did not tell anyone before . . . but only when you were publicly addressed. You might never have admitted the truth, and still you have not told me all."

She stepped closer to him and he likewise advanced. "I did not lie. I first warned Verel not to fight you, and later I thought it would be better for the rest of us if he fled."

"Since you did not impede his escape, how am I to believe that you did not aid him?"

"I cannot say who helped him, Hyatt. 'Twas not I, I swear it."

"Do you doubt that he had a good horse? Weapons?"

"I believe that he did, but I provided none of that."

Hyatt stepped yet closer. "You lie to me, Aurélie," he said threateningly. "And I know it. It is in your eyes when you lie; you do not hide it well."

"I could do nothing," she insisted, yet tears fell from her eyes. His many faces tore at her heart.

"He got clean away, and someone here is my enemy, pretending to be my ally."

"I thought I had convinced him it would be foolish," she said. "And you would have killed him, had you known."

"And for that reason you did not tell me?"

"Nay," she shouted. "For the reason —" She stopped herself abruptly. She looked into his hard, angry eyes. Her tears subsided instantly and her voice came softly. There was no reason to deny it any longer; Verel was gone. She lifted her chin. "For the reason that he planned to take me with him. I hoped that my refusal to go would end his plans and replace his lunacy with reason."

Hyatt's features relaxed into a superior grin. "I thought you would finally admit it was his lust that drove him. He was a fool to desire a woman to the extent of such risk." He raised both brows. "Did you think I did not know it?"

"Ooooo," she growled, insulted to the depth of her sensibilities. "You insufferable oaf, I should have kept silent." She tried to turn away from him, but he yanked her back, forcing her to face him. "Let go, Hyatt, you mean only to humiliate me."

"How could you have taken him seriously? Did it please you to know that the boy was so smitten with you, he would risk his life to have you? And how did you answer his love, Aurélie? How did you keep yourself from fleeing with your ragged, beaten knight?"

She struggled to free herself from his grasp, but he held her fast by the upper arms. "You rancid churl, he had more regard for me than anyone has since your coming."

Hyatt laughed cruelly at the statement, holding her wrists securely. "Truly, madame? I give you your home, your rule beside my own, a warm bed, and food for your belly. Yet you prefer the hot-blooded notions of a boy who lives on naught but childish dreams? You think to flee whole armies through a dense wood is *regard?* What could he give you but danger, a low fire to keep away captors, a few grains, and a long, harsh journey? And above that, if he offers passion, 'twould be an adulteress he would make you. Nay, I say he is a selfish idiot, with little regard for you."

"At least he is able and strong and does not insult me. *He* thought I was well worth the risk."

"To die needlessly is a high insult, madame. Further, if he had any loyalty to you, he would not suggest that you endanger yourself. Do you think you would have gotten away? I do not care much about Verel; he can have a horse and some grain for his journey. He travels toward Hollis, and that hearty knight does not like to witness a Frenchman who yet draws a breath. But you are too valuable a prize to sacrifice to Hollis or any other scavenger."

"Perhaps Verel will slip by your ruthless English armies and return with a French force to . . ."

"Giles is dead," he said slowly. "You were the only heir. You are my wife — bound by vows. If John comes to claim this demesne, he claims it against the will of God and the Church. Even your French king is not that stupid. Verel is lucky you refused him. Had you gone, you would have been found and returned, and I would not have been so gentle as I was when you were newly widowed."

She held herself rigidly in his grasp, her fury growing even more at his insensitive threats. "You have captured me once, Hyatt. If I choose to flee from you, you will never capture me twice. I will leave you nothing better than my corpse."

His smile vanished and he shook her abruptly. He could think of no reason for such a statement, save one. "Do you love him? Do you love the knave?"

"Why do you care, Hyatt? Do you perchance place some value on me after all?"

"You are the lady of this hall and your talents are well used. Your marriage to me rises above this English and French war and binds this property to my name. You are the mistress of De la Noye. Whether we share any affection does not matter, but the larger question must be answered lest there is some plan between illicit lovers to attack De la Noye. Answer me now; do you love him?"

She stared calmly at the anger in his eyes. Deep in her heart she wished that this rage came from his own feelings for her. But she knew his truth was well calculated; he considered her a possession and he would neither share her, nor accept any risk to have her. "Nay, I do not love him, Hyatt." She raised her clear blue eyes so that he could judge the truth for himself, as he had claimed he could. "Nor did I know his feeling for me went deeper than a man's allegiance to his lord. And, I did not welcome his confession."

Hyatt looked deeply into her eyes for a long moment and she saw that he was satisfied. The grip on her arms slowly slackened and he released her. He turned toward the door. Once that portal was opened, he looked back at her.

"When did he tell you the truth about his lust?"

"When you suspected he did. The day the prisoners were released."

"And you rebuffed him then?"

She stood tall and proud. "I warned him in earnest that even were you less inclined to kill to secure your possessions, I would not welcome his affection."

"Yet he asked you to flee with him?"

" 'Twas not of his doing. Verel is not that stupid. Someone convinced him there was a chance I would agree to go."

"And will you place a name to your suspicions? Now?"

"I cannot," she said, lowering her eyes. To accuse Faon would make Aurélie seem jealous and embittered in Hyatt's eyes. She would not be brought so low; she would not be branded as a conniving woman.

"You are my wife," he said softly. "If there is someone here who plots against me and you do not confess it, your hand joins him on the blade that slays me."

She slowly let her eyes rise. "If I thought you would come to any harm because of my silence, Hyatt, I would place names to my worries. But 'tis truth I speak when I say that the one I do not trust would never harm you. Others may fall by the way, but you will be safe." And then in a very soft whisper she added, "I pray you believe me, messire, for I value your life if for no other reason than that it assures mine."

He winced slightly with her words, blinking his eyes closed as if she touched some tender spot and caused pain. "Enough said," he said without looking at her. He seemed to regain his composure and looked across the room at her. "The guards accompany the farmers and their women for their protection, not as sentries to prevent escape. We have seen the makings of camps in the forests around De la Noye and do not know by the ashes of cookfires whether they are bandits, scavengers, English armies, or escaped French exiles. Whoever they be, they travel and camp in small groups, which does not bode well for our people, and they are at risk unguarded. An English army engaged in Edward's siege would be welcome here and need not conceal themselves, but the wolves who roam the forest after a war prey upon that lone sheep who wanders too near the woods."

"You did not tell me, Hyatt."

"You did not ask."

He left abruptly then, not waiting for the apology that was close to her lips. She had misjudged him again, and in her request that her people be shown more trust by fewer guards there was the sound of accusation. She told herself throughout the rest of the day that it did not matter if she failed to show proper gratitude for the good things he did. It did not matter to him whether she was thankful or whether she despised him, so long as she did what was expected of her.

But an ill feeling surrounded her all through the day, for she knew she had been unjust. Aurélie had no trouble keeping a proud façade, though she was beaten. Nor was she too subdued to throw her share of insults when the bantering began. But justice was essential to her, even when it concerned her treatment of a man who was her known enemy. Admittedly, his treatment of her had been decent.

As she groomed herself for the evening meal, taking more time than usual on her appearance, she thought not only of how she might show Hyatt that she was just and reasonable, but of how she might cautiously lead him toward more trusting companionship. There had not been only changes in De la Noye, but within herself. Her body was changing, her heart was softening toward Hyatt, and a growing need to be at peace with him was emerging.

When she descended into the common hall for the evening meal, she wore her best gown, the cream-colored one that she had worn on the day Hyatt had taken her to the priest. The room was nearly full, and the trays of food were already being put on long trestle tables. She could see from Hyatt's eyes that he approved of her attire. He stood as she came down the stairs and held a hand out to her to seat her at his side.

"King Edward would be well pleased to see how agreeably these French swine have come to heel."

Aurélie did not look in the direction of Faon's intentionally loud voice. She went to her seat beside Hyatt, hearing the voice of a man who was well oiled of ale respond to his dinner partner.

"With all the boasting about these French armies, we thought there would be plenty of fighting, but the French are a cowardly bunch. They've come quickly to submission . . . but then, we heard they were weak. Now the Scots . . ."

"At least the French know their betters," Faon laughed, cutting the man off. She was not interested in war stories, but wished to keep the subject turned to slurs against the conquered. "Though few will admit it, Edward's forces did nothing but put an end to their misery and incompetence, that a better rule could be formed, especially here."

Aurélie's jaw tightened, but she looked at Hyatt. His eyes were fixed on Faon for a moment, then he sat down beside his wife. There was no amusement in his features.

Faon's laughter was joined by some of the men at her end of the table, but their jokes were cruel. Much was said of the beaten French, their ingratitude at being rescued by the stronger warriors; their quick, frightened servitude. Giles was liberally ridiculed for his lack of warring skills and was named the poorest soldier in the whole De la Noye troop. One voice delivered a remark that stung Aurélie deeply. "Even the Sire's widow appears pleased with her new ruler. Mayhap she thanked her conqueror for removing the monkish moron, else she'd have had to spend the rest of her days as his wife."

"Girvin," Faon called out loudly. "Are you bored now that your days are spent hunting rather than fighting? Do you wish to meet with a challenge of some strength?" Girvin grumbled something low and inaudible. "What say you, Girvin?" Faon pressed.

Girvin raised his head. "Was your question whether I'd rather hunt or fight, mistress? I like a good fight, but so do I like the hunt. To slay a boar satisfies me now, since it fills grateful bellies. I enjoy helping to feed the farmers; they work to earn it. It chafes at me to work to feed the stomach of a drone."

"What?"

Girvin chuckled. "Mistress Faon, I am only a soldier and not a learned man, yet I am wise enough to know that anyone who works gets a return on his labors, whether from my hunting or my lord's protection. I wager that every person kept by Hyatt knows how he earns his lord's hospitality, or how he strains it. He who does nothing will find equal reward, mistress."

Rather than risk an insult like the one that had nearly reached her, Faon turned her attention to the knights who would appreciate her wit. She collected more these days, since Hyatt seemed to have his affection focused elsewhere and it was beginning to look as though Faon was accessible. Aurélie stole a glance at Girvin. She decided, when the man did not return her glance, that it was unlikely Girvin had put the audacious woman in her place in any gesture of loyalty to Aurélie. It was well known that Girvin did not tolerate Faon well. But Aurélie smiled inwardly, feeling less alone since Girvin nearly announced Faon's laziness.

Aurélie ate most of her meal in silence and when she was nearly finished, she touched Hyatt's hand as he paused with his knife over his plate. "*Monseigneur,*" she said in a quiet, humbled voice, "my tongue was quick today and before I thought better of my words, I had cast unfair doubt on your actions."

He raised a brow and peered at her in question.

"I would have told you of Verel's plan if I thought any other men would join him, but he alone fled De la Noye, and it is better he is gone, I think. I give you my word that I know of no other who plots an escape."

"What assurance do I have that I can trust your word, Aurélie?" he quietly asked.

"None, messire, but I will tell you the truth just the same. He was foolish in this desire he claimed to feel for me, and I think it was bent more of loyalty and his wish to return to our old ways that moved him to confess so much."

Hyatt smiled. "You said that Verel was not stupid."

"That is why I have not understood him," she said with a shrug. "As God is my witness, Hyatt, he was never so foolish before. I was frightened of you, and of him. I did not want such nonsense to be harshly punished."

Hyatt smiled. "I think I understand, Aurélie. Are there others here who fancy themselves in love with you?"

Her cheeks pinkened delicately, yet a slight rueful chuckle escaped her. "Nay, Hyatt. Only once has a person claimed such passionate love, and he escaped your rule in rags."

"Then 'tis better that you hold little hope on his rescue."

"You may believe me, I do not hope for that. But Hyatt, forgive me for questioning your use of your men. It was wrong of me. I should have known you did not worry over the flight of a few farmers, and I welcome your protection of them. I am sorry."

Hyatt's brows rose in surprise. "My ears fail me. You are asking for forgiveness?"

She folded her hands in her lap and looked down. "I was wrong, Hyatt. You have done well by your possession in most cases, and I wish only good to come to these people. I shall not question you again."

His hand covered both of hers. "Are we bent on a common purpose at last, *chérie?*"

She turned to look at him. She wondered for a moment if there was something more for them than master and slave, but warned herself not to take much heart in his momentary softening. "I gave my word to see my people well served. I shall not fail in that."

He frowned slightly, as if he was not completely satisfied with that response. "You are forgiven, madame. I find I am hard put to deny you anything."

He watched her as she finished her meal. He made a silent oath to see her fitted with cloth for better gowns once the harvest was in and there was money to spare. Perhaps before winter he could send to neighboring cities that had been quelled some men to buy things needed at De la Noye. He liked sitting beside her more when she was richly dressed; her beauty was deserving of jewels and expensive cloth, but she was modest. He suspected that there was more hidden away and he did not question this, for he believed that when she felt secure, she would draw out anything she had.

He glanced at Faon, who wore her jewels liberally. He supposed many, including Aurélie, believed he had given her gems and gold. Actually, her gifts had come from some of his men seeking to win favor either from her or from him. He had always seen to it that she had plenty of money with which to buy things as they traveled, and though he meant it more for Derek than Faon, once money was given he did not consider it his right to question its use. And Derek always appeared well kept.

But Aurélie, he silently decided, should have gifts. Her pale, silken flesh would shine under the weight of gems. Her small but full figure would be even more alluring in a few new gowns. Even the one she wore, though her best, seemed to fit her poorly, although he could not deny that the strained décolletage pleased his eyes.

In spite of her efforts to keep herself safe and distant from his lordship here, it was obvious that even she was thriving. His memory could not have failed him so completely; her eyes were brighter, her cheeks and lips had a healthy pink flush, and she appeared more robust, more beautiful, than when he first arrived. She had covered her long, lustrous hair with a wimple, but when she was bereft of these garments, it was her hair that he loved most. He could not keep his hands from it. As he studied her, his hand idly moved to her bare shoulder to gently caress her flesh. She turned toward him to catch him in his brooding stare and she let a smile flirt at the corners of her mouth for just an instant before she rose to see to the cleaning of the room.

"I will conquer even her," he thought, watching her move about the room. The swing of her skirt, the swell of her breasts when she stooped or bent to some task, and the strong but feminine grasp of her hands as she lifted an object, every movement enchanted his thoughts. She grew more breathtaking with every passing day. He would guard his emotions and never be her victim, but a proud smile grew on his lips as he watched her and conceded that a man could hardly do better in getting a wife. "If she ever comes to heel," he thought, "I might even admit that I have been smitten with her since the first."

"At dawn, so says Sir Hyatt."

Hyatt turned as Girvin's voice loudly interrupted his thoughts. He frowned in worry that he'd been caught gazing with longing at his wife. The meal was done and the occupants of the room were settling into their evening routine. Some of the men had filled their horns with ale and the duties for the following day were being discussed. A half-dozen men stood leisurely around the lord's table listening.

"We hunt at dawn's break, Hyatt?" Girvin asked.

"Aye, in the south forest. I will accompany you, but you select the hunters to go, Girvin. You are more aware of the most skilled."

"You hunt, Hyatt?" Faon asked, laughter ringing in her voice. "You must have reached the height of leisure of a prosperous lord now. I have never known you to hunt unless you are bored."

"Perhaps he wishes to shoot a few arrows for himself, lest his desire to feed his villeins be questioned," Girvin said loudly. "I say these people are well fed, Hyatt. And almost everyone here present works as hard as the lord for their keeping."

Hyatt wondered at Girvin's wisdom in taunting Faon, for

he knew that was what he did. He tried to disregard the man's jeering. "I am anxious to see if the same evidence of raiders exists in the south wood. If so, we must brace ourselves."

"Not only the search for camps, Hyatt, but for better game." Girvin lifted his horn of ale. "I thank you most kindly for conquering a castle endowed of such good cooking talents. I swear I've never eaten quite so well as this." He gave his middle a pat. "I think it has begun to show," he said, getting a round of laughing agreements from the other men.

"It has proven a good place," another man said.

"Even the women here are more to my liking than in England," said another.

"Hah, the women *anywhere* are to your liking."

Hyatt had to laugh at the heightened color on the cheeks of the young man in his group considered to be the most vulnerable to a swinging skirt.

"Since I guard this place and spend more time here than any of the riders, I take a good, long look at the town each day. The people of De la Noye regard this occupation with considerable respect now. And they are showing the signs of my hunting efforts as well as I." Girvin leaned back in his chair and seemed to survey the room.

There was another round of laughter and several well-fed men gave their firm stomachs a hearty salute. "I am glad we all agree it is a good and plentiful place. Let's see if you still think so when you rise before dawn to hunt." Hyatt stood from his place at the table and, seeing that Aurélie was finished with her duties, held an arm out to her. She looked more lovely than ever, and he was eager to leave all the toasting and jesting to his men.

"Even your wife is of stouter frame these days, Sir Hyatt," Girvin said as Aurélie came near the table. She stopped short beside Hyatt, looking with questioning eyes at Girvin. His manner was more jovial and louder than usual. "Have we toasted the beautiful lady? I think a toast has been too long neglected, since we had no wedding feast. To Lady Aurélie."

Someone thrust a horn into Hyatt's hand and he drank,

though he did not hold it high. He could toast her beauty better than anyone, but she seemed rigid and uncomfortable beside him, as if embarrassed by the attention being drawn to her. As he drained his cup, he let an arm casually encircle her waist.

"I vow she grows more beautiful," Girvin chortled. "Does she admit she prefers this marriage to the last?" Hyatt frowned at his knight, not getting much pleasure from Girvin's light mood. "To what do we owe the bounty of goodness that shows itself, my lady? Sir Hyatt, did your seed strike a fertile place where Giles's failed?"

Hyatt slowly turned to look at his wife, meeting her eyes. There was a proud swell of emotion there as she tried to remain composed. His gaze slowly dropped to her bosom, and then to her waist. He had eaten many a meal beside her, and unless her habits in his absence had been gluttonous, Girvin had just voiced an explanation for the changes Hyatt had earlier sensed.

"He means to keep us guessing," someone laughed.

"Nay, it is that he does not want too many toasts on the night before an early hunt."

"I think he is jealous of his privacy. Hyatt leaves us last to know when he has wed and no doubt will share the news of some new heir when we hear the squalling infant from behind his chamber doors."

Hyatt's gaze burned the question into Aurélie's eyes. She saw no escape and slowly turned to the guffawing knights. They stilled their tongues instantly, almost reverently, when she looked at them. "I hope you do not drink yourselves into illness, for Hyatt's child will not be born for many months. You may toast your lord, for he has begun to seed his dynasty."

A round of cheers went up and Aurélie turned back to Hyatt, her voice barely heard by him, for she did not choose to share her words. "I would have chosen another time to tell you, *monseigneur*. I have only just become certain."

"To Hyatt's son," someone shouted.

Hyatt's eyes were as gentle as she had ever seen them. In that instant she understood all that had motivated Faon, for the light in her husband's eyes at the prospect of a child equaled her own feelings of joy. The mistress had seen this in Hyatt and had used the power that such devotion could wield. "Would you like to escape this, *chérie?*" She nodded and he pulled her along past the table toward the stair.

"What is this? You drink to Hyatt's son?"

"His next son, we should say. Lady Aurélie is with child."

"*Nay!*"

The voice had the quality of a scream of pain, and all heads turned to see Faon standing at the end of the table, palms pressing flat against the solid oak and green eyes ablaze with defiance. As Aurélie watched her, Faon slowly collected herself, but the struggle to resume her usual confidence was obvious.

"She is with child?"

"Yea," Hyatt said quietly.

Faon began to laugh, an almost hysterical sound. "What makes you certain it is yours, Hyatt? If not Giles, perhaps the lusty lad, Verel. She toyed with him aplenty while you were away."

A piercing feeling assailed Aurélie's stomach, not from the accusation, but from what she saw. Faon's face was white with panic, her eyes glittering with rage. The mistress had obviously assumed, as many did, that Aurélie was barren and would fail to produce children for Hyatt. The woman's single asset was publicly stripped away. Aurélie stole a glance at Girvin, whose loud jesting had finally ceased. That hearty knight leaned back in his chair and looked with shrewd satisfaction at his prey.

Hyatt's hand gently squeezed Aurélie's waist. "The child is mine," he said sternly. "And that question need not arise after tonight."

"You may wish it so, my lord, but 'tis well known the lady lies to you. Perhaps when you conquered this keep, Giles had finally succeeded with her."

Hyatt glared at Faon for a long quiet moment, and then his eyes slowly shifted to Aurélie. She stared at him, pleading in her expression that he not shame Giles's memory with the truth. His hand tightened at her waist for a moment and she saw his slight, almost imperceptible nod.

He looked back at Faon. "The lady's child was sired by me, not because I delude myself, or because I graciously accept another man's offspring. 'Tis mine because it is. I know it. And that is what matters."

Faon straightened as if slapped, her lips pursed in a tight line. "What about Derek?"

Hyatt shrugged. "I made my oath to Derek, though he was not old enough to understand. I make my oath here and now to this child, since there is no question it is mine. If you wish to raise any questions, Mistress Faon, raise the question of your own future. You are the one to worry."

Her voice was strained and hurt. "Hyatt, do you warn me before your wife, your men?"

"You are the one person foolish enough to question my intentions before this woman and these men. Shall I answer you before them?" He shook his head and frowned at the panicked look on her face. "I have said that you would be cared for as long as you mother my son to my liking and you heed your place in my household. Yet you strain my generosity. If you do not like your circumstances, you are free to go. If you wish to stay, mind your behavior carefully. I am very weary of the trouble you create."

"Do you warn *her?*" Faon asked in a trembling voice. "Or is it so different because you have made her your wife?"

"Everyone who lives on my mercy knows it, except you." He turned his head to look at Aurélie, but her eyes were downcast as she quietly listened to what he had to say. She was amazed that there was little anger in his voice. "You, who have the most cause to be careful, practice the least caution. You assume some rights that have never been granted to you, publicly or even privately. Yea, the lady was warned, and further, she heeds the warning. She has quickly learned

200

the one thing that you fail to grasp. I value her while she serves me faithfully. If the loyal service fails, the value drops. Likewise, the greater energy put to honoring my lordship, to lending dignity to my name, the higher esteem she gains in my house.

"Now I see that my generosity with you bites me, for you are ungrateful and unwise. I regret that I let you think I could be used so easily."

He turned to mount the stairs, holding Aurélie's elbow.

"Hyatt . . . please . . ."

He turned back to her. "My last warning to you is this — if you destroy what you have by your own lips, your own foolishness, I will not attempt to rescue you. I have not betrayed you yet. Will you betray yourself?"

Aurélie's eyes narrowed in confusion, for what Hyatt said caused the woman to clamp her mouth shut and turn away from him. She followed him up the stairs, letting out her breath in a sigh when the door was closed behind them. She stood, feeling oddly out of place, as Hyatt moved away from her to light candles and open shutters to let the cooling summer breezes cleanse the stale air in their chamber. There was a heavy silence that she did not break for many minutes.

"She hates me so, Hyatt. I cannot blame her; she thinks I have taken you away from her."

"If she does, she lies to herself."

"But she does . . . and I alone know that you dislike all women and only value their work and the children they might give you."

He smiled slightly. "I have never cared much for women; they are treacherous and use their feigned devotion as brutally as a soldier uses his sword. They pledge it, remove it, cripple men with it, and then hold it as a chain around their lives. I do not wish to allow any woman that kind of dominion over me. Yea, I see that Faon wishes to do this to me, and I refuse to be drawn into her plan. Yet I know the worth of loyalty. Do not betray me, Aurélie, and perhaps you will be content."

"You could do the same to me," she said softly. "Mayhap you will be pleased with me for a few years and then cast me aside for another."

"My lady, Mistress Faon has not been deposed from her position by my marriage to you."

"Of course she has. She was your woman before you . . ."

Hyatt shook his head. "Faon has assumed some sense of privilege because she is the mother of my son. She has taken liberties with servants and even guards, all on behalf of Derek. But she was never at my right side, never granted privy authority on my behalf, and was never seated above the salt. Faon is a servant in my household. She holds a high position of servitude since Derek is her son, but nothing about her life has changed at all since I wed you. If she held onto some hope that I would marry her one day, she did so despite my many assurances to the contrary."

"Do you mean to say that you got her with child and kept her as a servant? A slave?"

"Would I have been a better man to abandon them both? To fail to follow my own act with responsibility? Or to deny her the right of motherhood by taking away her child? Perhaps I should have chosen not to be a father, though in truth the boy is mine. Or would you say me righteous to marry her despite the fact that she would be a poor wife?"

"But do you not see how she hurts for want of you?"

He sighed. "Does it appear, because of the woman's suffering, that I am not steadfast? That I am without honor? Need I plead my case to you? To my men? To a priest?"

"Your men seem not to judge you, Hyatt. I do not wish to judge you, but . . ."

He approached her and grasped her gently by her upper arms. He looked deeply into her eyes and then slowly covered her mouth with his. She was amazed at the way his kiss caused her to tremble, weaken, and give herself to his embrace. She did not lie to herself that she obliged in the obedience he demanded. She relished the taste and touch of him. It was not for her rightful place in her home or for the people who depended on her that her pulse quickened and she returned his caress. He had only just come to her, by route of the most skilled sword, and it was already becoming impossible to think of living without him.

He released her mouth and looked into her eyes. "Judge me, Aurélie. I welcome it; I encourage it. But do not ask me to defend myself against the slurs of others, or explain myself in the face of another's unhappiness. Ask no other how I should be judged. Look at my acts and decide for yourself. I will not argue that I am honorable and loyal. I will not beg to be believed or understood. I will never win my good reputation by laying down in speeches the low virtues of another. I did all that once and learned that there is only one way to the truth — through what a man *does,* and not through rumors and accusations."

"It may prove the harder way, Hyatt."

"It is *always* the harder way. But the surest."

❧

There burned a single candle on a small stool near the open window. The hour was past midnight and the summer sky was filled with luminous stars. The air was cool and a half-moon sat high against the black velvet of the sky.

Faon knelt on the floor beside the candle. Nima sat on a bench before the open window. Derek and the servants slept soundly, but still Faon's voice was hushed.

"You must *kill* her."

Nima's old hands trembled. "I cannot. I will not."

"If you refuse me, I will tell Hyatt all. All!"

"Even though you are foolish enough to jeopardize your only shelter, you are not foolish enough to end your own life."

"She must not have this child. Nima, she must *not.*"

"Do not ask me again, Faon. I have obliged you in too many evil things. I will not do this for you."

"We will perish if he does not become my lover soon. Derek will perish."

"Nay, to Derek he is committed. You must accept the

truth soon. If you do not, he will cast you out with nothing."

Faon fell into soft tears. "I was good enough once. He denies himself, but he wants me. I know it. I know it. I have always known it. Why does he do this to me?"

Nima's shaking hand reached forward and gently brushed the hair away from her granddaughter's face. "You tricked him into siring the child, as was your plan. It served, Faon, for he took you from your father's house as you wished. You have not worn a bruise since we escaped Montrose. But Hyatt is clever and has avoided the bindings you would tie about him. Nothing has worked to change him. Nothing will. Accept his charity and abide here in peace, or give him his son and let us go."

"I could have gone with Verel," she wept. "He said that he would take her away. He lied to me so that I would secure the horse and weapons for him. He used me. All I asked of him was that he take her away and leave Hyatt for me again, but I should have bidden him to take me."

"Faon . . . did you dally with the man? Did you —"

"He is young and handsome . . . and one of her own men. As a captain of a troop, he had any woman of his desire, but longed for the woman, Aurélie. He wished to take her away. I would have done *anything* to get her out of here."

"Faon," Nima issued in a breath, "did you tamper with one of Hyatt's enemies?"

Faon looked away from her grandmother as if in shame, but her mouth was set in a petulant line. "What do you expect? That I will go to my grave as a spoiled virgin who has known the touch of a man but once? Even in your old age you must understand the loneliness of such an existence."

"Oh Faon . . . did you not learn with Thormond? The only men who will ever touch you are those who hate Hyatt. That is not love, but revenge. You have but to seek freedom from Hyatt and you will be allowed to wed a man who will be faithful to you. But to dally with those men who would kill Hyatt . . ."

"I thought he would take her away . . . but he failed," Faon went on, as if she did not hear a word of Nima's advice. "If he returns, I will go with him. I will have to."

"Faon," Nima whispered urgently. "If you come with child . . ."

"You will give me the herbs. Do not worry."

" 'Tis dangerous, Faon. Women die . . ."

"I did not die the last time."

"Hyatt does not care what you do, Faon. Find another man, one who will be smitten enough to take you to wife."

"But Hyatt is rich and powerful. Who is more so? Not Verel. Not Thormond. And some of his men play with me, but none will leave Hyatt. Nay, Nima. I have followed him all this time, living in tents as some extra baggage. I deserve to be his lady. He will come to me again."

The old woman straightened and looked out the window. "He has not lain with you since Derek. He promised you that he would do his duty to this child, but no more. You should have taken him at his word. You know he never loved you, but I think he hates you now. If you are wise . . ."

The old woman's voice trailed off. She did not finish because it was hopeless. Since leaving Montrose's house with Faon and Hyatt, she had begged her granddaughter to listen to reason. But Faon thought only in terms of plots and schemes to get the knight under her spell. Nima feared the girl would meet death before realizing her error.

ELEVEN

ISTRESS Faon has released me from service since the woman Perrine mostly cares for young Derek," Thea told Aurélie.

"How interesting, since your mistress was most demanding of additional servants."

Thea shrugged. Her expression was insolent and unhappy. "She finds she does not need so many after all."

"Then, does it not occur to her to return my servant to me?"

"You may ask her, if it pleases you, but I think Perrine's service is more to her liking than mine. She has sent me to you to seek a position in your bedchamber."

"My bedchamber?" Aurélie glanced over her shoulder into the room. The hour was so early that Hyatt was only just strapping on his spurs and Baptiste had not yet arrived to begin her own chores. Overhearing the conversation in the opened portal of his bedchamber, he peered at Aurélie with a raised brow and an odd smirk.

"My woman, Baptiste, is much younger than you, but she is my handmaiden and you would have to take instruction from her. And I will not allow laziness or insolence. Do you wish to labor under these conditions, or are you better placed at some other castle chore?"

Thea cocked her head slightly, her mouth turned in a grimace of distaste. The young woman's thin, sharp features made her seem constantly perturbed. "Since I have done nothing other than aid Mistress Faon by attending her and caring for her child, there is nothing else I have learned to do."

"Do not despair, Thea," Aurélie said, her teeth showing in a cunning smile. "If you prove incompetent in my chamber, I know of several women who would willingly teach you cooking, cleaning meat, harvesting grain, emptying pots, or perhaps laundry."

The maid actually winced slightly.

"I am certain that you will work hard to please me," Aurélie continued. Baptiste, on her way to Aurélie's bedchamber, came down the hall and stopped short behind Thea when she viewed the maid and her mistress in conversation. The small blond girl held her hands clasped before her and stood in nervous silence. "Baptiste," Aurélie urged, holding the door open wider for her maid to come forward, "you will be most pleased to know that Mistress Faon, in a rare and generous mood, has sent one of her own maids to assist you in my bedchamber." Baptiste's eyes grew round and alarmed at the mere prospect. "It will be your responsibility to teach Thea, for I am certain my ways are not the same as Faon's, and if she fails to meet your high standards, you must tell me at once so that I can find another chore for her somewhere in the castle. And do not delay, for poor Thea would only suffer ennui without work to occupy her."

"Yea, my lady," Baptiste said quietly, passing her mistress and going into the bedchamber. She kept her eyes downcast as she circled the room, keeping far from Hyatt's brooding stare as she always did.

"Go ahead, Thea," Aurélie urged. "Baptiste will show you how I like things done. And do remember, Thea, if you fail to please Baptiste, it will be impossible for you to please me."

Aurélie stood in the opened door while Thea joined Baptiste on the far side of the room, where the latter passed her the basin of dirty wash water to be dumped. Aurélie watched Hyatt as he looked at them for a moment, then picking up his gauntlets, made to leave the room. He paused for just a moment in the door, a small smile curling his lip and a twinkle in his eye. "If you mean to be such a difficult taskmaster, my lady, why do you not save Faon all this trouble and simply send the girl back to her?"

"We make good use of our people, *seigneur*. No one has ever been idle in this castle or town . . . until very recently."

"Do you not see that she wishes to have one of her own women in your rooms? Otherwise, she would release Perrine."

"Of course, Hyatt."

"Then why do you —?"

He stopped abruptly as he noted her clear-eyed acceptance of the fact. His hand deftly reached around to slap her posterior with a snap of his gauntlets. "Do not make trouble where there is none," he quietly warned.

"Humph," she grunted, rubbing the insult with both her hands. "I am ever getting warnings, and ever trying to set things aright. You are most unfair."

He began to turn away, but stopped abruptly, studying her face again. "You have never bemoaned Faon's treatment of you. Why do you go to such lengths to bite your tongue against criticizing her? I know you could sound many complaints; why do you voice none?"

"Hyatt, would it do any good?" she asked dismally. "Nay, do not answer me. I do not seek to win you from Mistress Faon; 'tis much the other way around. I pity her for that. I know she would be less cruel and easier to abide if only she felt that you desire her."

He shook his head and a pained expression came into his eyes. "My lady, you do not know the woman at all. She —"

He was cut off by a shout from below. A runner had been sent from the outer wall to alert Hyatt and other knights of an approaching army carrying an English banner.

"Hyatt," Aurélie gasped. "Is this a trick?"

"Trick?" he echoed, looking at her quizzically.

"Sir Hollis, of the Château Innesse?"

"Who told you about that?"

"I have heard your men talk, Hyatt. You never mentioned that you visited an old enemy who had roosted nearby."

He sighed and took her elbow, leading her down the stairs with him. "My lady, if you are given to listening to gossip, you would be better placed in coming to me for confirmation of the facts. Sir Hollis and I despise each other and have had repeated contests, but I doubt that he will ride up to my gate, his banner raised, and beg admittance. That is my way; his methods are much more treacherous.

"But, come along. We will not open the gate hastily. The countryside has quieted a great deal since the landed armies arrived, and whether we will it or not, we will be having visits from neighboring towns and keeps."

She went willingly through the hall and into the courtyard. Hyatt's efficient squire had speedily brought his destrier to the inner bailey that the lord might ride the distance to the gate. He released his wife's arm and mounted. She looked up at him and nearly sighed in admiration. He cut an elegant figure when astride. "Do you go out without armor, mail, or a shield?"

He broke into a wide grin. "Do you worry for me, *petite?*"

She was instantly sorry she had asked. Whenever she inquired of him for the sake of safety, he failed to return the compliment by showing similar concern for her, but rather teased her as if she had finally weakened and had fallen in love with him. "You are a conceited lout," she said. "I simply worry that we will be conquered again and again when new attackers slay the last warlord, and my misery will be repeated over and over."

"You needn't doubt my skills to that extent, my lady."

" 'Tis not your skills," she said, whirling away from him and beginning the long trek to the outer wall afoot. " 'Tis your good sense I doubt," she flung over her shoulder at him.

She had taken perhaps a dozen steps at a quick, agitated pace when she heard the horse hooves come up alongside her. She did not turn in his direction, which proved her major mistake, for he leaned low on the side of his destrier and circled her waist with his competent arm and whisked her effortlessly off her feet, pulling her up onto his lap. She gasped in surprise as she found herself seated in front of him on the huge steed. "Sometimes, Aurélie, I think you are softening your opinion of me. I have heard apologies from your lips and betimes I swear I hear your fear for my safety in your voice. Come, madame, and we will greet whoever calls together, as lord and lady."

"Hyatt! Let me down! What will people think, especially since they know I am *enceinte.*"

"Oh, the very worst, I am sure," he laughed. "How terrible for you if they think that your husband, father of your child, holds some affection for you."

"Bah, 'tis not of affection, and we both know it. You taunt me and seek to embarrass me. You only do this so that all who see, your people and mine, begin to assume that we have accepted each other."

" 'Tis time, is it not?" he asked with a shrug.

"Time or not, it would be a lie. Just another of your games, Hyatt."

His arm tightened about her waist. "Don't be too sure, Aurélie."

She turned to look into his eyes. Her smile was superior and mocking. "Do you now wish to speak of affection, sir knight? Of devotion? Of love? Does my husband and father of this babe wish to pledge something greater than utility of services to this union?"

His eyes narrowed, but his smile was bright. "Do you admit that you hunger for such promises?" he countered.

She strained against him suddenly as if she would throw herself down from his steed. She was infuriated by his refusal to issue tender words. The strength of the arm that held her tightened. "Nay," he said softly but firmly, "do not in a foolish moment hurl yourself to the ground and do injury to yourself and the child. You prayed for a baby for many years, Aurélie, and now one is quickening in you. Be still, for your own sake."

She looked at him closely. "What makes you so certain I prayed for a child?"

"It is whispered by all your villeins, yet only you and I are aware that more than prayers were required to ease your barren consequence."

"Do not be cruel, Hyatt," she whispered.

"Then do not be rash, my Aurélie. Take what I willingly give you and cease in your demands for more and more of me."

"What have you given me?" she argued, feeling the injustice of his words. "A husband to bury. A hall that was once mine to rule is now yours, and I am instructed to see it kept for you. There is a child to be born, but from whence did it come? From a loving spouse, or a conqueror? And now, before scores of serfs and knights, I warm the great warrior's lap en route to the wall, but before you came, Hyatt, I walked to the donjon proudly, with my head raised, to command my knights and archers."

He pulled on the reins and the horse paused. The glitter in his eyes bespoke anger. "You are ever ungrateful, my lady. Yea, you have buried a husband: a man who did not lie beside you, did not consummate your union, did not rule his house or his men, but forced you to be the man he was not. Yea, you ride with your *lord* to the wall, confident that the knights and archers will be firmly led and victorious in protecting you and yours. And within you now is a child. Conceived in love? I cannot say. But, 'twas not wrought of rape, nor brutal conquest, nor indifference. You ask for oaths, promises, deference, and the verses of love sung by lesser men — but I give you an honorable marriage, a legitimate child, the strength and experience that should ensure you many future nights of peaceful sleep, and in our private solar you share sweet and tender bliss with me. To keep these assurances for all your days you need be only honest and loyal. I beg no simpering words of love, for words are only as good as the person who utters them, nor do I ask you to be grateful for what you have. You know you have never had so much, nor been so safe and well kept. We both know it."

He silently urged his mount forward, almost daring her to

argue. By the stern set of his jaw, she knew better than to voice any further protest. The truth of his words angered her, but in the back of her mind there was a jeering. *Giles said he loved me, and gave me no love. Hyatt will not say he loves me, yet his actions bear out more than I dreamt of. Where is the sense of this confusion?*

They passed into the outer bailey and toward the great gate. Paused there in wait was Girvin, clad in armor and outfitted with his weaponry. A glance around the perimeters of the wall showed Aurélie that many archers were in place and De la Noye was well defended.

"Sir Hyatt, it is Ryland."

She felt Hyatt stiffen as if an arrow had pierced his back. For herself, she flinched, for she knew not what horror had passed between brothers that would induce Hyatt to call himself a bastard, but she reasoned it must have been vicious.

"What does he want?"

"He brings word of your father's death," Girvin said. "He seeks friendship and kinship, his messenger says."

"Damn him to hell," Hyatt barked.

"Hell is in Innesse," Girvin rumbled, low. "Ryland comes from England, Hyatt. He was not sent with Edward's forces, but his troop is not small. I think that his army, coupled with Sir Hollis's, would be a bad omen."

"You know the bastard as well as I," Hyatt grumbled. "Do we invite him in? Coddle him, and pretend that he seeks *kinship?*" Hyatt leaned away from Aurélie and spat in the dust of the road. " 'Tis a lie, and I do not deal in lies." He glanced briefly at his wife and then looked back to Girvin. "There was nothing in the way the sun rose this morning to indicate that this would be a black day, yet everything that has transpired thus far has been a burdensome lot of trouble — and I have not yet broken my fast."

"Invite Ryland in with half his troop," Girvin suggested. "There is no reason you must accept kinship with him, yet I would wish to see how Ryland instructs his men. Will they camp outside our wall and await Ryland's orders, or do they travel straightaway to Hollis? I would know, Hyatt."

Hyatt began a smile that was wholly sinister. A silent chuckle shook his shoulders. "A wager? I say Ryland is too clever to send his men to Hollis."

Girvin smiled, and his grin was the devil's own. "Aye, but I say Hollis comes here."

Hyatt gave a sharp nod of his chin toward the gates. "Handle him gently, Girvin. He is afraid of you."

Girvin put on his helm, and the slate eyes that shone through the narrow slit glittered like steel blades. By his eyes alone it looked as if Girvin craved bloodshed.

Hyatt turned his mount abruptly, not staying in the courtyard for even the sight of Girvin crossing the moat. He hurried his destrier toward the hall and when Aurélie looked at him, his eyes were cast far away, perhaps into the past.

"Who is Ryland?" she asked gently.

"He is a centaur from Hades, but instead of the body of a horse, he has the mind and heart of a jackass."

"Is he kin of yours, Hyatt?"

"When I was a small boy there was one I called brother whose name was Ryland, but I have known no brother since, for many years."

She placed a hand on his chest, but still he would not look at her. His eyes remained on the road ahead. "Will you tell me about it, Hyatt?"

"Yea, but on a day when the telling does not cause my head to pound in fury. There is a chance you will be an old woman before you know. But do as you are fond of doing, Aurélie. Listen to the gossip of the men and see what you learn."

His voice had the sound of anger and pain, and she knew it was best to shrug off the insult. "Hyatt, if it is true that your father is dead, I am sorry."

"You needn't be, for I am not. It means that his pain is finally at an end."

213

"Was he ill for a long time?"

"Yea. His body was fit enough, but his heart and mind were twisted by the treachery of his wife and his son . . . and the word was that he never recovered."

❧

Aurélie sat beside Hyatt at the trestle table, a bowl of pork and coddled eggs before her. Her hunger had fled with the coming of Ryland, but her husband ate. He devoured his breakfast in a defiant mood, stabbing his meat and tearing his bread from the loaf in a vicious swipe. His bowl was emptied and filled again, two tankards of cool milk were gulped, and through the meal his brows were fiercely drawn together, his movements tight and jerking.

"Have you not seen this Ryland for a long time?" she asked with hesitancy.

"I would have preferred not to see him, madame," he grumbled without looking at her. "Unfortunately, he is a knight bidden to the king and our paths often cross."

"Why does he come?"

Hyatt's mouth turned in a sarcastic line. "Perhaps in answer to your prayers, Aurélie. Surely you have prayed for my comeuppance, and I assure you, a worthy opponent is at hand. Ryland conspires with Hollis."

Aurélie gulped at the memory of her sworn oath to Perrine on that day so long ago. She knew better than to try to soften Hyatt's agitated mood. "Does he mean to harm you?"

"In fact, he has always meant to."

Aurélie looked again at her bowl of food. She could not suppress the fear she felt for her husband. His angry attestation of what he had given her rang back through her thoughts many times. Three months before she would have delighted in the arrival of one of his enemies. Now she feared she might lose him before she really had him.

She looked askance at him as he ate. It had been such a long time since she had enjoyed the luxury of a friend or advisor to whom she could talk. The priest had never served in that capacity, but in the past there had been Guillaume

214

and Perrine. In matters of manning the castle or managing the villeins, Guillaume had been like a father or older brother. And while she had never confided the truth about Giles, Perrine had seemed to know. The older woman's gentle advice, support, and faithful service had helped her through many a confusing and lonely hour. She wished for someone to talk to about her husband.

He is right, she thought forlornly. *I complain for the sake of pride, for never have I had so much. The route of our alliance was all wrong, but our existence as man and wife is right and honorable. He is the enemy, yet I hunger for his touch, yearn for his child, and pray for his long life, for a son would need a father such as he. He is enemy no more, for he guards this castle and these people from any avenger, English or French — something Giles could never do. And though he may never love me, in his manner there is the promise that he can be steadfast if he is not betrayed.*

The door to the main hall finally opened and Aurélie knew instantly that the man was Ryland. He was older than Hyatt; taller and of a thinner build. His face was slightly narrower, but his brown hair, deep-set brown eyes, and square chin were remarkably like Hyatt's.

He wore a deep green cloak that swirled as he entered. He carried his helm in the crook of his arm, and embroidered upon his surcoat was the blazon of a hawk with golden lightning jutting out behind it.

Hyatt's gaze slowly drifted to the tall man and when their eyes met Ryland smiled, but his was not a smile of greeting or delight. "Well, Hyatt, you seem to do better for yourself each time we meet."

Girvin came in behind Ryland and stood just inside the door, grimly watching the reunion. He stood tall and silent.

"What do you want of me now, Ryland?"

Ryland looked around the large room, his brows raised and his lips turned up in a smile as he surveyed the wealth of the holding. His shoulders trembled slightly as if in a rueful chuckle as he glanced at each candlestick, tapestry, and wooden furnishing. He was slow to return his gaze to Hyatt. "I think I have never quite understood your continued hostility toward me, Hyatt. 'Twas not I who cast you out."

"I asked you, what do you want?"

"I bring you tidings of your father's death."

"I have no father. 'Twas his choice, not mine."

Ryland approached the table and placed his helm in front of Hyatt's plate. "As the old man neared death, he had come to regret his hasty mood. I thought you should know that."

"How do I know you do not lie?" Hyatt asked calmly.

"Why would such a lie serve me?" Ryland shrugged. "To the contrary, 'twould be better for me and my English lands to be the only son of the old lord. But you were your father's favorite, and he was ill from the day he sent you away."

"It has been many years since I left his house. He had abundant time to send his regrets to me."

"Pride, Hyatt. Surely you understand that."

"I have understood none of what happened, nor do I perceive a change of kinship now."

"You are too cold, Hyatt," Ryland said, smiling slyly. His eyes shifted from Hyatt to Aurélie and one brow lifted. "This castle held a good booty, I was told."

Hyatt slowly stood, his hands pressed down on the table. Aurélie could sense the stiffness of his body, the tension in his words. "The lady is my wife. If you cannot keep your eyes from her, regard her with the highest respect. You will find I am hard in this concern."

Ryland smiled in surprise, a laugh escaping him. "Wife? Hyatt, you have changed greatly." He made a sweeping bow before Aurélie. "Madame, it is a rare pleasure to make your acquaintance. Despite my brother's bitterness, we are kin now, you and I. I am Ryland Laidley, Lord of Lachland, which lies in the north of England."

Aurélie gave a slight nod, lowering her eyelids to acknowledge him, but she responded no further.

"Where is Faustina?" Hyatt asked.

"Wales, my brother. With her countrymen and family. She has been gone from Lachland for a long time."

"He sent her away?"

"Nay, Hyatt. She fled, finally. I gave her escort to her home."

"And the child?"

"Child?" he laughed. "Man, Hyatt. The child you were accused of siring on your stepmother is six and ten now, and long ago left Lachland to pursue his training. But, alas, he has gone the way of his mother and defends some hostile Welsh chieftain in Faustina's homeland."

Aurélie had to be quick to stifle a gasp of surprise when she heard Ryland's reference. She cautiously turned her gaze to Hyatt and saw his coloring deepen and a pulsing appear at his temples.

"Did she ever name the boy's sire?"

"Nay, Hyatt. But you will be pleased to know that she finally admitted it was not you. And I suppose you still deny the fact?"

"Did she deny it before Lord Laidley?"

"Nay," he said, shaking his head. "Upon her journey to her Welsh tribe she told me it was not you, but she said she feared to name the man lest Lord Laidley kill him. She said that one of his own sons would survive the accusation."

"Yet she named the younger son. I have often asked myself why she did not let you stand as the accused."

Ryland smiled lazily. "Perhaps out of some loyalty for me. I did bring her to Father, after all."

"And, I think, kept her free of loneliness. Did you fill Father's shoes?"

Ryland's smile faded. "I did not know she was evil, Hyatt. I thought she would restore a bit of lost youth to the old man. She maligned you, but you did survive, very well, didn't you?"

Hyatt did not answer, but looked evenly at Ryland. "My custom is to claim any child of my loins, legitimate or otherwise, Ryland. Unlike yours, there are no bastards of mine scattered about untended."

"Ah, yes. You do have a bastard child in keeping, don't you?"

"You are making a mistake, if you think to banter with me while you are in my home, Ryland. On the tourney grounds or the battlefield you may taunt and challenge me, but in the walls of De la Noye there will be none of that. I am lord here. First landed, soon to be declared by Edward. And in due time, King John will have to accept my lordship, for my wife, Lady Aurélie, is the widow and only heir of the former lord, who was killed in battle. Anything you say to me will be courteous, for I have the authority to see you chained, or worse. And, I confess, it would give me great pleasure."

Ryland seemed somewhat surprised by the calm, direct speech. But he stood erect and listened. Gone was his superior and insolent smile. His eyes were serious. "Hyatt, let us bury this hatred. I could not help you, but I did not knowingly hurt you."

"You wish kinship with me now? It is too late, Ryland. You have coupled yourself with my enemies."

"Hollis? Come, Hyatt, I need not choose between you. You are my brother and he is my friend. If we can find a means to lay our old battles to rest, Hollis will keep his distance. I should think that would be incentive enough."

"Ah, now we come to it! You offer protection through kinship, is that it? If I will name you brother, Hollis will not attack me?"

Ryland sighed. "I do not know whether Hollis will attack you, Hyatt. I have not seen him this past year. I have not come this far for Edward's war, but to bring you the news of our father's death and my offer of brotherhood, late but sincere. And you should know, lest you hold your hope on some distant promise, there are no more English troops crossing the Channel. Edward has stopped moving armies. His claim to Aquitaine through his mother is satisfied for now.

It seems, then, that you and Sir Hollis will be neighbors for some time."

Hyatt regarded Ryland coldly for a long, silent moment. He turned his gaze to Girvin and gave a slight, almost imperceptible nod and the huge knight turned and left the hall.

Ryland, too, looked at Girvin, noticing that the knight had taken some silent command from Hyatt and departed. "I see you still have Goliath panting at your heels, lapping up your orders. What, pray, do you feed the monster?"

Hyatt smiled, showing his teeth for the first time since Ryland had entered. "The blood of those who betray me."

Ryland stiffened indignantly. "Do you give me shelter, Hyatt, or do you send me on my way to seek the hospitality of another?"

Hyatt slowly lowered himself to his chair. "I shall give you and half your men shelter inside the outer wall. You, your squires and pages will be allowed rooms in the main hall, but the other knights who come inside will have to find their own accommodations. And know this, Ryland: I do not accept brotherhood with you, now or ever. I give you shelter because you are an English knight of Edward and have journeyed far from home. Your stay will not be long."

"You expect me to leave half my troop outside the protection of the wall?"

"Do what you will with them. We are crowded enough; De la Noye possessed a large troop and many villeins when I arrived. Your men will be allowed to share in our hunting and we can provide some game and provender from this hall, but they will have to make their own camp." He cocked his head slightly. "If they are attacked from without, I shall lend arms."

"How very generous you are." Ryland smirked.

"You are free to go, if you prefer," Hyatt shrugged. "If I were you, I would . . ."

Hyatt's words trailed off slowly as Ryland's eyes moved

toward the stair. Hyatt turned to see where his brother's attention was drawn and found that Faon stood at the bottom of the stair, looking into the room.

"Who is this lovely creature, Hyatt?"

Hyatt grunted dourly. "Mistress Faon, the mother of my son, Derek."

Ryland threw back his head and laughed loudly. He approached Faon and took her hand, pressing his lips to its back and bending low in a bow. She gave a brief curtsy. "Mistress, it is indeed a pleasure. I am Ryland, long-estranged brother of Sir Hyatt." He backed away from Faon and looked at Hyatt, his eyes twinkling in devious delight.

"Oh, I shall stay, Hyatt, no matter how uncomfortable you try to make me. Such an experience should not be missed. I have heard that your manner of ruling is different from that of other men and now I am curious to see for myself." He glanced between Aurélie and Faon. The wife blushed lightly and the mistress smiled victoriously. "Indeed, this should prove to be very enlightening."

❧

Girvin and Guillaume were dressed in animal-skin leggings and soft leather boots, and wore leather vests that covered lightweight linen gowns. Each had a thick belt on which he could carry pouches of grain and dried meat. Bows and quivers were slung over their backs, and their only other weapons were stout hunting knives and axes, but it was not the four-legged animal they hunted.

After the sun had set the bridge was lowered, but the gate was kept closed so that no one but the tower guard would see who departed. The two had lowered themselves over De la Noye's wall by a rope; Guillaume led the way through the thickest portion of the north wood and Girvin followed.

Both men were large, Guillaume being only a little shorter and slighter of build than Girvin, but their boots made no sound on the leaves and grass on which they stepped. They walked silently for several hours until the sun began to rise. They camped by the bright afternoon sun in a heavily concealed copse and ate of a freshly speared, roasted rabbit. As the sun lowered, they began the trek again. The moon was high up when Guillaume stopped. He pointed to a rocky ledge on a hill that could barely be made out in the dark of the night. "The road from Innesse toward De la Noye passes under that ledge. There is a shallow cave that can be reached, but 'tis best done in daylight."

"Good," Girvin said. "We can camp here until dawn."

Guillaume moved a bit off the path, kicking around in some shrubs as if making a space within the brush for a concealed pallet. "No fire?" he asked.

"Not unless you wish to draw raiders," Girvin returned. The other knight followed suit and stamped down some tall grass and vines, finally dropping from his back and belt the packs and supplies he carried. "You've done well, Guillaume. I thought you would know a place."

Guillaume unrolled the skins he carried for a pallet and sat down, taking from his pouch a thick slab of dried meat and gnawing on it thoughtfully. "What makes you so sure that we shall see an English troop pass between De la Noye and Innesse?"

"Hyatt's brother will betray him. There is no kinship there and Ryland has long been associated with Sir Hollis, who holds the Château Innesse now. It will be either knights of Ryland's troop, traveling to Innesse to deliver word that Ryland is inside, or troops of Hollis's, come to view the situation from the wood. Whichever it is, Hyatt must be told."

"I do not understand these English ways," Guillaume said, shaking his head. "Your king sends armies here to conquer us, and now that two knights of the same kingdom have landed and taken possessions in his name, they will fight each other? And Hyatt's own brother will betray him? For what?"

Girvin laughed, a low, rumbling sound. " 'Tis not the way of us English, but the way of certain men. Ryland allied himself with Hollis many years ago, for Hollis is strong and has a large troop traveling with him. In the beginning, Ryland was dissatisfied to see Hyatt live, fearing that the favored son would one day return to Lachland and make amends with the old lord, laying some claim. When that fear diminished with the passage of time, Ryland was moved by jealousy, for Hyatt has become steadily richer in reputation, favor, and, now, possessions. Ryland has his stinking Lachland, which is not worth a quarter of this Aquitaine demesne. Ryland is a lazy and selfish man and cannot endure Hyatt's success. This has been a long feud, begun many years before Hyatt left Lachland. I do not know how Ryland holds Hollis's friendship, but it must take a large supply of silver, for Hollis has no principles save greed."

Guillaume laughed. "Do you draw me out to do this service for Hyatt by trying to convince me that this has nothing to do with the war between French and English, but some battle between brothers?"

Girvin tilted a skin of wine to his lips and drank greedily, then passed the skin to Guillaume and wiped his mouth with the back of his hand. "Whether the battle be of countries or brothers, there is one fact. Sir Hollis is well known for leaving a path of death and waste where he conquers, and Hyatt's reputation has him building into greatness whatever he claims. Soon to come to De la Noye is the offspring of France and England, for Lady Aurélie will give birth and this child will be the heir."

"I was told that the boy, Derek, whom my wife tends, would be heir."

"Oh, Derek will have an inheritance, for certain. But not De la Noye. There are other lands for him."

"English lands?" Guillaume asked. "Does Hyatt leave this domain to go home?"

"Nay, he will stay in this new possession until Edward calls him to arms elsewhere. And what Hyatt plans for his firstborn he does not share with me. But unless I did not hear him correctly, he means to keep the lordship of De la Noye safe for many generations by passing it on to a legitimate heir.

You may be assured," Girvin said with a smile, "that Derek will not be neglected."

Guillaume grunted a sour reply and tore at his meat with his teeth, chewing the dried stuff with difficulty.

"It does not matter whether your new lord is English or French, Guillaume. What matters is that your mistress and your people live." Guillaume looked away into the darkness. "Do you reckon with your new leader yet?"

"Not yet," Guillaume replied without looking at Girvin.

"Bah, you follow orders like any loyal vassal. Why do you withhold your oath? You could have your arms returned."

Guillaume looked back at Girvin and a chuckle escaped him. He patted the stacked goods beside him; his pouch, quiver, bow, knives, and ax. "I do well enough with these."

Girvin leaned closer. "You have these for the sake of Hyatt, Lord of De la Noye."

"Nay, for the sake of Aurélie, Lady of the castle."

"Humph! You are as much Hyatt's knight as I."

"Nay. Not until you are as much Aurélie's vassal as Hyatt's."

"It cannot be. I killed her husband."

"She will learn the truth to that one day."

Girvin's eyes shot to Guillaume's in stunned surprise. "What truth?"

"There are many slurs applied to the former lord. Most of them are only pompous jests, but some of them I think are true. I listen."

Girvin eyed Guillaume suspiciously and then he snatched the wineskin from where it rested beside Guillaume. He took a hearty gulp, spilling much of the dark liquid on his shirt. "If you listen to idle gossip and battle tales from drunken knights, you are as stupid as a mule."

Guillaume laughed loudly and heartily. "Stupid as a mule, eh? And when did you know a mule who refuses to carry his load or walk a narrow ledge to be stupid? Stubborn, perhaps. Determined. But stupid?" He laughed all the more and held out his hand to have the wine returned. Girvin nearly thrust

223

it at him in what appeared to be petulance. "Never mind," Guillaume replied. "The time will come when both Hyatt and Aurélie will have to reckon with what they have captured and the truth will be revealed then."

"Hyatt *and* Aurélie? Hyatt has captured the castle and the woman, but the lady has captured nothing."

"Oh?" Guillaume chuckled. "Has she not?"

TWELVE

URÉLIE did her part as the lady of the hall and helped Ryland, two squires, and a page to settle into a comfortable chamber in the south wing of the castle. Her rooms, shared with her husband, were in the north wing. Hyatt had made no special request but that she see them housed. However, with the protective instincts of a lioness, she took Ryland far from her mate.

She stood in the frame of the door and watched as Ryland entered and leisurely surveyed his quarters. She was struck by the likeness Hyatt bore to his brother, yet some subtle differences, perhaps more of character than features, stood out in her mind as only a wife might notice them.

Ryland's fingers were longer, thinner, and his hands moved in smooth, graceful lines, while Hyatt's hands and arms seemed to move with power and determination. Ryland's advantage was in his height, but his frame was not as well muscled as Hyatt's. And something Aurélie sensed about Ryland left her shivering, but she did not know if her own instincts were reacting to a man who should not be trusted or if she had acquired this feeling of dread and doom because of Hyatt's warning and ominously foreboding mood. Whichever it was, she decided at once that Ryland was evil.

Hyatt did not ride the perimeters of De la Noye, hunt, work in the stables, or partake of any of his customary duties. He indulged himself in a brief practice of arms with some of his men the day after Ryland arrived, but that was the extent of his usual activity. To an untrained eye he might appear busy at all times, either walking through the baileys, along the wall to the various parapets, or sitting in the main hall for meals or polishing and honing the weapons he carried. But Aurélie and most of his men cast furtive glances his way, for his constant presence among them was unusual and suspicious. Hyatt's custom had been to trust his men to guard his possession, and he went about his duties with confidence that they would keep safe his house. Now it seemed as if he refused to leave the castle complex, nor did he dally too far from the main hall. And he was broodingly silent.

"It is either that Hyatt watches Ryland, ready for his brother to make some move against him, or that Hyatt plots Ryland's death," a knight whispered under his breath to a comrade as Aurélie passed them.

"Were it I, I would have killed the knave twenty years ago. 'Tis certain that Ryland plotted the argument between Lord Laidley and Hyatt. Mayhap Ryland got the woman, Faustina, with child, for it was well known that the old man could not."

Aurélie did not intend to eavesdrop in order to gather information about the conflict between the brothers. Yet after overhearing that exchange between Hyatt's knights, she sharpened her ears. It was not difficult to learn, since Ryland's appearance had prompted much talk. There were several snatches of conversations that she had, over a period of a few days, pieced into a story that would fit her husband's circumstance. She soon understood that Hyatt had endured a terrible shock as a child, and an even worse one as a youth just embarking on his manhood.

"After he buried his first wife, Lord Laidley was near death from grief and his estate fell to ruin, but he was still rich and influential. 'Tis a pity he did not die of his broken heart before Faustina came to claim him. Faustina meant to have wealth and power . . . and indeed she did, for a time. But before she fell, she destroyed a loyal boy who should have risen to glory in his father's house."

"Do not pity Hyatt. The time to pity him has long since passed. When he was a small lad of ten or twelve years and the Lady Laidley died, then he was much alone and bereft. Still, I think that was better than the evil day that Faustina accused him of tampering with her, and Lord Laidley beat him and turned him out for the wolves to feast upon. But he showed them, did he not?"

"It is said that Hyatt welcomed Faustina . . . ," the knight continued.

"Anything to relieve the old man of his melancholia would have been welcomed. 'Twas Ryland, fighting in Wales, who found the young widow, daughter of a wealthy chieftain, and brought her to Lachland. But did you know Hyatt's mother? It is said that Lady Laidley was like the sunshine and Faustina more resembled the cavernous black of a devil's tomb. Wicked, she was. How did Lord Laidley not know that she lied?"

"The story goes that Hyatt was but five and ten. . . ."

"Nay, older. Six and ten, perhaps. But his age at the time of the feud is unimportant. The crushing blow was that Hyatt was the favored son, the light in his father's eye. There was such a bond there that such a betrayal is inconceivable."

"But not shy of good fortune . . . the poor boy, beaten, turned away, stripped of his colors and name, thrashing through the wood without blade, quiver, or bow . . . and whom did he stumble upon but Girvin. He was not a knight then, but the Master Huntsman of Lachland Hall. He followed the boy out of Laidley's house. Together, they have managed to gather more than Lord Laidley could have bequeathed Hyatt."

" 'Tis a simple matter to understand his hatred of the fairer sex, after Faustina, the bitch."

"And Faon . . . equal in her devilry. I would not have kept the wench, child or not, for Hyatt knew she tricked him from the first. But I think the boy must surely be Hyatt's; his looks are strong."

"Mistress Whore . . . why does she stay? Hyatt has not used her since that time the child was sired . . . and will not again, I am certain. She does not value the child, yet she will not release him to Hyatt's care and be on her way."

"Nay, she will stay until she is an old woman. And mark me, she will pretend for all her days that Hyatt eases himself on her. Forsooth, she thinks all of us believe it so."

"Hyatt has never denied it. . . ."

"Hyatt does not speak of personal matters to anyone, but 'tis most obvious that he looks the other way when Faon tarries with certain knights who would try to best him by using his whore. Do you know so little of your leader after so many years? Hyatt watches and waits. He does not care what she does, nor with whom, but he judges the men who will guard his back in battle by their actions off the field. He learns much about the loyalty of one of his own by watching his behavior around Faon. Yea, that is perhaps why he allows her to stay; she brings the quick betrayal from his men. 'Twas said that even Thormond . . ."

"I have seen Faon cast a lusty look at Ryland. Mayhap an alliance will form there."

" 'Twould be like Faon to find a knight of any color to bed and she does not care whether 'tis friend or enemy of the man who provides for her. She is not wise. She is a bitch in heat. Her time is short."

"Short enough? I doubt it."

Ryland had been in residence for four days. Aurélie had heard more than enough. There were few words passed between Hyatt and Ryland, but her husband watched his brother scrupulously, and not a word that left Ryland's lips was ignored. She could see by the expression on Hyatt's face, the slight turning of his head or a pulsing in his temples, that he was alert.

She entered her bedchamber after the evening meal and found Hyatt seated before a flaming hearth, sweat beaded on his brow and staining his linen shirt. He pounded and polished his broadsword, a chore better done at the smith's fire, for he had made the room sizzle with unnecessary heat.

He glanced her way briefly, then looked back to his work.

She sensed his need to remain close to where his brother lingered, yet it was obvious he had a strong desire to keep his hands busy. Hyatt abhored idleness. If much more of time like this passed, Hyatt might be driven to mending for want of tasks.

Aurélie said nothing about the hot, steamy room. She went to the far corner and removed her gown, placing it carefully away. She unbraided her hair and separated the plaits with her fingers, pulling the long tresses over her shoulder. Barefoot, clad in only her shift, she went to stand behind Hyatt, placing a hand on his shoulder. She leaned close to his back, her middle pressed against his straining shoulders, and lowered her lips to the top of his head. He did not turn to her in this unusual display of affection, but his movements of the oiled cloth against his steel blade did slow. "Hyatt, do you remember her? Your mother?"

She felt the stiffness in his spine, but it was a brief reaction. "Aye," he said. "She brought Lachland to my father through marriage. Why do you ask?"

She placed her other hand on his other shoulder, softly kneading his tense muscles. "It is said that she was good and kind, and very devoted to her family."

He leaned his head back against her breasts. "I suppose she was. She died when I was little more than a child."

"And then came an evil woman into your father's household."

Hyatt gently closed his eyes, though Aurélie did not see. "You have listened well. You surely have the story now."

"You urged me to come to you for confirmation of the facts," she reminded him.

He sighed heavily. "It was a hasty remark on my part," he said with some chagrin. " 'Tis not a matter I can easily discuss with anyone. Leave it to say that I have had no family for many years . . . since I was a young man. Perhaps it has really been since the death of my mother, though it was later when I left Lachland."

"Had your mother lived, you would not have come to

France. The woman would have had no chance to betray you and your father would not have died without you near."

Hyatt groaned at the thought. "The blame is not entirely Faustina's. She lied, but Lord Laidley chose her word over mine. 'Tis a sad day when a man will choose a woman's lie over the truth of his own flesh and blood."

There it was; the original seed of all this distrust. Hyatt had failed to remember the good love of his mother, and could not forget Faustina's treachery.

Aurélie lowered her cheek to rest on the top of Hyatt's head. For the first time since he had come, she felt that he was vulnerable; that he, too, had a soft, bruised place on his heart that could be touched by a lover. She pitied the boy whose mother had died, whose father had failed him, whose brother betrayed him.

"Come, Hyatt. Your shoulders are stiff from your practice of arms today. Lie down on the bed and let me knead away the pain."

He chuckled a bit and burrowed the back of his head into the softness of her breasts. " 'Tis a foolish thing, what a man will do to save himself from the ill of ennui. This room is like a simmering hell."

Perhaps, she thought, to match the hell of sad memories. There was a fluttering in her womb. She had only felt such movements a few times over the past days, but with the evidence that the child grew she knew great joy. She had not expected Hyatt to feel the slight fluttering, but he had. He pulled away slightly and turned to look up at her. "My son?" he questioned.

"Or daughter," she said with a warm and yielding smile.

He looked away, a pensive darkness in his eyes. "It is a sign of strength when the child moves so early."

She caressed his jaw with the palm of her hand, causing him to turn his face and look up at her. "Of all worries, Hyatt, do not doubt the child's strength. That much is proven already. This child was conceived in the midst of a war, the seed of a ruthless conqueror that burrowed itself into the womb of a frightened and unwilling bride. 'Tis a child meant to be born, a child who was strong since its genesis."

Hyatt rose slowly from the stool before the fire, laying his broadsword down in front of the hearth and using the poker to scatter the logs a bit so that the fire could die out more quickly. He moved toward the bed and stripped off his short linen gown and chausses, casting them aside.

Hyatt sat heavily on the bed and Aurélie noticed that the lines of fatigue burrowed deeply into his face. His shoulders appeared slightly slumped with exhaustion, though she knew it was not wrought of physical labors. She passed him to blow out two tall tapers and open the shutters to the room, daring to look at him only from the corner of her eye. Her husband was energized by his work and beaten down by boredom and suspicion. He was better placed in a war with weapons braced than waiting in his house for some lowly serpent to strike.

She went to the opposite side of the bed and climbed on, kneeling. She gestured with her hand for him to lie down, and without hesitation she began to rub his back and shoulders. He wore only his loincloth and his body glistened with perspiration. Under her fingers the tension in his muscles stood as taut as cords of heavy rope. He sighed deeply as she used all her strength to soften the knots of strain in his back, shoulders, upper arms, and thighs.

She began to realize more as she touched him. Perhaps he had not slept well since Ryland's arrival; that would explain the penetrating fatigue that showed on his features. And surely the other man's presence caused a dreadful pain in recounting all those old memories. Hyatt still felt the deep betrayal of his mother's death; one woman had loved him with devotion and loyalty, and she had died. Faustina had made him the pawn in a relentless pursuit of her own selfish gains, tearing his father's love from him. And Faon, it was said, had somehow used him, tricked him, and now held his beloved son in a strained balance between her success and failure. How did Hyatt so stoically endure the betrayal of these women? It was no wonder he could not love a woman.

231

"Hyatt, do you sleep?" she whispered.

"Nay, Aurélie," he sighed. "Your ministrations are welcome. I had not realized how I overtaxed myself."

"You must have used the lance and sword fiercely," she murmured, willing to let that be the excuse for his weary frame.

"I shall use better judgment in the future," he replied tiredly.

"You must sleep, Hyatt. A good night's rest will serve you well. Come morn, you will not feel this ache."

"Oh?" He chuckled ruefully. "Do you mean to utter some sorceress's incantation over me as I sleep?"

Aurélie lightened the pressure in her fingertips, stroking his back with her palms. How aptly they avoided the details of this strife! One day, perhaps, he would share the pain in his heart with her. And she might even tell him of the many hurts that she tried to lay to rest to reconcile herself with this new life, this new beginning. But for now it hurt him to speak of his past and he could bear no more pain. Still, he did not seem to mind that she knew . . . however sketchy her knowledge.

"You are wise to refuse to love women deeply," she said. She felt him tighten under her hands. "If you hold yourself in control of your heart, what happened to your father can never happen to you."

"How do you mean that?"

"I can give you my promise for a few things, Hyatt. I can promise you that I will love this child that I carry; I will tend him well and faithfully. 'Tis true, I have longed for a child — and one born of a strong father. Now that the life of my longing moves within me, you need not wonder how I shall cherish him, for he is born of strength and he is my desire. I will not use him as a pawn in the inheritance of your possessions, nor will I seek to bind you closer with him, for I can accept the oath you gave the priest and will ask nothing more. But Hyatt, I cannot swear that I shall never die. And should I meet some angel of death before my child is grown,

I'd rather that you'd never loved me than that your loss of me would drive you to madness, that the child would lose both mother and father."

He was still and silent for a moment and then very slowly he rolled over, looking up at her. Aurélie knelt still, her long honey-streaked hair falling forward over her shoulders. He gently caressed the silky softness of her arm, sending shivers of delight through her. The light in the room was suffused and dim, the fire giving its last to glowing embers. But still, she could see the uncertain cloud in his dark eyes.

"Do you mean, my Aurélie, that you would rather have my sworn love given to my child than to you?"

She let her chin slowly drop. "If that is the best way to assure that he will never lose his father's love, yea."

"And what of his mother's love? Should I be removed from this castle by some heathen sword, what will become of my child? If you fancied yourself filled with some desperate love for me, you might, in your misery, forget that part of me I leave behind. You might, in your loneliness, welcome some unscrupulous devil into your house, your bed; one who means only to use you." He shook his head. "Do you see, my Aurélie, why it is unimportant to me to hear these troubadour's words and poems from your lips? I wish only that you know who your husband is, but that your love is steadfast unto your own flesh. I have seen the treachery that some women disguise as love, and I am certain there are men who likewise cripple their prey from the same empty words and promises."

His hands were closed about her arms and in his eyes she could see how earnest he was. How frightened he was to commit from his heart, how terrified to feel the depth of devotion, lest it be cruelly revoked. Perhaps, when some time had passed and Hyatt was less afraid, she might talk with him about the man his father had truly been. They might learn together that Lord Laidley was not made weak by grief, but was weak all along and had lost his only strength when his wife died. It would have been thus with Giles, had Aurélie died. He was not strong or wise enough to endure alone. Hyatt seemed not to understand that in this union both of them were equipped of wisdom and strength and beating them would not be so simple, whether they stood singly or together as a pair.

She knew it would be a long while before they could speak any more freely than they did now. By the tone in Hyatt's voice she could tell that he desired a greater closeness with her, but there was a fear and distrust that rang through his words. He had bought his fears at a high price. She pulled one arm from his gentle grasp and lovingly brushed the errant lock of hair from his brow, leaning low to place a gentle kiss where her fingers had touched. "Worry not, Hyatt. I know who my husband is, and whether you live or die, the child I carry shall be nurtured with devotion and love. And I am not so unwise as to yield to any devil in my grief . . . as you are well aware."

He gave a brief, rueful chuckle. "For some reason I forgot that I conquered a widow. 'Twas a virgin widow I forced into wedlock to protect my newly acquired lands. Yea, you are not easily tempered, wench, but I see that you begin to come around."

"Lest you become too arrogant, messire, I would have you know that I reckon your lordship here because 'tis a better lot we bear with you than the alternatives. Ryland, I can plainly see, is wicked and should not be trusted. And what I have heard of Sir Hollis makes you seem much the avenging angel, rather than the heathen we thought had penetrated the walls."

He smiled and ran a finger from her throat to the valley between her breasts. "From devil to angel, woman? My face has changed in your mind. You've grown soft. The truth, Aurélie; is it not that now that you have found those pleasures that lie in the marriage bed, you refuse to be without them?"

She raised one finely arched brow and smiled at him. "What pleasures are those, Hyatt? Forsooth, since Ryland's coming I have shared no fleshly pleasures with any man, angel or devil. You have been too beset with worry to notice me. Perhaps my memory will be refreshed when your beastly brother has finally gone. . . ."

". . . Or sooner," he said hoarsely, pulling her down to meet his lips. She yielded with the ardor that had become common in their private hours together. And when their passion was spent, they lay in each other's arms, Hyatt's head resting gently at her breast. She tenderly stroked his hair and knew that he slept well, fortified by the very love he could neither claim nor acknowledge.

☙

The first faint rays of morning sun were just beginning to rise over the farthest eastern knoll when Aurélie heard a movement in the bed behind her. As Hyatt stirred, she turned from the open window to look at him. She smiled inwardly as she noticed that the first thing he did upon waking was to reach toward the place she had occupied, and then with a jolt he turned to look for her.

He relaxed instantly as he found her nearby, at the open window. " 'Tis unlike you to rise before me."

She smiled at him and took two steps to the bed, bending to place a wifely kiss on his brow. "You often rose and watched me sleep. You have rested well, messire. Are your muscles yet sore?"

"Nay." A roguish grin graced his handsome lips. "I always sleep well after such a night, madame. But why are you up and about so early? Whither are you bound?"

"With your permission, messire, I would go to Perrine's household before she comes to Faon's rooms. I have not shared a private word with her since your arrival some months ago, and I do not like to go to her when she labors for Faon."

He frowned slightly. "Where is the need, Aurélie? Do you require privacy for some plot you hatch? Does Perrine spy for you?"

She sat down on the bed beside him and pulled one of his hands into both of hers. "Nay, Hyatt, never that. Perrine is my closest friend; she was my confidant and adviser for many years. She was the one to coddle and shelter me when I came here for Giles, for I was only nine years old and a bride. And over the years she gave me comfort. I have not needed her shelter, nor am I in want of advice, but I do miss her, Hyatt. In times gone by we would sit before a winter hearth and talk of women's things, or gather summer flowers and share our ideas on the raising of children, the baking of bread." She shrugged and looked down. "If it worries you, I need not go."

He squeezed her hand. "I will take your word that it is only woman's chatter you long for."

"It is no more serious than that, Hyatt," she said, rising to leave him. Her hand instinctively went to her middle. "I find I have a great deal of concern. Perrine's counsel will be welcome."

Hyatt stood and gently lifted her chin. "Aurélie, I know nothing about what a woman feels as she prepares to give birth and I fear I cannot ease your mind or give you advice. I will be useless to you. You are wise to seek out Perrine."

Aurélie smiled and touched his cheek. "You needn't feel useless, Hyatt. I believe you've done your part."

A roguish grin appeared on his handsome face. "It was my pleasure, *chérie*." He kissed her nose. "Go ahead, you needn't fear my suspicious nature this morning."

"Thank you, Hyatt," she said most sincerely. "That means a great deal more to me than you know."

As dawn struggled to rise, the sky was a gray tinged with streaks of gold against the clouds, the air cool and misty. There was no need for a wrap, and the dampness that came with the morning dew promised an afternoon of simmering, boiling heat. Once outside the hall and past the inner bailey, Aurélie could see the rising of smoke above the cottages from peat fires that were started to boil some morning meal or warm water for washing. The same rising cloud came from the seneschal's house, and when Aurélie knocked and called out to Perrine she was quickly admitted.

Perrine had not yet bound up her hair and a loose braid,

still messy from sleeping, trailed down her back. She wore her wrapper and padded around her large room in her bare feet. "Come in, love. Sit down and I'll give you a drink of milk drawn from the goat just a moment ago. What brings you here? Are you in some trouble?"

"Nay, Perrine . . . but it seems I never see you anymore, never talk to you at all. And I did not want to go to Faon's rooms."

"Aye," the woman smiled, understanding at once. When Aurélie found a stool by the single table in the room, Perrine dipped a ladle into a bucket and passed her a cup of goat's milk. "You're wise to stay far from that woman's quarters. She'd slit your throat in a trice, lass. She is a hateful creature."

"But the boy?" Aurélie asked.

"A joy," Perrine said, her wrinkled flesh folding around her mouth and eyes as she smiled with genuine sincerity. "Talk to me, lass, while I dress."

"Guillaume is already up and gone?" she asked.

Perrine went to stand behind a curtain that separated their eating and living quarters from a sleeping space. "Aye, we're all alone, lamb. Tell me how you've been."

"I am well, Perrine. Have you heard . . . I am with child?"

There was a long silent moment in which Aurélie did not even hear the rustling of clothes. Perrine must have stood shocked still in the next room. "Aye," the servant finally replied, "I had heard; this must please you well, my lady. 'Tis what you've wanted for a long time."

"A long time," she said in a breath.

Aurélie sipped her milk and heard the sound of Perrine dressing. She relaxed a bit, looking about the seneschal's house. She had always liked this room. Although it was modest, there was a warm feeling here. Perrine and Guillaume had raised a family here, their sons grown and about their adult responsibilities. One had gone to a monastery, one to a larger city to take up a trade, and two were still living in the village with their wives and children.

"Do you remember, Perrine, when I first arrived, how

frightened I was?" She laughed at the memory. "I did not know what to expect of this man I was to wed, this son of the bold and arrogant Sire de Pourvre. And then I met Giles; he was only a few years older than I . . . and almost as frightened as I."

The curtain pulled back and Perrine came again into the room wearing her gray wool tunic and a scarf tied around her bound hair. "It does not seem so long ago, does it?"

"Oh, now it does. Lifetimes ago." She knew the sadness in her own voice. "Did you know that he slept on the floor beside the bed? Walked with pebbles in his shoes? He slept only in a monk's habit and was mostly unwashed." Perrine sought a stool nearby her mistress, but said nothing. "He had overcome the flesh, sought no pleasure, did not hold money away from God, and confessed every day. Betimes he beat himself with ropes into which he had tied knots that bruised his flesh. *Salvandorum paucitas, damnandorum multitudo.* Few to be saved, many to be damned. Perrine," she said, looking at her woman, "was he one of the few?"

Perrine reached into her mistress's lap and squeezed her hand. "Madame, do not torment yourself over Giles. If he is not saved now, there is nothing you can do."

She shook her head and bit her lower lip, tears welling up in her eyes. "Was I a good enough wife while he lived, Perrine? I did not betray him, did I? I did not hurt him too badly, did I?"

"Let it be, lass. You cannot bring Giles back, nor can you undo any harm done while he lived. Any pain, Giles brought to himself. He was possessed."

"Yea. And he possessed nothing. I pity the manchild that is born, for too much rests on him. He is never to seek a mother's love, yet craves it. He is never to be weak, never to doubt, never to need, never to let another soul know that he stands on sand and not rock . . . all the days of his life. You knew Giles was beset, did you not?"

Perrine looked at Aurélie for a long moment before she spoke. "Yea," she whispered in a breath.

"Did you know my torment, Perrine? We never spoke of it in clear words; never spoke of Giles's strange obsessions and how much alone I was. Perhaps I was not so alone — I had you and Guillaume, my parents and friends. I had the wall — I commanded the archers and knights, sometimes through Giles, sometimes forthrightly. I rode as well as a man, ciphered the sums, and hid away livres to buy food when the harvest failed. I worked; merciful Holy Mother, I worked so hard that I slept exhausted, ofttimes without even my prayers." Tears slid down her cheeks. "Perhaps I fell into sleep without my prayers too often."

Perrine saw that she was becoming distraught, though the reason remained unclear. The older woman opened her arms and Aurélie fell into her embrace, sobbing onto Perrine's soft shoulder. "There, my angel, you did not cry so when you were brought word of his death."

Aurélie cried heavily for many long moments. The sound of a rooster's crow could be heard by the time the mistress was able to pull away and wipe at her tears with her sleeve. She straightened her spine and sniffed back the emotion. "I had wanted to be a mother, and did not see that I had been for many years."

"You must let go of Giles soon, my lady. 'Tis unwise to be so filled with his memory while you live as Hyatt's wife."

Aurélie shook her head with a laugh. "Oh, Perrine, I buried Giles long before he died. 'Tis for this that I burn with guilt and shame. I cared for his house with great zeal. I was comfortable with Giles because he was familiar; there was never any surprise. As his wife I had great power. The people came to *me!* I ruled; there was never any question. I had no strength but my own; I had no love but what I felt for De la Noye, which became my child. When Giles was killed, I did not mourn the husband I lost — I grieved for the power that was taken from me. No kingdom on earth would allow a woman alone to rule, but a woman wed to a weak man could rule and no one would argue. I knew exactly what I lost when I buried Giles; I lost my lordship here.

"Perrine," she went on in a whisper, "Hyatt found me a virgin; Giles never even consummated our marriage."

Perrine's eyes flared slightly, but she kept her reaction small. Her mouth pierced into a tight line as she held her angry emotions back from her mistress. "I had wondered. . . ."

"But conquer he did, in every feasible way. He holds this castle most firmly and the people herein are the better for his lordship. He has conquered me, for I carry his child and it even moves in me. To feel this life within my body brings me joy. He is the strong arm I longed for, and however heavily I lean, he does not show the strain. He has the wisdom in his disciplines that allow those who know him to trust him. And would you think ill of me if I told you that in those private moments when we share a pallet, I hold him dearly? He brings me pleasure, Perrine, such as I had not known was possible."

Perrine's hand caressed Aurélie's damp cheek, her eyes softened by understanding and sympathy. "Then do not weep, my lady, unless you weep for joy."

"He does not love me. He is most suspicious of women, and with just cause."

"In time, my lady. Since he can be good, strong, wise, and tender, can you not nibble on those tasty bites until the full feast arrives?"

"He fears to love a woman. His mother died when he was young, abandoning him to a failing father. His stepmother was wicked and accused him of adultery with her, which had him beaten and cast from his father's house in shame, though he was innocent. His mistress, whom you serve, tricked and betrayed him, and he houses her to keep safe his son. Perrine, he is as tormented as Giles was, though their demons are of another sort."

"My lady, listen to me. Do you fear him?"

"Oh, nay. I am not frightened of him now."

"You depend on his strength? His ability?"

"Aye, Perrine. I told you so."

"You feel joy in those tender moments? You are pleased that you have brought his seed to life?"

"Aye. Why do you ask me these things?"

"Many a mighty warrior has sworn no need of love and yet has sung that light verse with great gusto when he feels love come. Be easy on him, my lady. Grant him acts that show your worth and devotion. Leave him be till he mends his own hurts. Time willing, he will admit that he can love."

"But Perrine, how should I wish this from him? He is my enemy. The enemy of my country."

"Nay," she whispered. "He is your husband, father of your child. And, I think, a worthy man."

The tears came anew. Aurélie's eyes first welled up, deep and liquid in emotion, dropping over her lower lids and spilling down her cheeks.

"Aurélie," Perrine whispered, "you have buried the man who could not be your husband, and wed the strong knight. Forget that he is the enemy. Here, why do you weep?"

"Perrine, I love him so . . . and I am so afraid. . . ."

"Hush, Aurélie. Afraid? I have loved my Guillaume for thirty years and I know there is strength to be found in the love a man and woman share."

"Did you not tremble when he battled and met the enemy? Worry each time he rode away and collapse into exhaustion when he returned, safe? Did your heart never bleed with the stabbing fear that he would never feel this for you? And the shame of such wanton desires; to love a man who sees only utility in the marriage. Oh, Perrine, do you know what I feel?"

Perrine put her arm around Aurélie and led her toward the door. "Oh yea, my lady, I know what fragile strings hold your heart together now. But was it better with Sir Giles, living with his torment, his obsession? Perhaps it was easier, for his pain did not really touch you. But was it better, my Aurélie?"

Perrine opened the door of her house and Aurélie saw that the sun was shining brightly outside. She sighed heavily and turned to Perrine. "Better? I cannot say. But I was not so afraid. I did not need Giles. I did not love him."

Perrine chuckled softly. "And so you need the bold and lusty knight? Ah, my lady, how your life has changed."

"What will I do?" she asked, a catch in her voice.

"What all women do. Let your need of his love transform you; bring dignity and honor to his name, give him the goodness in your heart, and be not weakened by what you feel, but strengthened. Only a misguided fool sees love as weakness. You are above such nonsense."

"You will be late to Mistress Faon's rooms. Will she punish you?"

"Nay, I think not. Come, my love, we'll walk together. You were right to come; you have been alone with no counsel for too long and have forgotten, I think, that yours was not meant to be a simple or pampered life." Perrine squeezed her shoulders and they looked much like mother and daughter, out walking. "Do you forget also that we cannot grow or challenge the strength of our virtues if we do not face new trials? Ah, I think Hyatt was lucky when he found you, for this once he will not suffer the treachery of a lying woman. Be steadfast, my lady, and trust your heart. And thank the Virgin that those things you prayed for came to you . . . albeit, by the sword."

"He could not have come in the gentle mist of morning, riding a friendly horse," Aurélie sighed, knowing for the first time the truth to that statement. Had Hyatt been of French blood, Giles would not have been slain. She could only have loved him as an adulteress. She would have been excommunicated, or stoned, or left to live the private shame of such debauchery. The only way she could have found herself with Hyatt, carrying his child, was by the sword.

"Thank you, Perrine. You are ever patient and wise."

"Thank you, my lady," she said with a smile. "You are ever in search of truth. And this is rare in those who also have power."

"Power?" Aurélie laughed bitterly. "Oh nay, Perrine, I

have none. I am the vanquished here. That power I had when I was wed to poor Giles is gone forever."

Perrine slowly shook her head, but she smiled. "Gone? Your power is not gone, my lady, but different than with Giles. Pray do not forget the strengths you once knew, in the event your husband has need of them. Where once you felt your power in your ability to command, it will be doubled now as you stand beside a strong and able lord. Once you ordered troops because your husband was unable to protect you, but you have an able husband now and can lend him support. Once it was loneliness and despair that drove you, now it will be love and loyalty. Hyatt has need of a strong woman. Remember what you have learned."

"Excellence, wisdom, courtesy, and humility," she murmured. "He spoke those words to me."

"Then do not pretend that you don't know what he wants from you. And do not fool yourself, Lady Aurélie, that he could seek these virtues from a woman he does not love."

❧

Aurélie had been so intent on observing Hyatt and Ryland that she had not noticed that Girvin was not about the keep. The knight's presence about the hall, wall, outbuildings, and baileys was only strong in Hyatt's absence, as he guarded the place on Hyatt's behalf. When Hyatt was ruling De la Noye, Girvin generally remained aloof, occupying himself with hunting, attention to the horses, weapons, and the surveying of the outlying lands. For these chores Girvin mostly chose Guillaume as his frequent companion, which made for an odd couple. Their similar qualities of stubbornness, pride, loyalty, and strength that had made them natural enemies with the siege was seeding a friendship in them now.

The sun was setting when Girvin came to the hall carrying a dozen strung rabbits. Aurélie had never seen him dressed so. He wore skins, boots, and a wide leather belt heavy with provender, and carried only the weapons of the crudest hunter. On previous hunts Girvin had donned mail and carried his sword and shield lest he meet some opponent in the wood.

Girvin's hair had become shaggy, his face was shadowed with a heavy growth of beard, and his condition spoke of many days away from shelter. "Sir Girvin, have you been hunting this whole week?"

"Nay, my lady, but I did go deep into the wood to judge the game for the taking."

Hyatt came closer to his wife and his messenger. "And is the game in the wood interesting?"

"Yea, my lord. 'Tis a good lot we spied, though there were odd breeds from many different groups. They gather in the forest."

"How did you view the game?" Hyatt quietly asked. Aurélie listened, looking between the two men, not understanding their strangely hushed tones or descriptions.

"Sir Guillaume knows the forest very well and found a concealed cave above the road from which we might see the animals that pass. 'Twas a good loft to make count and name the beasts."

"How clever. And the hunting will be good?"

"Aye, Hyatt, if we are the hunters and not the hunted. I would not hasten to kill any animals within the small groups lest we chase away the lot." Girvin smiled wickedly. "I have left Guillaume to watch. You will be interested to know that we sighted a wounded stag. One limb was missing."

Aurélie's eyes rounded at the prospect of a three-legged stag. "A leg missing?" she gasped in interest, disbelieving. "You should have killed it and brought it here, Girvin."

"I will my lady, in good time," he said with a smile, bowing away from them.

She stood silent and still for a long moment before she looked up into her husband's smiling eyes. She finally concluded that the animals they spoke of were not the kind one cuts into stew.

"Hyatt, what is Girvin about?"

"The protection of De la Noye. Of course."

"And Guillaume?"

"The same, I assume."

She raised a brow. "Have you brought my seneschal over to your side?"

"I think not, Aurélie. It appears that he serves you still, by keeping the castle safe."

"My seneschal and your henchman. 'Tis an unlikely couple they make."

"So long as the peculiar brotherhood works for the good of this, I would not question it. But speak not of Girvin's hunting, my lady, lest the hunted become suspicious or get warning."

"I would do nothing to risk De la Noye; you know that. But are we safe?"

Hyatt sighed and looked around the room. Some of his men were entering to have their evening meal. Ryland lounged at a long trestle table, sipping an ale, looking much at ease. Servants were gathering to serve and clean up.

"I think so, my lady. But I accept your prayers, just the same."

THIRTEEN

ATHER Algernon replaced the communion chalice, covering it reverently with white linen, and blessed himself before the altar before leaving the sanctuary. He genuflected before the crucifix and moved into the vestry, his head bowed and hands folded. Once inside the bare little room he jumped in surprise, for a man had startled him by somehow slipping in without being seen.

"You should not have come here," he said in an angry, hushed voice.

Ryland smiled confidently. "No one saw me. Not even you."

Algernon stiffened. "What you seem to misunderstand is that your brother has no religion. He is a heathen. Should he discover that I have traffic with you, I would be stripped and turned out onto the road. He does not worry about his soul; he does not know the dire consequences of working against a man of the Church."

Ryland laughed good-naturedly. "But the man of the Church understands fully the consequences of working against Hyatt. You are right, Father; my brother cares nothing for his soul, his spiritual bread and wine. He would *not* cast you out of the castle for working against him. Rather, he would slay you instantly. But that will not happen, will it? We shall show Hyatt the road out."

"And this man you promise will help you to replace Hyatt?"

"You will be very pleased, Father Algernon. Have I greased his entrance with enough silver? Do you require more?"

"I must know the state of his soul; I would know that my place in my church is secure. It is costly business, this thing you ask of me."

"That is an utter lie; it costs you nothing but courage. And I have sworn that the man who comes with troops will secure you in this church. Have you received permission for the pilgrims yet?"

"I have not asked it."

"Soon?"

"Have patience. Pilgrims come here in droves, for De la Noye has always received them."

"That was before Hyatt. You could seek him out today. . . ."

"I could, but 'twould seem odd to seek permission to admit groups of prelates on a pilgrimage many weeks from now. If you will only wait, the plan will not fail. Do you swear that no one will be hurt?"

"Not one of the friars or monks. Of that I can give assurance because they will travel unarmed. Within these walls, yea, there will be death and injury, inasmuch as these people of Hyatt's fight to preserve De la Noye for him. But was it not so when Hyatt came? If you wish to remain under his rule, say so now, Father."

"Nay, we cannot remain under a faithless lord. 'Tis better, I think, that your friend overtake him and bring the religion back to this place. We simmer just above Hell now."

Ryland's eyes twinkled. "And with the Sire de Pourvre it was so much better?"

"The Sire was a devoted man; he had risen above those mercantile desires of the fleshly man. He was free of the sins of the godless knight."

"I see," Ryland said. "We grow impatient, Father. De la Noye must be restored soon. The priest in Château Innesse was not deposed; his robes are richer and his church grows larger than it was before the battle. I am anxious to have this business settled."

"If you do not await the harvest, sir knight, you will not succeed. That is the time of the largest pilgrimages."

247

"Do not betray me, Father. I warn you."

Father Algernon inclined his head in an affirmative nod and Ryland turned abruptly to leave the vestry. He peeked out the open door and crossed in front of the altar through the chapel. Being seen leaving the chapel was not a problem, but had anyone been praying there and realized he was closeted with the priest, grave suspicions would arise. Ryland knew how carefully he was watched and this excited him.

Ryland walked from the chapel toward the hall. He purposely wished to pass through the mistress's gardens. His pace was leisurely, his manner relaxed. He liked to wander about De la Noye. After Innesse, De la Noye was a lovely surprise. This was a rich and robust place, not at all like a castle recently besieged by war and death, but a flowering little blossom in the midst of a stormy land. If all went according to plan, and if he could stay Hollis's harsh hand, De la Noye would barely be bruised in the siege. The dead would belong to Hyatt's men-at-arms.

Ryland had a liking for flowers and found the gardens in the inner bailey behind the central keep to be perfectly groomed at all times. There were always women and young boys at work there. This was the one place completely untouched by the conquering forces, for a wall that was about knee-high to a full-grown man surrounded the place, and the clumsy knights had not ridden nor led their warhorses through the flowers. He touched a rose, stooped to pluck a marigold, and inspected a large, fragrant white flower. He inhaled deeply, smiling.

A figure kneeling not far from where he stood caught his eye. It was Aurélie, stooped beside the herb patch with a small knife and a basket. A chuckle rose to his lips. How unlike a noblewoman to be engaged in menial labor. Any of the women he had known would have sent a servant to collect herbs. But then, he had seen her involved in many tasks beneath her station. She poured ale from her pitchers, delivered wine from the closet to the table, brought dinner eggs from the village. Mayhap she curried horses when she had a spare moment, he thought wryly.

He approached her. "Is there no one to do this for you, my lady?"

She turned and looked up at him. "There are many who would do as I bid them, sir. I choose to do this myself."

"Ah," he acknowledged with a smile, "you must enjoy the garden. The selection of herbs brings you satisfaction."

She began to rise and his hand was ready to lend assistance. She warily allowed this and came slowly to her feet. There were two round brown spots on her apron from kneeling in the soft dirt. "I planted the herbs myself, sir, and so it is my wont to harvest them myself."

"In England it is not considered good fashion for a noblewoman to engage in the labors of serfs and servants."

Aurélie smiled in spite of herself. Did Ryland mean to educate her on the style of the English? But she had watched Hyatt, who she suddenly realized was quite like herself in this respect. He was not too high a lord of men to perform even the lowest task if it was a chore that needed doing. He liked activity and detested extended leisure. He was no less able to delegate work to others, nor did anyone ever dare to question his command. Hyatt would be amused to have someone criticize him for shoveling up a pile of horse dung or pounding the dents out of his own shield.

"I think I would be most bored in your country. In our fashion, work is noble and laziness is a sin. I doubt you will find that any of my people do not know who is mistress here, despite my poor costume."

"Yea, this I have noticed as well. You have trained them very nicely."

"Trained them?" She chuckled. "Sir Ryland, I beg you consider how seriously a servant will follow orders to cure meat if the one who issues the orders cannot say how 'tis done. That, as in any task, is the essential: to give instruction in the chore. Since I was a small girl I have been taught each task to be done in my home so that I can see each is properly completed. Can you order work done without ever having done it yourself?"

"Certainly," he said rather stiffly, tucking one hand into the central fold of his gambeson and seeming to look skyward.

"And your English estate prospers?" she asked.

He seemed nearly to flinch and his eyes were on her face instantly. "What do you hear of my lands, my lady? Does Hyatt criticize what I have?"

She bent to pick up her basket. "He has never mentioned you, nor what you have. Even now that you are here, he does not wish to discuss you with me."

"Ah, and have you not wondered why?"

"Nay, I have only . . ."

"I will tell you why. Though I was the firstborn, I was weak and small as a child. Three years after my birth came Hyatt, large and strong from the beginning. We were the same size when I was ten and he seven. Yet he was the robust child, and our father decided early that I would not survive and Hyatt should be taught the workings of the land and keep; Hyatt was prepared to take what I would not live to inherit. He was the favored one, always. My father, I think, was disappointed to find that I survived and, in fact, became stronger and larger each passing year. But he was glad that I survived when that black day came when Hyatt was accused of tampering with his wife."

The tone of self-pity mixed with anger in Ryland's voice caused Aurélie to listen carefully to his words. So the jealousy was the first impetus to all their problems. Lord Laidley had wrongly shown favoritism to his younger son, and the problems had begun. Before the end had come, all of them had been deeply hurt, not only Hyatt.

"Messire, by your own words, Hyatt was not at fault . . . but your father."

"I do not dispute that. But neither did Hyatt strive to set that problem aright."

"Oh. Does he threaten your demesne?"

Ryland looked off, irritated. She remembered what she had overheard from the knights; had Ryland been responsible for the breach of love between father and favored son? Had he done the dreadful deed with Faustina because he was so tormented he could not resist revenge? If so, Ryland had tripled the crime now, for he seemed propelled by a vengeful cause, driven by bitter memories from his childhood.

"Sir Ryland," she said as gently as she could, "I think you and your brother have been hurt enough by your father's poor judgment. You have your father's demesne and it is safe from Hyatt. He has fought and won his own lands despite his impoverished beginnings. 'Tis done now. I think you only do yourself harm by clinging to bitterness and hate."

"How odd, my lady. You sound as if you are very devoted to him, when I was told that you begrudge this marriage and only acquiesce to keep yourself and your people safe. He killed your husband. I would think you would hate him."

Aurélie felt deep pity for the man, though she knew she should not soften toward him. "Giles fell in battle, messire. I could have been stripped and chained, but I was wed. Hyatt is a difficult man to please, but he is honest and fair, and his authority here is indisputable."

"You speak with great pride, madame. I believe you love him."

"If I speak with pride, 'tis because I respect him. What more there is, I will not share with you. When you seek to slander him and cast a doubtful light on his deeds, you should not do so before his wife. And I am a wife, Sir Ryland, whether loving or grudging. And in wifely loyalty I am bound."

"You are wrong to chastise me, my lady," he said as if deeply chagrined. "I have come here to make amends to my brother. 'Tis Hyatt who refuses to accept kinship with me, yet I did not turn him out of Lachland as a youth. Perhaps he has a right to his hostile notions, but it is all wrought of Faustina's treachery and his father's betrayal. In this he is not alone, for it was I, shunned as a boy, turned away from my father, and protected by my mother and my nurse. I would lay away my miseries with Hyatt's . . . but he refuses to call me brother now."

"Then do not demand it, Ryland," she advised in a soft voice. "Say your piece and go on your way. You have what you desired and Lachland is yours. Leave Hyatt be. Your presence here reminds him only of his unhappy youth."

"*His* unhappy youth?" Ryland laughed, but it was a bitter and empty sound. "I see that you have not heard me. Never mind, you are right." He took her elbow and turned her to leave the garden. How swiftly his anger had turned to indifference. "You are right; 'tis done. I am only a guest of English blood. I have Lachland, Hyatt has his Aquitaine demesne, and King Edward is well pleased. I require no more. Perhaps I will go for a ride. Will you join me, my lady?"

Aurélie was a bit jolted by the change of mood, the abrupt reversal of a boyish temper to a courtly flirtation. "Nay, Sir Ryland, I have a great deal that needs to be done."

"Then I shall leave you to it," he said, bowing away from her and walking briskly through the garden along a path that would take him toward the town.

Aurélie stood for a moment in some confusion, watching him go. He did not use a determined step, but dallied somewhat along his way. She followed for a while, carrying her basket of herbs into the village where Ryland was meandering. He nodded amiably to each person he passed, chatted for a moment with a man wearing his own livery, climbed the ladder to the northeast parapet to look at the castle and town and outer bailey from a loft.

Something about Ryland so distracted her that she found herself wandering without direction or intention. She seemed to follow his path somewhat. Soon she stood before the gate and bridge. Ryland was looking over the outer wall toward the forest and farming plots. Nothing in his posture or actions suggested the earlier anger and hostility she had heard.

She stood back as there came a shout and the bridge was lowered. Hyatt rode in ahead of a wagon heavily burdened with felled trees. Upon seeing her, he dismounted and pulled his destrier aside. "This load should be taken to the inner bailey, where you will find Delmar waiting. When these trees are stacked to his liking, return to the clearing for another load." He turned to his wife then, smiling. "Do you come to greet me, *chérie?*"

"Hyatt, what is this? Why are you bringing unsplit logs into the bailey?"

"Delmar claims that with a few additional men he can construct wagons for me."

"Wagons? Whatever for?"

Hyatt put a casual arm about her shoulders and led her away from the outer wall as the massive gates slammed closed behind them. "We can hardly carry goods from De la Noye in the few wagons this place has available. The villeins have a few, but they are needed to move tools, seed, and other necessities from town to fields."

"But where on earth will you carry goods?"

"From our fruit trees and gardens we will take food to the Sebastian Monastery. They will trade us good Gascon wine for necessary stock and crops. We will keep a bit of wine for the castle and send some to England. In return, we will receive cloth and wool and hardware that cannot be found here. There have even been promises made to your father in Flanders, but until I am certain how the land is settled, Lord Lavergne will wait."

"But Hyatt, surely scavengers will halt the wagonloads and . . ."

"There are plenty of guards. Do not worry."

"But . . ."

"Did Giles never send what he had grown here to trade with other keeps and towns?"

"Nay, Hyatt. We made do on what we had. We always had enough."

"Enough? My lady, there is no need to make do. This is a rich farming burg. We cannot send vegetables and chickens to England to sell, but wine and cloth and ironworks travel quite well. I sent a man to deal with the Sebastian brothers, and they were delighted by the trade since they cannot sustain themselves on grapes alone. We shall soon have better than enough. This can be a place of plenty."

"You mean to make money on our goods?"

"Of course, Aurélie. Now, what have you been up to? What brings you to the gate, if not to greet your husband?"

She shook her head as if to shake away one subject and approach another. "I have seen your brother this morn, messire. He spoke to me in the garden."

"Did he offend you somehow?" Hyatt asked stiffly.

"I find his presence to be an offense by itself. But I must tell you that Ryland's complaints of his childhood seem to exceed even yours. He claims a bitterness wrought of being shunned by your father. He says that he carries a burden of anger from his youth, for you were the favored one."

"He has always said that." Hyatt shrugged. "My memory of our childhood at Lachland does not bear it out to be true. I was a heartier lad than Ryland, but I could not become ill to make him appear more lively, nor could I fail so that he would appear smarter or stronger. He was always jealous and perhaps with just cause, but it is not the same as being deliberately cast out."

"He would lay away that sad memory with your kinship now."

"It is not possible, Aurélie. Ryland may have many complaints about his early life at Lachland, but it is his estate now. He stood beside my father when the old lord denied that I am of that family blood. You do not take such words back and declare them unsaid. But even that does not sustain my hatred. I could forgive anything done by a boy, but Ryland has committed many crimes against me since he has reached manhood."

"But Hyatt, what can he gain as your enemy? How does he mean to profit by plotting against you?"

"Oh, I am certain that he seeks to own what I have. He committed so much to wresting Lachland from me, and it is laughable since Lachland was never mine. He engaged Faustina to help him and what he got was an estate impoverished by the bitch and a treacherous woman as an accomplice. Lachland, it is said, is not worth a damn. Ryland is poor, for he has spent his money foolishly." Hyatt had one arm about her shoulders and threw the other wide to indicate the town they walked through. "And I have become quite rich by comparison. I have oft been accused of being miserly."

"Hyatt, you do not believe he speaks the truth about wishing kinship with you, do you? There is too much hatred in his voice when he speaks of you, his family, his home."

"Is there now? I am little surprised. I have not believed for one moment that he wishes to bury the past. Indeed, he is here about another business entirely."

"Hyatt, why is he here? Please, tell me what you know. This brother of yours tarries about my home, greeting the peasants, viewing the lands, and all in the best of humor." Hyatt stopped walking and looked down at her. "He looks at De la Noye as an heir-apparent views his future demesne."

Hyatt smiled, but there was a certain sadness in his eyes. "That is what he does, madame. He fully intends to wage war on me."

"That is what I feared. Why have you let him enter?"

"You will learn in time, my lady, that it is better to watch the devil than to turn your back on him."

"Hyatt, there will be a dangerous moment to come. I am afraid."

He lifted a brow. "Do you doubt that I can keep you safe?"

Her hand went to his of its own accord, giving him a tight squeeze. "Nay, Hyatt. I am worried for you."

"Ah, the truth finally comes out. Have you finally given your heart to me?"

"Oh Hyatt, cease. You carry on as if naught is amiss. You build wagons and prepare to harvest your first crops in De la Noye. It has not missed the notice of your men that you are much in residence, making only brief sojourns outside our wall, but beyond your watchful eye, you seem to do nothing to protect yourself."

Hyatt smiled and kissed the end of her nose. "Aurélie, my vixen, you have just given me a very large compliment."

"How so?"

"If it appears to you that I do nothing to protect myself, then surely it must seem so to others, for no one watches me as closely as you do. And that is exactly the appearance I wish to give."

⁓

In the south wing of the castle two squires nodded off sleepily on makeshift pallets outside Ryland's bedchamber door. The hour was late and the disturbing noises from within the room had finally ceased, dulled into the soft whispering of conversation, which lulled the lads into a dozing stupor.

Inside the room Faon snuggled closer to Ryland.

"Ah, wench, I shall sorely miss your company. Would that I could tell Hyatt how much pleasure this visit has been."

"But you would not. You swore."

His hand swept over her naked bosom in a casual caress. "I will not confide in him, but . . ." He lifted her chin so that he could see her eyes. "But I think you have led me to believe there is more between you than there is."

"Why do you say that?"

"If Hyatt frequented your bed, how would you dare come here?"

Faon lowered her eyes. "Since his marriage, his demands are . . . less frequent."

"Ah! Do you mean, not at all?"

"Nay, that is not what I . . ."

"Stop pretending. If he does not appreciate you, he is the fool. I can see that this marriage is all that Hyatt desires. And the woman adores him."

" 'Tis not true! She fears him!"

Ryland stroked her brow almost lovingly. "You must reckon with this soon, dear Faon. I have seen the way Hyatt watches her, and though he might not admit it, he is smitten with her. And she told me with her own voice that she is loyal to him. In every way. Hyatt is finished with you."

Faon took a deep breath. "I am his son's mother. His son will inherit his estate."

"In time he will turn even Derek against you, my love. If you are wise, you will find a way to best Hyatt before he casts you aside for good. By the way he regards you, that time fast approaches. His woman will not abide your presence much longer."

"The bitch," Faon snarled. "Poor mother of a bastard child, what am I to do? Where am I to go?"

Ryland began to laugh. "Somehow, I do not see you as suffering. But, if it is a place to go that you seek, you are welcome to come with me. But I warn you, I will not have that brat along. Or that old woman."

Faon was quiet for a long moment. She snuggled a bit closer to Ryland, her head in the crook of his arm. She could not lie to herself any longer; Hyatt's intention toward her had never been one of love or longing, not even in that first coupling. She had, in fact, served him so much drink that he fell asleep. At dawn's light she had shown him the stains on the bedding and wept at her virgin's loss, which was a lie. He then took advantage of what he thought he'd done and bedded her with zeal. She became pregnant easily; Montrose pressed the lusty knight for satisfaction.

It had not worked much to her advantage, though, for he not only refused marriage with her, but did not lie with her again. He bought prostitutes on occasion, but rarely. He kept her closely guarded and watched her grow with his son, but he never returned as her lover. She made comments and gestures occasionally, to make the others think they were intimate, for it gave her power with his men. But he shunned her more publicly now. And what Ryland said was true — he watched Aurélie with unmasked lust.

At first there was the pain of disappointment when he had married, but now she had begun to despise him. And she longed for Aurélie's death. Perhaps she would see them both punished for the way she'd been cast aside.

"Where do you go, Ryland?"

"Not far, my love. I shall be in France for some time to come."

"And you will keep me safe from him, if I go with you?"

Ryland chuckled. "Do you think he would search for you?"

"If not out of devotion, most certainly to keep me from taking his secrets out of De la Noye and giving them to his enemies. And though you try to conceal it from me, I know you are his enemy."

Ryland pulled her closer. "How are you so sure?"

"Because I am his enemy, too. He has shamed me enough."

❧

Aurélie had been busier than usual throughout the morning and still had a great many afternoon duties she wished to do when Percival's grandson, Paulis, came to the common room of the hall in search of her. He had been helping Delmar with some building, and his hand was cut and filled with large splinters.

The room was empty but for Girvin and two young squires. The squires were occupied with mending chain mail and Girvin, it appeared, had come to the hall for a midday meal. She had only just arrived herself, nodded briefly to Girvin, and had not had time to speak when Paulis had arrived with a rag tied around his hand.

"I'll fetch my supplies and see if I can help. Sit down by the hearth; I may need the fire to tend your hand."

The lad's face bleached white and he sank weakly onto a stool. Aurélie laughed lightly and placed a soothing hand on his shoulder. "Don't be frightened, Paulis. I use the flame to clean my tools and to warm salves. I will try to be gentle."

She went from the room in a hurry and was back quickly. She unwrapped the hand and looked at his injury. "Ah, this is not so bad. The cut will heal itself nicely, but the splinters must be removed, Paulis. They will fester otherwise. Now, you're a brave boy. Mmmm?"

"Yea, my lady. Do what you must," he said as resolutely as possible, but he swallowed convulsively.

"First, I should like it best if you watch this bowl for me.

I have to place it close to the flame to warm it, but it must not burn or boil. Can you watch the dish while my eyes are busy with your hand?"

He frowned uncertainly, his eyes unwillingly drawn to the cut and surrounding splinters. Finally he tore his eyes away and watched the dish, and Aurélie began to work.

"What were you doing, Paulis?" she asked.

"We were trimming down a plank for the wagon. The ax needed to be very sharp to plane the wood . . . and I slipped."

"You're fortunate that you did not hurt yourself any worse. Carpentry is dangerous work for one so young. Ah, there's one."

Paulis's eyes shot to his hand and Aurélie held up a splinter with the sharp point of her dagger. Paulis's eyes grew large. "I didn't even feel it."

She smiled and gestured with her eyes toward the bowl. "Do not let my salve burn or boil," she advised. She bent again to her task, dabbing away bits of blood with a rag. "Now, tell me, how many wagons do you propose to build?"

"Oh, my lady, a dozen," he said proudly. "There are several boys my age who are not needed in the fields, and Delmar promises to teach us to build many. . . . Oh!"

"Another," she said, holding a large splinter up. "Paulis, my salve."

"Yea, madame. Delmar promises to show us how to build *and* carve. In winter, when there is not planting or harvest to occupy us, if Delmar has a room in which to do his woodworking, we will learn how to do many things. And then in summer, we shall . . ." His voice trailed off as Aurélie dug for a deep splinter.

"Nearly done, Paulis. Watch my bowl, please, for I cannot."

"I do, my lady."

"Very good; now why is it you are so taken with wood? Your father works with leather, and I thought every boy of twelve wished to be a knight?"

"But my lady, a boy has to be selected as a page before he can train as a knight."

There was a long shadow thrown over her work and Aurélie turned to see Girvin behind her. The huge knight was bent at the waist, watching her pluck slivers from the boy's palm. She looked up at him with an exasperated sigh. "If you mean to stand so close to my work, Sir Girvin, you may tear this linen into strips. I will bandage Paulis's hand in a moment. I'm nearly finished."

"Nearly finished?" the boy asked.

"I told you it was not very bad. Paulis, dear, you must watch my salve. Now," she said, when he had turned his head away again. "Why is it that you cannot become a page?"

"Oh, my lady, these knights of Sir Hyatt do not need pages, and they are too busy to train any new ones. And all the pages who once served knights of de Pourvre are now working as serfs. And I am neither of the English army nor the de Pourvre troop. I would be the last to be chosen. And my grandfather says we must be grateful that we have a home at all, for the English army north of here destroyed every thing and person in its path."

"You must not accept defeat so easily, Paulis. Perhaps these knights of Hyatt can be persuaded to take you on one day."

Paulis turned bright eyes and a hopeful smile toward Aurélie. He whispered his secret. "I practice with a mock sword and lance, just in that case," he said.

"A page does not use a lance or sword," a rumbling voice interrupted.

Aurélie turned her head and glowered at Girvin. She did not think it was kind of him to dash the boy's hopes. "Paulis, my salve. Sir Girvin, the strips."

They each resumed their tasks like good lackeys. But Girvin did not hold his tongue. "A page is more set to earning the right of training through hard work. 'Tis very hard, and breaks the desire of many boys. There is the keeping of the battle gear and horses, serving the knight's table, study in the late hours of night. You have been misinformed if you think it is playing with weapons that a boy is invited to do."

Paulis looked bravely at the big knight. "I know it is hard work. I have watched the pages of Hyatt's knights and I know what they do."

"And you think you could sustain such a rugged life?"

"As easily as they do, sir knight," he said. "Also, they fix their master's pallets, mend their clothes, and shave their faces. And there is a special rite at mass they perform for the knights. I know the routine."

"Do you now? But you are slight for a lad of twelve and the armaments are heavy."

"I am not quite twelve and I am strong," Paulis said indignantly. "Besides, I am strong enough to pull a bow."

"You are? Who gave you permission to practice arms?"

He dropped his gaze. "I did not ask permission."

Aurélie reached past Paulis to lift the bowl. "I am finished with the splinters," she said gently. "A little salve on your cut and we shall bind the hand."

"It did not hurt," Paulis said happily.

Aurélie touched the boy's cheek. "I lied when I said it was not bad. It was a terrible wound and you are very brave. Now let me bandage it and you may go. But no more chores today. And tomorrow you must tell Delmar that I insist you have a less dangerous task."

Aurélie cast Girvin a damning look for baiting and insulting the boy and jerked the linen strips out of his hand. She tied the dressing and nodded her head. Paulis rose and made his way toward the door, his eyes studying the bandage.

"So happens I am looking for a page."

Paulis whirled around and stared in awe at the huge knight.

"I do not believe you are strong enough for the job, however."

"I *am*," Paulis insisted. "I swear I am! Do you mean it, truly?"

"The wagons are more important and I am too busy to train a page as yet. But on the morn after the wagons are complete, I will have need of a page. I keep my gear in the rear of the stable. Be there at dawn."

"Aye, Sir Girvin! At dawn!" Paulis hurried toward the door, but turned back. "Sir Girvin, may I tell my grandfather?"

"It is essential that you tell him. A page must have his elder's permission to serve a knight." Girvin frowned darkly. "It seems, lad, that is the thing you have trouble learning about. Permission."

Paulis beamed as if his whole life had changed for the better. "Yea, sir knight. But I will learn. And I will be the best you ever had." He fled the room and a burst of giggles could be heard on the far side of the door.

Aurélie rose from her kneeling position and sat tiredly on the stool that Paulis had occupied. She shook her head and laughed, looking up at Girvin. She pushed a wisp of hair out of her face, exhausted but pleased. "That was very generous of you, Sir Girvin. You've made the lad very proud."

"He will earn it," Girvin said. "I am not known to be tenderhearted."

"Not many know you, then," she chuckled. "Sir Girvin, you are at once the most frightening, yet most docile knight in all Christendom. Your fierceness is all for demonstration." He grunted a sour reply, but Aurélie just sighed, tired to her bones. "Does it ever seem there are not enough daylight hours?"

"Hyatt should gather more serfs to do your bidding. If he wishes a healthy child, he must not work you so hard."

Aurélie laughed. "Hyatt seldom notices my work, Sir Girvin. He does not bid me labor. Like his, it is my desire to be occupied. It takes my mind off more unpleasant things, like Mistress Faon . . . and Sir Ryland."

"That will be over soon. Lady Aurélie, I know you are already beset with more tasks than you can easily do, but there is a need I have, and you are the one I would request."

"What is it, Girvin?"

He bent and rolled down the legging over his right shin.

A gash and a bloody bruise were exposed. The wound had already festered and Aurélie gasped at the sight of it.

She stood up from the stool and with an impatient wave of her hand, requested that he sit. "When did this happen? You did not even limp."

" 'Twas days ago, and Guillaume is good in the wood, but miserable at treating injuries. He slopped some swamp muck on the cut for a poultice, and I do believe it has worsened."

"Indeed," she huffed. "Tell him for me that he need not be jealous of my healing skills. I shall gladly teach him, lest he maim some innocent soul with his ineptness."

Girvin's rumbling laughter answered her. "With pleasure, my lady. 'Tis a contest we have, to see who can fail whom."

"No doubt, but you should cease before one of you wanders about with a stump where a limb was. Why didn't you come to me straightaway? More to the point, why do you not go to the old woman in Faon's household? I hear that she is the true healer."

Girvin grunted. "I would go nowhere near Faon, even facing certain death. The old woman may be good, but she yet allies herself with the whore, and there is no way to trust her. And I could not draw you from your duties any sooner." He smiled broadly. "I liked the way you handled the boy Paulis."

Aurélie cocked her head to one side. "Your wound is dreadful and my tending will cause much pain. I will have to cut it open. Would you like to watch my salve for me, or can you bear it?"

Girvin took a deep breath. "Do your worst, Lady Aurélie. I trust your skill."

"Truly?" She shook her head and bent to the task before her. "I swear, this is a day I never anticipated."

"Forsooth, I thought you were a woman of greater faith."

She looked up at him in question, but could read nothing in the cold silver eyes. She tended the wound to the best of her ability, cutting the festered thing open, applying medicine and bandages, and finally pulling the legging up.

Girvin stood, testing the leg. "It feels like new. You missed your chance to maim me."

She sighed heavily. "Why would I do that, Girvin? Something tells me I may need you one day."

He smiled again, amusement showing all over his face and his eyes twinkling in delight. "Ah, now there is the faith I spoke of."

FOURTEEN

URÉLIE was slow to rise and was just standing before the washbasin when Hyatt was strapping on his belt, ready to leave the room. She splashed cool water on her face and sighed deeply. She moved slowly back toward the bed and rather than picking up her dress, she sat heavily.

"Aurélie? Is there something amiss?"

"Nay," she said. "I think it is the hot weather, Hyatt. I began to notice yesterday that in the afternoon heat I am not very able. I was in the garden and . . ." She sighed and looked at him. "You will surely think I've become lazy."

"Are you unwell?"

She rubbed a hand over her abdomen, which was just beginning to swell with her pregnancy. "I felt in the best of health until just the last few days."

Hyatt approached her and stooped to grasp her ankles. He lifted her legs onto the bed and she reclined obediently. "I shall ask Perrine to find at least one other woman to help you. And you, my lazy wife, shall rest more. I am anxious for another son."

She smiled and reached out to touch his hand. "You are letting your soft heart show, *seigneur*."

"Do you think I've gone soft because I speak good sense? Do not deceive yourself that you are pampered, madame. I take good care of my possessions and would no more abuse a perfectly good wife than I would ride a horse beyond its endurance. Stay abed for a day."

"Oh, Hyatt, I cannot lie abed. I would lose my mind. Especially with Ryland about. He creates mischief and I like to pass him in the hall just to see what he stirs up."

"You need not worry about Ryland much longer. His men are breaking up their camp and he prepares to leave."

"Today?"

"Aye. After the noon meal."

She took a deep breath and put her hand on her brow. "Good heavens, that's one problem solved."

"Name another you wish solved and I will do it for you."

She laughed at him, her eyes twinkling. "Oh no, Hyatt, you shall not trick me into pleading my case to you. You know my troubles well enough."

"Know them? I share some of them." He walked toward the table and picked up his gauntlets. "You need not rise to accomplish this chore. I have need of your advice. A matter has been put before me and before I give my answer, I would like your opinion. Your priest has asked for my approval for a sojourn. There is a pilgrimage to Avignon, where a conference will be held. He wishes to go."

"Father Algernon?" she questioned. "What conference is this?"

"I have no idea what meeting he speaks of, but then there is little possibility that the Church would inform me of their business. It has long been an understanding that any prelate may travel as is his like, but Algernon wishes a modest sum to pay for his journey, and he came to me."

"It seems odd, Hyatt. When does he go?"

"He says that he can meet a group of traveling monks in late August and ride with their group to the city if I release him."

Aurélie was perplexed by the request. She was not aware whether Father Algernon had asked permission for such trips from Giles, but if he had, certainly every request must have been approved. "Monks and brothers and nuns often travel at harvest time, but much of their mission is to trade summer wines and collect tithes along their path. They are smart enough to do a great deal of traveling when there are goods and money enough along the way to better their collections. You can be assured that we see few such pilgrimages before planting."

"Do they pass here?"

She nodded and her eyes became somewhat sad. "De la Noye has a reputation for being generous with such bands of prelates."

"They will be disappointed this time."

"Hyatt, do you mean to spurn them?"

"I share equally with the Church. But what I have heard is that Giles was more than equal. If you count on me to give them more than is fair, you will be disappointed as well. A kindness, shelter, shared meal, a few coins . . . my generosity has a limit, and I doubt I shall be as admired as de Pourvre was."

"I would not have them denied," she said.

"Father Algernon shares your concern. He wishes to ensure that our gates be opened to the clerics. Perhaps you should draw out your hidden silver, my lady, for I will not have this estate thrown into ruin because of the begging Church. A man cannot praise God if he dies of starvation." He looked at her scarlet cheeks. "Yea, my lady, I know you have hidden away some pittance, but I allow you that. If you think you save against my indiscretion, do so. I'm sure it was necessary with Giles."

"How long have you suspected that?"

"Since I arrived," he said with a shrug. "It is unimportant, since you do not steal from me until you attempt to take it out of De la Noye. Now that I will punish."

She frowned slightly, curious at the ease with which he accepted this. "You are no longer afraid that I shall flee?"

He smiled roguishly. "You are a stubborn woman, but not stupid. And, we have common purpose." He let his eyes drift over her reclining form, burning a lusty path from the top of her head to her bare feet. "And many common desires."

She reached obliquely and threw a small stuffed pillow at

him. "I am unwell and you bother me with your rutting ways."
He fended off the pillow easily and laughed in good humor.
He tucked his gauntlets into his belt and went to the door.
"Go lightly today, Aurélie. 'Tis my pleasure you are meant
to serve. Let the hearth go unscoured and floors unswept. I
shall tell Perrine you have need of another woman."

"Hyatt, what will you tell the priest?"

"I think I shall let him make his request again and again
before I answer. Perhaps I shall find out why this journey is
so important to him."

She smiled brightly. "That would have been my suggestion."

"Do you see?" he asked, opening the door. "We are very
much alike, except that I am not as stubborn as you."

He left then and Aurélie lounged for a moment, hugging
a pillow closely. She mused on how he spoiled her, then
pretended that he was only being wise, not indulging. There
was no mistaking the warm glow of passion in his eyes when
he studied her. And whether he took her advice or not, he
sought even her wisdom in combination with his own to
manage this castle.

She jumped in surprise as a stray castle cat jumped up on
her bed, and once recognizing the golden-furred creature as
the same one who had chased a mouse through their chamber
earlier, she gave the feline friend a gentle petting.

"Do you see how he tends to me?" she asked the cat. "Is
it true, Puss, that his horse can attest to the same comforts,
or do you think I lie gently on the harsh knight's mind? He
claims that he looks forward to another son, but when first
we met he told me it was fortunate that I was barren, for he
desired no more children." She laughed happily. "Oh, the
fierce warrior wishes to keep secret his true passions, and so
we shall allow. He does not speak the words, but I begin to
hear them just the same."

As if a cloud passed over, Aurélie's face darkened with
grimness. Her hand trembled slightly as she touched her
abdomen, for she was overcome with nausea. Her brow began

to perspire and she swallowed convulsively. When she lay very still and breathed deeply, the ill feeling began to subside slowly. It was not constant, but for nearly a week she had been plagued by spells of nausea and weakness.

She was afraid to move from the bed, although she felt better almost as quickly as she had become ill. She knew women frequently suffered with this illness early in their pregnancies, and other problems like puffiness and backaches and headaches assailed some women as their time drew near. But it was commonly believed that the time after the child had begun to stir and before the day of confinement was near was the most comfortable. She was frightened by these spells, afraid that something was wrong, that she might not bring the child to life.

The cat stirred beside her and stretched. Aurélie rubbed the cat's stomach abstractly. "Pray God I do not fail in this, since I have longed for a child. It would make my husband proud. I do not admit this to anyone but you, but I wish to make him proud. I wish to have him love me."

⊱

Aisla dallied in the garden, sniffing a flower, humming, and generally trying to keep herself far from the work. She was Thea's opposite; short, plump, dark-haired, and giggly. They looked a bit odd together, since Thea was slim and had such sharp features and reddish-gold hair and was commonly known to have a sour expression on her face.

Aisla longed for Thea's company. Faon cared nothing about tidy rooms, cleanliness, or the keeping of her clothes. The only thing that Faon was fussy about was being seductively dressed to draw Hyatt's eye, and it took no time at all to help her dress. Then Thea and Aisla were free to roam about, flirt with Hyatt's men, gambol across the fields and gardens, and play tricks on the other servants.

Aisla, at four and ten, was two years junior to Thea, but they had been like sisters since Faon collected them into her service nearly three years ago. For the first time Thea was occupied with real work, for Aurélie would not let her have

269

an idle moment. It was much easier to escape work with someone than alone. Aisla was lonely and bored.

"Aisla!"

She jumped at the sharp sound of her name. She turned to see Faon striding toward her, an irritated grimace on her face.

"There you are, you lazy whore. Here," she said, thrusting a tray of food toward Aisla. "Her royal ladyship, Aurélie, is sick abed today and I was told to have this tray of midday food delivered to her. You were nowhere to be found and I'll not wait on her myself. Take it to the lady's rooms, and mind you, do not be tempted by it yourself or you'll be beaten."

"Lady Aurélie is sick?"

"Aye, so it goes. There's a deal of fluttering and complaining and worrying about the witch when she's down. Perrine can't keep her mind on Derek and I don't have anyone else. Now you take this tray and don't you *dare* touch it. Leave it with the lady to eat at her leisure. Then you go back to my rooms and you stay there until I tell you otherwise. Now I mean to look for you; you had better mind for once or I'll slap you obedient."

Aisla curtsied nervously. "Is Sir Hyatt with her?"

"Nay, Hyatt does not care for women's troubles. He's ridden off with his men." Faon grunted derisively. "He does not even bid his own brother faretheewell. Now get on with you; I've had enough of your flighty ways."

"Aye, madame."

Aisla took the tray quickly through the hall and up the stairs. She knocked hopefully on the chamber door and grinned when Thea answered it.

"What have you got?" Thea asked.

Aisla peered past Thea into the room, seeing no one within. "I was told the lady was sick abed."

"Humph," Thea smirked. "She was for a time, and a fitful morning it was. She was in a high-flown temper about the way I'd put away her clothes and threatened me with every curse in the land. 'I don't have much, but what I have will be taken care of proper or I'll give the job to someone who can do it,' she says to me. Then she puts the little girl to teach me the task. Then she says that she'll show me how to scrub pots, since I can't take care of a lady's dresses. And then . . ."

"She does not sound sick," Aisla said.

"She does not seem sick. Not too sick to growl and curse. Then she says that if I scrub pots as bad as I clean her bedchamber I can shovel horse dung, since the good fellow who did that ran off." Thea grimaced. "I would ferry off, if this heathen place weren't so bad with soldiers."

Aisla shrugged. "What do I do with this?"

Thea thought for a moment. "She's gone up to the looms with her little brat, Baptiste. It might serve to ease up her bad temper if I take it to her. Let me." Thea took the tray from Aisla and flashed a rare smile. "When I come back, help me straighten her gowns, Aisla."

"I can't. Mistress Faon yelled at me, too. She told me to get back to her rooms and wait for her and said if I didn't, I'd get a beating." Aisla shuddered suddenly. "The whole castle's gone mad."

"At least the women," Thea agreed, closing the chamber door and walking past Aisla with the tray.

Thea walked slowly up to the next level of the castle to the room where six looms stood and several women gathered daily for weaving. She thought about what she would say and how she would win Aurélie's favor. Thea had begun to hate the lady. She was not only difficult to please, but almost daily Faon pulled Thea aside to question her about the events that took place behind Aurélie's bedchamber door, and there was nothing to tell.

There was Thea's greatest burden; she could not please either mistress. Her work was not good enough for Aurélie, and Faon was becoming more angry each day, for Thea had no conspiracies to report. She had never felt more alone.

She kicked a stray cat that had followed the smell of food

out of the way and went into the weaving room. Aurélie sat on a stool beside an active loom and pulled a piece of yarn between her finger and thumb. The cast of the lady's skin had a grayish pallor and Thea almost felt pity, for she did not look well. But then jealousy sprang up anew, for Perrine stood close by with Derek hanging onto her skirts, guarding her old mistress. Faon had fallen far from her post of importance, which put Thea farther still.

Thea checked her snappish mood and approached Aurélie. "My lady, I have brought you food. If you will not stay abed, you must at least eat."

Aurélie looked up in surprise. "How very thoughtful of you, Thea. That is a high virtue: to anticipate the needs of others."

Thea tried to smile and, holding the tray with one hand, drew back the cloth that covered the food. A cup of spiced wine and a bowl of caudled brewis emitted a luscious aroma of herbs and meat, but the lady blanched white at the sight and smell and clutched her stomach.

"Take it away, Thea. I am sorry, but I can't even abide the . . ." Her hand rose quickly to her mouth and she blinked her eyes tightly closed, fighting for control.

Perrine dashed forward, her face wrought with worry and impatience. "You heard the lady, miss. Get the stuff out of here. At once!" Perrine roughly pushed her out of the way and at once all those nearby bent over Aurélie, fussing and petting her.

Thea backed out of the room, near tears. She hated this heathen place. She had been separated from her only friend and there was no possible way to win favor. She had expected her show of concern to at least get thanks, and if not that, some demonstration of acceptance. Instead, she was treated as if she'd done something wrong. Such injustice hurt her pride and brought a new swell of anger.

She went back to Aurélie's bedchamber and plopped down on the bed in a huff. She still held the tray on her lap and the same pesty cat jumped brazenly onto the bed. "She gives me more work than I can do and doesn't care if I get a meal. No concern for the lowly servants, no thanks for what is done well, but great scorn for any minor mistake." She picked up a crust of bread from the tray and nibbled on it and the cat meowed, begging. "What's the difference; she won't touch it. I may as well have it."

Thea dipped the bread in the bowl of brewis and lifted the mug of spiced wine. She chewed ravenously, gulped the liquid to wash down her mouthful and dipped the bread again. Her spine stiffened suddenly and her features hardened in pained wonder. A searing fire spread from her throat to her stomach and her whole body was gripped in a spasm of horror. The tray fell from her lap and crashed onto the floor while Thea's hands gripped her belly and she rolled back onto the bed, groaning in a vicious and sudden agony. But the pain was short-lived and her limbs relaxed as she lay still.

⚬❦⚬

Aurélie swayed slightly on the stool and Perrine caught her shoulders.

"This is such foolery, madame. There is little sense in pretending you are not ill. You must heed Hyatt and go back to bed."

Aurélie recovered herself and tried to sit upright. "This is so difficult for me to understand, Perrine. What is this strange illness that comes and goes? Will I lose this child that I carry?"

"Thus far you have had no trouble carrying the babe and 'tis my thinking that you've had a piece of bad food and it will pass. How can you hope to recover from this spell if you do not rest? Come back to your bed and let me fix you a balm."

"Perhaps you are right. But you will have to find something for Thea to do outside of my chamber, for the girl tests my wrath. I went in search of a wrapper this morn and found my clothes stuffed into the coffer, nothing laundered, folded, mended, or even put in its proper place." She sighed. "I thought to give her my clothing to keep would be the simplest chore." Baptiste touched Aurélie's shoulder and the latter looked up at her with grateful eyes. "And this little one works so hard to cover Thea's laziness."

"Come along, my lady," Perrine urged. "To bed."

Aurélie nodded in assent, a look of defeat on her drawn features. She stood and took a step and the room immediately began to sail around her in a wild spinning motion. Her sense of balance was gone and her stomach lurched in wretched nausea. She stumbled and swooned, and Perrine caught her.

"Lay her down here and get a blanket and pillow." With the help of the other women they rested Aurélie on the floor. There were several women present and much fluttering about made for a chaotic scene while they fashioned a pallet for their mistress. Aurélie closed her eyes until the room stilled somewhat and she felt safe in opening them. Perrine knelt on the floor beside her. "We shall not attempt the stairs, lass. You lie here until a strong man able enough to carry you can be found."

"Perrine . . . I am afraid. What if I should lose the child?"

"None of that, sweetheart. You lie still and let me take care of you. All will be well."

"Perrine," she whimpered. "Don't . . . forget Derek. He could fall down the stairs or hurt himself on a loom."

No sooner did Aurélie mention the lad than she noticed him crouched on the floor right beside her. He looked at her most curiously, as if he could not understand the reason for a woman to lie supine on the floor. He reached out a chubby little hand to touch her wimple.

"Baptiste," Perrine instructed. "Take Derek out of —"

"Let him stay, Perrine. He does no harm and he must stay with you. Should Faon see him with Baptiste, she will seize the moment for some trickery." Aurélie smiled up into Perrine's eyes. "We both need you at the moment."

From a safe, concealed position in the wood, Hyatt watched his brother's group leave and travel down the road away from De la Noye. The distance was too great to make out small details, but the number of people, horses, and carts could be seen. And the road that Ryland had chosen was due west, as if he traveled to Bordeaux, but there was a crossroad a few miles farther that he could take toward Innesse, if he chose. Guillaume was watching from the small camp he and Girvin had made. The two men had spent many days and nights in their hidden copse, but on this mission Girvin was with Hyatt.

"If they choose the road to Innesse, Guillaume will see them?"

"Yea, Hyatt, though it amazes me that they still travel that road and do not creep through the trees to do their meeting. It seems brazen and foolish to me."

"Did you instruct the guards at the gate to search Ryland's carts?"

Girvin smiled. "Ryland will not take anything out of De la Noye that you will miss."

Hyatt looked over his shoulder at Girvin. "Do you think she has gone with him?"

Girvin shrugged. "My orders to your men were very clear; they will let Mistress Faon escape, but not the boy. You can see that no woman travels with them. If she has gone, she dresses like a page or squire."

An oddly placed look of disappointment crossed Hyatt's features. "Why would she escape me when I have offered her so much? I would pay her fare, give her protection on her journey, and buy her a decent lodging. Yet she would *flee?* Disguised?" He shook his head. "I admit that I do not understand women."

"There has been much whispering, Hyatt, that she found a warm place in Ryland's bed. If she goes away with him in some disguise to keep you from seeing her depart, it can only mean she plots against you now. She hoped for a long time that you would come to her side one day, but when you wed the lady, Faon lost her greatest wish."

"But she knows the reason. She admitted that she played me false, but I was generous. I accepted my own part in being made a fool and would not give her another opportunity to use me."

"You may not have given her the chance, Hyatt," Girvin grumbled. "But she saw her chance when you took a liking to your son. You should have removed the boy from her at once."

Hyatt was mute. That Girvin was right brought him no satisfaction. A small boy needs a mother's love, and Hyatt had hoped that Faon would be a satisfactory mother even if she could not be a good wife or mistress.

"If we find the woman still waiting at De la Noye, I shall begin making plans for her departure. But I think we are too hopeful, Girvin. She does not appear to be finished with me yet. I suppose she waits even now with some plan meant to trap me and bring me back to her."

The troop that Ryland led was over the farthest knoll when Hyatt turned his small party about and led them back to De la Noye. Their passage was unhurried and some game that was spotted along the way was speared or shot from the bow. The sun was setting its path to rest before the gates were in sight, and Hyatt felt a ravenous hunger. He looked forward to his first relaxing evening in his own hall since Ryland's arrival. He had let his brother stay for over a month, which was far longer than he had intended.

He dismounted just inside the wall so that a page could take his steed and was just pulling off his gauntlets when the crouched figure of the old woman who served Faon came rushing toward him.

"Messire, messire, I did not know what she would do . . . and now the lady is ill and no one will let me help. *Seigneur,* you must let me tend your lady. Only I can save her."

"What is this?"

"Faon, Sir Hyatt. I have searched everywhere, but she has stolen my herbs, my roots. I cannot find Faon to question her, and she alone would be so bold as to take those medicines that I mix. 'Twas poison, Sir Hyatt." The old woman twisted her hands and shuddered. "And Lady Aurélie is ill. I fear Faon has tried to kill her."

Hyatt grasped the old woman by the arms and nearly shook her, but her frail, withered body felt like brittle sticks in his hands. "What do you say? Where is Faon?"

"My most dangerous herbs are missing and Faon may know their use, for we have talked about my medicines. And I cannot find her, but the lady is ill and cannot be moved."

"Where is Lady Aurélie?"

"In the weaving rooms, milord. Her woman won't have her moved."

"And you know the remedy?"

"If there is a remedy, messire, I could find it. I could purge her of the poison. That she is not dead means she did not have much. But they won't accept my offer of help. The women won't let me near her."

"Come with me," Hyatt barked, taking the old woman's arm. He dragged her toward the hall and within just a moment he was aggravated with her slow pace. Without releasing her, he grabbed a mare that was being led to stable and heaved the old woman on the horse's back. He took the reins and ran in a panicked stride, the ancient woman holding onto the mane for dear life.

When they reached the hall he helped Nima down and dragged her through the doors and up the stairs. "You cannot find Faon?"

"She is nowhere, messire," Nima huffed.

"My son?"

"With the woman Perrine and your lady."

"Did Faon tell you what she would do?"

"She hates your lady wife, messire. She is torn with jealousy and asked me to mix a brew that would kill her, but I refused." Nima gasped for breath. "You must believe that I refused."

Hyatt reached the second level, and the old woman slumped, already exhausted. He looked at her with a frown of impatience.

"I can go on, messire. We must see to your wife."

Hyatt pulled her along and finally reached the weaving rooms, throwing open the doors. Hyatt went straight to the pallet where Aurélie lay and knelt down beside her.

"Oh Hyatt, I am sorry. I am ill."

"Your stomach? Your head?"

"A fearful weakness, and each time I try to rise, the room spins round and round. I cannot walk for fear of falling."

"We did not try to carry her down the stairs, Sir Hyatt," Perrine informed him. "And this old woman has pestered us the day long."

"Perhaps she can help. Did you not listen to her?"

Hyatt turned and regarded Nima, who stepped cautiously closer. Nima's brow was furrowed in confusion. "The poison is quick and frightful, messire. Perhaps that is not the lady's malady. Let me look at her, I beg you."

Hyatt scooped his wife up in his arms and carried her to the door. "Come to my chamber and have a look. Perrine, come along and watch this old woman, lest she trick me somehow."

Hyatt carried Aurélie down the stairs. She looped her arms around his neck and laid her head on his shoulder. "Why are you so hard on the old woman? What is this business of poison?"

"Faon is nowhere to be found and the old woman claims that her most dangerous herbs and roots are missing. She fears you have been poisoned by Faon."

"But that's absurd. What poison causes one to be dizzy? And I have suffered with this strange ailment for days."

"I thought I ordered you to bed."

"I tried, Hyatt. I cannot abide such." She held him closely. "Hyatt, if I fail to bring your child to life, will you hate me?"

He stopped in midstride just before his chamber door. "Hate you, Aurélie? I know you would not purposely end the very life you have longed for. Not even to spite me. Stop such talk."

Hyatt stood still for a moment and moved out of the way so that Perrine could open the chamber door. She gasped at the sight within, frozen in shock. Hyatt, too, was immobile, for there lay Thea on the bed, motionless, and on the floor by the bed were the spilled remains of a tray of food and beside that, the dead body of a cat. Aurélie tried to lift her head to see, but any movement caused her senses to reel. "What is it, Hyatt?"

Nima pushed through them though they blocked the door. She alone had the courage to look at the corpse. Thea's face was twisted in agony, her eyes open and her palms facing up. The cat lay stiff and cold on the floor and the wine and brewis had stained the rushes.

"This is the work of my poison," Nima said. "Thea brought this tray to Aurélie, but my lady refused it. She could not abide even the aroma."

Nima turned watering eyes toward Hyatt, who still stood in the doorway. "Messire, this is the work of my granddaughter. Yea, Faon is of my flesh, though she kept it secret. She was twisted with bitterness and hate. I beg you to believe that I would not do such a thing. My mixes have always been for healing only, and not for death."

"Then how do you explain possessing dangerous mixings, if not to use them?"

"It is many years of mixing and testing that I have endured to find the best of this and that. A certain root mixed with a certain vine can cure the flux, but the same root mixed with another plant can kill. 'Tis a mysterious occupation. The same potion that will draw pus from a wound and help it to heal will kill if swallowed. But I give my potions to stray animals to be assured they are not harmful and some of my strongest liniments have healed an aching back, but killed a rat. I have never meant to harm anyone, but Faon made me keep my talents mostly secret. I have been wrongly accused of witchcraft."

"She was your granddaughter, then? And you lied when you said you were her nurse."

"I am her grandmother and her nurse. I helped to raise her. Montrose threatened to have me tried and killed for sorcery, but I was only a healer, never a witch. Anyone who came to ill after my ministrations was not hurt by them, I swear. Faon protected me."

"To have your witchcraft at her disposal, no doubt."

Nima's face fell. "You are right, *seigneur*. She wished to have me mix brews that would be useful to her . . . but I did not. Betimes I told her something would work, but I tricked her and never gave her anything that would do any harm. I am an old woman. I have to have a means to live."

"Hyatt?" Aurélie murmured. "What do I hear? Thea is dead by Faon's hand?"

"It seems that Faon meant to kill you, madame. You had better tell me what you've eaten."

"Naught, Hyatt. The last I ate was beside you in the hall, from the same plate. We drank from the same pitcher. Poor Thea; is it too late?"

"Aye," he said. He glanced briefly at Perrine and then turned with Aurélie in his arms, taking her back to the pallet in the weaving rooms rather than to a room befouled with death.

"Hyatt, bring the old woman to me. I have heard she is skilled. I will do anything to save this child I carry. Anything."

He laid his wife down and looked at her through pained eyes. "You are young, Aurélie. If this child does not live, you will have another in a year. But without you, there cannot be another. 'Tis your life I would save."

Aurélie lifted her hand and touched his brow as if she would smooth away the lines of worry. She knew not how pale her face was, how dull her eyes, how weak her touch. She did feel that her sickness worsened. "Hyatt, my besotted knight, how poorly you conceal your heart when you are met with some crisis." He looked away uncomfortably. " 'Tis of no matter, the words. You need not speak them. But know you this, lest even the old woman cannot help me. I love you."

FIFTEEN

perceive that I am not gravely ill, but beset by some temporary difficulty and must see it through," Aurélie told Hyatt. When Thea's body had been removed, a brigade of women had entered Hyatt's chamber and scoured the place from floor to ceiling. A new mattress stuffed with freshly cut, sweet-smelling grass replaced the old one, which was swiftly burned, even though the death that had befouled it was wrought of poison and not plague. It came as no surprise to find all the castlefolk of De la Noye to be concerned about their mistress, for it was well known they loved her. But fully panoplied warriors wearing the red and black of Hyatt clamored about, restless for any chore that would somehow aid the lady. When Hyatt selected one hulking lad to take Thea's body from his chamber, the young knight did so eagerly, as if chosen for some elite position. Only a few hours had elapsed when Aurélie had been returned to her bed, her room, and despite Hyatt's worried frown, Nima sat at her side.

"I do not feel well," she said, "but neither do I prepare to die. A few days of peace and rest will do me well enough. Especially with Faon and Ryland both gone from my house." She smiled weakly. "Your house," she whispered, closing her eyes.

Hyatt meant to sit at her sickbed, perched on the edge and holding her hand, but after an hour of this Aurélie protested.

"There is nothing you can do, messire. Seek a pallet of your own. Or lie here beside me and sleep."

"I would stay, Aurélie. I do not wish to sleep and I am best placed watching over you."

"Though Faon wished me harm, this ailment is not wrought of her evil hand, but the hand of fate. I will recover. No one else here means me harm. These are my friends. Go about your business and come to me when I am well."

Thus he was rousted from the sickroom and left meandering about the hall and grounds without his mind, for his thoughts were in his chamber with his wife. His gaze was faraway, his steps errant and unguided, and his attention difficult to draw.

Percival approached him. "Sir Hyatt, is there anything my family can do for the lady?"

"Nay, Percival. It is best that we all leave her be for now. She needs rest."

A knight who had ridden with Hyatt for six years sought him out. "The word passes through your troop that Lady Aurélie is ill, Sir Hyatt. She has always been kind to us; is there a way to help her now?"

Hyatt smiled with a touch of melancholy. "There remains some doubt that I have completely conquered this castle, but I see the lady has quelled my troop. Nay, there is nothing to do but hope that she recovers quickly."

As the sun set and the hall emptied after the evening meal, Hyatt was without purpose. He could not find a comfortable place to roost, and he chose not to disturb his wife's rest. He would have preferred a place at her side, but the old woman sat near and he would find no sleep with a spectator.

He tried the chamber that had been Giles's and now housed ten men-at-arms, but could not abide their undisturbed snores. He tried the stable, seeking work to ease his tension, but both the animals and serfs protested with grunts and snorts at such an ill-planned venture in the dead of night. He walked the wall, finding his guard ever alert and awake, for those hearties took their chores seriously, but Hyatt was not in want of conversation, so this did not suit him either. And of course his distressed presence and wakefulness bore out the proof that he was plagued with worry over a woman.

The setting moon had begun its downward path to yield to dawn and he had not blinked even once with sleep. He crept to the chamber where Aurélie lay and opened the door with all the silence of a thief. He moved quietly toward the bed and stood looking down at her peaceful face. In sleep there was nothing to indicate the tortures of fear or illness. Her hands were relaxed at her sides and her eyelids did not even flutter. He turned his head toward Nima, whose weak gray eyes glittered slightly by the light of a single candle.

"You do not sleep?" he asked in a whisper.

"A curse of old age, *seigneur,* is that one sleeps but little."

"Old woman, will my wife die?"

"Nay, messire. The child moves in her womb, and her rest is peaceful. This illness need little concern you; I cannot say what plagues my lady, but I think that rest, food, and peace of mind will see her fit in a short time. You need not fear."

"Would you harm her, old woman? I would kill you if you . . ."

Nima slowly shook her head. "Sir knight, I tried in vain to help my granddaughter. I prayed to the saints and gave her good counsel. I did not have the courage to betray her to you, but now she is gone, and if I can undo but one of her wrongs, I shall be satisfied."

"I fail to understand why you seek to win my favor by helping my wife now. You do not know her goodness as I do; you do not owe her good service as I do."

Nima smiled patiently. "You are wrong, my lord. She will raise up my great-grandson and by her love he will be as strong and powerful as you. I owe her a great deal. And I will not rest until she is well."

"Derek . . . ?"

"Do you think your success in life has been born of the pain of your father's betrayal? Do you think you were driven only by hate?" Nima laughed softly, a cracked chuckle of an old hag. "I know your sad story. Perhaps you are strong because a good woman once loved you. Perhaps Derek will thrive on this lady's love. I know she is capable of it."

"If that is so, old woman, explain Ryland's evil. He was more coddled and protected in childhood than I. He had much of our mother's devotion, for he was sickly when he was small."

Nima smiled tolerantly and reached out a crooked, withered hand to touch Hyatt's. Her whisper was strained. "Ryland is still sickly and small. It is a pitiful waste when one does not accept one's gifts. Faon did not accept all the good that befell her, but demanded more. She would never have been pleased with her life, and she will not find pleasure now, though she seeks it with a miser's zeal. Had she been a virtuous maid, seeking to do good and not evil, she would be a proper lady now.

"I am glad for you that you have taken everything that was given to you. You made use of all that came your way and did not cast one gift onto the waste heap. You took mother's love and let it make you strong. You took your father's betrayal and let it firm your strength with determination. You took the bastard child into your keeping and let him know your loyalty, though I know you saw his conception as one of your mistakes. You even pitied poor Faon and allowed her too much tolerance, but I think you have made good use of even the gift of her treachery, for she showed you a way to judge the worth of a mate.

"Go about your duties to keep this precious jewel safe, Sir Hyatt. I shall guard her for you."

Hyatt looked down at Aurélie. Her lips were parted slightly in sleep, her breathing slow and easy. He stooped and touched his lips lightly to hers.

He made to pass the old woman, placing a hand on her shoulder as he did so. "Make her well, old woman. I need her."

Hyatt went to the stable again, but this time he did not seek work to occupy him. Instead he found a change of clothing and some light gear and woke Girvin. Knowing there was nothing he could do in his own bedchamber to make Aurélie well, he sought an escape from the oppressive fear that she would not rise. He gave Girvin the command of his house and learned the way to Guillaume's camp from the older knight.

No horse could manage the way to the secluded place that Guillaume and Girvin had occupied for better than a month and Hyatt walked through ten hours of the heat of day. Dark clouds that promised a drenching storm gathered in the west, and the lightning in the distance brightened the graying sky with intermittent flashes.

There was a break in the trees and brush, and silhouetted against the purple-orange sky was the tall, broad-shouldered figure of Guillaume, standing on the path fifty paces in front of him. The older man smiled. "You're in luck, Sir Hyatt. The storm will drive in a thousand renegades and wild beasts, and we can enjoy the warmth of a fire."

Guillaume turned and led the way up a brush- and tree-covered hill, along a steep and winding path to a shallow cave. All the comforts of a long established camp lay behind the bushes that concealed the opening. The first large drops of rain began to patter down onto their heads as they entered and Hyatt sank gratefully onto a pallet of skins. Guillaume passed him a wineskin and worked at starting a fire while Hyatt eased the tensions of the trek, the fear, and the exhaustion.

"You are not the man I expected, Sir Hyatt."

"Nor did I think to see your camp, Guillaume. I had need to be away from De la Noye. My lady, your mistress, is sick abed and I cannot abide the role of nursemaid." He shrugged lamely. "I am unable to make any sound decision as to her care, so I left her in the hands of my betters."

"How has she come ill?"

"I thought at first that it was by some evil hand, but it appears that it is the simple work of fate, and not an enemy." Hyatt related the story of Faon's attempt to poison Aurélie, the fate of Thea, and Faon's disguised departure from De la Noye with Ryland.

But his conversation with Guillaume did not end with the events of the past few days. Rather, he talked on about himself as though the whole of his life were burning a hole in his gut and the time to expel the demon was at hand. Guillaume as a chosen confessor was an odd choice, or perhaps not so odd, since the seneschal was both devoted to Aurélie and one of the few men Hyatt knew who was not familiar with all the events of his life.

"Lord Lavergne allied himself with the English and traveled to a conference with King Edward when the Prince of Wales was forming and collecting his armies for this siege. He bemoaned the state of his daughter's life with the Sire de Pourvre and asked that if De la Noye would be conquered, Lady Aurélie would be spared. Yet she mourned Giles grievously, as if he were a great lord."

"He was a good lad," Guillaume said. "Not all men are born to be kings and lords."

"I have not understood why she loved him so," Hyatt confessed. "I did not travel here with the notion to kill him and wed his widow, but the events made that solution the best for all, including her. I believe that, Guillaume."

"I think it is true," the seneschal said, a grave concession on his part.

"Explain her devotion to Giles. I must understand that."

Guillaume chuckled low in his throat and tipped the wineskin. The rain collected at the orifice of the cave and ran in little rivers into the enclosure, but did not dampen the men or douse the rare fire.

"Why is it necessary to understand her devotion to her dead husband, Hyatt? Like all men, Giles did what he thought was best. If he misspent his life, he did so in innocence, for Sir Giles was not wicked. If he was weak, it was because he could not be strong. He did not abuse her, unless it was abusive for him to wed her though he did not want a wife.

He did the best he could." Guillaume shrugged. "His best was not much."

"His reverence for Christ should have given him strength."

"Perhaps it did. He did go to battle."

"But . . ." Hyatt stopped himself. He would not divulge the secrets of the battle.

Guillaume did not press Hyatt for those details. "You must understand, Hyatt, that for Giles to don his mail and take up his shield required more courage from him than you need to face one hundred strong, skilled, armed knights. Giles was a coward. But he tried harder than any coward I have ever known. At least he did not creep up to the backs of his opponents and strike from behind, as many cowards do."

"Did he love her?" Hyatt asked.

Guillaume smiled wistfully. "He worshiped her, placing her above all other women. He believed that God had given him an angel to guide his errant step and protect him from himself. Indeed, as the Sire de Pourvre stumbled, Aurélie spread her angel's wings and shielded him from the slurs of those who were stronger or wiser. She never chastised him for his weaknesses, nor did she criticize his failures. I never heard a complaint from her lips, never saw her look in his direction with scorn. I was not so strong. I rose in fury when Giles squandered too much on the Church and left us short of necessary supplies. My lady cautioned me to be silent and promised that we would make do as we always had, but she would not blame Giles.

"Love her? Perhaps not in the way other men love their women. He praised her for her loyalty, her fortitude. He envied her, for he believed she was stronger and wiser than himself. Once he said to me, 'I know not why God set me to the task of keeping this precious flower, for I do not deserve the right, but when the purpose is known to me, I shall rejoice and give thanks.' "

Guillaume looked at Hyatt with sentiment misting his eyes. He shrugged. "It was Giles's way to believe everything came from the Father. He had many failings, Sir Hyatt, and I know he did not keep my lady well, but there is one thing of Giles that I respect and admire. If he lies in his grave now and knows that his enemy has taken his land, his woman, and his life, but that there is good rising out of the flames of his demise, he will praise it and give thanks. That was his way."

Hyatt looked hard into Guillaume's old eyes. "Did she love him?"

"She did him honor as his wife and never failed him, to my knowledge. Love? That secret is locked in the lady's heart."

"I would know."

"To know the answer to that you will have to exhume her husband's bones, lay them before her, and ask that she denounce the duty she once paid him. And . . . the truth, that she loved him true, or that she loved him not at all but paid homage to her duty as a wife, will not change what she feels today. I think it would be foolish of you."

Hyatt dropped his gaze to the flames.

"You could ask her, but not before you are willing to tell the secrets of your own heart."

Hyatt's eyes bolted upright and there was anger in them. Gradually, the anger ebbed and his brown eyes softened. He reached for the skin, drinking deeply of the red wine.

"We sound like two doddering dowagers, trying to grip the strings that bind a heart or mind; or worse, two old troubadours, too tired and withered to chase our maids, so yet we sing of the entrapment of their musk." Hyatt drank again. "What good are all such words of promise? What becomes of these boyish words of love once they are all spoken? Bah! Let the poets say the words. A man must live by his actions."

Guillaume laughed good-naturedly at Hyatt's surly protest. " 'Tis well that your king did not feel so when he extracted his oath from you. That is the good of the words, young man. If you can both say them and live by them, then you are fully a man. To act without promise or to promise without action, these are the boyish whims of one who cannot voice his commitment because he fears he cannot keep it."

Hyatt was mute. He picked up a piece of dried meat that lay by the fire, chewed it thoughtfully, and washed it down with another swallow of wine.

"Take your time, young man," Guillaume advised. "Lady Aurélie is no whimsical lass, and she is wiser than most women. She will not whisper her feelings to you until they live in her heart, and she will not wish to hear your tender oaths until you can live them as well as say them."

Hyatt kept silent, but his mind was afire with the words. *But she has spoken the words. I would not, he thought, lie to her in a hasty moment and make a mockery of what I felt. But upon my return to De la Noye it would be truth to tell her that without her at my side, my life is over.*

"Sleep, Hyatt," Guillaume instructed as the fire began to die. "It is usually foolish to try to form the words before you hold the woman in your arms. When you return to the castle to find her risen and in health will be soon enough for that. Then, if you cannot speak of love, perhaps you can tell her how you depend on her life."

❧

Ryland and his troop of nearly fifty made their camp in a clearing, for Ryland was ill at ease in a war-torn country. It was fortunate that the worst of the English aggressors was his friend.

"You must have a great deal to tell your friend about De la Noye, after a month within her walls," Faon said.

"Aye, and what I have to tell is that she is nearly impregnable."

"Nonsense. Does not this fierce knight to whom we travel have war machines? Battering rams? The peasants huts are all thatched with dry grass, and mud and fire arrows would . . ."

"You are misinformed, Faon. I do not wish to oust my brother at the cost of the castle. I want the burg, the hall, and the . . ." Ryland's voice trailed off. It was enough for

Faon to know that he meant to have Hyatt's possessions. "The only killing will be of Hyatt's men."

"Then it is impossible. You will never take it."

"Oh . . . I think it is possible. I have a plan. One that Hollis will admire."

"If this Hollis is so treacherous, so bloodthirsty, how do you trust him?"

Ryland laughed. "There is one thing Hollis likes better than spilling blood. Money! I shall pay him a handsome *pâtis* for his protection. And I shall take the fruitful castle and make myself both rich and influential. The king will be pleased."

Faon laughed openly. "Pleased? That you have taken your brother's demesne when the king himself sent Hyatt to De la Noye? Are you truly so foolish?"

Ryland leaned closer to Faon. "You misunderstand, madame. Hollis will kill Hyatt, and I shall step into De la Noye, negotiate for the fair treatment of the prisoners, save the burg to produce for England and Prince Edward, and roust the heathen, sending Hollis home to his own conquered lands. It will look as if I am more clever than Hyatt, for I shall be able to deal with Hollis without further bloodletting."

"And save the prisoners. Humph! There is nothing amongst that useless bunch worth saving."

Ryland looked skyward. "There are a few hardworking souls. And one very beautiful lady."

Faon's eyes shot to Ryland's face. "You, too, Ryland?"

"What do you ask? Hyatt had both wife and mistress, and yet his men held him in the highest esteem. Where is the problem? With me, you will not be driven to some low position of scorn while the great lady rules over the dominion. Nay, you shall have the authority of one who shares my bed, and she shall yet serve my whim, as well as she did his."

Faon's eyes were round with disbelief. Suddenly her gaping mouth formed a smile, then her white teeth gleamed and she was torn with wild laughter, loud and haunting.

"Shut up, wench," Ryland cautioned. "Do you mean to draw the wolves on us?"

"Forgive me, Ryland," she chuckled, finding it difficult to contain her mirth. "I did not know you desired the bitch."

"I do not desire her, but if she paid such loyal homage to Hyatt, she will pay better to me, for all the years that . . ."

Faon continued to chuckle, tears wetting her cheeks. But she shook her head. "She cannot, Ryland. She is dead." Ryland sat in a stupor. "I took Nima's poisons and fixed her food. I poisoned her. The bitch is dead."

Ryland stared at Faon in a wonder of disbelief. His features hardened and his eyes took on a glitter of rage. He raised his hand and slapped Faon so hard that she reeled backward, her face bruised and her lip cut. Ryland was on his feet looking down at her. "You ignorant whore! Don't you *ever* take action out of my authority again!"

Faon raised herself on one elbow, rubbing her cheek with her other hand and looking up at the tall figure who stood before her. "You *valued* her? But —"

Ryland kicked her in the stomach with all his might, and she tightened into a moaning ball, gripping her middle. "Stupid bitch. How dare you mete out your vengeance on my possession."

She looked up at him again, tears of pain smarting in her eyes. "You said you would take care of me," she choked out.

"I will take care of you, dearest. I will make a gift of you to Hollis, and then you shall know your betters." Ryland whirled away, his cape swirling, one hand flying into the other in a series of angry punches. "Insolent, bumble-headed slut. I'd kill you if you couldn't bring a good price."

Faon stared at him in wonder, her insides splitting with both physical pain and the anguish of truth. She knew it was over for her now, for Hyatt would kill her for what she'd done, and now Ryland had proven to be worse than the devil she had heard he was. How had she been so ignorant as to believe him? And the worst was yet to come, for she would be given to Sir Hollis for his entertainment, unless she could get away. At the moment, the only escape lay in the deep woods where hungry wolves roamed.

She laid her head down on the damp earth and sobbed, for all of her life every opportunity she had ever seized died a cruel death before she could achieve anything of comfort.

Hyatt awoke to the sound of animals rising in the wood. The birds chirped, squirrels ran up the trees, deer fed on the sweet grass by the brooks. The rain had left glistening gems on the moss and grass, and the sky was clear and beautiful.

Hyatt stayed through the day, hunting and fishing with Guillaume, and their conversation was less than the night before. There was no downpour of rain to cover the voices of men deep in the wood and they moved about stealthily. Hyatt had hoped to spy some soldiers or scavengers on the road, but as the sun set on the day it appeared there was no one else in the forest.

They did not enjoy a fire at night, for Guillaume would not chance drawing anyone toward his secret camp. They shared the skin of wine and at dawn's light Hyatt prepared to leave the cave to make his way back to De la Noye. The two men stood on the path below the hill together.

"I should thank you for making me welcome," Hyatt said.

"You left the game you killed." Guillaume shrugged. "That is thanks enough."

"Then I thank you for good advice. It is obvious you have raised sons."

Guillaume smiled and held out a hand in friendship. "I did so with the help of a good woman, Sir Hyatt. Tell my lady I wish her well . . . and tell her we shall best these devils who mean us harm."

Hyatt took the proffered hand. "She will be glad to hear it, Sir Guillaume."

"God's speed, lad. Safe journey."

As the sun rose in the sky, Hyatt moved resolutely toward De la Noye. He felt as if a decade had passed since he left. It was not possible so much of his mind could be changed in fewer than three days in the deep forest. Yet it had.

He shared very few qualities with the Sire de Pourvre, but yet there were certain things he was beginning to understand about the peculiar young lord whose demesne Hyatt had conquered. Hyatt, too, believed that very few things were coincidence. And as Nima had given voice to his thoughts, he had taken everything life had offered him and made something out of it all, the bad and the good.

Hyatt had enjoyed the flirtations of many a woman over the years, yet never had an English maid tarried on his mind for the whole of a day. On campaign in Crécy and Calais he had fallen to the subtle seductions of French demoiselles, but even then he did not find anything to bind him. But upon entering this captured castle he felt his desire stirred the very first moment he saw the widowed mistress. Even though the marriage was a sound negotiation and Hyatt believed marriage was business, he would not have wed the woman had he not desired her. He had been suspicious of his strong feelings, at first believing it was poorly timed lust. But as the days grew into weeks and the weeks became months his desire for her grew apace with his trust in her wisdom and loyalty. Everything he did and said had a purpose that was directly meant to keep secure the home and the wife he now possessed.

And none of this could have been without the many sad coincidences that had led him to the council room of King Edward and the Prince of Wales. His prowess in battle directly resulted from the necessity to prove himself to the father who would disown him. Had all the difficulties of his life been planned, that he would make himself worthy for this?

My God, I love her, he thought. *I'd sooner lose my arm or my eye than be without her. And she loves me. Is it desperate we are to become because of it, or strong?* He laughed aloud in the woods. *If it is weakness love brings, why do I feel as though I could kill a wild boar with my bare hands? And if love truly blinds a man to a woman's treachery, then why could I never love*

Faon, even when I wished to? And while I tried to keep myself from loving Aurélie, she proved gentle and devoted. I drew myself the conqueror when, in fact, she conquered me.

He walked on, amazed at the beauty of the day and the joy in his heart. He was eager to be again at her side, no longer in fear that her illness might rob him of something dear, but anxious to speak these words at least once, lest she leave him through some cruel trick of fate without hearing from his own lips what he felt.

And indeed, everything felt different. He would henceforth enter battles and contests with a new reason to fight hard — his lands and his family. His life was no longer just empty pride, but pride in what he called his own. He no longer had to prove his worth to an embittered old man who would disclaim him, but to himself, that he could feel deserving of what he now held. He thought of what he could teach Derek and the children to follow about his life, about pride, about the principles that made a man whole.

His pace was quick, though the wood was thick. He cut back shrubs and vines with his stoutest blade, moving relentlessly toward his home as if he moved toward a new life.

A twig snapped and he paused, his neck stiff and his head turning like a great stag that sniffs man. He ventured on with a softer step and beyond him the brush rustled. With the stealth of a cat he crouched and pulled a short-handled ax from his belt. With ax in one hand and hunting knife in the other, he slowly turned in a complete circle, but saw nothing. He took another step and without a sound to warn him, his arms were pulled around to his back and though he struggled, he was firmly held from behind.

They let themselves be seen, stepping out from behind trees, bushes, and rising from the knee-deep brush. It was a ragged group of makeshift warriors and thieves, obviously such because of their lack of knightly garb. They wore leather jerkins, rudely fashioned fur boots, and they brandished roughly honed weapons. A dozen such men circled Hyatt, their eyes hungry for a fight. And then Verel stepped onto the path before him.

"What luck!" The young knight laughed. "I could not have dared wish for so much. I thought I would never find you outside of your strong walls. The walls you stole from another."

"And so, Verel, this is what you've become. Do you kill me while your friend holds my arms?"

"Yea." Verel smiled. "And it will feel so good."

Hyatt smiled mirthlessly. "Perhaps you can boast of the fact to Lady Aurélie."

Verel's superior grin faded. "She would thank me."

"Would she? Even now, as she carries my child?"

"You lie! She is barren!"

"Nay, Verel. Nor was she ever. The Sire did not make her his wife. I did."

"Lies!" Verel let his fist fly into Hyatt's stomach with such force that Hyatt bit his lip and a drop of blood dripped from his mouth.

"Ask her," Hyatt said in a breath.

Verel stepped back away from Hyatt and drew a sword from his belt, the very one that had been stolen for him.

" 'Twould be the easier way, Sir Verel. Once I am dead, no one need ever question which of us is stronger. You may say it was you."

"It is I, my lord fool, for you are the one captured now."

"Aye, it is you, with the help of ten men."

"Do you taunt me with *honor?* This is no tourney or contest for the king. This is the wood, where men live and die by their quickness and wits. And you, Sir Fool, have stumbled into my land."

"So I have. But if you have fallen so far from honor, you cannot blame me, for I did not drive you away from the chivalry of knights. I took you in fair battle." Hyatt smiled lazily. "Aurélie said you were the best knight — strong, honorable, good. She will be disappointed."

Verel stood motionless for a long moment. Hyatt eyed the group. They varied in age and strength. A young golden-haired lad with thin arms and hollow eyes held his wooden pike weakly. A man of forty years with thick arms and a heavy beard wielded a monstrous broadsword with finesse. All of these, Hyatt assumed, were driven into the forest to save themselves from one enemy or another.

But they all watched Verel. Aurélie must have been right about Verel, for he had become the leader of this group, as he had in Giles's troop. Where the young man traveled, whether in groups of thieves and scavengers, or with honorable soldiers, he made himself leader. A man had to have something to offer to become revered so quickly.

Hyatt eyed the young man warily. "I await your pleasure, Sir Forest Knight. I would give you a fair fight, left unbound."

Verel stood his ground, his cheeks pulsing, his blue eyes glittering with hate. Hyatt smiled at his rage. The boy would be a worthy knight, if it were possible.

Verel turned abruptly, issuing no command, but his silent orders were followed, and Hyatt was dragged from that heavily shielded piece of woods down a long and dense path to a place where there was a small clearing. He espied the camp, four tethered horses, only the one stolen from De la Noye boasting a saddle. Verel had not even spoken to these ragged men, but they followed his orders as ably as Hyatt's trained knights would. A bit of respect for his opponent began to rise in Hyatt.

Verel stood, legs braced apart, sword in hand, and a feral gleam in his eyes. "Loose him."

Hyatt was immediately released and stood for a moment, still gripping his ax and knife, but his arms were numb from being dragged through the forest so tightly gripped.

"Is it our contest, Verel? Or do your men only await a sign that you are in some trouble before they lend assistance?"

"Do you fear them?" Verel asked with a superior grin.

"Aye, Sir Verel. Only a fool would be at ease, one against a dozen."

Verel bowed most elaborately. "It shall be our contest, Sir Hyatt, for Lady Aurélie and De la Noye."

"And if I win?"

"Your life."

Hyatt looked around the group, convinced from only a glance at the faces they would take Verel's orders. They were a tattered group indeed: remnants of beaten armies, villagers without homes and families, dependent on any kind of leadership. And in this case, good leadership.

"Fair enough, Sir Verel," Hyatt said. He looked at the weapons in his hands and put the short-handled ax back in his belt.

Verel took a ready posture to fight: knees bent, legs spread, and arms wide. Hyatt did likewise and they circled each other cautiously. Verel took a wide swipe at his opponent, but Hyatt easily drew back with a jump. "Nay, Verel, too soon. Watch your man and let him be hasty, while you are cool."

Verel grimaced with the insult. He did not wish to receive instruction and took another hasty swipe.

"Nay again, sir knight. You show your anxiety when you attack too soon . . . before the fight begins."

"Shut your mouth!"

Hyatt circled with Verel, swirling his thick, sharp hunting knife to distract him.

"Don't let your opponent heat your temper with taunts, Sir Verel. Your necessity is to fight; arguments are best placed in the bedchamber. This is not a contest of words."

Verel's face became red and he took a third swipe at Hyatt, but Hyatt jumped back on one foot and the other rose high in a kick that landed under Verel's chin, forcing him off the ground and back onto the earth in a heap. He lay stunned, his sword lying next to his hand, looking up at Hyatt.

"The Scots," Hyatt said with a shrug. "If you are not weighted down with armor, save your life first, worry about a chivalrous contest later. Now, sir knight, your weapon lays at hand. Get it."

Verel rose a bit shakily, wondering why Hyatt had not

killed him. He quickly concluded that it must be the sure knowledge that the others would fall on him and slay him instantly. But a good warrior would die willingly if he took but one with him.

Again, they circled each other. Again, Hyatt twisted his knife in his hand. Verel noticed the flashing of the silver and when he looked in that direction, Hyatt struck. But he held the knife against the younger knight's chest while he held Verel's wrist with his other hand, preventing the sword from reaching him.

"Never let your opponent distract you so easily. Watch his arm, not his weapon, lest he entrance you with ease."

He shoved Verel backward hard, causing the younger man to fall on the turf again. Verel rose, blood lust in his eyes. They circled each other another time, and this time Verel kept himself alert and would not be tricked. He waited until they had rounded each other twice and let Hyatt make the first move. Hyatt's stout knife whirred past Verel's belly and Verel moved quickly, deftly, bending his knees and thrusting his sword hard forward. Hyatt jumped, dropped and rolled, but not quickly enough. The sword caught his thigh and when he was again on his feet, a gash swelled with bright red blood and the pain throbbed in his leg. He knew the contest had best be short.

"Good point, Sir Verel," Hyatt said with a smile. He readied himself for combat anew, a smile on his face. "The pity is, now that you've drawn blood, we best be done. I can't parley any longer. Remember that. When your opponent draws blood or batters your head, it's time to be done, lest you lose too much blood or good sense to finish. Come lad, give your best, and quickly, or the fight won't be fair."

"What care I for a fair fight, Hyatt? So long as you die!" Verel made to stab at Hyatt, again hasty and hot-tempered, and Hyatt deftly knocked the sword from his hand, sending it flying. He grabbed a wrist, twisted Verel's arm behind his back, and positioned the blade of the hunting knife under the young man's throat. He looked around the dozen men who looked on.

"Well, lads? One landed knight for a leader?"

None approached him. They obviously valued Sir Verel greatly. Pulling Verel with him, Hyatt backed away from the group, out of their circle, until he had reached the tethered horses.

"Kill me quickly, you black-hearted bastard," Verel snarled.

"Why? These men need you. I shall warn my own not to travel in this forest unarmed, for I would not sacrifice even one to you, but you need not die, Sir Verel."

"I would rather die than be beaten by *you!*"

"Why so? Is a good knight never bested? You show your inexperience and youth, Verel. A good knight learns from each contest, bettering himself. Don't be a fool. Don't accept death as an honorable venture. Once dead, you will never again raise a blade to defend what is right."

"I despise you," the young man uttered, pain drawing each word.

Hyatt sighed, backing toward the horses. "Such unnecessary passion will only slow you down. Take ease; clear your head. You are a good fighter, Verel, but I have been a scavenger in the forests of England much longer than you. For me, it was a challenge to learn to fight by courtly rules, but for you the reverse will be true. You must learn to fight as scavengers do, if you are to live like this. 'Tis a pity, if you are satisfied with such."

Hyatt threw him to the ground and Verel lay face-down in the grass. In a single motion Hyatt had the tethered reins in hand and was astride the stallion that had been taken from De la Noye.

"If you change your mind, Sir Verel, you may present yourself at your old home. Perhaps you will be allowed to earn a position with a decent troop of soldiers."

That said, Hyatt gave the stallion a firm heel and whirled away from the camp. He bent low over the horse's mane, tucked his legs in tight, and rode like the wind through the trees, under low branches, down narrow paths. The steed's hooves were swift and graceful and not once did the beast stumble or falter. It was a good horse Verel had gotten off with.

Hyatt heard the three horses behind him for a time, but not for long, for as he neared De la Noye the scavengers gave up the chase. Hyatt paused when he reached the forest's edge. The sun was setting and the distance from the wood to the gate was long, but he sat in pause, admiring the silhouette of De la Noye at sunset. From the distance the castle seemed to sit in three tiers; the wall surrounding the outer bailey with a massive gate and bridge and seven parapets made the first layer. Within the outer bailey were peasant housing, a huge stable and smith shop, and room for a thousand horsed men-at-arms. Next was the inner wall, with portcullis and iron gate. Beyond that was the rising structure that was the main hall, shaped like the cross of Christ, with four wings and a rising citadel, the donjon, from which Aurélie had viewed the conquering forces.

There was room there for even more than they now housed. Yea, a dynasty. Hard to win . . . hard to lose.

He thought about Verel for a moment and dismounted, tethering the horse at the forest's edge. Let one knight from De la Noye ride away from the magnificent castle on a worthy steed, for her sake.

It was dark by the time Hyatt called to the gatekeeper for entrance. He was met as all were met when they came to the wall, by a group of armored knights astride, lest there be any threat or trick at play. His chest swelled with pride at the way they carried out his orders even when he was away.

He spurned their worry at the sight of the blood on his thigh, but accepted a mount to make the hall in shorter time. He left that borrowed horse with a page and took the stairs swiftly for an injured man. Within his chamber Aurélie sat upright, her face colored again with health, her loosed hair brushed to a high sheen, and a tray of food on her lap.

He stood in the doorframe studying her. There were comfort, softness, beauty, and strength in her sweet smile.

"My lord, you have chosen to return to us," she said brightly.

"And you have chosen health," he replied.

Her chin slowly fell in a single nod, her eyes glittering with happiness. "Of course," she said. "I told you it was nothing."

He approached her quickly, leaning down to kiss her lips. Her arms went instantly around his neck and she answered his kiss with enough energy to convince him that she had fully recovered.

Oblivious to the servants still in the room, Hyatt released her lips and smiled at her. " 'Tis well. I would not have wished to live without you."

"Of course, my love," she whispered. "We must henceforth be cautious not to ask it of each other, for it is not my desire to be without you, either."

The room slowly emptied of unwelcome spectators and Hyatt and Aurélie were left to say the many things that thus far had not been said. She did not remember she had been ill, and he forgot the wound on his thigh. The most important tending to be done was done to the hearts of lovers.

SIXTEEN

Y the first of September the fruit trees were heavy with their crops, piglets were fat, and chickens were laying. Baby goats born the previous spring were leaving their mothers' udders, giving village women plentiful goat's milk to serve their own children. The largest crop of vegetables ever seen at De la Noye were harvested, and fourteen calves had been born.

Lady Aurélie rose from her sickbed, more ravishing than ever before as she began to round most proudly with her first child. But she stood under Hyatt's watchful eye, for the knight was insistent that she not be weakened by work or pregnancy, and the noble dame was ordered to bed by husband and a bevy of servants each afternoon, whether she protested or not.

Nima was no longer confined to a bedchamber, kept out of sight to wither with age and loneliness. The old woman sat in the main hall, ever near the hearth, watching her great-grandson play on the rushes with his toys, and offering advice on medicines and poultices and philters. Though she was ancient of form and face, her eyes held a new glitter of usefulness, for finally she made some contribution other than covering the evil flaws of her ward.

"Humph," Hyatt snorted as he entered the hall one afternoon. "I don't know that this is an improvement," he said, gesturing toward his son. The boy scampered among Nima, Aurélie, Perrine, and Baptiste. "Now he will be made soft by all the skirts that indulge him. Dolls, balls, and what is this? A pillow that he clutches?"

"You may have him soon enough, milord," Aurélie said with a smile. "He is too tender for your brutish ways. But if you protest his keepers, you may perhaps ask Sir Girvin to swaddle his bottom and rock him to sleep."

A snort came from the corner, and Girvin looked up with a scowl on his face. Hyatt glanced about the room and noticed many a weary soldier. The outer bailey was stacked with goods; fruits, hens, sacks of grain, vegetables, barrels of ale, large bolts of cloth from the looms, and every product rendered by the people of De la Noye. After the lord had taken his share and selected the goods for trade, the people would have theirs. There was a great plenty to divide. And the effects of hard work was obvious all around. His men had given assistance, but not in replacement of their knightly duties. Those who guarded the wall by night, harvested by day. Those who guarded the wall, protected the farmers, and rode perimeters of the demesne by day, stacked goods by night. Everyone therein, it seemed, hoped for some bonus.

"Is our work done?" Hyatt asked, glancing around the hall. "Everyone seems much at his leisure, and it is not yet noon."

"Hyatt," Aurélie said in an admonishing tone. "These men have worked hard. Let them enjoy a meal, at least."

"Why? Do I take my rest before the work is done?"

"Humph! You should have been given a whip, rather than a broadsword." Lady Aurélie frowned at her husband, for there was not much left to do.

"Sir Trevor," Hyatt barked at a young knight who had worked night and day and appeared to be near dozing. "Is there some feast or fair I have not been told about? There seems to be a mood of laziness and frivolity amongst my men."

The youthful knight blushed and rose wearily, straightening his aching back. "Nay, my liege," he sighed, moving toward the door slowly.

Aurélie grunted some sour, disapproving remark that Hyatt

303

did not quite hear as the knight reached the door. Girvin muttered, "There will be burying to do when these poor lads die of their labors."

"You are right, Trevor," Hyatt said to the young man's back before the door for the hall was opened. " 'Tis a feast I have not been told of. Did no one have the courage to suggest to your warlord that we celebrate our good fortune? Am I such a cruel taskmaster as that? Sir Trevor, find a good-sized hog to slaughter. And beef; we need not take so many calves from the castle. There is no time for a hunt, and I think there is too much ale for the wagons Delmar built us. Why not drink a bit and lighten the load?"

Everyone turned wide, surprised eyes toward Hyatt. He stood in the center of the large room in his dark chausses, boots, a linen shirt rolled up to his elbows, and a leather jerkin belted at the waist. He looked more like a farmer than a knight, his hair tousled, a thick blade at his waist, and growth of beard that spoke of more time spent on work than grooming. Aurélie's eyes sparkled, for she thought him almost more handsome when he wore the effects of hard labor. And Girvin smiled, proud of the young lord he had reared. The others, stunned, sat in silent wonder.

"Very well, if you are not interested . . ."

"Consider it done, Sir Hyatt," Trevor said, bolting out of the hall. A dozen men followed, one with his hand ready to draw out his short blade for the slaughter of good meat. Perrine jumped up, clutching her mending, and ran in the direction of the cookrooms to give instruction. Baptiste hoisted up young Derek, making for the stairs. Nima struggled to rise and follow. Soon there was a flurry of activity that could be heard all over the castle and courtyard as the word was passed, and only Hyatt, Girvin, and Aurélie were left in the large room.

Hyatt nodded toward Girvin. "Let's see what we can do to keep our wall safely tended and yet enjoy the day. Can you divide the men into groups that will relieve each other?"

"Yea, Hyatt," he said, rising. "And I shall keep fifty, thirty of whom will be sober enough to call a guard and fire an arrow straight."

Girvin lumbered toward the door and Aurélie rose with a sigh, leaning her head against Hyatt's chest. "Are we unsafe for even a day of harvest feasting, Hyatt?"

"I am never too sure of our safety, my love, but 'tis their day more than mine. I shall be mostly at the wall, myself."

"But Hyatt, you deserve to celebrate more than anyone."

He touched the softness of her cheek with his roughened hand. "I shall, *chérie*. Later, when the others have fallen on their pallets."

Pleased with him, Aurélie did not interfere with his design for the feasting celebration. She cautiously supervised the preparation of food, most often from a chair. This was the one day she did not indulge in her afternoon rest, but Perrine's hovering frown warned her that she would not be allowed to overtax herself. "I am treated like an old woman," she complained.

"You are treated like a woman we would all like to see become old," she was reassured.

The meat was pitted in the inner bailey rather than the hall so that more of the farmers and villagers could gather together. Huge pots were carried out and placed on large fires, the steam, smoke, and savory smells rising to fill the early fall air. A villager entertained with a gittern and songs were sung. The meat was nearly cooked, the brewis boiled, bread was baked, and huge trays of fruits and vegetables graced the trestle tables that had been brought outside. The sun was lowering in the sky and the feasting would begin when Aurélie went in search of Hyatt.

Good to his word, he was more attuned to safety than to celebrating and could be found in the donjon, looking out over his keep and lands, simultaneously watching the wall and parapets to be assured his own men did not slump at their task. Aurélie climbed the steep, winding stairs without spilling a drop of the cool ale she delivered. He frowned when he turned to see her.

"You should not come up here, my lady. The way is steep and the climb is demanding."

She smiled at his worry, finding that this suited her very well. Being protected by him was nearly as gratifying as being his wife. "But this is my favorite place, Hyatt. I came here daily before I was sick, and I mean to again, after my lying-in. It is from here that De la Noye is most beautiful."

He took the ale and drank down a hearty gulp. He gestured toward the wood with tankard in hand. "Look there, my love. At the forest's edge." Aurélie strained to see what Hyatt pointed toward and finally she saw a slight stirring and gasped. "Nay, be at ease," he said, watching.

"But someone goes there. Sound the horn."

" 'Tis Verel, my love. I venture it is more the smells of feasting than want of fighting that draws him near."

"Verel? How do you know? You can barely see."

"I caught a glimpse of the stallion I left him." Hyatt sighed and dropped an arm about her shoulders. " 'Twas Verel I met in the wood as I returned to De la Noye. We had a contest and he made his point on my thigh."

"Hyatt, you told me that was a mishap. You did not tell me about Verel."

"Aye, my love. I thought to spare you, and myself. But Verel has not gone far. He is a woodsman now, leading a little troop of scavengers through the dense wood. When he left De la Noye he must have quickly learned that there is no French force nearby and the other English warriors are more dangerous than I. He keeps himself deep in the forest."

"And you did not kill him? You left him a horse?"

Hyatt nodded. "Verel is good stock, though angry and misguided right now. This is the pride of youth, yet untempered, not yet honed with wisdom. When I judged the hatred and shame in his eyes, I saw myself, for as a youth I was driven into the woods, left there to fight my way back to a decent life. I left Verel a horse, but when I was imprisoned in the forest I had Girvin. It was a better lot I had to aid me." He turned her shoulders and looked into her eyes. "Can you send Sir Trevor up here? I would speak to him."

"Do you mean to go after Verel now?"

"Nay, my lady."

"I am surprised you did not kill him."

"On an earlier day, I would have. I am glad for us both that my temper has eased. The young knight is too good to waste. Leaders of men are hard to find."

Aurélie looped her arms about his neck and rose on her toes to kiss him. She pressed her body close, wove her fingers into the errant locks at the base of his neck and parted her lips under the flaming heat of his. She yielded all, moving her mouth under his and drawing a deep sigh from the hearty warrior.

"You make me forget my watch, my lady."

" 'Tis well, Sir Hyatt. You have come nicely to heel."

"Have I now?" he laughed. "And who better to conquer a brutish knight than the vanquished one? Go, my love. Find Trevor for me."

She looked down into the inner bailey, as did Hyatt. They saw village girls dancing with Hyatt's knights, captive knights turned serfs in contests of strength against armored knights, with much laughing and swigging of drink to accompany them, and serf and warrior together turning spitted meat. A scene like the one that lay below them had not been possible even with Giles, and with her eyes she flashed him a look of love that melted his heart and filled him with longing.

She left him to his high tower and beckoned away from an arm-wrestling match the young knight her husband sought. She tarried over a steaming pot, pinched the bread, and sampled a fresh, cool bean before Trevor returned to the courtyard, shaking his head in bemusement.

"Whatever troubles you, Sir Trevor?" she asked.

"My lord troubles me. He has not suffered enough drink to go daft, yet his instructions are a mite strange to bear out. I am to find a dozen armed men not bidden to the wall and take a wagon of food and drink to the forest's edge. We're to unload it there and return with the wagon." He shook his head again. "Does he mean to feed the beasts of the forest as well?"

Aurélie laughed, covering her mouth. "And if he does, Sir Trevor, are you bound to argue with him?"

"Nay, my lady," he said, still shaking his head in confusion.

"Then you had best find the men that Hyatt requires."

As the young man went off to do as he was asked, Aurélie looked up toward the donjon, but she could not see Hyatt. He was obviously intent on watching over the whole of this property singlehandedly. She beckoned to a squire and asked him to carry a tray to Sir Hyatt, and the lad was overjoyed to be chosen for the task. And then a swirl of robes caught her eye and she saw Father Algernon among the group, near the food. She made her way toward him.

"So you have decided to join us after all, Father. I'm glad you came."

He frowned at her. "I suppose you are very enamored of your able warrior now, since under his sword he has provided so much. But do you ask yourself what there is of Christ in this burg?"

"We have you, Father. Is not your task to deliver us the gospel, the saints, the salvation of our souls?"

"It was my mission under Giles, but under this new master I am not bidden do my cleric's chore."

"Nonsense, Father, you do Hyatt wrong. He has tried hard to support your word, your Church. You ask too much of him, I fear, for he will not indulge you the way Giles did. And we are all the better for it, I think."

"You would think so, madame, for your heathen ways match his."

"I will not let you spoil the day, Father. Partake of this feast in good spirit and say a prayer over the labors of these good people, or go back to your cell and eat your dry bread alone."

308

"You could change his mind."

"I doubt it, Father, for we are too much in agreement."

"He has forbidden me to journey to Avignon."

"Forbidden? But . . ."

Aurélie looked at the red-faced priest with something of confusion. Hyatt had not mentioned that he had finally delivered an answer to Father Algernon's request, and it was above all a very strange answer.

"I'm sorry, Father, I do not understand. 'Tis like Sir Hyatt to refuse to put the Church's needs above those of the people, but I don't see why he would forbid you to travel to the Pope's see. Are you certain you understood him?"

"He was easy to understand. He would not permit me to go unless I told him the business I traveled to complete, and he said I might not travel with pilgrims, but would take knights of his colors with me."

"And that was not to your liking?"

"A cleric's business is not a knight's. My conference in Avignon is none of his business, and I will not travel through France with an English escort."

Aurélie frowned. "Hyatt must fear that you plot against him."

"Priests do not plot. The faith and the souls of our people are our concerns. He does nothing to lend spiritual help to this place."

"Look around you, Father. What do you see? The people are fed, happy, and protected for the first time since I came here. You decry my lord's faith, yet he has done better by this place than you and Giles ever did together. If you wish to go to Avignon, go on his terms and be brought safely back. If you will not abide by Sir Hyatt's request, then he is right to refuse you."

"I am his priest!"

"He is your *host!* I am sorry you have not gone to your papal see. You should venture down the road but a league and see what these knights of Hyatt have seen. You would return to this humble keep and give thanks for a score of days and nights for your life, your Church, and any tolerance from this lord."

"You lie," he growled.

She smiled with rare superiority. "Nay, Father, 'tis truth. Edward had but a few with the wisdom to rule and not just devastate the land. Ask Percival; his town was leveled to ash; babies and women who begged for mercy were slain." She gestured impatiently toward the one she named. Percival had one arm casually drapped over his wife's shoulders while with a free hand he lifted a mug to his laughing lips. "If we sin because we live, Father, then we shall sin for a long, long time."

"You heathen wench, you conspire with him to lies. You try to make me believe that 'tis worse borne through other lords, when I know otherwise. I have been cut off by your English swine. In other French burgs overtaken, the priests are revered and obeyed."

"You old fool," Aurélie angrily snapped. "Go back to your prayers and pray for truth. Hyatt has saved your life. Anywhere else you'd have been lucky if only turned away from your chapel in rags . . . and on the road you would surely be killed if not stoutly guarded." She dismissed him with an impatient wave of her hand. "Life with Giles spoiled you and made you greedy. May your soul yet be saved, O faithless monk."

She whirled away from him, angry to the depth of her bones. In her mind there was nothing worse than a bad priest. Algernon cared not for souls, but for the money he could earn in pretending to save them. She had seen and heard of evil priests before and knew that Algernon was not the worst, but she wished they had a sincere cleric.

She fumed so with anger at his disloyalty, his selfishness, that rather than partaking of the feast, she climbed the high tower again. When Hyatt turned angry eyes her way, her flushed cheeks stayed his chastisement. "Leave me be, husband," she said hotly. "I have just had a few unkind words with a fat priest and I am ill disposed to be reprimanded by you." She let out her breath in a huff. "Ungrateful churl!"

Hyatt chuckled at her anger and lifted to his lips the thick, brown-roasted drumstick from a healthy hen. He chewed thoughtfully and gestured with the bony point of the meat toward the forest. A rug was spread on the ground by the edge of the trees and on it rested a keg, a pile of food, a mound of bread. Hyatt said nothing, but watched. The small troop who had delivered the goods was just making their way over the bridge and inside the wall. The creaking of the wheels that turned the crank and raised the bridge finally stopped.

A man came into view from out of the trees. He looked around very cautiously. Another appeared. A third. A group converged on the mound of food. Two hefted the barrel of ale while the others lifted their share, and finally the cloth was closed over what was left and the whole lot disappeared in an instant. All that could be seen finally was a man astride a dark stallion, who stood looking at De la Noye. A better eye, Aurélie suspected, would show a wistful look of longing on Sir Verel's face. And then he gave the stallion heel and turned into the trees.

She touched Hyatt's face. "Why do some fail to see your goodness?" she asked, thinking of Algernon.

"Because," he said with a shrug, still chewing, "I am not good to all. Some, like Verel, Algernon, even Guillaume, will have to abide on less because of me. That is the way of it. Not all can willingly accept their lessened share. If it were I, I would accept no less than I had before.'" Hyatt looked up at her and smiled. "You, my lady, have less than before. I took your command from you. Are you angry still?"

"Nay, Hyatt. I have more than ever before. And I thank you."

꧁

The feasting was five days past. Hyatt had sent a train of wagons with goods to trade with vineyard monks on the following morning, though many people were bleary-eyed from celebrating. Twenty-five soldiers were required to guard the entourage, but fortunately it would not take them long to empty their wagons and return with cases of wine. A group of nuns were housed overnight and given the gift of a heavily laden wagon of vegetables to carry on the remainder of their journey.

Hyatt had proven to be more generous with the pilgrims than Aurélie had expected, but then, he had not said he would spurn them. And truly, Giles had given too much to them, whereas Hyatt had been generous, but fair. Even if their winter proved to be the worst ever, the people of De la Noye would have enough.

Aurélie awoke at dawn and impulsively kissed Hyatt's bare chest, waking him. His arm was instantly around her. "Had I known the delights of waking up with a woman at my side, I would have tried it before."

"You mock me," she said, pushing against him. "You have slept with hundreds of women; I know it."

He chuckled. "A time or two I slept, but deeply, from the help of too much drink. But I never slumbered at a lady's side by will, until the wedding night."

"Not so!"

"True, Aurélie. More than true. I have been afraid of women. They are all soft and pliant, and while their victims sleep, their claws come out." He pulled her closer. "Or, so I thought."

"You fear me, sir knight?"

His voice trailed off as a fierce knocking at the door interrupted him. He cast a glance over his shoulder. "And so the day begins. Is it yet dawn?" He sighed. "Cover yourself, my love. I do not wish to kill anyone over you today."

Aurélie did as she was instructed and Hyatt called out to the intruder to enter. Girvin stood in the frame of the door, sheepishly looking inside. His business was more important to him than decorum, and he entered despite the state of undress within, closing the door behind him.

"Sir Hyatt, I beg your pardon, but Guillaume is not about our camp. Something is amiss."

Hyatt's spine straightened and Aurélie sat up straighter, clutching the covers over her naked bosom.

"What is it you fear?" Hyatt asked.

Girvin shrugged. "We had a plan; if some troop ventured near our camp, Guillaume was to leave a lance stuck in the ground, standing upright. There was no sign, and nothing there was disturbed. And he would not leave the cave to venture closer to knights or travelers."

"Perhaps Verel . . ."

"Nay, again. Verel would do ill to any of us, but not to Guillaume. I do not know what has become of him, but the wood is deep . . . and dangerous. Will you give me ten men?"

"To search?"

"Aye, Hyatt."

"But we have sent twenty-five out, and with ten more . . ."

" 'Tis important, Hyatt. 'Tis *Guillaume!*"

The sound of his voice, the devotion mixed with command, was an order that the highest lord would not dare dismiss. Aurélie reached out a hand and touched her husband's back. He looked over his shoulder and in her eyes there was a sentimental gleam, a plea. The two warriors were as brothers. Hyatt looked back at Girvin. "Who knows the wood as well as you and Sir Guillaume?"

"You, Sir Hyatt."

He looked again at Aurélie.

"Go, my lord. Take ten men and find my seneschal. We have need of his wisdom; his talent. Please."

"Find my squire and have my gear and horse readied. The wood has some two-legged dangers and we will be forced to travel as knights would. The scavengers are crude, but desperate."

Girvin stood for a moment longer, his cheeks darkening with what could have been a blush. "Thank you, my lord. My lady." And then he was gone.

Hyatt gathered his clothes and gear quickly. "I shall leave you Trevor and Maximilian. They can command archers and pikemen in my absence. I will give them orders."

"And I have Delmar and others." She shrugged. "They have not forgotten so soon. And they would hold the wall."

"Do not be afraid, Aurélie."

"Hyatt, I am not. I have had you as my very own, and you have had me. If fate is cruel to us now, we will have the strength to carry on in memory, if nothing else. Nay, my liege, I am *not* afraid. Nor will you be. Hyatt, let us be strong, not fearful. Go with God. Come back swiftly."

"I shall be quick."

"Be careful. Be strong."

❧

It was a great strain on all of De la Noye to have the best gone together. Girvin, Guillaume, and Hyatt were all away. Trevor could barely take the time for a meal, and Aurélie suspected by the look in his eyes that he did not sleep. The residents were all flinching at the slightest sound, the merest movement in the trees. Hyatt and Girvin had been out three days. The watch was tired.

A group of monks had passed the castle and a fully armed group of knights rode destriers out to their entourage, judged them to be safe, and the gates were opened to let them enter. A lucky charm must have accompanied this pilgrimage, for they carried loaded carts of jugged wine and were eager to trade it for lodging, fresh bread, vegetables, and a bit of roasted meat. It was an abbot and his friars, and they were a worldly bunch from the Dominican order, of which Father Algernon did not approve. But Aurélie both welcomed them and enjoyed their company, for they were not so devout and sang songs, laughed, and made no crippling demands for offerings.

When Hyatt was gone four days and Abbot Charlisle was about to ready the brothers for travel, Aurélie stood with them in the inner courtyard. The abbot's carts were loaded with crated chickens, fresh food, cloth, and barrels of good ale. Beside the carts were cases of the abbot's wine. "My husband will be pleased, *monseigneur*. Will you not stay a day longer and make his acquaintance?"

"Nay, child, we'll be along our way, for our journey has only just begun."

"But my priest is not yet come."

"I shall bless the travelers, madame. Your priest is of another order and does not approve of us."

Aurélie knew it was true, but it galled her that Algernon was so superior. He had no right; he had fallen far from the Divine. "That's preposterous, Father. Wait, and I shall get him."

She made to turn away when a call came from the gatehouse. "My lady. Flagellants. Almost a hundred."

Aurélie sighed. She did not like to face these pilgrims. They were too much like her late husband — peculiar, obsessed. They beat themselves as they traveled. They did not come to trade but to show their penance and collect coins. This lot would not be satisfied with lodging and food. They would request silver.

"Where?" she asked with a shout.

"Far out. More than five leagues."

"Let them come closer. We can meet them with a troop before we escort the abbot out."

She lifted her skirts then to make a fast trip to the chapel. An ill feeling had surrounded her because of the priest, for she did not know how to deal with him. He was not satisfied with his plenty; he could only be satisfied to rule through a puppet lord. He had had so much power when Giles was alive. Aurélie was often betwixt them, fighting religion with reason, an impossible battle that she frequently lost.

"Father Algernon," she said upon entering the chapel.

He turned from the altar and looked at her.

"The Abbot Charlisle is prepared to leave. Do you not give him a blessing and wish him a safe journey?"

"He is capable of that, my lady."

"But you are the priest of the burg. 'Tis your obligation."

He shook his head. "He is not of my order. He worships worldly goods and fleshly pleasures."

Aurélie shook her head in frustration. "Oh, Father, will

you not? You are to be above jealousy, above judgment. Come be our priest; be the Word again, I beg you."

"Ah, you beg, my lady. How I've waited."

She stiffened. "You may disapprove of the abbot, but flagellants approach. Do you wish to have them admitted? Will you bless their number?"

"How many?" he asked with acute interest.

"A goodly number. One hundred."

"Yea, my lady, you must admit them straightaway. They do penance for God. For all of us."

"Will you come?"

"In time, my lady," he said, his voice strangely nervous. Aurélie saw that his hands trembled. "Let them in and I shall come."

Her mind tumbled. Father Algernon had been acting too oddly. It could not be ignored. He did not believe Hyatt's rule was good; he believed that outside the gates of De la Noye priests prospered under the English siege.

"Father," she said, stepping nearer. "Father Algernon, you have not left De la Noye for a day or night since Hyatt has come. We escaped much death. Do you know it? Did you ask Percival what his village suffered?"

" 'Twas not necessary. Hyatt gave him shelter, so he spoke for Hyatt. I understand the give-and-take of such politics."

"Do you know of Sir Hollis?" she asked. He stiffened visibly; his eyes wandered upward. "The priest from Château Innesse was castrated and left to bleed to death in the street. Ask one of Hyatt's men. They witnessed the rape of the château. Hollis laid it to ashes. Sir Ryland is his friend."

Father Algernon's eyes drifted back to her face. She heard the sound of the horn that signaled that the gate would be opened. "You have listened to idle tales meant only to make you believe you have a good leader here. 'Tis a familiar trick. The priest of the château has a larger church than before."

"My God," she whispered. "The flagellants! One hundred!"

It was all suddenly clear. The castle and wall could not be impregnated unless the bridge was down. Ryland would have seen how strong they were, how ready. But the discontented priest who hungered for power, for money, would believe Ryland. And Algernon had assured himself that pilgrims would be admitted. In addition he had asked to be relieved for a journey of his own — to be away from De la Noye when the flagellants arrived to open the gate.

"My God, you utter *fool!*" She whirled away from him, bolting out of the church and running down the length of the gardens, the street, toward the courtyard. The creaking of the bridge screamed inside her skull. She heard it hit the opposite side and the horses of the escorts, ten mailed knights . . . *only ten* as they rode out. She knew as she had never known anything that the cowardly Hollis meant to get into her walls by a monk's costume.

She flew past the inner gate, screaming. "Secure the gate! Raise the bridge! It is a trick! My God, a trick! 'Tis Hollis! Raise the bridge! Close the gate! Secure the portcullis! Your arms! Your arms! Men! Arm the wall!"

SEVENTEEN

IR Trevor was at the portcullis gate and stared at Aurélie with wide, disbelieving eyes as she ran into the outer bailey. Maximilian, older and more experienced, needed no further prompting. He manned the bridge and gate and jabbed the squire at his side to sound the horn. Ten knights only just on the other side of the moat looked back in confusion, for the horn and subsequent raising of the bridge made the attack alarm.

Abbot Charlisle ran through the portcullis behind Aurélie. "Madame, madame, these monks . . ."

"Our priest, abbot, has sold us to the enemy. These are English raiders, murderers, who mean to enter by a cleric's costume. They are not here about a Christian war, but bent on killing us all." She turned away briskly. "Delmar, form a group of archers to lend aid. We are sorely in need of men. Percival, gather any of yours who can string a bow, throw a spear, carry arrows to the bowmen. Maximilian, sound the horn for the pikemen. Full armaments, all from the wall . . . no destriers. It is a trick to get inside." She looked back at the abbot. "If your faith prevents you from saving our lives by aiding our fight, at least bind my priest. He is the cause of this."

The abbot whirled away and Aurélie went straightaway to the wall. She requested a hand up, but was rebuffed immediately. Her cheeks heightened to a fiery red and her eyes blazed. "My lord is gone and the wall is *mine!*" And while the knight who would prevent her from climbing to the platform stood in awe of her, she pushed him aside and made the familiar climb without assistance.

She was barely up with both feet secure when she heard Maximilian mutter, " 'Tis Hollis, the *bastard!*"

Across the rolling hills the brown road stretched. Approximately one hundred clerics dropped brown robes off their shoulders and revealed chain mail and helms. Visors were pulled over faces, and shields, longbows, and quivers appeared. A cloud of dust rose from behind the now kneeling advance, and armored destriers could be seen thundering toward De la Noye. "Fifty," Aurélie muttered. "Sixty horses. We have loosed ten knights astride. Dear God, we are doomed."

The sky became black with arrows as the English bowmen fired them rapidly. Until Hyatt's coming the archers of De la Noye had used the crossbow, accurate and deadly, but slow to arm and fire. The longbow was lightweight and quick, and a rainshower of arrows began to pelt the wall and flow into the inner bailey. The knights of De la Noye covered their bodies with shields while Hollis's horsed troop neared.

"How many bows do we have ready?" Aurélie asked Maximilian.

"Fifty at most, my lady."

She turned and looked into the bailey. "Delmar," she shouted. "Loose all the weapons confiscated by Hyatt's troop and arm our men. Serf and knight alike. Match our crossbows with Sir Hyatt's longbows at the wall. And your axes, knives, and hammers."

"Yea, my lady." Delmar turned and began shouting. Aurélie watched in wonder at the scene below her. Hyatt had fewer than a hundred archers and knights, but there were close to forty good knights of De la Noye, though bereft of armor and shield. And squires and pages were running wildly through the baileys, from stable to town to keep, gathering their weapons and passing them to able-bodied men. Shields that still bore the de Pourvre crest were pulled from tackrooms and sheds, crossbows considered obsolete and useless were quickly strung by women and boys, and the short, heavy arrows for that weapon were scrounged from every corner.

Bows and full quivers of arrows were handed up the wall, while below on the nether side of the moat Hyatt's men stood their ground, protected behind shields, in wait for the horsed knights. A scream pierced the air, and Aurélie saw one of Hyatt's archers tumble from the north parapet with an arrow in his chest. And then she saw the sky blaze as arrows laced with fire began to hit the outer wall.

She watched in horror as a thatched roof was caught and a woman screamed. Aurélie grabbed the arm of the knight beside her. "Get the women and children to the hall and have the gate at the portcullis closed. Forget the fire. We can rebuild the town if we have our lives. Tell them to let it burn and hold the wall."

He gave a nod of agreement and made his way down the ladder. He was barely to the ground when Percival was beside her, one crossbow in hand and another tucked under his arm.

She took the heavy bow from under Percival's arm just as an arrow whirred past her right side. Aurélie did not give notice to the near miss. She stooped to grasp a full quiver as it was handed up and armed her bow. At a weight of twenty pounds the weapon was heavy and clumsy. She looked askance at Percival, who was aged and somewhat frail. She gave a slight smile. "Our aim will have to be sharper than most, Percival. We shall not get as many arrows off as the young and strong."

"Aye, my lady, but in my youth I was a fair contestant in the tourneys."

"You?"

"One does not speak of his knightly oaths to the conqueror, madame," Percival said with a grin. He released the catch and his arrow sailed. An archer from the other side fell. "Good point, Sir Percival. Make every one count."

In the time lapsed the archers on the wall had begun a good shower of their own arrows and with a few well-placed shots from the crossbow, a fair number of opponents fell.

The wall was manned by armored knights, squires, serfs, and the like. Men whom Aurélie had seen ride out to meet the English were lined up on behalf of Hyatt and De la Noye now. She saw knights in red and black who wore chainmail pass their shields to serfs wearing naught but quilted gambesons and thin linen gowns. Paulis and other boys who were not yet even pages were running from hall to outer bailey with as many swords, full quivers, and knives as could be carried, while a stream of women with small children were aided by doddering old men toward the main hall. Here and there a monk was seen, running supplies, carrying babies, or herding chickens and goats out of the outer bailey. Smoke rose in a thick black cloud from a peasant hut struck by a flaming arrow.

The horn sounded from the donjon and Aurélie looked about for the cause. From the wood she saw destriers emerge and her breath caught in momentary panic. They wore red and black surcoats, one with a plume of red atop his helm.

Hyatt.

"Maximilian, my lord is come. Cover his passage."

Hyatt rode out of the wood and paused at the head of his troop. He pulled out and braced his lance and behind him the others did the like. She caught sight of Girvin, for he was the largest and always wore black armor, making him look more the heathen than ever. But before Girvin, draped over his saddle, was a large, hulking body. She knew that they had found Guillaume, and he was dead.

Hyatt's troop began a slow advance toward the castle, but Girvin held back. He dismounted with care, pulled Guillaume from the horse and held him up. Guillaume was not dead, but injured. Girvin placed his friend on the ground at the forest's edge, leaning him against a tree and propping his own shield before him to ward off any wayward arrows. Then he mounted again and from his lips issued forth a cry of rage that rose above the cacophony of battle. At the cry Hyatt's troop bent over saddles, lances braced, and charged the destriers of Hollis as they came up behind the archers.

Girvin, void of shield, swung a battle-ax, slaying an archer even as his steed rode over two more. The knights who had ridden over the bridge earlier, only ten, saw Hyatt's move and charged the arrow-slinging band, running warhorses over those in the way, and pressed on toward Hollis's approaching troop. It was a melee of twenty of Hyatt's men against sixty of Hollis's, and Aurélie shuddered in absolute terror at the odds.

"My lady, look west."

She strained at Maximilian's instruction and saw a cloud of dust rising from down the road. Fear choked her heart. "Holy Mother of God," she prayed. She armed her bow again, desperate to lend aid to Hyatt. Archers who had not been shot or crushed by the destriers rose and ran in a line toward the wall. Aurélie fixed her aim toward the horsed troop, however. She spied the red plume of Hyatt's helm and, with a prayer, fired toward his opponent. The arrow hit the man's back between his shoulders and he slumped and fell from his horse.

The thing she had failed to worry over happened. Hyatt looked toward the wall and spied her. He was frozen as he saw whence the arrow had come, and as he stared toward her two knights charged him from other directions.

An earsplitting cry came from the field as Girvin, ever suited to guard Hyatt's back, rode in a fury toward his lord. One of Hollis's men fell to Girvin's ax, while Hyatt's broadsword finished the other. Aurélie sighed and armed her bow, the thundering cloud of another advance of horsed men coming closer. The air was filled with the clanging of swords against swords, shields raised to axes, the shouts of combatants, the shower of arrows flowing from De la Noye and toward her, and smoke, rising from within the wall where peasant huts burned out of control.

And the horn sounded again as a galloping herd came into sight. "Most merciful God," she breathed, for they wore Hyatt's red and black. It was the escort that had taken out goods on

Delmar's wagons. Along the wall there was the sound of cheers.

But the horn sounded yet again, and this time there was a battle cry from the forest's edge as a tattered group, only four of whom were astride, charged onto the field. Aurélie knew the man on the dark stallion must be Verel, charging without benefit of helm, armor, shield, or lance, but swinging a sword with deadly intent. He rode low in his saddle, head down to escape arrows, straight for Hyatt. Aurélie held her breath and aimed her crossbow. She had held it up for so long that her hands trembled, but she was ready.

With a sigh of relief and a choked sob, she lowered the bow. Verel took down the knight approaching Hyatt's back, sending him to the dust. The empty destrier reared up and fled the field. Verel raised a bloody sword high in the air and brought it down on another of Hollis's men.

Aurélie saw a knight in blue livery edge to the outside of the melee and take flight. Another followed. The contest was equal in numbers, with Hyatt's men doing abler fighting. She turned to look into the outer bailey, where fire blazed. "Archers lower bows and check the fire," she shouted.

There was swift action all around the wall. Bows were lowered and men jumped into the bailey. Outside the knights were one for one and Hollis's archers were fleeing in numbers around the horsed melee, to the outskirts of the wood to get away. The gate at the portcullis was raised and women, old men, and boys came flowing through to the outer bailey, tearing down buildings not yet burned, with pitchforks, axes, shovels, and hoes. The well squeaked and buckets were passed. Aurélie looked again to the field and saw more of Hollis's men take flight down the road. The red plume of Hyatt's helm still wobbled like a rooster tail as he used his broadsword fiercely. Verel was unhorsed nearby and engaged in a weighty test with an armored knight boasting a broadsword. Verel's sword flew from his hand and he took a dive, rolling once, twice, thrice, coming up alongside the body of a felled knight. He searched frantically for a weapon on the person of the dead warrior while his opponent loomed nearer, sword raised. Girvin's ax came down hard between the knight's shoulders and he fell atop his fellow on the field. And Girvin pulled a short-handled broadsword from his saddle strap, tossing it to Verel, and turning his horse back to the fray.

A cry went up from the blue-liveried knights and a dozen turned to flee. A score more ran, and Hyatt's troop gave chase down the road, due west. Aurélie threw back her head and looked up at the sky, her eyes alive with fire and ice, and a cry of proud victory left her. She watched her husband as he led the chase over the knoll and further, the only sign that they were still in pursuit being the brown dust cloud in the distance.

One of Hyatt's did not follow his lord. Girvin galloped toward the forest and dismounted there. He stooped and lifted Guillaume into his arms and carried him back toward the castle. A few archers from Hollis's troop could be seen fleeing into the wood in all directions, but not one stopped to arm a bow. Girvin did not pay them any regard. Some of Verel's ragtag group chased archers, but did them little harm except to drive them into the trees.

"Lower the bridge and open the gate. We'll pass buckets from the moat," she told Maximilian.

"What if there are Hollis's soldiers hiding in the wood?" the knight asked.

She nodded toward Girvin. "He would have smelled them," she said. She turned to climb down from the wall, passing Percival as she went. "Keep watch, Sir Percival," she said, giving him the knighted role with much resolution. She glanced toward the field. Bodies littered the earth. She would have to go forth and discover which were theirs, but not until Hyatt had returned and the fire was out.

Aurélie watched as monks, serfs, knights, archers, and even children passed and ran buckets into the bailey. She knew that theirs had been good fortune with only a battered wall and a dozen homes burned, for the stable was saved and almost all their produce was in the inner bailey and hall. Had Hollis thought of a way to disguise war machines as nuns, the castle would have been completely destroyed. But the offending knight could not carry battering rams or pull trebuchets and still make his trickery work. There was a smoldering ache in her chest as she realized what would have happened to them had the bridge been lowered for one hundred armored archers with a troop of sixty knights close behind them. Hyatt would have returned to De la Noye to find blood, bones, and ashes.

Girvin passed through the confusion of pail-bearing, bucket-passing people. Guillaume slumped in his arms and Aurélie ran forward to meet them. "A broken leg, fever, no food or water for days," Girvin said. "He does not know who I am."

"Take him to Nima," she instructed. "I shall come."

Guillaume lifted his head and opened his eyes. He looked at Aurélie briefly, blankly, and then collapsed against Girvin's chest again. She watched Girvin's departing form as he strode purposefully toward the hall, his burden carried with such ease that Guillaume might have been a child in Girvin's arms. But the mist of fear and pain in Girvin's eyes had not escaped Aurélie's notice.

The smoke in the bailey blackened and turned sour as the water from the moat drenched the flames. A few small structures were dismantled and pulled away to starve the fire. A woman of her village lay in the dust weeping as knights searched the destroyed hovel for her child. In another corner of the courtyard a group of women hovered over injured archers. Aurélie turned toward the injured.

"Madame. My lady."

The sound of Algernon's voice sent a shivery spasm up her spine and she whirled to face him. His cheeks were streaked with tears, his eyes paled by the destruction all around, and his hands were tied behind his back. Two brothers who had traveled with Abbot Charlisle held his arms.

"Sir Ryland swore that the Innesse priest was revered by the conquering English and applied his power with that of the knight, Sir Hollis, to bring the people to peaceful acceptance. Sir Hollis was to have added silver and labor to their church, making it better than it was. My lady, he said no damage would be done, but only to Hyatt's fighting men!" He dropped his gaze to the ground.

Aurélie looked at him with disgust. She wished to slap his face, to see his head ride a pike on her wall. There had been many failings within this castle over the years, but never had one of their number betrayed the secrets of their wall to an enemy. She could have even understood a traitor amongst the beaten French knights, a betrayal from a widow of a soldier of Giles, or any deposed or abused villein. But her priest had suffered only one loss; he had lost the lord he carried in his pocket.

She spat in the dust at his feet and turned away from him. She heard Algernon's whining as he was dragged away. He begged for pardon, mercy, forgiveness . . . but she closed her ears to him and bent over a young lad, formerly of Giles's troop, who had taken an arrow in the arm because he fought without armor, shield, or even a thick leather gambeson. But the lad was brave as the wound was tender, as were the next ten.

Two hours slipped by like minutes. Wounded were brought from the field; Hollis's dead were left where they had fallen. Piles of ash were soaked with water while cloths and tents were raised to house the homeless. Aurélie had not yet ventured so far as the hall, where she assumed she would find a scene of confusion and upset equal to that in the courtyard.

The horn sounded to alert them that troops approached, and she knew from the long blasts that it was Hyatt who returned to them. She was kneeling to the task of wrapping the gashed head of a knight who lay on the ground, and she tied the final knot and sat back on her heels. The bridge and gate were left open, receiving, and so she assumed her husband's good health and watched for his horse with a rapid beating of her heart.

Hyatt entered ahead of his troop. He stopped the huge

warhorse just inside the gate and removed his helm. As he looked around the courtyard at the fire damage, the injured, and mass confusion, his brown eyes took on a feral light. All voices were hushed to a deadly silence as Hyatt surveyed them all. He stabbed his broadsword into the earth, rested his helm atop it, and stared across the rubble toward Aurélie.

She rose slowly, meeting his eyes across the distance of thirty paces. A smile grew on her lips.

"My lord Hyatt," she called. "Your castle yet stands. Your people are bruised but mostly alive."

He shook his head as if to clear her image. "It almost appeared as though these knights took instruction from you, my lady," he shouted back.

A muffled cough and a choked wheeze escaped someone in the crowd. Aurélie let her head drop back as she laughed. She took a step forward, then another. Hyatt advanced toward her. They came together slowly, a prideful gleam in his eyes to blend with the regal light of victory in hers. They stood but a pace apart, looking at each other more like lovers standing in a garden than the battered survivors of a siege.

"Aurélie," he said in a breath, "I don't know whether to thank you, or throw up your skirts and beat you for what you dared."

"Before these people, messire?" she asked, lifting a brow and smiling in delight. "If you cannot decide, my lord husband, why not just kiss me?"

Hyatt opened his arms to her and she filled them instantly, clinging to him with all the ardor in her heart. Their lips came together in a fierce and passionate kiss, and without releasing her mouth, Hyatt lifted her into his arms. A cheer came from a horsed knight, and another joined him. Within moments there were dozens to shout and cheer, in both Gascon and English, praising the lady, the lord, and De la Noye.

Hyatt paid no mind to the deafening shouts of victory. Aurélie's arms were looped around his neck and he carried her in the direction of the hall. "You are a foolish, brave, and beautiful wench," he muttered.

"Oh, Hyatt," she laughed. "I would fight a thousand battles for you. Would you not for me?"

"Nay, woman. A million."

At the gate, not yet inside the wall, Verel stood. He watched Hyatt carry Aurélie away. He saw the strength in the knight's stride, the way his gaze lingered only on her face. Her arms were locked about his neck, her lips against his beard-roughened cheek. The cheers of French and English rose above the rubble in a unified sound of joy and pride. There was a tear that wet Verel's cheek and his lips trembled. His closed fist rose into the air and he joined the chanting.

"Victory to Hyatt! Victory to Aurélie! Victory to De la Noye!"

Guillaume was slow to rise, but his story came out in a week. He was abed in the seneschal's house, his leg stretched out on a board, and his delirium cured. He was weak, as he would be for some time to come, but not too feeble to tell the tale. He had been hunting for his daily fare at dawn when he heard the approach of horses on the road nearby. Reasoning that they could be soldiers, he climbed a nearby tree until they passed. The trip down was not so good, for he fell and broke his leg. It was impossible for him to drag himself up the hill to his camp, so he pulled himself into a sheltered copse in hopes of rescue. A murky bog greeted him there, for it was not a good, secret thicket that he hid in, but a covered marshy hole. For a week he held himself out of the murk by grasping a tree root, no food to sustain him and only dew off the nearby brush to quench his thirst.

He was still there when Girvin came thrashing through the wood in search of him. And he did not know his own name or the name of any friend or foe.

Aurélie had visited Guillaume nine times and heard the story, with better embellishment as the days wore on, an equal number of times. To her seneschal she reported the progress in De la Noye. "We lost a few good men, but Hyatt proudly adds some of the de Pourvre knights to his troop, among them Sir Verel."

"Ah, he's come about then," Guillaume sighed. "Good. It's coming together now, lass. De la Noye will rise above the war and be whole."

"There is good reason we should come together now, Sir Guillaume. Without Hyatt and Girvin, you would be dead now."

Guillaume's eyes became wistful and sentimental. "My lady, there is a thing you must know. There is gossip whispered amongst Hyatt's men, but he forbids them to speak of the battle with de Pourvre knights. And our own will not even yet speak out against the Sire de Pourvre. But what is told is that Giles died fleeing from the field. He fell from his horse and broke his neck."

Aurélie's eyes widened. "But I saw him, Guillaume. His chest was covered with blood and Girvin admitted it was his sword."

Guillaume nodded solemnly. "Girvin's blade. He knew the shield was that of the lord, the leader. He gave Giles a deadly wound to make his demise seem more honorable." Guillaume shrugged. "He does not admit his own tender heart, but I suppose he meant to spare us some dignity in our downfall. We thought we buried a fighting lord, though most of us doubted it was possible. Girvin's act gave us a little pride. Only one fled from battle. Giles."

Aurélie felt tears come to her eyes. "Why do you tell me this, Guillaume? Do you mean to punish me for some crime I am unaware of?"

"Oh nay, my lady, nay. But I shall not rise to my former strength." He patted her hand and looked on with sympathy as tears coursed her cheeks. "The leg will never hold me upright without a staff; it was broken a week without tending. I can hobble about and give instruction for a few more years, but I shall never again have my former worth. You must look to Girvin. You must not let Giles's death come between you."

"Oh, Guillaume," she wept, laying her head on her seneschal's chest. He gently stroked her back as she cried. "He need not have died. He could have refused the king's order and stayed behind his wall. Hyatt would have spared him and sent him away."

" 'Tis done, Aurélie. Edward means to secure Aquitaine, if not all of France. And so he has."

She raised her eyes. "Do you count it done, Guillaume?"

He shrugged again. "But for this business with Hollis, we are nearly at peace. And my lady, Sir Hyatt burns with the desire to lay Hollis low . . . along with Ryland, may God help them all."

Aurélie's hand went to the slight rounding of Hyatt's child. "I pray every day and night that my child will be born to a castle and family united. And I had such hope, before Hollis attacked. Now, I don't see how it can be."

"After all that we've seen, my lady, do you fail in faith now?" Guillaume squeezed her hand. "We are better fixed than we have ever been, my Lady Aurélie. At least when you pray, you do not rely on prayers alone. We no longer pray for mercy and miracles, but only for the right to use the hard-earned talents that defend our home. Tell your husband that if he is interested in the sworn fealty of a crippled old man, I am ready to make my pledge to his service."

She wiped the tears from her cheeks and smiled. "I shall tell him, Guillaume. He will be honored."

❧

Sir John Chandos, the highest ranking knight in Prince Edward's army, rode through much of Aquitaine on the business of gathering word of the English progress, and delivering news to the knights who had fought and secured land. De la Noye received him warily, for it would not be unlike Hollis to disguise his army by the prince's livery and a royal banner, if he could but afford the cloth.

Fifty armed men rode out of De la Noye to meet the approaching troop, Girvin at their head. The gate was promptly opened and the bridge lowered as the royal entourage entered. Hyatt met Sir John with Aurélie at his side. He bowed before the esteemed knight under whom he had fought more than once.

"You hold the wall most agreeably, Sir Hyatt," Chandos teased. "But we've passed a countryside at rest. Is it not a waste of good horseflesh to arm so many?"

Hyatt was deadly serious. "The countryside might be at peace but for my hearty neighbor at Innesse, Sir Hollis. He has already caused us much damage and death by way of his attack. And it was in monks' clothing that his archers and bowmen crept up to our gate. We nearly let them in, thinking they were but a wayward pilgrimage of flagellants."

"Monks' garb?" Chandos bellowed. "Courageous man, Hollis! How did you fare it?"

"Better than he."

"Good, Hyatt. Then it should please you to know that the battle ends. King John is taken prisoner by Edward and he bids you come to Bordeaux for the tournaments and ransoming."

"Captured? My God!"

Chandos smiled. "I think we can count Aquitaine settled, if not the whole of the country. I am making a fast sweep of the newly settled lands to deliver the word. Edward the Prince will wish to award you full title in his demesne at the celebration."

Hyatt stood proudly, not looking askance at Aurélie. He was a bit afraid to see the pain in her eyes at the word that her king was captured and held.

"Sir John, 'tis well known that I would ride into Hell on a peacock for the prince, but if I leave De la Noye and travel to Bordeaux this castle will belong to Sir Hollis before the dust has settled in my path. And for the next attack, I suppose, he will come dressed as a dowager with a sword up his skirt."

Chandos laughed heartily and for the first time regarded Aurélie. He looked at her briefly, smiling, and then looked back to Hyatt. "Hyatt, do I hear you say you are afraid to leave your home because you are too wary of Hollis? Why do you not finish with him?"

"I shall, when he comes next. But I do not launch an attack on Prince Edward's own castle of Innesse just because my enemy resides there. That is Hollis's shallow loyalty to his king, his overlord. Not mine."

"Sir Hyatt, you have just cause to take him out. The prince will not chastise you, but support you. Do it in Bordeaux." He gave his belly a pat. "I am sorely hungry and thirsty, but if you feed me well and give me some decent wine, I will deliver your challenge to Hollis myself . . . and escort him to Bordeaux to meet you in the lists. Hollis cannot beat you in a tournament of rules. Well?"

Hyatt glanced warily at Aurélie. He expected to see grave disappointment at the news that her country was settled within the reign of an Englishman. And if not that, fear that her husband would go against the treacherous Hollis. But he saw that her eyes were fixed on Sir John, and a smile of confidence graced her lips.

"So happens, sir knight, we have the best Gascon wine in these parts," Aurélie said. "And enough good food to make your journey to Innesse a comfortable one."

"Most women are wary of such conflict and beg their lords to avoid such battles."

"I can understand such women," she said with a shrug. "How could they be otherwise? They have not been wed to Sir Hyatt."

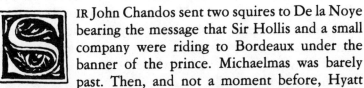IR John Chandos sent two squires to De la Noye bearing the message that Sir Hollis and a small company were riding to Bordeaux under the banner of the prince. Michaelmas was barely past. Then, and not a moment before, Hyatt gave the order to make ready for their own departure. He selected a good troop of thirty knights with squires and pages, a balanced combination of longtime de Pourvre knights and his own men. Sir Guillaume reigned over De la Noye as the seneschal, his voice cracking like a whip from his portable litter. Girvin prepared to travel with Hyatt and was heard to remark that Guillaume's booming voice had more than compensated for his immobility.

Carts, horses, wagons, and people stood ready to depart, but Hyatt had misplaced his lady. She was not in the bedchamber, the hall, the inner bailey, or ready to mount her palfry. Finally the gatekeeper in the portcullis whistled, then pointed, and Hyatt strode impatiently over the bridge. He stopped short when he sighted her at the graves, her wrap pulled tightly over her shoulders and her head bowed as if in prayer. He approached her more slowly then, as he realized that she stared down at de Pourvre's grave.

She had voiced no protest at the capture of King John. No tears were shed for France, nor did her spirits seem to lag while Sir John Chandos boasted of the battle in which twenty-five hundred English met over twenty thousand French at Poitiers. All he had heard her mutter was "Your English prince must be a most brilliant warrior." And feeling some sympathy for her, he had replied, "Edward will hold Aquitaine well, *chérie*, and you need not fear for your future, or the future of your children."

He stood behind her in silence for a moment, his hands gently squeezing her upper arms. She turned to face him and there were tears in her eyes.

"I did my best as his wife, Hyatt."

"I know. He knew."

"There was nothing of passion in what we had. No passion of the mind, heart, or body. I served him out of duty and I tried not to complain if there was anything lacking. Many women dislike their husbands. But oh, I did long to be a cherished wife . . . to be made whole."

"Aurélie, do not . . ."

She lifted a hand to stop him. "Marriage is nothing more than a settlement of property, and any love and desire that come are fortuitous. Most marriages are duty only. It could have been far worse for me, a mere child of nine years. I could have been given to a mean-hearted old knight, or a cruel and abusive man. Giles was not a great man, but he was not terrible. Hyatt, Giles never intentionally hurt me." She placed a hand on his chest. "You knew, all along, what Sir Girvin had done?"

He nodded, his eyes clouded with doubt. He had not seen any reason to hurt her with the truth. No harm would have ever come from her burying her lord with pride.

"I fought you hard, Hyatt," she said. "Do you forgive me?"

"Aurélie, my love, had you not fought me, I would have doubted your worth. I did not expect you to coddle your conqueror."

"I did not expect such a conqueror. I am not a skittish woman, my lord. Had you been any other kind of man, I would have held fast to my hate and perhaps finished your life as you slumbered by my side. But you owned this land by right of arms; you could have cast me aside and searched about for a rich wife and doubled your booty."

"No," he said softly. "I could not."

"Hyatt, do we go now?"

"Aye, love. All is ready but the lady."

"Wait," she said, turning from him and kneeling on the ground. She scraped a little hole with her hands and sat back on her heels, pulling off the ring that bore the de Pourvre crest. She put it in the ground and covered it. She stood, and after brushing the dirt from her hands she reached again into her cloak, pulling out a purse of silver livres.

"This is what I had hidden away when I learned that Giles was dead. It is yours. For armor, weapons, ransom; anything that will help you in the contest."

"What is this, Aurélie? Why do you do this?"

Tears sprang to her eyes again. "There need not be money or goods hidden to guard me against the future. I have need of nothing but you. Should anything happen, Hyatt, I shall not return to De la Noye. I go with you."

"My lady, we do not joust for you, but for land. I would enter no contest for you."

"I know that, my love. But it is important to me that you believe I shall never take another. Never. No matter what . . ."

"It is not like you to be cowardly, my lady. It is not like you to think the worst. Do you doubt me now?"

"Oh nay, Hyatt, my dearest love. I believe you will win. I would ride in the lists with you and guard your back. But I see now that this silver protects me from nothing. If I somehow lose you, I have lost the one thing in my life that matters most. I love you, Sir Hyatt. And I shall love you through all eternity."

"Then continue to keep the silver and the faith, my lady. Let love make you strong. Your love gives me strength and I will win."

She smiled and put her hands on his arm. "I doubted I would hear that from your lips."

"I don't know why, madame," he said with a chuckle, leading her back toward the wall. "You put the words there with yours."

Faon tried to pretend she was asleep so that Hollis would not bother her again. She lay still on a straw tick in a loft of a merchant's house in Bordeaux. The family had been ousted by the surly knight, tossed a few coins that would hardly keep them, and were sent cruelly on their way. Now the humble abode housed too many and they were all uncomfortable, but Hollis was here on business and did not listen to any complaints . . . least of all hers.

Hollis was large and fat, and he did not wash. He was stupid and cruel, but fighting was his forte and he almost never lost. From the talk she had overheard, he had lost but one contest, and that was not so much because of a lack of skill, but because he lost his temper and breached the rules.

That incident was with Hyatt.

I have not yet reached a score of years, she thought dismally, *and my life is over.*

Hollis made grunting sounds as he banged around the small loft in search of clothing, gear, and food. He threw open the shutters and relieved himself out the window, the urine splashing into the courtyard below. This was what Edward wished to take into battle, this grunting, snorting pig. Hollis fought like a wild boar, even with eyes blinded by blood and sweat. He was an animal trained to fight, but trained in nothing else.

Ryland had been good to his word, and punished her properly. Upon their arrival at Innesse, the devastated keep that sat in a pile of putrid waste and rubble, Ryland had pushed her toward Hollis and said, "Ease yourself on this for a while. She was Hyatt's."

Hollis hurt her, mating with her like a wild bull, slapping her if she whimpered, crushing her with his huge, clumsy body. And then he ignored her. She asked for something to clothe herself in and was shown a coffer full of discarded gowns that had belonged to the old mistress of Innesse. They did not fit her, being too narrow in the waist and far too short. And horribly ugly. She had made away from De la

Noye with her bag of gold and gems that she had acquired while with Hyatt, and Hollis had taken them from her.

But Ryland was the evil one. Hollis was ugly and stupid and mean-tempered, but Ryland was the one who plotted and schemed and planned out acts of viciousness and murder. It was Ryland who devised the plan to clothe Hollis's archers in monk's robes to attack De la Noye, and Faon had smiled slyly, though carefully, when Hollis returned, defeated, and told the story of the battle. Somehow they had known he was coming, Hollis raged. Hyatt's troops emerged from down the road, from the woods, from the keep. And the gate was not opened. The priest must have warned them.

And the lady yet lived.

Faon heard Hollis leave the room, slamming the door, and sighed in relief that she had been forgotten. She sat up gingerly, rubbing her back. Her whole body ached. She longed for a bath, for though she had never been fastidious about her personal cleanliness, she had not been granted servants or grooming tools since leaving De la Noye. No mercy was bestowed on her even after it was learned that Aurélie lived. She no longer knew why she was kept with them.

The door opened and with a start she pulled the blanket to her chest, covering herself. It was not Hollis, but Ryland. And he smiled with ruthless superiority.

"Good morning, my love. Dress yourself in something. We're going out to find where Sir Hyatt keeps his lodgings."

She glared at him without response.

"You are not interested in your lover any longer? Well, I am. And you shall help me."

Faon said nothing. For once she feared to open her mouth, for between Hollis and Ryland she had suffered enough beatings.

"Tomorrow is the contest that Prince Edward will view for the pleasure of his victorious court . . . and your lover's challenge will be met. You would not wish to lie abed while Sir Hyatt and Sir Hollis do battle, would you?"

"What is it you wish of me now, Ryland?"

"You shall help me secure Hyatt's son."

"*My* son, Ryland," she said, rising in the bed, a note of panic in her voice. "You would not harm my son!"

"Do you pretend to care for the boy? Well, perhaps you shall see him again, in that case. He is here, in Bordeaux, with Hyatt's household." Ryland laughed. "I could have sworn that you disliked the child, and used him to gain a place in Hyatt's household."

"Ryland," she said in a desperate whisper, "you must not hurt the boy!"

"I do not mean to harm him, dear Faon. But do you see? If Hyatt should somehow best Hollis, we shall find ourselves in a sorry state. I have very little silver left to feed the hungry bear. I think it wise to keep a little booty at hand. You do wish to be reunited with your son, do you not?"

"If you plot against Hollis, he will kill you."

Ryland laughed heartily. "Good God, dear Faon, I am not that kind of fool. Now get up! I am in no mood to tarry."

❧

Hyatt took a drink of wine and passed the chalice to Girvin, who took a drink. The huge warrior looked down at Hyatt. "I don't think I shall like this plan. I have always ridden at your side or guarded your back."

Hyatt slapped his gauntlets into his open palm. "That was before there was so much more to guard. And Sir Verel wishes a chance to prove himself."

"He is not as good as I," Girvin grumbled.

"You are right; he is not. That is why you have each been given your proper chores."

Girvin gave a slow nod. "All will be well, Hyatt."

Hyatt stepped outside his pavilion where the destriers, saddled, decorated, and being fed from grain bags, waited. He looked to the spectators and saw the faint blur of rose-colored velvet that was his wife's new cloak. Across the field there was a wide expanse of blue that was Hollis's tent.

Hyatt looked around at the collection of men that would ride in the melee. Some were his own of many years; six were of de Pourvre's troop who had practiced with them before leaving De la Noye. All were ready and wore serious faces. If Hollis somehow managed to win, most of these men would be serving a new lord. The stakes were quite high; if there was not loss of life, the knights would be ransomed to the extent of their worldly goods.

The two knights had met with Prince Edward and Sir John Chandos the day prior, and Hollis was confident of his skills, easily putting on the line his own conquered keep, plus the costly armor that outfitted his entire troop and each destrier they rode. Hyatt nearly winced at the cost, but covered his shock. Before he spoke, Chandos whispered in his ear. "Finish with Hollis once and for all, Hyatt. All or nothing!"

Hyatt had glanced briefly at the shrewd, handsome eyes of the young prince. Edward could hardly criticize the warring skills of one such as Hollis, but did not rest easy while the same man held property in his demesne. A good mercenary did not often make a good lord of lands. Hollis's troop was comprised mostly of criminals with orders of pardon bought by Hollis. Hollis and his group were a good war-machine to take to battle, but sorry keepers of the larder. Could the prince be so confident of Hyatt's skill in the contest that he would risk having Hollis own it all?

In the eyes of the prince there was a firm request to finish Hollis's treachery . . . before it worked against England. And Hyatt obliged. He had pledged his worldly goods to the outcome of the contest, and Hollis had smiled with an evil gleam in his eye.

The trumpets sounded and the knights mounted up. Squires began to race around the tents and pavilions, readying lances, swords, shields, and additional armaments. Hyatt led his troop around the field and paused before the prince, bowing low over his horse. Edward was young, strong, and in his glory. He held the King of France and many French lords and knights. The ransoms were high and to be paid by Christmas. A great deal of wealth was changing hands even now, and Prince Edward sat in the midst of it all.

King John occupied a prominent, if heavily guarded, position to observe the contest. Not many places to his right, Aurélie slowly stood. She was proud and erect, her eyes alive with courage and love. She touched her fingers to her lips. She did not show the fear that Hyatt knew had burned in her heart. He was aware of her restless loss of sleep, her distracted mood, and the slight frown of worry that creased her brow.

Hyatt rode on and Hollis presented his troop to the prince and the spectators. Hyatt rode the length of the gallery and back to his pavilion to stand ready. He looked over his shoulder at Sir Girvin and slowly shook his head. Girvin disappeared instantly.

Hyatt had only one opportunity to look closely at Hollis's pavilion as he passed. He scanned the grounds and saw Thormond standing among the tents and horses. And nearby was the young squire whom Hyatt had asked to watch the scoundrel. He counted that matter done; Thormond would not ride in the melee, but it was important to see what he did later.

The rules of the contest were read, and cheers from the crowd went up all around when the trumpets sounded. Hyatt wiped his hands on a cloth, tossed it to a page, and pulled on his gauntlets. He accepted a blunted lance, for it was property for which they fought and not to the death. He looked at the line of one dozen fully fettled knights wearing his livery. "For De la Noye," he said. He heard the cheer. He looked directly behind him. He met Sir Verel's eyes. "Let us best this devil for my lady's sake, Sir Verel."

"For my lady and De la Noye." Verel's strong voice carried conviction.

Hyatt turned back toward the field and dropped his visor. His hands were steady, his mind focused on one thing only. Hollis. The mark of a good leader was to give orders and believe them done. He had assigned each man to an important task in the melee, and if any one failed, they might all lose. But if each did as he was instructed, the contest would be between Hyatt and Hollis. Now that the plan of attack was set, he could not dwell on the details. He focused on the huge knight whose destrier stood ahead of the rest. At the trumpet's blast, he heard their visors all drop. Lances were braced; squires released the reins and ran out of the way. A third blast was the call to charge.

The destriers crashed together. The sound of cracking lances, grunts, and cheers filled the air. Only two were unseated; one from each side. The felled knights ran for new horses and the remaining group, now lined up before their opponent's pavilions, waited for the trumpet sound to repeat the charge.

Hyatt's lance held through the second charge, but he threw it down and called for a replacement. As he passed Hollis, he noted a gleam of satisfaction in his eyes. After three passes, six knights were unseated and had almost depleted their alloted number of new destriers. Hyatt meant to keep throughout the steed he was riding. At the fourth pass a total of nine were unseated and points were awarded to Hyatt, whose troop had the most astride. The crowd was wild with cheers. But Hyatt longed for the strength in Aurélie's clear blue eyes.

At the fifth pass Hyatt's blunted lance found Hollis's chest and the man was pushed back, his feet hard in the stirrups and his knees tight on the horse, but Hollis was too heavy. He fell. More points to Hyatt's side, for a leader had been unhorsed. And the crowd roared with pleasure. Hyatt knew by the sound there were very few spectators yearning for Hollis's success. But the position of the crowd was the least of his concern. He knew, as he had known from the first, that there was more at stake than De la Noye. He knew it because Ryland was somehow pulling the strings that caused the puppet knight, Hollis, to work.

Hyatt looked around the field. He had the advantage still, for his side had more men astride. He dismounted and pulled out his broadsword, while Hollis chose the mace. Hyatt's steed was whisked away by a squire. He dared not look about to see what his men did, for if they followed their orders, they would busily push back Hollis's men. The win was not so important, at the moment, as keeping the opposing side at bay, for it would be like Hollis to have a plan to worry Hyatt from the rear.

Hollis swung the mace as he approached. "Come, bastard," he growled.

Hyatt heard the clanging of metal and crunching of armor all around him, but there was not the slightest indication that any of Hollis's men approached his back. To turn and look would give an advantage to Hollis, and he reminded himself to trust his men to do their part. He fended the mace aside with his sword, sweat running down his forehead under his visor and into his eyes. He swung and stabbed and swung again, and the dust around their feet rose in a choking cloud. He saw blood dampen Hollis's gauntlets from the fierce grip the latter had on the chain. The mace whirred past Hyatt's stomach and as it passed he crouched suddenly, bringing his blunted broadsword into the fat knight's side.

Hollis grunted in pain and fell to one knee. Hyatt gave him leave to rise, which was the rule of the chivalrous match. By the cheers, the move had been seen and counted. Hollis rose with a growl, the mace wildly swinging toward Hyatt's head. It struck the side, dazing him for a moment, his helm so badly dented that he pulled it off and let it fall, but his opponent did not give him time to recover from the blow, but brought the mace back around on the backswing. Despite the fact that Hyatt's vision was clouded with pain, he saw the bulk descend on him and rather than trying to escape the second blow, he raised a knee to Hollis's gut. A round of booing and hissing from the gallery could be heard as Hollis stumbled back. Hollis would not give a felled knight a chance to rise, despite the rules.

"You're losing the contest, Hollis. Don't be a fool."

Hollis growled again and righted himself. He glanced toward the prince's pavilion and slowly pulled off his helm, casting it aside. Hyatt did not seize the moment when Hollis looked away, but waited as he should, wondering at his opponent's next move. It appeared that Hollis meant to equalize their terms by taking off his helm.

Hollis swung the mace and his eyes gleamed. "Fall to my next blow, bastard, and you may have your wife and son."

Hyatt did not look at the pavilion that housed the spectators. Instead he smiled shrewdly. "Fall to mine, and you may have your life."

The mace whistled as it came close to Hyatt's face. He ducked and swung the mighty blade, hitting Hollis again in the gut. Hollis grunted in pain again, falling to one knee. He looked up at Hyatt with blood lust in his eyes. "I have your wife and son," Hollis growled. "If I lose the match, they shall be ransomed."

"Nay, Hollis. It is you and I . . . at last."

"Look for yourself, fool!"

Hyatt did not glance around. By the lack of clanking armor and grunts he knew the field was nearly clear; there was an almost fearful quiet. He did not know the points collected, but he realized that the others had finished their contests. If Hollis's men had bettered his own, he could still take the day by beating the leader.

Hollis rose uneasily under his own weight. His face was streaked with dirt and sweat and he charged like a wild boar with a snarl of hatred on his lips. But Hyatt's lighter weight served him well as he jumped out of the way of the swinging mace and applied his sword again to the same side he had struck twice before. This time Hollis sprawled.

Hyatt looked down at his opponent. "You're a fool," Hollis muttered. "Ryland has them. He will kill them."

"You're the fool. If you get up, I shall only have to knock you down again. Yield the day!"

Hyatt watched as the man rolled in pain, his mace lying far from his hand. Hyatt turned, bowed to the gallery, and plunged his sword into the dirt beside his victim. He began to walk toward the prince, straining his eyes not for Edward, but for the rose hue that marked Aurélie's cloak. Blood ran from his temple into his right eye, but his left was clear.

Aurélie was not there. Hyatt mumbled a prayer that bore the name of Girvin.

He had taken twenty paces, panic rising, when the audience seemed to rise as one and the sound of a galloping horse could be heard. He looked first in the direction of the horse and saw Verel charging onto the field, an unsheathed broadsword raised high. He was gaining on Hollis, who was charging with Hyatt's broadsword. A moment of stunned wonder paralyzed Hyatt. Hollis would attack his back.

Hyatt dove out of the way, sliding into the dust, while Verel screamed a battle cry that held all the outrage the lad had stored for many months. The sword Hollis held was blunted, but Verel's was not.

Hyatt got to his feet as quickly as possible and a piercing whistle left him. Verel reared the destrier with a sharp turn and maneuvered the steed between the combatants, his sword still high.

" 'Tis mine to do, Verel," Hyatt called out sharply.

Verel stared for a moment, then with a smile on his lips he threw the broadsword to Hyatt and pulled the destrier out of the way.

Hyatt tossed the hilt of the sword from hand to hand. "Unsheath your blade, Hollis," he ordered.

Hollis tore the blunted sword from its cover and swung the blade at Hyatt. Hyatt stopped it once, twice, thrice, and when Hollis made a wide, powerful sweep at Hyatt's middle, Hyatt moved back a half-step and plunged his mighty sword into Hollis's gut.

Hollis dropped his weapon and clutched the heavy hilt of the sword that ran through him. His eyes widened for only a moment, a trickle of blood running from his mouth, and then he fell for the last time.

Hyatt stood and wiped the sweat from his eyes, oblivious to the roaring of the crowd. He saw a rustle of movement in the direction of Hollis's pavilion and saw Thormond push a squire down and clumsily mount a destrier. Hyatt whistled again, a short blast to alert Verel and two long, calling for a horse. He turned and began to run toward the prince's pavilion.

A knight astride met Hyatt before Edward's seat and quickly dismounted, giving the steed to Hyatt. Hyatt bowed briefly over the saddle. "Does that satisfy Your Highness?"

Edward gave a half-bow. "The contest is yours, sir knight, and not from your opponent's disgrace. You took it fairly. He will not attack your back again."

"Nay, Your Highness. But the contest goes to the streets, for Hollis claimed he somehow held my wife and son."

"Then do not dally here, Hyatt. I was told the lady went to see about a sick child."

"Aye, sir. The sick child is my brother, Ryland. By your leave."

"Godspeed, Hyatt. And good luck!"

Hyatt bowed and gave his horse a firm heel, leaving the grounds and making for the streets of Bordeaux.

❧

Hyatt was still in the saddle and Aurélie's breath was still caught in her throat when the page arrived. "The child, Derek, has taken a bad fall, my lady. Mistress Perrine begs you come quickly."

Aurélie had looked around frantically, not knowing what she should do. She looked toward the prince, her host, and he gave a slight nod. Hyatt's heir was more important than his wife, especially in the eyes of a future king.

She rose with great hesitancy. She had an odd tightening in her stomach. It was not like Perrine to call her from something like this, especially since Aurélie could do no more than Perrine could do in an emergency. And Aurélie's advanced pregnancy, coupled with Perrine's protectiveness, made the request even more strange. She followed the page out of the gallery, across the grounds. The afternoon sun was bright and the air was brisk, but Aurélie's cheeks were hot. A deepening fear for Derek and a deep apprehension for herself began to bloom.

The lodgings Hyatt had secured for them were in a hostel

345

in Bordeaux kept by an elderly couple. The page had brought her a palfrey to ride, and led the way. Behind her she could hear the shouting from the lists and imagined the crashing of metal. "Oh, Hyatt, be strong," she silently prayed.

The sounds faded as she rode. In the streets there was an eerie quiet with almost everyone gone to the pavilions to catch a glimpse of the captured king, the English prince, the knights called to contest. The clattering hooves of the palfreys echoed, the sound surrounding her.

She stood before the humble hostel. The page tethered her horse, bowed, and departed. She opened the door and stepped inside. There was a stony silence within, not typical of a place that was both heavily guarded and where a bad accident was to have occurred. She looked toward the staircase and down the hall ahead. "Perrine," she called. "Perrine . . ."

The door was not yet closed behind her, when an arm encircled her waist and another closed over her mouth. She could not see who held her and struggled in vain. On the stairs leading to the room where she had left Perrine and Derek, Faon appeared. She held the boy on her hip and under her reddened eyes were deep, dark hollows. She stared at Aurélie with a mixture of hatred and pity. And then the demon's voice came to her ears.

"Be still now, my lady, or we shall have to do you harm," Ryland threatened.

He relaxed the hand that covered her mouth, but the arm around her waist tightened.

"Ryland," she said in a breath, "what do you dare?"

"We're going to keep you safe until the contest is done, my lady. Perhaps, if the cocky knight is very lucky, there will be a ransom. It should be a tidy sum, to equal what he holds, for a wife and son, both valued."

"Was it not enough to pit him against Hollis in Aquitaine, and again in the lists?"

"Hollis will win," Ryland said with a laugh. "And I shall

take you back to De la Noye, where the saddened brother of the slain knight will keep his lot for his son."

"How have you secured Hyatt's son? Where are the guards? Hyatt left two of his best here."

Ryland laughed wickedly. "Would I come here alone and ask very kindly that they yield me Hyatt's son? I brought some of Hollis's with me. Hyatt's are dead and the other knights guard the back of this humble place, lest we be interrupted."

Aurélie gasped in spite of her wish to be strong. "Perrine?" she asked with hesitancy.

"Tied. She will not scream."

Aurélie stiffened and tried to think clearly. She watched Faon warily, wondering what to make of the woman's blank stare. "And if Hollis loses?" she asked.

"Then we have a little plan, of which you and Hyatt's son are an important part. But do not worry, *chérie.* When your man is down, Hollis will tell him that I have you . . . and Derek." He let go with a vicious laugh. "Hyatt will turn his head to look, and . . ."

Aurélie stiffened suddenly. "He will not look," she said.

"He will look! And his skull will split as he turns his head!"

There was a crash that caused all heads to turn. From a rear door, Sir Girvin appeared, an evil smile on his lips and his short-handled ax in his hand. He tossed the heavy weapon about effortlessly and there was blood staining its edge. "He will not turn his head from the contest, Sir Ryland," Girvin rumbled. "He entrusted the lady's welfare to *me!*"

Faon stood paralyzed on the stair and Derek began to squeal, not knowing that death lay at hand. He murmured and fussed and reached out hands toward Aurélie. Aurélie looked and saw the glint of steel in Faon's hand. She held a sharp dagger in the hand at her side. Her eyes were hollow and blank, her face void of emotion.

"Girvin, hold, I beg you," Aurélie whispered. "Faon, do not! He is your own flesh!"

Faon drew her breath sharply in, lifting her proud chin as she did so. She had been cast aside by Hyatt, tricked by Ryland, and used most brutally by Hollis. What next, she dare not think.

"She will kill him," Ryland said. "Tell Goliath to step back and drop his ax, and come with us peacefully."

Aurélie disregarded Ryland, though he held her so tightly that she felt cut in half. Still, she focused on Faon's green eyes. The dress that the haughty mistress wore was tattered and ill-fitting. Her hair was not its usual mass of coppery curls, but dirty and unkempt.

"Faon, Hollis does not win this contest. As I left the lists, Hyatt was ahead by much. 'Tis Hyatt you will have to deal with, not the brute. Do not harm the boy."

"Come, Faon," Ryland urged in a cajoling tone. The blade moved in her hand, rising toward the boy. "Come with us, Faon, and we'll have the best of them yet."

Faon's raging eyes darted to Ryland's face. Then the green glitter went back to Aurélie.

"He is a noble babe, Faon. Hyatt will rear him to take his due. You cannot doubt that."

The glitter increased as tears gathered in Faon's eyes. The sound of horse hooves pounding down the lane could be heard, a sound like no other. In these narrow city streets, emptied because of the tournaments and feasts, only one person would ride so. Aurélie smiled. " 'Tis not Sir Hollis," she said shrewdly. " 'Tis Hyatt, come to settle this."

"Nay," Ryland shouted. "He'll not find one of you alive!" He tossed Aurélie aside in a move of sheer panic, lunging for the stairs. His hands were stretched out toward the boy and the knife. Faon backed away and gasped in sudden fear. But the ax was swift and sure and the sound was faster than the sight. There was a whiz and thump and only the weapon's handle stuck out of Ryland's chest. A look of terror gripped his face as he slumped. Faon seemed not to react, but still held her own blade at about the waist of her child.

The hooves came closer, the noise echoing between the

closely built houses. Aurélie raised herself quickly. She stepped toward Faon, but not too near for the woman to pass her if she would come down the stairs. Aurélie reached inside her cloak and produced the leather purse she had offered to Hyatt.

"By the rear door, Faon. Girvin will let you pass. I wager his horse is tethered yonder."

Her eyes darted toward the huge servant. "This last time," Girvin agreed.

Faon's eyes teared again and she did not lower the blade. "I tried to kill you. You will ask him to chase me down."

"Nay! You are the boy's mother. I know what that means."

Faon stepped down. She pressed the blade close to the boy and used him as a shield as the sound of the approaching horse came closer and slower.

"Let me have the child, Faon. Please."

"Tell him to move," she said, indicating Girvin with her frightened eyes. Girvin did not require the command, but moved quickly, the blade still precariously close to Hyatt's son.

Aurélie stepped closer, caution guarding her step, sympathy clouding her eyes. "Take the silver, Faon, and leave the boy. If you take Derek, I dare not say what he will do."

"Will you take care of him? Do you swear?" she asked, a tremor in her voice.

"Yea, Faon. I give you my word." The sound outside of the gallop slowed to a stop. "Quickly, lass," Aurélie breathed. "Take flight. I can forgive you, but if he cannot . . ."

Derek reached toward Aurélie, and Faon choked on a sob. She dropped the dagger and reached for the silver. In a flurry of skirts she ran out the door that Girvin had kicked open. Without pause Aurélie whirled to face the messenger. "Let her go," she commanded.

Girvin let his chin fall in a nod.

"How did you know where to come?"

"We saw them yesterday, my lady. I followed Ryland from Hollis's pavilion today, sensing his plan to come here."

Aurélie sighed. "Someday you must tell me how one so large gets about so easily without being seen."

Girvin smiled devilishly. "And you may tell me how one so small commands troops with such finesse."

Hyatt hit the door to his quarters with such speed and force that he nearly tripped over the body of his brother. Straight ahead, standing like a sentry at the door that led the way out through the back, Aurélie stood, holding Derek. She did not react to the blood on Hyatt's face because she was determined that he would not follow Faon.

"It was Faon and Ryland," Girvin reported. "My ax."

"Where is she?" Hyatt snarled.

"Gone, my lord," Aurélie said. Hyatt took a step toward his wife. "Nay, Hyatt. Leave her be." She stopped him with a hand on his chest and slowly let her hand rise to touch the blood, dried now, on his cheek. "She is alone now and can do us no harm. You have no cause to hunt down a woman."

"She may return with yet another scheme. I have let her go for too long."

"Nay, Hyatt . . . she is beaten."

Aurélie rose on her toes to place a light kiss on Hyatt's lips and in the close exchange, Derek encircled his father's neck with chubby arms. Hyatt took the boy and slipped an arm around Aurélie's waist. "You are sure, lady?"

"Yea, Hyatt. If we are strong enough to love, we are strong enough to be merciful." She sighed and leaned against him. "Please, my love. I shall never ask you to pardon an enemy again, but let us not raise up your son with the knowledge that his father killed his mother."

Hyatt's eyes clouded with doubt, but Aurélie's voice pressed him. "If the contest is met, take me home."

He looked down into her eyes and a smile grew on his lips. " 'Tis met, my love. Did you doubt it?"

"Never, Hyatt, 'Tis met . . . and done."

EPILOGUE

HE ground outside the De la Noye wall was covered with a fresh blanket of late snow. All through the night the wind had howled, the snow coming in ruthless blasts against the castle walls while Lady Aurélie labored with her first child. The morning dawned clear and bright, the sun shining on the fresh, new whiteness, and yet the lady struggled to give birth.

At dawn, unable to bear the moaning pain of his wife any longer, Hyatt brooded in the hall. It was Guillaume who said, "When my wife labored with children, I found they were born much more quickly when I chopped wood."

Hyatt knew good sense was at work. He donned a heavy fur jerkin and high leather boots, and took a long-handled ax outside the castle wall. He plied the ax with all his strength, bringing down a tree at the forest's edge. It was not the lord's duty to split logs for the fire, but Hyatt could not bear the idle wait while his wife labored.

A tidy stack of split logs grew and Hyatt was damp with sweat under his heavy garments despite the chill of the air. A blast of the horn from the high citadel caused him to bolt upright, leaving his ax standing in the log. The lady had given birth.

He looked toward the castle, his breath drawn in as he waited. There was a long pause. There was to be one blast for a girl child, two for a son. Yet there was naught but silence.

He turned and began to run toward the gate. It would not end in injury . . . did the child not live?

As he neared the wall he heard a blast of the horn, but he continued to run. Ah! A second blast. It was a boy.

A third blast came. Hyatt's face went pale, but he hurried on. They had not discussed what signal to use if the child did not live, or if Aurélie . . . It was Guillaume who had promised the call from the donjon.

His feet thudded across the bridge.

"Sir Hyatt, what is it? What has the lady delivered?"

He did not pause to answer for he was driven only by dread. He could not imagine the meaning. Perhaps they meant only to call him back; perhaps the child had not come. Or his wife lay in mortal peril. Or worse. He thundered through the portcullis and ran to the hall.

Guillaume sat before a winter fire, a mug of ale in his hand and his stiff leg propped up. Girvin stood nearby, also hefting ale. They did not wear the faces of doom or death.

"Sir Hyatt," Guillaume said cheerfully. "You are getting slow in your old age. You should have taken a horse to the wood."

"Guillaume, *three* blasts sounded! What is amiss?"

"Aught amiss, lad. We did not cover all the possibilities with our code."

"She is well?"

"See to your lady wife, son," Guillaume said quietly, a smile on his lips.

He needed no further prompting and took the steps to his chamber two at a time. Aurélie lay in the bed, two pillows to prop her. She held a bundle in her arms and he heard the baby crying. Nima sat close by and Perrine was turned away at some chore, her back to the door. He rushed toward his wife.

Aurélie pulled back the blanket and proudly displayed a small, pink, screaming little girl. "Your daughter, messire."

"My God," he said in a breath. "I was sore afraid. The lout

in the tower sent forth three blasts and I feared the worst. I'll have the boy horsewhipped!"

"Here now, that's a feisty mood when the boy did my bidding," Perrine interrupted, pushing him out of the way and producing a second bundle. She placed another babe in Aurélie's free arm and drew back the cover to show Hyatt another child, a small, whimpering boy. "We were at odds with how to tell you from the tower, milord." Perrine beamed. "Small, but strong."

Hyatt's face lost color as he gazed down at his wife and two children. "Aurélie, are you all right?"

She smiled tiredly. "I feel wonderful. I am at least as surprised as you."

He looked at Nima. "They are healthy? Not too small?"

Nima nodded her head. "They are perfect, milord. Do you not think them beautiful?"

Hyatt sat weakly on the edge of the bed. He laughed suddenly, greatly relieved. "Oh, they are indeed beautiful! But, my lady, if you bring them forth two at a time, I shall be hard pressed to feed them all."

Aurélie let her lips touch the top of one tiny head. "We have need of a large family, Hyatt, to hold all the possessions you bring to your name. There is so much."

There was a soft knock at the door, and Perrine went to answer it. Hyatt touched a tiny hand, kissed his wife's brow, and covered the babies again. Perrine returned to the bed and whispered in Aurélie's ear. "Let him come in," Aurélie said.

Hyatt turned to see who disturbed them. Father Algernon entered with his head down and his hands folded together. He approached warily, his eyes soft and his lips held together with a slight trembling.

"My lady, will you let me bless the new babes?"

Hyatt stood, stepping back from the bed slightly and glowering at the priest. It was Aurélie who had insisted that they not cast the priest out or punish him, but his continued presence at De la Noye bothered Hyatt. Still, he could not deny his wife.

"I would like you to bless them, Father."

The priest leaned over the bed, making the sign of the cross on each little head and muttering his prayer.

He turned toward Hyatt. "I have much for which I must atone, my lord. If you can forgive me for my betrayal, born of a foolish heart, I shall try hard to serve your family with my knowledge of God and the Church."

Hyatt looked at Aurélie, frowning. She held him with her eyes and a slight smile appeared on her lips. This was the first time Algernon had dared to approach him. He looked back at the priest.

"It has been said that it takes greater courage to love and have mercy than to fight and rule lands. Atone with good works, Father, and you shall have a place here for many years."

"Thank you, my lord," he said, turning to leave as quietly as he had come.

Hyatt sighed and went again to his wife. "You said you would not ask me to forgive any more enemies."

"I do not have to, Hyatt. You have the wisdom to know when to forgive with no word from me."

"Somehow, madame, the whole world believes you the loyal and steadfast wife, all servitude and compliance, and yet without even a word of request, you have your way with me on every turn of the hand. How shall I hold together armies of men if they ever learn that a small and quiet woman rules this warrior's every whim with such ease?"

Aurélie lifted a baby and placed it on her other side, next to his sister, and then put both her arms about Hyatt's neck and drew him down to kiss her lips. Though she was weak and tired from childbearing, her kiss caused him to tremble.

"Just tell them that we have a common purpose, my love, and that is all that matters." She smiled sweetly. "Now and forever."